2008

1G

continued . . .

Much Ado About Magic

"The magical Rice takes Trev and Lucinda, along with her readers, on a passionate, sensual, and romantic adventure in this fast-paced, witty, poignant, and magical tale of love." —*Romantic Times* (Top Pick, 4^{1}/2 stars)

This Magic Moment

"This charming and immensely entertaining tale . . . takes a smart, determined heroine who will accept nothing less than true love and an honorable hero who eventually realizes what love is, and sets them on course to solve a mystery, save an entire estate, and find the magic of love." —*Library Journal*

"Rice has a magical touch for creating fascinating plots, delicious romance, and delightful characters both flesh-and-blood and ectoplasmic. Readers new to her Magic series will be overjoyed to learn that she has told the stories of other Malcolm women and their loves in previous books." —*Booklist*

"Another delightful, magical story brought to us by this talented author. It's a fun read, romantic and sexy with enchanting characters." —*Rendezvous*

The Trouble with Magic

"Rice is a marvelously talented author who skillfully combines pathos with humor in a stirring, sensual romance that shows the power of love is the most wondrous gift of all. Think of this memorable story as a present you can open again and again." —*Romantic Times* (Top Pick, 4½ stars)

"Rice's third enchanting book about the Malcolm sisters is truly spellbinding." —*Booklist*

Must Be Magic

"Very sensual." — *The Romance Reader*

"Rice has created a mystical masterpiece full of enchanting characters, a spellbinding plot, and the sweetest of romances." — *Booklist* (starred review)

"An engaging historical romance that uses a pinch of witchcraft to spice up a tale with a rarely seen uniqueness. The story line mesmerizes. . . . Fans will believe that Patricia Rice must be magical as she spellbinds her audience with a one-sitting fun novel." — *Midwest Book Review*

"I love an impeccably researched, well-written tale, and *Must Be Magic*, which continues the saga of the Iveses and Malcolms, is about as good as it gets. I'm very pleased to give it a Perfect Ten, and I encourage everyone to pick up this terrific book. It will brighten your summer."
— Romance Reviews Today

Merely Magic

"Simply enchanting! Patricia Rice, a master storyteller, weaves a spellbinding tale that's passionate and powerful."
— Teresa Medeiros

"Like Julie Garwood, Patricia Rice employs wicked wit and sizzling sensuality to turn the battle of the sexes into a magical romp." — Mary Jo Putney

"*Merely Magic* is one of those tales that you pick up and can't put down. . . . [Rice] is a gifted master storyteller: with *Merely Magic* she doesn't disappoint. Brava!"
— *Midwest Book Review*

Other Historical Romances by Patricia Rice

The Mystic Isle Series
Mystic Guardian

The Magic Series
Merely Magic
Must Be Magic
The Trouble with Magic
This Magic Moment
Much Ado About Magic
Magic Man

Other Titles
All a Woman Wants

Mystic Rider

A MYSTIC ISLE NOVEL

Patricia Rice

A SIGNET ECLIPSE BOOK

SIGNET ECLIPSE
Published by New American Library, a division of
Penguin Group (USA) Inc., 375 Hudson Street,
New York, New York 10014, USA
Penguin Group (Canada), 90 Eglinton Avenue East, Suite 700, Toronto,
Ontario M4P 2Y3, Canada (a division of Pearson Penguin Canada Inc.)
Penguin Books Ltd., 80 Strand, London WC2R 0RL, England
Penguin Ireland, 25 St. Stephen's Green, Dublin 2,
Ireland (a division of Penguin Books Ltd.)
Penguin Group (Australia), 250 Camberwell Road, Camberwell, Victoria 3124,
Australia (a division of Pearson Australia Group Pty. Ltd.)
Penguin Books India Pvt. Ltd., 11 Community Centre, Panchsheel Park,
New Delhi - 110 017, India
Penguin Group (NZ), 67 Apollo Drive, Rosedale, North Shore 0632,
Auckland, New Zealand (a division of Pearson New Zealand Ltd.)
Penguin Books (South Africa) (Pty.) Ltd., 24 Sturdee Avenue,
Rosebank, Johannesburg 2196, South Africa

Penguin Books Ltd., Registered Offices:
80 Strand, London WC2R 0RL, England

First published by Signet Eclipse, an imprint of New American Library,
a division of Penguin Group (USA) Inc.

SIGNET ECLIPSE and logo are trademarks of Penguin Group (USA) Inc.

Printed in the United States of America

PUBLISHER'S NOTE
This is a work of fiction. Names, characters, places, and incidents either are the
product of the author's imagination or are used fictitiously, and any resemblance
to actual persons, living or dead, business establishments, events, or locales is
entirely coincidental.
   The publisher does not have any control over and does not assume any
responsibility for author or third-party Web sites or their content.

ISBN-13: 978-0-7394-9816-3

Acknowledgments

As a reader, I've always considered acknowledgments pages to be wonderfully edifying, but as a writer, I've considered them too literary for the fantasies I have so much fun spinning. But there are so many wonderful people who have brought this series into existence that I can no longer get away with saying "to all those who helped me; you know who you are," because I'm not certain they realize how important they really are.

In no particular order:

Ellen Edwards, the editor who understands my vision and helps me realize it

Robin Rue, the cheerleader who offers encouragement and keeps my evil twin from slitting throats

Mary Jo Putney and Susan King, my fellow cauldron stirrers and coconspirators, whose fantasies and friendship I can't do without

The Wordwenches, one and all, who understand the need for history

The St. Louis convocation, who accepted a stranger into their midst like an old friend

Everyone—and this list is much too long to name— who listened to my ravings, read my trashy beginnings, and supported my insanity

And my husband, who bears my ups and downs with patience and love and an occasional dose of shopping therapy

Thank you all!

Prologue

Smoke rising from the Mystic Isle's highest peak dimmed the glow of the quarter moon, casting a foreboding shadow over the drooping leaves of the tropical jungle at the mountain's foot.

Undeterred by the prophetic gloom, Iason Olympus gripped his six-foot-tall oak staff with both hands and adjusted his breathing until he reached the center where his soul resided. As the island of Aelynn's only Sky Rider, he was attempting his visionary journey once more in an effort to subdue the abnormal weather that was crippling his home and his people. Previous efforts had failed, but perhaps this time . . .

He swung the staff over his head with practiced hands. As the staff spun faster and faster, he gazed into the starlit bowl of the heavens, searching for answers. The tropical night was humid, and beads of moisture formed upon his brow.

His torso stripped bare, he strained for greater swiftness, compelled by the urgency of the situation. The staff became little more than a blur of motion against the sky as images poured through him.

Sweat glistened on bronzed shoulders and arms bulging with muscle. His abdomen was taut from years of practicing this exercise. Standing half-naked on a rocky hillside above the lush forest of his island home, he was as much a part of the natural world as the trees below—a human windmill catching the energy of the skies.

Electricity danced along his fingertips like a thousand fireflies. As the staff spun faster, sparks flew from its ends.

Iason took no notice of sparks or speed. His inner eye fixed on the familiar image rising in the stars, a womanly vision fine and fair, caught in a cacophony of stormy music. Thunderous deep bass notes joined in symphony with the high-pitched melodies of woodwinds. He didn't understand the significance of the music, but the chorus of screams in the distance, the background of blood and soldiers . . . Those he interpreted from reports he had received. *Revolution.*

The woman had entered his visions before, capturing his imagination. Cylindrical blond curls framed high cheekbones flushed with pink. Skin like ivory silk, a high intelligent brow, and thick gold lashes provided a perfect setting for crystalline blue eyes. Her music pulsed through Iason's veins, filling an emptiness inside him.

Women had told Iason that he had a hollow heart, and he'd acknowledged the truth of the accusation. He'd never loved, never known passion. He'd hoped someday that might change, but it didn't seem reasonable at this late date. He was what he was, and his detachment had made his days exceedingly efficient. Until now . . .

He'd never known such stirring music, or been so thoroughly aroused by the sensual promise in a woman's winsome smile. His lonely soul awakened and craved life.

Why do the stars continue to summon this vision?

He caught his breath as the image unexpectedly sharpened at his question. There, just past her round, bare shoulder, hovered the sacred Chalice of Plenty. Its disappearance two years ago had marked the start of the deteriorating conditions on the island. The *chalice*, with a woman not of his world. Did this mean . . . ?

Iason had given up all hope of ever finding his physical and spiritual equal, the rare *amacara* only a fortunate few were granted. If he read the stars correctly, he'd found them both—his mate and his duty—in a woman who was caught in a storm of violence.

He rarely saw himself in his visions, but he recognized his staff in a man's hand reaching out to the woman and the chalice. And there, beyond the chalice—*Murdoch!* In a soldier's uniform. The vision exploded in a painful swirl of red and the thunder of drums, striking him with a blow as effective as if it had come from a club.

Gasping at this psychic attack on his senses, Iason slowed the motion of the oak staff until it became visible. Staggering, he steadied himself. He couldn't stop now while the vision filled his head. He needed to puzzle out its meaning.

Slowly, he worked out the kinks in his extended arm muscles by lowering the pole to the height of his shoulders. He crossed his arms to grasp the top and bottom of his staff and spun it from hand to hand in looping figure eights while he pondered.

What did the blood in the vision signify? His own death? Or that of the woman who was his destiny? And how did Murdoch, a banished renegade, fit into the image?

That he himself should die anywhere other than on Aelynn was unthinkable. Who would lead their people into the future? His sister? Like him, she had no mate. If neither brother nor sister produced an heir, Aelynn would eventually be left leaderless. In a time of upheaval such as this, that could spell disaster for their gifted, ancient people.

He sought other meanings.

The people of Aelynn had been assigned the duty of protecting the chalice, and they had failed. The fate of his world could rest upon his recovering the sacred object—and finding the woman.

As it had more than once before, the conflict between the fate of his line and that of the chalice kept him twirling his staff until this time he saw resolution. Only after he began his cooling exercises did the visitor waiting at the bottom of the hill dare to approach him.

"Ian," Kiernan the Finder shouted, reducing the regal family name of Iason to the more familiar one that Ian preferred.

Kiernan's presence had not intruded upon Ian's trance. Now he resented returning to mundane matters after the vision of golden curls. But he had been taught since birth that his responsibilities came first, and he acknowledged the Finder with a nod. Several months earlier, Kiernan had been sent to retrieve the chalice and the woman in Ian's recurring vision, but he did not appear to have returned with either of them.

"I assume you have Seen the news I have come to tell you," Kiernan said.

"She is lovely," Ian agreed obliquely. "The chalice recognizes her, but if she has gifts, they are too common for her to be aware of them." He seldom spoke of all he'd Seen in his visions, but he hoped Kiernan might provide more insight into the woman.

"You See more than I," Kiernan replied, to Ian's disappointment.

The Finder looked weary as he came closer, Ian noted. The youthful humor that had once defined his friend's smile had worn away these past few years into the harsh angles of an adult who had seen more than he liked. Ian was sorry that he'd had to ask so much of him.

"I See *differently*," Ian corrected. "I know nothing of the Outside World except what others report. The woman appears foreign and exotic to me. I simply recognize the chalice. I possess just a small portion of your skill and can guess only her direction."

Kiernan did not have visions, but he could locate any object once he'd been told of its existence. "The woman is in Paris," he stated bluntly. "The city is a maelstrom of discord, misdirecting my insight with the smoke of anger and hatred. The chalice lies in the center of it."

With great patience, Ian waited for the Finder to explain why he had not returned with either prize— the chalice or Ian's mate—as he'd been instructed to do.

Kiernan shoved a callused hand through his long, ragged hair. "I went to Paris," he stated with a rough edge to his voice. "But the chalice is not a . . ." He hesitated, apparently searching for a means to explain. "It is not an inanimate object."

He seemed to be waiting for the obvious protest about the inability of lumps of silver to have minds of their own, but Ian acknowledged the possibility of sentience with a nod. "The gods work in strange ways."

With relief at Ian's understanding, Kiernan continued. "Tracking the chalice is akin to tracking our exile. I know its general direction, but like Murdoch, it does not stay put. I have the feeling that the chalice is deliberately avoiding me, just as Murdoch does."

Ian frowned. He disliked the idea that Murdoch Le-Droit might be in the same country as the chalice. The renegade had been banished for killing Ian's father, Council Leader of Aelynn. Whether the death was an accident or deliberate was still debated, but either way, the lightning Murdoch brought down had demonstrated the danger of his unruly physical and psychic gifts.

Murdoch had the ability to invoke earth, wind, fire, and water. After causing Luther's death, he had supposedly been stripped of his perilous gifts and exiled. The immovable ring of silence that he wore would prevent his ever speaking of his invisible home. Still, the dangerous fool seemed to hold the fate of Aelynn in his hands. Two years ago, he'd nearly killed the island's Guardian with Greek fire. What havoc might he create if he claimed the chalice?

"Murdoch should not be able to sense you," Ian reminded Kiernan.

"I know." Kiernan's troubled expression revealed his reluctance to acknowledge what must be said. "I think it is as Trystan warned us—Murdoch's abilities may have been muddled, but they were not entirely destroyed. Is it possible that he has more gifts than was known?"

Ian spun his staff. As usual, the movement helped him concentrate. "Anything is possible, although I suspect it is more a case of no one being able to completely erase what the gods have given. Could he be the reason you cannot find the chalice?"

"I think the chalice is avoiding Murdoch as much as it avoids me. And I sense that your mate is the reason."

Ian's head jerked up, and his eyes narrowed. "You think she has the ability to conceal it? That she knows of its worth to us?"

"I have no good explanation for why the chalice and your mate keep disappearing at the same time."

Kiernan straightened his shoulders and met Ian's gaze boldly. "I think the chalice is challenging you to claim your mate in person."

At this confirmation of Ian's own thinking, a ripple of shock hit him. His family never left the isle, not since the beginnings of time. Their abilities were too valuable to risk elsewhere.

Because of that risk, he had never sailed beyond the island's waters. It was his duty—as it had been the duty of all generations of Olympians—to lead the Mystic Isle of Aelynn. As the only son of the late Council Leader Luther, and the presiding Oracle, Dylys, Iason led the island's government. Among other things, he ensured that those of his world followed his mother's edicts.

Ian was also the last Olympus male on Aelynn.

Even Kiernan was painfully aware of the enormous consequences of what he was suggesting. The Finder dropped to a boulder seat and bowed his head, waiting for the gods to smite him for speaking such heresy.

They did not.

Perhaps it was time to think the unthinkable.

Although Ian had abilities beyond those of mortal men, using them to cause harm in the Outside World was forbidden except in self-defense, and even then, their use was dangerous. Mankind often killed what it did not understand, and Ian was an enigma even here, where he'd been born. In the Outside World, he would be akin to a statue come to life, with little knowledge of his surroundings beyond what his instincts told him.

"She is a revolutionary," Ian murmured, keeping his horror—and his secret longing—to himself as he pondered the fate he had been assigned.

"She has the chalice." Since he hadn't been struck dead by the gods, Kiernan dared lift his head. He had no fear of Ian's wrath. The Oracle's son had been raised to be as dispassionate as the rock upon which Kiernan sat.

Aware of his duty and the expectations of his peers, Ian spun his staff. His path became more clear with each rush of air. "I'll retrieve the chalice," he said in a tone that brooked no argument.

Kiernan's jaw dropped. "France is a country at war. You could die there."

Ian had already pondered that possibility. If he died, it would mean more than just his death, for he carried the souls of his ancestors. Should he die in the Other World, those souls would be lost in a place that did not recognize them, rather than on the island where his blood was revered. His gifts would also be lost forever—unless he left behind an heir to carry them on. Yet the woman destined to be his mate lived in the maelstrom that could kill him. The challenge intrigued him.

"Nonetheless, I will go."

"The Council will never allow it," Kiernan argued.

Ian grunted acknowledgment of the Council's inevitable opposition. Its members stubbornly resisted any break with tradition. Although they were extremely gifted people, many were elderly and accustomed to his father's rule. Luther had had fewer psychic gifts than Ian did and would never have used them to coerce the entire Council.

Ian had no such compunction. He had obeyed his elders' decrees all his life, but the time had arrived to assume leadership. He had been given his abilities for a reason, not to let them molder unused.

And if his choice led to his death, then he alone was responsible.

Ian did not make his decision lightly. He had given the problem careful consideration since he'd seen the unthinkable in the skies these last months. "What is the point of my living if the chalice is lost in the Other World?" he asked. "And if I do not have a mate to pass on my abilities, of what use am I to Aelynn?"

Without waiting for a response that he knew Kiernan was unprepared to give, Ian strode down the hill toward his home, leaving his friend alone in the starlight to contemplate a future without a leader.

The Council unanimously agreed upon that future several days later, after Aelynn expressed her disapproval of the chalice's loss by spewing steam and hot ash from the volcano's peak for the first time in the memory of even the eldest citizen. At Ian's suggestion that the gods wished him to retrieve the chalice and prevent Murdoch from using it to blackmail them into abetting his lust for power, the mountain grew silent in approval.

All hastily concurred that only Ian could ensure their future, that only he could appease the angry gods by returning the chalice to the island. They left the fate of the renegade Murdoch in his hands.

Ian very carefully did not mention the revolutionary mate he had foreseen in the stars. The Council had little use for rebels.

One

Paris, June 1791

Chantal Orateur Deveau gasped with horror as she read the note the messenger had delivered. "This is not supposed to happen!" she cried, then abruptly stifled any further protest.

The walls had ears these days, even in a humble printer's shop. She had learned to keep her thoughts to herself, but she was having difficulty staunching her hysteria. With ink-stained fingers, she scrubbed hastily at a tear that portended an imminent deluge. Valiantly, she hummed beneath her breath to keep her rage and fears at bay while rereading the note.

The ragged urchin on the other side of the counter shrugged and waited for the coin he had earned. "Things change," he said carelessly.

"They're supposed to change for the better," she argued, suppressing her resentment that she had so little control over those changes. The arrest of her beloved Pauline—and the children!—was just one small example of how petty greed and hypocrisy were muddling the glory of a perfect revolution.

She rummaged in her pocket and produced a piece of silver. The urchin bit into it. Satisfied it was real, he smiled, bowed, and ran out the door of the pressroom, back into the streets where he lived.

Behind her, the printing presses clattered, producing

the pamphlet her father had written last evening. It was a spectacular essay, deriding the radicals in the Assembly for trading church property for political influence instead of distributing its wealth to the poor. He was to deliver the speech today, and the pamphlet would be all over Paris by evening.

She was proud of her father, but his brilliant oratory would not save Pauline.

Emile emerged from beneath the press, wiping his hands on an oily rag. "Bad news?" he asked sympathetically, noting the message in her hand.

"Pauline's been arrested for harboring a defrocked priest." She held out the note to her father's friend. "She's not just my sister by marriage, but my best friend since childhood. Do you think someone heard of Papa's upcoming speech and planned this to distract him?"

The burly pressman scowled. "Pauline is just another aristocrat who thinks herself above the law. Maybe this will teach her a lesson."

Emile could have been the source of the gossip that had sent the militia charging into Pauline's attic, Chantal realized. "The priest is her brother!" she exclaimed in frustration at this reminder that even friends could no longer be trusted.

At her cry, the printer grimaced as if in pain and slid back beneath the press to escape her protest. She let him go. It wasn't as if she could change his prejudice with her tears.

She'd spent these past two years since her husband's death establishing a safe, stable world that shielded her from grief and anger. Even while Paris rioted around her, and her father stood on street corners shouting for revolution, she calmly taught her music students, obediently wrote out her father's speeches, visited the ill, and had tea with her friends while they politely discussed how the Assembly would make life better.

She didn't doubt the worthiness of her father's cause. She loved him and aided him as best she could, fully believing the nobility had no right to deny others a chance to better their lives. Unfortunately, the only area of her life she'd ever controlled was her music. Were she to allow her emotions free rein, she'd no doubt shoot the toes off anyone standing in her way. Better that she pacify her unruly sentiments by staying behind the scenes, writing music for the Revolution.

She had thought that in the two years since its formation, the Assembly would have finally created order out of chaos. Pauline's arrest not only destroyed her serenity, but also raised her anxiety to new levels.

Helplessly, she tapped her nails against the silver bell a student had given her in lieu of payment for his music lessons. She had taken to carrying the bell with her in her errand basket, in hopes of finding someone to replace the missing clapper. But all the decent silversmiths had deserted Paris for more peaceful, profitable markets. Mostly, she carried the bell because the charming chime of her nails against the silver helped her believe that all would be well. The bell had become her comfort when nothing else succeeded.

As always, the melodic notes cleared her emotional stress sufficiently to light a rational path. *Bribery* might rescue her sister-in-law and her two adorable children from the horror of prison. Paris ran on bribery—mainly because coins were scarce and the Assembly's paper notes were almost worthless. She didn't think she could find sufficient coin to free a priest charged with treason, but innocent women and children . . .

While Chantal tried to imagine where she might acquire enough coins to bribe a guard, she smoothed her palm over the polished curve of the peculiar bell, and her ring caught on one of the gemstones embedded in the ornate handle. She would have thought the stones would reduce the bell's harmony, but they somehow enhanced it. A very skilled musician must have crafted it.

She set her basket on the counter and lifted out the bell by its broad handle. Frowning, she looked under it, trying to determine why it no longer possessed a clapper, or how one had been affixed to the interior, but she was no silversmith.

Her eyes widened at a wild thought. Would the guards take a broken silver bell as a bribe? The gems alone must be worth a fortune, and silver was always valuable. The possibility that someone might melt down the harmonious object horrified her, but . . .

She cringed. She hated to destroy such a treasure, or give it up at all, but she had to be practical. The silver and gems gave the bell a monetary value far higher than even her piano, and the bell was easier to carry. Since it was broken, its musical value was small.

For Pauline, the sister she'd never had, she would sell her soul.

Verifying with the printer that the pamphlet would be ready when her father came for it, Chantal wrapped the bell in the wool she used to disguise its gleam. Then, lifting the skirt of the sturdy twill gown she wore when she worked, she hurried into the bustling streets of Paris. Once upon a time she would have had a grand carriage to take her the mile to her family's home, but in these days of the glorious Revolution, her father's position in the Assembly required that they suppress any conspicuous show of wealth. They kept the carriage and horses out of town, where her father could use them to travel long distances.

Chantal did not mind the walk home or the necessity of wearing old dresses. As long as she had her music, and life stayed on the path she knew best, she was content.

But Pauline's incarceration had thrown her off her safe path onto an unknown side road. She wished she had someone wise to talk to, but she couldn't bear to think of Pauline and the children locked behind bars while she scoured the streets for sage advice. Even if her father arrived this evening as planned, it would take time to negotiate a release. Travel in France was erratic, based on politics as much as weather and the condition of the roads. Anything could happen to Pauline before Papa returned. Chantal shuddered in horror and walked faster.

The massive wrought-iron gates enclosing the carriage drive to her father's home did not swing wide at her approach. Instead, a small door in the block wall opened to let her in. Chantal nodded a worried greeting to the guard, then hurried up the marble stairs. The town house was not so grand as their country home near Le Havre, but she preferred the coziness of the smaller rooms, and the acoustics of the music chamber were ideal.

A maid met her at the door, and Chantal handed her the bell. "Shine it until it gleams, if you please. Then ask Girard to join me in the music room as soon as he arrives. Madame Pauline and her children have been imprisoned for helping her brother."

The maid gasped, curtsied, and hurried away.

Pauline had her own small townhome, but she and the children ran in and out of Chantal's suite as often as they did their own.

Chantal lifted her skirts with both hands and raced up the stairway to the family wing where she kept her rooms these days. After Jean had died—almost two

years ago today—she'd sold their flat and moved
home to share her grief with her recently widowed
father. So many deaths in so short a time . . .

The mansion had been built for a large family, but
the Orateurs were not fortunate in that way. She was
an only child, and Jean had never given her an infant
of her own.

She did not regret that she had no child to worry
about now. Her work with her father on France's revolutionary course and her music lessons kept her well
occupied. All in all, her new life would be almost
perfect—if not for the hotheadedness of these new
radicals who condemned all royalty and believed the
poor and uneducated should rule the kingdom.

If it hadn't been for the protests of members of the
middle class like her father, the Assembly would never
have been created, and the decadent nobility would
still be in power, so she couldn't argue with the need
for change. She simply wished the radicals weren't
so . . . forceful in their demands. Or so extreme. Com-
promise was essential. The alternative was civil war.
She hummed to shut out that unpleasant idea and
turned her thoughts to her immediate concerns.

Gentle Pauline had never caused anyone a moment's grief. To imprison a young mother because she
loved her brother . . . it was barbaric, even if Pierre
had refused to take the oath of loyalty. He was a
priest. He owed his loyalty to the church. One could
not ask a priest to forswear God.

Hastily washing, Chantal discarded her drab twill
and replaced it with a modest flowered muslin dress
wrapped with a bold satin sash. The chemise à l'an-
glaise was all the rage, and its simplicity suited her,
but her father's chargé d'affaires, Girard, was elderly,
and preferred the stiff elegance of panniers and satins
from an earlier time. As a concession, she chose the

delicate muslin instead of the twill in hopes of persuading him to do her will without enduring his silent disapproval.

She had always enjoyed fashion. Even if all France was in a state of unrest, she could maintain a sense of normalcy by following the latest mode in her home.

Bribery, however, was not only not normal, but illegal, and considering such an action disturbed Chantal on many levels. Her father, Alain Orateur, was a lawyer sworn to uphold the law, as had been Chantal's husband and her maternal grandfather. But the latter were gone now, Jean to consumption, followed by her grandparents in the same typhoid epidemic that had weakened her mother and led to her death not long after. Their losses, one right after another, had deadened her soul.

Papa and Pauline's family were all she had left. She would fight to the death for them.

Girard appeared in the music room as requested. He still wore an old-fashioned gray wig over his balding head, and the gold braided frogs and silk coat of the previous era. But his stature and the sword at his side protected him in a way that Chantal couldn't command for herself. Her petite size was a hindrance in a city tense with violence.

"They caught Pierre in Pauline's attic," she said without preamble. "She's been harboring him despite the Assembly's edict."

Girard's stoic features revealed no opinion. "Where was he taken?"

"I don't know." Chantal paced the parquet floor, working up her courage. "He should have left Paris for Italy when he had the chance. He knew we would not let Pauline and the children come to harm. It was reckless foolishness on both their parts."

It had been foolishness to refuse to take the oath,

also, but Pierre had become a priest because he held noble ideas. Chantal was more pragmatic. Noble ideas seldom fed the poor and often led to death. Dead was dead, no matter how one got there.

"You know your father will not approve of whatever you are thinking," Girard warned, well versed in Chantal's ability to wheedle her way into getting whatever she wanted.

"He would not approve of Pauline rotting in prison through no fault of her own either." She pivoted on the marble tiles, her skirt dragging on the floor behind her.

"Supporting a traitor is an act of treason," Girard intoned without inflection, giving no indication of his opinion one way or another.

"He's her *brother*!" Chantal clasped her hands nervously, not certain she dared ask Girard to break the law. But she could not very well go to the prison on her own. She'd survived so far not because she was strong, but because she wasn't stupid.

The maid hurried in with the silver bell wrapped in clean felt. How fortunate that the clapper was missing, or Chantal felt certain it would be ringing in warning of her rash behavior.

"This is a gift to the guards who keep Pauline." The declaration appeared on her tongue without conscious thought. She was not usually quick with a lie, but once she considered the words, she found they truly were not a lie. "Find out where she is being held; then present it to them and ask if I might secure the bond of the prisoners and have them released in my name."

How amazing that she should suddenly utter phrases she'd heard since childhood, as if *she* were the lawyer in the family.

"Oh, madame, you cannot bring a defrocked priest

here," the maid whispered in horrified tones. "It is a sacrilege!"

"That depends on whether you're speaking of Rome or Paris," Girard corrected. "There, he is a hero. Here, he is a traitor to our cause."

Chantal waved aside the rhetoric. "He is my brother-in-law, and his sister and her children are suffering for his beliefs. He is the same man who blessed this house a year ago, not the evil Inquisitor the radicals would make of him and others like him."

"It is not our place to change the laws," Girard insisted. Once his mind was made up, it became an immovable object.

She might be merely an idle lady with musical talents, but Chantal had devoted her life to the well-being of her small family. She hummed beneath her breath to suppress her frustration as she'd learned to do. Hysteria would never aid her cause. There were times when she wished herself a foot taller and a hundred pounds heavier so she could pitch obstacles out of her way. As it was, she had only her love and determination to move them.

She took the bell from the maid and unfolded the cloth to admire the gems twinkling back at her. She tapped her fingernails against the silver, breathing deeply of the happiness resonating from the clear chime. Warmth and assurance instantly wrapped around her like a cloak.

She did not want to let the bell go, but she must. Lifting it from the cloth, she hugged it, then shoved it at Girard, who grabbed it instinctively.

"Go," she said pleasantly, modulating her voice into persuasive tones she had learned at a very early age. Her toddler tantrums had caused people to flee her presence, but sweetness never failed her. "Be swift, and be kind. Bring Pauline to me once you have found her."

At the maid's anguished cry of protest, Chantal turned and bestowed a comforting smile upon her. "Pierre will not wish to harm his sister again. Do not fret."

The calming effect of her voice produced the desired result. She knew she played upon their emotions, but she would not regret her manipulation if it saved Pauline. The maid's frown disappeared, and she curtsied. Girard smiled approvingly and bowed himself out. No further argument strained Chantal's already fragile patience.

Her father had scolded her often enough for using her appealing ways to encourage others to do what they should not, but sometimes it was difficult to differentiate between right and wrong. This was one of those times.

The law was unfair and ridiculous. Pierre had done nothing except remain loyal to his beliefs. Let the pope go to jail if he did not approve of the new Constitution. Let the Assembly go to hell for claiming the Church's assets as state property and expecting priests to be loyal to state instead of church.

She paced the floor, allowing her true feelings to emerge in an angry hum. She must calm down. She did not want to be out of sorts when her father arrived. He'd not been himself lately. The schism between the radicals and conservative Jacobins was widening, fraying the glorious Revolution that had made all men equal.

Wiser minds would surely prevail, Chantal told herself. There'd scarcely been a riot since the Assembly had taken over and begun ruling France. It took time to institute change and establish a new order. She would secure Pauline's freedom, and this episode of wrong thinking would be forgotten in a few weeks. That was the way of it here—the mood of the city shifted with the wind.

She should order rooms prepared for the children. They would be horribly frightened. She would write them a song!

With the relief of returning to some small part of her ordinary routine, she retreated to the marvelous piano her father had ordered all the way from Austria. She'd been told that Wolfgang Mozart composed on one just like it. The lighter tones suited her ear better than the heavy English one she'd learned on.

The bass wasn't heavy enough to achieve the rollicking notes of the "Carmagnole," the dance tune she'd recently heard in the streets. She'd composed some simple lyrics, adding notes to suit her ear. Trying to buoy her sagging spirits, she played through the triumphant opening of another revolutionary song bearing her mark—"Ça ira!"—"We will win!"

Then she recalled that since that first innocent version, new lyrics had emerged to express bloodshed as victory. People were fond of desecrating pretty tunes with violent images.

The songs no longer made her feel optimistic. She was like the clapperless bell, echoing the empty chimes of others and not ringing proudly with her own music.

It wasn't like her to be out of sorts like this. She sat on the piano bench and forced her fingers into a tune that the children would enjoy. Little Marie was only three—Chantal ran a light trill of notes that she heard when Marie laughed. Anton was five and much like his big barrel-chested father, who had died last year from an infection after being maimed in a duel. Foolish man. Deep bass notes crashed from her fingers.

Dead, all dead played from the keys.

Shoving the bench back, she stood and paced again. She could not expect Pauline's immediate return. Girard would have to find the right prison, locate a malleable guard, grease many palms, negotiate, and maneuver. Perhaps they would let him visit with Pauline, reassure her. Nothing was ever done swiftly these days. Maybe tomorrow . . .

She couldn't bear to think of Pauline rotting in prison for even so long. Her sister-in-law was gently raised and frail, and the children were too young. This was such *foolishness*.

Chantal returned to the piano and crashed a few chords of thunder and lightning. Her fingers tumbled across the keys like rain. She was a whirlwind of anxiety and doubt. These past months since she'd owned it, the bell had soothed her, but now that it was gone, her fears raced out of control.

She let her emotions flow in her voice and released them in song.

She didn't hear the maid announce a visitor. She turned because a large block of silence mysteriously absorbed her chaotic chords.

She gaped in shock.

A monk in long brown robes stood just inside the doorway. A cowl hid his features, but the soft linen of his robe did nothing to disguise his wide shoulders, lithe grace, and air of authority as he strode into the music chamber. A rope belted his narrow waist, and his long brown fingers clenched a gnarled oak staff.

"I have come to retrieve my chalice," the monk intoned in notes that shivered up and down Chantal's spine like a sensual caress.

She had no idea what chalice he meant, but there was something about the confidence with which he spoke that almost convinced her that he had every right to take it.

Two

Exhausted by his extraordinary journey inland to a gated city teeming with the best and worst of humanity, Ian Olympus controlled the effect of the exotic female on his gyrating wits by gripping his staff. Her musical voice had reeled him into this cold chamber as effortlessly as if he were a fish on a hook. He, the powerful Council Leader of Aelynn, had been caught by a shimmering minnow.

Accustomed to Aelynn's fresh sea breezes, open spaces, and the silent peace of his countrymen's shielded thoughts, Ian had chosen to travel as much as he could by water. On rivers, he needn't deal with the maddening blasts of excessive passion from Others. Upon arrival in the city, he'd shut his mind to the thoughts bombarding him, leaving open only his Finding ability. But the stench of sewage and unclean bodies, the crowded, shouting masses of humanity, the hundreds of beasts and vehicles in one small landbound area, had assaulted his physical senses as much as his psychic ones. There was more than one good reason why sensitive Oracles did not leave Aelynn.

If fate decreed it, he would gladly sacrifice his life in noble battle with enemies or in saving the sacred chalice. But he seriously objected to losing his mind to an unwashed mob.

Except that the final jolt threatening to knock him

over was not the city, but the shock of finding his intended mate.

She was an oasis of peace. In her presence, all else fell away.

And she was *exquisite*—a frail gardenia blooming in the midst of hell, a lady of the finest sort in a city of Philistines. The stars had not given him any sense of her delicate perfume, or showed the poise with which she moved, or the golden melody of her voice. As he'd entered the chamber, her song had pierced his chest.

She was so . . . fragile. He could snap her delicate wrist with a twist, encompass her waist with his hands. All Aelynn men were warriors by training, gifted to protect the island and its sacred objects, but he felt as if he'd just been dealt a blow that laid him flat.

Her complexion was as pale as the silvery moon, with hearts of heightened color on her high cheekbones—probably due to his rude stare. But he couldn't help himself. She had hair like sunlight, and eyes . . . intelligent eyes, the rarest magical blue of topaz—to his disappointment, not multihued Aelynn eyes.

But right now, that did not matter so much as the song thrumming through his blood and the sense of coming home to a woman who soothed his senses.

"I beg forgiveness for my rudeness," he said, still seeking balance. "The journey was long, and I came here directly without resting. The chalice is extremely important to my people."

Rising from the piano bench, she pressed slender fingers to her expressive lips, and her silver-blue eyes narrowed. Her golden ringlets dangled temptingly, and he almost reached to stroke one. Instead of answering him, she tilted her head as if listening to distant bells.

Ian clenched his staff harder and wondered if the beautiful mate the gods had chosen for him was a lackwit. It did seem an ironic fate for a man who had been privileged from birth to have everything except what he most wanted—freedom, and the support of a woman who matched his strengths with her own. Perhaps only feeblemindedness could complement his highly trained abilities.

"The church no longer owns property," she finally replied, in a voice that sang sweetly, even though her words made little sense to him.

Frowning, Ian tried again. Without the usual emotional or mental cues he received from those with whom he conversed, he could not tell if he was speaking her French language correctly. His gift for understanding foreign words was not so well developed as those of his kind who traveled more frequently. "The chalice does not belong to your church. It belongs to—"

He could not explain Aelynn. The ring of silence would not allow it. He wished he had more experience in the Outside World so he could circumnavigate these limitations as easily as Kiernan did. But this was his first time, and he must think twice about everything he said.

"The chalice belongs to me," he decided to say. The gods would forgive him since the sacred object belonged to all of Aelynn.

Her eyes widened in shock, and he stole a moment to admire the long golden brown lashes that made her eyes appear to fill half her face. He tried to concentrate on her expression, but he was weary and as easily tempted as any man, perhaps more so, given his extended abstinence. His gaze fell to the high curves of her creamy bosom framed in a filmy froth of lace. He desperately needed to touch her to see whether she was real or just a vision.

"Someone *stole* your chalice?" she asked with a

perplexity that indicated he still wasn't communicating clearly.

"Exactly," he agreed, to keep the confusing conversation to a minimum. "I am willing to pay for its return."

Chantal drifted back to her seat at the piano, away from her disturbingly intense awareness of her robed visitor. She assumed the maid had allowed him in because he was a man of the cloth. The erotic timbre of the monk's voice thrilled her to the marrow of her bones, which must border on religious perversion.

Pauline would say she had been too long without a man, but Chantal had never had much interest in that part of her marriage. Jean used to say she lived inside her head, not her body. She wasn't entirely certain that was true either. She knew desire. She often woke in the night overheated by inappropriate dreams. She recognized the devil's need rising in her now. She'd simply never known a particular man who inspired it, and certainly not a *monk*!

She swallowed hard and tried to quell her reaction.

"Why do you think I have your chalice?" she asked, simply because her thoughts were too rattled to allow her to know what else to say. She needed to render his stimulating voice into music that she understood. Perhaps then she would be able to think clearly.

"I saw you with the cup," the monk replied, not raising his rich voice.

She wanted to explore his intonation, understand the highly unusual harmonies she heard when he spoke. She relied on her ear for character when she listened to people speak, but with this man, her physical excitement hampered her understanding.

She turned her back on him and hit a note on the keyboard, attempting to locate the key that resonated with his pitch. He was a baritone. A deep reed instrument would more accurately represent it. "How could you have seen me, if you just arrived?"

This was probably the most senseless conversation she'd ever engaged in, but they seemed to be talking on different planes. They hadn't even been introduced.

She didn't hear him move, yet he was suddenly standing so close that she could feel his heat. Did she imagine it, or did she sense him resisting a desire to force her to face him?

"All things are possible if looked upon from the right angle," he said.

His voice vibrated chords of desire that she'd thought long lost. Rather than respond to his declaration or oddly compelling attraction, she found the right key, then played a few notes to reproduce the rise and fall of his voice. She often did this when someone puzzled her.

But what she felt wasn't precisely puzzlement. Like a tuning fork, the depths and honesty of his desire resonated with her own, and excited her beyond measure. She simply didn't understand why or how this was happening.

They knew nothing of each other, but on some primitive level, they were connecting physically. The notes of his voice that she imitated on the piano were ones of enthralling intimacy that whispered sweet secrets in her inner ear. He longed to touch her!

She didn't know whether to be flattered or appalled. Mostly, she was basely thrilled. Parts of her that had not stirred in years stirred now. It seemed she hadn't entirely dried up from disuse as Pauline had predicted. Or perhaps anxiety had robbed her of her wits.

"Do you have the chalice or not?" he asked patiently.

Do you want me or not? is what she heard. He may as well have spoken inside her head, so certain was she that he was a hairsbreadth from circling her waist like a lover. She could almost feel his kiss upon her nape, and the fine hairs there rose in anticipation.

Rather than act on her imagination, she responded with the notes that said, *I want you very much.* It was a game she played, one no one else could participate in. Only musicians could hear music speak, and few musicians listened.

Behind her, the monk stiffened. In the polished surface of the piano she saw him lift his hand. . . . She held her breath, but he fisted his fingers and dragged them back to his side. Surely he could not understand her music! She closed her eyes and drank in his enthralling presence.

He did not smell like an unbathed monk. Despite his insistence that he had just arrived, he radiated the fresh, clean scent of an ocean breeze. She'd grown up near Le Havre. She missed the quiet lap of waves, the cries of gulls. This man reminded her of happier times.

In response to her unusual joy, her fingers played an arpeggio of notes of their own accord, flying up and down the scale, communicating the passion she hid inside her, the raw emotion she never displayed. One of her curls flew loose and slipped along her jaw.

Shockingly, the stranger reached out and caught it, sliding the curl between exploratory fingers before tucking it behind her ear. "I have never met anyone as soft as you," he murmured with a puzzled awe that whispered through her ear to her fingers, producing provocative chords. "I could never have imagined . . ."

Standing, he towered over her. She gasped as his fingertips grazed her nape. His touch was flame, and she was tinder. She was suddenly aware of the stimulating fragrance of her musky perfume blending with his masculine scent, and her breasts swelled with a need long denied.

"I have many chalices," she countered, playing faster to hide her shiver of desire. "Most came from my mother, or as wedding gifts. They are mine."

He generated intense heat, though the salon was chilly. He was wider and broader than she was, and she was alone with him. She had no fear for her safety, however. Instead, she was imagining improbable scenes of rising from the bench and turning in to his arms. . . . No one would come unless she called—

"You are married?" he asked.

Was it her own disappointment she heard in his inflection? Or his? She used both hands to find the keys but couldn't tell. Something was happening to the notes. They were blending, harmonizing— *His notes were entwining with hers.*

"Widowed," she answered curtly, becoming a little afraid of her frenzy. She never acted on the turbulence in her heart.

She jerked her fingers from the piano before they smoldered, and closed the lid. Attempting a less subordinate position, she stood and turned her back on the keyboard to face the man who had her behaving like a foolish adolescent.

"Such magnificence," he muttered in a dazed voice. Now that he could see her face, he stroked her chin with a wonder she felt through his touch. "Like a rare gem among the coals . . ."

Bracing her hands on the mahogany piano lid behind her, Chantal tilted her head to study this startling stranger. Despite, or perhaps because of, his concealing garb, his . . . masculinity . . . was overwhelming. The cowl shadowed his face, but she knew when his gaze dropped to her bosom. Her nipples sharpened to stiff points.

Impatiently, he shook back the hood. It fell to his wide shoulders, and eyes the sapphire of the deep blue sea met hers. She nearly evaporated with the power of them.

May the saints be praised, but he was the most striking man she had ever met. Coal black hair rippled from the peak on his forehead, tied back in a thick sheaf. She wanted to stroke it, to see whether the waves were real or some artfully constructed wig.

Altogether, his features weren't handsome, and a far cry from pretty. They were—manly. Like the rest of him. Hard ridges for cheekbones, deep-set eyes that burned like coal fires, a sharp nose, and full, sensual lips that parted to reveal white, even teeth as his body slanted closer.

"I hear the music even when you do not play," he said in wonder, whispering a kiss along the line of her jaw.

She gasped and bent backward into the piano. Her breasts strained at her thin bodice, and he noticed. Heaven help her, but his gaze dipped deliberately to her cleavage, and her nether parts moistened.

"Widowed." He repeated her earlier word with interest, capturing one of her carefully constructed curls and wrapping it around his finger. "The music you make"—he hesitated, as if looking for words—"it speaks to me."

She gasped. He could hear her notes? Her words? He *knew* what she'd played? Impossible.

"As your voice speaks to me," she tried to say lightly. She meant to skirt around him, but somehow she got lost in his eyes and forgot.

"We do not have"—he hesitated again—"music . . . where I come from. I like this manner of speech." His voice rumbled deeply, an erotic massage of her overly sensitized nerve endings.

"You're a man of the cloth," she protested, but she knew it was already too late. She heard the hunger in his voice, felt it in her bones, and somehow her logical mind slipped away, leaving her prone to the desires she'd denied for too long. Gravity drew them together.

"I am a man, yes," he agreed, although puzzlement creased his brow. He rested his hands against the piano on either side of her, entrapping her and pressing closer. "But my clothes are meaningless. If your music speaks truly, material things are no impediment to what we crave."

Amazingly, she still did not fear his encroachment, so lost was she in the wonder of his voice. Before she had the presence of mind to make the leap from *man of the cloth* to *clothes,* he pressed her back against the piano with his length and drove one hand into her chignon, sending pins flying across the Aubusson carpet.

The weight of him heated her breasts and lower parts. Releasing the safety of the piano, she rested her hands on the robe over his chest, pushing at him in a futile effort to deny the physical sensation of this man and her craving for what he offered. Chantal knew she should push harder, but curiosity and the compelling view of his sensual lips held her captive.

Instead of shoving him away, her hands drifted upward, and scandalously, she marveled aloud, "You have the broadest shoulders. I love broad shoulders on a man."

He cupped her head with a strong hand, forcing her to look at him while his thumb traced an exploratory path across her cheek, paralyzing her with his gentleness. "Not the broadest," he murmured honestly, "but I know more than most men."

Before she could respond to this confusing statement—know more about *what*?—his other arm captured her waist, crushing her fragile skirt and bringing her even closer. She could no longer free herself if she wanted. His robe concealed no soft priest but iron-solid muscle.

Despite the temptation of his caress, she opened her mouth to protest. She meant to protest, really. But his lips finally reached hers, and his tongue took possession of her breath, and all rational thought ceased.

Effortlessly, he lifted her limp form, crushing her in his embrace. Her skirts and petticoats protected her from feeling much below her waist, but she grasped his shoulders for balance and absorbed their magnificent strength while drinking in his kisses. She drowned beneath his hungry command, letting the nectar of his breath fill her starving soul.

A little voice far in the back of her head tried reasoning with her, but she slammed the door on reason. She wanted. He wanted. It seemed so simple.

He lifted her onto the lid covering the piano keys, propping her against the back while he made short work of the fastenings beneath the bow at her gown's gauzy neckline. No man had touched her in such a fashion in so long. . . .

He caught her gasp with his mouth as his marauding fingers slipped beneath the muslin and played a sinful tune on her aroused nipple. Desire shot straight to her loins. She moaned her pleasure and arched into his palm so he could touch more of her.

"What matter of wonder you are," he murmured in foreign accents that warmed her inner ear, "to both soothe and arouse. My pardon, but I cannot resist—"

He cupped her buttocks, lifting her from the piano lid to press her shoulders against the wall so they could feel more of each other. She needed no more encouragement to wrap her legs around his waist and return his fervent kisses, drowning in the avid possession of his tongue. She no longer thought at all, but responded to the prowess of pure male animal.

He growled against her mouth. His whiskers scraped her cheek, but the fresh scent of his skin filled her with longing. Her petticoats fell back until the heat of his sex pulsed where she needed to be filled. He carried no sword on his hip as gentlemen did. He'd left his staff leaning against the furniture. But he was not weaponless. Beneath his robe he was equipped as all men were. His robe dropped to the floor with a couple of shrugs, and supple leather breeches chafed her thighs.

He adjusted her higher, releasing her breast to tug her skirts free and find her needy flesh. Chantal cried out when his thumb parted her sex and caressed her there.

He nipped her lips, then lowered his head to suckle her breast at the same time that he expertly stroked the pulsing bud between her legs.

Chantal exploded in spasms of pure pleasure. Weeping, clinging, she was barely able to hold on while she surrendered to an ecstasy she'd seldom experienced. Had Jean been too young to know that they could enjoy this even when the consumption had weakened him? Why had she not known that the pleasure of simply touching could be so grand?

"You belong to me," the monk rumbled gruffly, holding her tight so she did not fall.

She did not know if she heard aright, for her assailant took that moment to shove aside the flap of his breeches. Before she had fully recovered her whirling senses, he thrust the head of his thick erection between the folds of flesh moistened by her pleasure.

Frightened, Chantal stiffened and tried to pull away, but it was far, far too late to protest. The stranger spread the strong trunks of his legs, stretching her wider and opening her completely before bringing her down on himself so swiftly and surely that she shattered.

She may even have blacked out, so overwhelming was the impalement of her long-unused body.

The pressure completely filled her emptiness. In moments, she was weeping with pleasure, tears flowing down her cheeks as she clung to his hair while he thrust higher, deeper. She feared he had surely penetrated to her very soul. As she came apart in his arms a second time, he muffled a cry of triumph and flooded her with the thick, hot essence that had the potential to tie her to him for all time.

Clasping her tightly in his arms, her powerful lover moaned his rapture against her mouth, then fell still against her while they gathered their breaths. Gently, he tasted her tears. He seemed to hesitate, waiting, as if she should say or do something in the aftermath of such glorious insanity.

But she was too spent. She leaned her head against his broad shoulder and allowed him to carry her to the chaise longue.

"No child came of this," he informed her courteously, almost with disappointment. "But there will be other opportunities. It is good to verify that we share equal enjoyment of this act."

His inflection was foreign. She didn't even know *his name*. She only knew she trusted him because of the character revealed in his voice.

Embarrassed, she couldn't open her eyes while he towered over her. Searching for reality, she absorbed the pain where he'd entered her, felt the whisker burns on her cheek, and knew her mouth was swollen. Still, she wanted him again, ached for a repetition of the act, perhaps in her perfumed bed. She wanted him naked. She throbbed with desire as she never had before.

He brushed aside her skirts—they hadn't even undressed!—and sat near her hip. She couldn't possibly keep her eyes closed any longer. Fearing that she had imagined him, she opened her lids to gaze into strange dark eyes that reflected the dying light from the windows. She could have sworn she saw straight to his soul, so transparent were his pupils.

He'd fastened his breeches but not yet donned his robe, so she could see more of the square shape of his shoulders, the powerful strength of his chest beneath a finely woven linen shirt, the narrowness of his hips. He didn't need the pretty beauty of court nobles. He was beautiful in his strength as a man.

"Who are you?" she finally had sense enough to ask. Remembering the monk's robe, she continued, "Surely you are no celibate."

He seemed to consider for a moment before answering in a clumsy French accent, "Ian d'Olympe. Again, I apologize for my discourtesy, but not for what we have done. You have granted me a gift greater than I deserve, and I thank you. But I still must have the chalice."

"I will have the servants bring every chalice in the house, and you may choose among them," she suggested generously. She probably ought to be calling for help instead of offering access to her entire household, but she was still acting on the honesty she heard in his voice. She did not detect a single untrue note in him.

"I wish only the silver one with the gem-encrusted stem. It is awkward and ugly, and by itself, it is of no use to anyone."

He spoke with such sincerity, she had to believe him. She must have his chalice—

Chantal stared at him in surprise. "The silver bell! You want my bell!"

A V formed over the bridge of his nose. "It does not ring," he argued, "but it is silver. Might I see your bell?"

Dismay filled her as she realized she must disappoint him. "It is gone. I sent it away hours ago."

Three

Ian would have liked time to process the amazing synchronization of his body with his mate's that had produced such pleasure. He'd known many gifted women on Aelynn, but they had wanted marriage, power, and heirs. They had expected him to use his empathic talents to make the encounter memorable, without making much effort to return their gratification.

Never had he experienced such natural responsiveness, such a giving sensuality as this woman's. Now he understood the spiritual as well as the physical differences between a legal wife and an amacara. She'd lifted the exhaustion from his overworked senses, harmonized his thoughts, and restored him. She was amazing, a rejuvenating elixir he didn't want to give up.

He would have liked to simply study her beauty and the alluring way her blood pulsed through her veins when she looked upon him. He'd given up hope of ever meeting his physical match, and he needed time to ponder what it meant that she was not an Aelynner.

And that was only the beginning of what he wanted to do. She looked so deliciously shocked at what had happened between them that he could not resist leaning over and enjoying the intimacy of stealing another kiss, to assure her that this moment could be repeated again in the future. He was not a sentimental man, but he sensed her hunger for his touch, and he willingly complied.

He lingered on her lips to imprint them firmly in his mind before he straightened and returned to his task. As heir to the Oracle, he must put duty before pleasure. He was disappointed that a child had not come of their joining, but he was not disappointed that his future obligation lay in a continued attempt to create one.

For now, he would return to his foremost task. "If you will tell me where you have sent the chalice, I will fetch it and return here as quickly as I can," he promised.

Her hair fell in a waterfall across the arm of the oddly shaped chair on which she lay. Ian filled his hand with gold and indulged in the sensual luxury of stroking the silken strands with his callused fingers, while he waited for her to gather her wits.

She shook her head, and he hastily released her hair, thinking his rough caress might not cause her such pleasure as it did him. She did not give off all the usual cues to which he was accustomed.

"I cannot call the chalice back," she informed him. "It is all I have that might release my sister-in-law and her children from prison."

Ian did not have time for disappointment. He should have known the task would not be easy if Kiernan could not complete it. But he had already found his amacara. Gods willing, he would have the chalice soon. Then he must ponder the problem of Murdoch. Leaving a man with powerful, unpredictable abilities, a man with overriding ambition who possessed the ancient knowledge of Greek fire, to roam in a world already torn with strife appeared to oppose the most basic laws of Aelynn.

He stood and picked up his cloak. "I will offer coins

to whomever has the chalice. Tell me how to find your family, and I will bring them back with me."

Theoretically, he was not supposed to interfere in the Other World except in self-defense, or if one of his kind had caused harm. But if the chalice was meant to save his amacara's family, then it seemed reasonable that he should assist it.

"You do not know Paris," she stated, pushing her hair from her face and looking a little less dazed.

He swelled with male pride that he'd been able to fluster her as thoroughly as she had disturbed him. Perhaps it had been a new experience for both of them.

"You cannot find Pauline until I know where she is being detained," she insisted. "I have sent my servant to find out."

Ian disliked delay. He preferred a methodical accomplishment of his duties before indulging in further pleasure. Proper meditation and gratitude for the gift given him in this gentle lady was called for as well. In his heedless youth, he had occasionally exploded into emotional tumult, disregarding the necessity of quiet contemplation—at great peril to his own life and limb and to the people around him. He did not repeat mistakes. Indulging in further passion would be dangerous until he had accomplished his goals.

He slipped his robe over the Other World clothing Kiernan had insisted that he wear. He found the breeches constraining, but the shirt was loose enough that he could swing his staff as needed.

He'd refused to wear one of the tight coats that would hinder his ability to act quickly, and waistcoats were frivolous baubles of no use for comfort or protection. Kiernan had found the robe when they'd first landed in Brittany. He'd presented it with a grumble about Ian's living the life of a monk, so he might as well look like one, a comment Ian had disregarded. Kiernan's disrespect for his leader's asceticism was well-known.

"I have been unforgivably rude," Ian said again, hoping she would give him clues as to how to solve the problem of the chalice's location.

"*Rude* is not the word I would use," she murmured, still attempting to straighten her clothing and locate her hairpins.

He almost smiled at her dry remark. They were very much in tune, it seemed. Once he had the time to do so, he would enjoy learning more about how they could play together. "I do not even know your name or how you would like to be called."

She looked startled and then ashamed. "I think your bell or chalice or whatever has affected my mind," she muttered. "I cannot believe what we have done. You're a stranger. Perhaps you should leave. My father is expected to return from Versailles this evening."

"There will be time to explain later, after I retrieve the chalice," he said soothingly. "I will present myself to your father, and we will have a discussion about your future. I promise, you have done nothing of which to be ashamed, but I am concerned I have given you a wrong impression. I am not usually so impulsive." That was an immense understatement. At home, he had all the leisure in the world in which to contemplate his intentions before acting on them. He had not anticipated giving in to spontaneous arousal. Or the need for apologies. He'd never had to apologize, until now. "Please forgive me."

She sighed, and pushed high by her confining garments, her beautiful bosom rose and fell. Ian had to tear his gaze away and study the plaster garlands and painted cherubs on the ceiling to prevent his body from responding again. He supposed if one must hide from the Other World's intemperate climate in these huge dark caverns they called houses, it was best to do so in artful surroundings.

"I think it is your voice that makes a muddle of my brain," she said distractedly, rising and offering her hand. "I truly do know proper etiquette and do not generally behave as an uncivilized heathen. I am Chantal Deveau. It is a . . . pleasure . . . to meet you."

Ian was aware of the custom of greeting others with outstretched hands. Conscious of the irony, considering the intimacy they had already shared, he took her offered fingers and bowed over them. "My pleasure," he said as he'd been taught, but truly meaning it. Just touching her was pleasing, and he stroked her palm, causing her to look startled and as interested as she had earlier. She had a way of lowering her lashes and appearing sleepily seductive that would divert him were he any ordinary man.

"Now, if you will instruct me as to where I might find the prisons in which your family might be detained, I will attempt to return with them before your father arrives."

Chantal couldn't decide whether it was the man or the lovemaking that was making her brain whirl unsteadily. Had she mentioned that Pauline was in prison? It was not a delicate thing to say. Had he just offered to break her family out of prison without even asking why they were there? And what had he meant about her future? Surely she'd misheard him.

"I don't know where you come from that justice is so easily accomplished, but it could take days to find Pauline and arrange for her release," she argued. "Most monks have fled France, since the Assembly confiscated their property. You cannot hope to pass even the first guard dressed as you are. Paris is in turmoil, and people are very suspicious of foreigners. I trust your passport is in good order."

"I am sorry; I do not have days to wait," he said with an impatient gesture that might be interpreted as arrogance in a man not wearing an ascetic's robe. "As much as I would enjoy learning more of your world, I have a mission to complete before I return home. I would discover the level of difficulty for myself."

He conveyed an implacable authority that she'd sensed earlier, a superior attitude that she resented in most men, but oddly, not in him. Perhaps because she trusted him to use his authority wisely? Her mind must be completely lacking. She hardly knew the man.

"Fine, then, I will come with you," she announced. "Let me have the maids instruct my students to return tomorrow. I will admit I am anxious about Pauline." She must truly be crazed to suggest this, but she could detect no uncertainty in his voice. He *knew* he could free Pauline. Who was she to argue with a man who was willing to give her exactly what she wanted?

She blushed as she realized how thoroughly he had given her what she wanted, even when she hadn't realized what that was. And she *had* needed their lovemaking, it seemed. She felt much better and braver now. Surely a woman of the world who could make love to a stranger had the courage to challenge a prison guard, especially with this odd white knight at her side.

She rang the bell for a maid before Monsieur d'Olympe could object. He hadn't raised his cowl, so she could see his thoughtful frown, but he didn't outright refuse her aid. *A man among men,* she thought dryly.

More than a man among men to have come here and turned her inside out as he had, but since she wasn't thinking clearly, she wouldn't try to puzzle him out. She would see how he behaved when confronted with circumstances beyond his control. That always revealed a person's character. She was terrified that for the first time in her life she had not interpreted the notes of a voice correctly. No mortal man could be so trustworthy.

She was in no humor to change from her fragile at-home gown. Instead, she retired to her chamber to wash away the evidence of their encounter. She was a widow and had done nothing that every other woman in this city hadn't done far more often than she. This was Paris, the city of love. The court could not function without sexual power plays. She had no reason to be ashamed of her behavior—other than that she didn't know this man.

She sent for her cashmere shawl in case the June evening turned cool. Then she donned her wide-brimmed straw hat to cover the shambles Monsieur d'Olympe had made of her hair—and to conceal her blush whenever she thought about what they'd done.

She returned to find her guest frowning at a large oil painting of a bloody cavalry charge. He turned at her entrance, and his frown disappeared. She took that for approval since he didn't seem to smile a great deal.

A footman hurried to open the front door for them. Girard generally accompanied her when she walked to her father's office, but she had sent him off with the bell—the chalice. Now she had her strange . . . beau? . . . to act as escort. Most of the people in this arrondissement knew her and would not harm her. Still, these were hard times. Anything could happen.

Ignoring polite etiquette, her escort did not offer his arm for her support, but picked up his staff and followed her as she swept down the circular drive.

The largest prison in the city, La Conciergerie, was located on the Île de la Cité, next to the Palais de

Justice, and since Pierre and Pauline had just been taken, they would most likely still be there. Girard would have driven over in the pony cart. Chantal could easily walk to her father's office and the market, but crossing the bridge where filthy radicals assembled to cast their insults could be unpleasant.

Oddly enough, while she hesitated, her companion began to twirl his walking stick in circles with ever-increasing speed. She blinked in astonishment as it became a blur of lightning that he whirled from front to back and over his head in a manner she could not quite follow.

"This way, I think," he said when the stick slowly came to rest. Taking her elbow—more to steer her than out of politeness—he led her toward the gate-keeper, who stared at them with his jaw hanging open.

Before she could ask the servant to hire a cart, Monsieur d'Olympe escorted her into the bustling street and turned in the correct direction, toward the main road that would lead them across the bridge.

He strode rapidly. She had to lift her skirts to follow him. He slowed with a frown.

"Perhaps you should not accompany me, after all. The degree of hostility around us indicates a high probability of danger. I did not realize I would jeopardize your safety out here."

He turned to lead her back, but Chantal dug in her heels. She had given up attempting a normal conversation with this man. *Degree of hostility*, indeed. "I walk these streets every day. You might wish to engage a cart and driver, though. The distance is great and you are already weary." She added the last with the same patronizing tone he had used.

He eyed her warily, apparently sensing her displeasure. "You would engage one of these men who appear to despise you?"

Truly offended now, she propped her hands on her hips and glared. "If you have just arrived here, how can you presume to know how people think of me? I have known them for years. Admittedly, there is a great deal of resentment for my father's wealth, but I cannot believe that they actually despise me."

Although she often sensed simmering anger beneath the resentment, she assumed that was because poverty ate at the soul. Once people understood how hard her father worked for their benefit, once times improved, the hatred and resentment would dissipate.

"Perhaps I am overtired and do not yet understand how your people think," he agreed with hesitation. "I have no desire to strike anyone for imagined insults. Show me which carts are for hire, and I will acquire one for you."

Chantal rubbed the place on her brow that had begun to throb. It was apparent he did not have complete command of her language. One did not *strike* others for *thinking* insults, did one? So she had obviously misunderstood, or he'd misspoken. She glanced up and down the street, saw old Jacques meandering in their direction with his cart empty of produce, and signaled him.

The old man nodded his graying head and steered his ancient mule toward the sloppy gutter, splashing passersby with the cart's wooden wheels. "Madame Deveau," he murmured in greeting, not offering to step down from his high seat. "You are out late this evening." He eyed her companion with disfavor.

The monk drew up straight in evident umbrage, offered Chantal a look of disbelief, and rapped his solid staff against the cart's big wheel with such vigor that even the old donkey started and turned to look.

"Out of the cart, old man! Your filthy thoughts condemn you as worse scum than those who have abused you. Get down, and I will take the lady myself. I will pay you for the animal's freedom."

Before Chantal could so much as gasp in shock, Monsieur d'Olympe threw a coin at the driver's boots, then bodily lifted Jacques to the street when the old man bent to grab it. Jacques spit at their feet, but thoroughly cowed by the encounter, he did not argue.

Without so much as a by-your-leave, her companion lifted her to the cart's high seat. Chantal stared in astonishment as all semblance of his tantrum dissipated, and he stopped to stroke the nose of the cantankerous old mule and apparently murmur pleasantries to it as she might her kitten.

After seeing to the mule, he swung effortlessly up to join her. His cuffed boots did not bear a single splatter of mud beneath his long robe.

"You're not really a monk, are you?" she said as he studied the mule's reins and called softly to the animal. Without need of a tug of the leather, the animal turned its head in the right direction.

"A monk?" he asked without inflection as he concentrated on steering the cart into the busy street. "That means a man of your church; am I correct? No, of course not. Why would you think that?"

Chantal rolled her eyes and began to hum beneath her breath. Perhaps she would let him buy back the bell—the chalice—then hit him over the head with it. That might produce a calming effect.

"You are wearing a monk's robes," she pointed out.

"Clothing does not make the man," he informed her as if she were the crazy one. Safely in the main stream of traffic, he clicked the mule down the street as if he knew precisely where he meant to go.

Four

Ian frowned at the defiant tune his amacara hummed, but he chose to study her moods as time went on rather than question, since his queries seemed to disconcert her. He had learned from his friend Trystan's wife that Other Worlders did not know how to conceal their emotions and thoughts as Aelynners did, though his mate seemed able to conceal hers with music. Even when she was silent, she vibrated with sound. It was a pleasant new experience that he would enjoy exploring, once he had the chalice and Murdoch secured.

He was obviously out of harmony with her world. That the vile old man could even think of Chantal in such violently sexual terms had shocked him beyond reason—so much so that even the poor animal's neglect had not registered as it ought. He could not remove his mate from this unpleasant environment quickly enough for his tastes. Once he obtained the chalice, he would speak with her father and settle the marriage arrangements.

He had learned about Other World marital customs from Trystan, who had taken a Crossbreed for his wife. Mariel had already borne Trystan a pair of healthy, delightful twins, so perhaps the gods knew what they were doing by matching Ian with Chantal. If a mere Guardian like Trystan could overcome the conflict of cultures, then Ian was confident he could.

Twins would be more than he could expect. He'd settle for a single heir, male or female.

Once he had presented the proper marriage gift and said the required words, he could take his amacara with him and protect her from the hostility of this appalling city. Trystan was fortunate he could live on the peaceful coast of Brittany when he and his wife weren't on Aelynn.

"You bullied an old man," Chantal said abruptly, intruding on his thoughts, reminding him that he might have a few hurdles to overcome before she understood his actions.

"I scared a bestial coward," he replied. "Never go near that man again. I should have tied him up and turned him in to your authorities. If a creature like that is allowed to roam the streets unhindered, I must ask why your family has been incarcerated. Surely they cannot be worse."

"Would you quit talking in circles?" She stamped her kid shoe, and the ancient floorboard cracked ominously. "You are giving me a headache. I cannot fathom how a man of such candor can be so impulsive, bigoted, and"—she hunted for a word—"and so lacking in understanding!"

"I would learn more of the nuances of your speech if I could read your thoughts, but I cannot, so you must bear with my clumsiness until I understand where I have erred."

"And quit being so reasonable!" she cried. "You make me want to believe you, when I have just seen you intimidate a poor old man. You have stolen his cart, his livelihood! I have known Jacques for years, yet you call him a bestial coward simply because he is cross-eyed and grumpy. Then you insult my family, and you do not even know them!"

"Go back to humming, please," he requested. "It is more pleasing and less confusing."

Trying to concentrate on his faint Finding ability, Ian steered the cart into the crowded throngs of a broader thoroughfare. The chalice lay straight ahead. He was almost there. Perhaps Kiernan had been right and the gods had wanted his personal attention in seeking the sacred vessel and his amacara.

A troop of soldiers in striped trousers marched past carrying a strange assortment of weapons, and Chantal broke into a song that Ian loosely translated as "We will win!" He didn't see the relevance, but people in the street waved their caps and smiled in response. She had a truly amazing voice. Aelynners did not have a tradition of music, and he rather regretted that. Over the generations, the gods had denied Aelynners less useful abilities and encouraged more practical ones. An island could hold only a limited number of people, so Ian could understand their purpose. But relaxation had a purpose as well.

"What do you intend to win?" he asked once she'd stopped singing, having vented her apparent frustration.

"Victory over those who would oppress us," she rejoined tartly. "You will have to show your passport at the bridge guardhouse."

Trystan had provided the necessary paperwork when Ian had arrived in Brittany. So far, no one had questioned his papers, but Chantal seemed nervous. "Those buildings ahead are where your council meets?" He sought a better translation. "Your court of law?"

"Yes." She nodded and began humming again, keeping time by tapping her fingers against her pretty skirt.

All gentle femininity and soft speech, she appeared to conceal an inner core of strength that fascinated him. He wished he had more time to enjoy her musical voice. He'd never suffered such a diversion from duty before, not even when he was young.

He might wish to delay sealing the unpredictable—irreversible—bond of amacara until he'd achieved his objectives. His intended mate was distracting enough without that visceral connection binding them.

He halted the cart at the end of the bridge. Blue-uniformed soldiers bristling with swords and muskets stepped forward and demanded their paperwork, as Chantal had predicted.

She continued humming as she handed over her passport, and the guard on her side smiled and tipped his cap, murmuring pleasantries.

The guard on Ian's side frowned at his papers. "You are not from Rome?" he demanded.

"I do not even know where Rome is," Ian replied truthfully. "Is it a place I should visit?"

Chantal elbowed him. He didn't know what that meant but decided it would be wise not to offer any additional information.

"Swiss," the guard said in disgust, examining the passport's writing with difficulty. "Why are you here?"

Ian didn't know what Swiss meant either, but Trystan had assured him that such papers would pass easily through this country. "The lady wishes it," he said pleasantly, not desiring to go into complicated explanations when he did not comprehend the necessity. On Aelynn, he was the authority who did the questioning, so this was a relatively new and irritating experience.

His reply was apparently acceptable. The guard nodded, handed back the papers, and stepped aside. Chantal waved gaily at the other handsome soldier, and Ian started the cart with a jerk that threw them both against the seat back.

To his utter astonishment, he had a strong urge to strangle the young man she'd favored with her smile. This could not be a good thing. A Sky Rider must be objective and dispassionate to effectively comprehend his visions.

His companion took a deep breath of relief, and his gaze dropped to the plump mounds pushing above the neckline of her tight bodice. Fortunately for both of them, she'd covered herself with a long cloth that molded to her curves but did not reveal tempting flesh.

The air coming off the river was sticky and windless, but the setting sun had fallen behind a cloud and brought with it a drop in temperature. He noted her shiver. "I will try to be quick so you do not catch a chill."

"You are going the wrong way." She pointed toward a menacing gray stone wall on the left side of the street. "You will need to ask at the Palais where Pauline is being kept."

"The chalice is this way," he insisted. "I would speak with whomever holds it. If you sent it for your family's release, then the possessor of the chalice should know where they are; am I correct?"

She shot him a mystified look. "How can you know where the chalice is?"

He shrugged. "Your language does not have the necessary words to explain. When we have time, I will try to answer your questions, but there are many things I cannot tell you without showing you. There will be time for that once I have done what I've come to do."

"I wonder if this is a form of madness," she muttered, "or if you are a magician like Mesmer who has stolen my mind, for I am surely out of it."

Since he could not read her thoughts, Ian had to put himself in her place and attempt to understand her unease. He did not need to stretch far to grasp that Other Worlders walked about in a world of psychic silence, unable to communicate in any way except verbally.

Not too different from his home, really, where everyone had learned to keep their thoughts to themselves and politely avoided prying into others' if they had that ability.

Although Ian could not always read their minds, he understood his fellow Aelynners sufficiently to comprehend and manipulate their behavior as needed. It was just that here, he was so bombarded with every violent thought and emotion that he assumed everyone felt and heard what he did. Sadly, Chantal did not seem to possess his empathic talents. Since she did not have Aelynn eyes, chances were good that she was not even a Crossbreed. That could cause grave difficulty in the future. He didn't want to believe the gods would bring him such grief.

"We have only just met," he assured her, and himself. "It takes time to understand each other. You must question me, or I may take your silence for comprehension."

As he brought the mule to a halt in front of the imposing edifice that contained the chalice, he added, "But save your questions for later. There are far too many people here for me to think clearly."

He refrained from adding that he dared not swing his staff to enhance his concentration in crowds. That was another of those details he must explain later. He'd thought learning the ways of the Outside World would be his largest difficulty, but it seemed that explaining himself was even harder.

He couldn't explain Aelynn at all, not unless they were properly bound by vows. Taking an Other Worlder for wife was fraught with difficulty. Most Aelynners left their Other World mates with their Other World families rather than bring them to the island. Ian couldn't afford that luxury. He might never be able to return here again, and he had no intention of leaving Chantal in this grim place. A solution must be found.

Climbing down, he stroked the donkey's muzzle, soothed by its uncomplicated affection. People might not completely understand him, but animals accepted him without judgment. He hoped his rebellious, glorious amacara eventually would, too.

He almost laughed when she hummed louder. He was not a man accustomed to laughing—or expressing any other emotion—but he was starting to grasp this peculiar reaction of hers.

"I will learn to hum my frustration as you do," he told her, lifting her from the cart. "Just think how I must feel trying to understand your strange ways." He set her on the muddy street and strode briskly toward the prison's entrance.

She remained where he'd left her, tapping her toe on the cobblestones.

Knowing he was close to the chalice, Ian was half inclined to leave her there. She would only slow him down. But this was not peaceful Aelynn, and he was beginning to understand mortality in this world where life was so little valued. He refused to lose her now that he'd found her.

So he returned and frowned down on the wide-brimmed hat that prevented him from seeing her expression. "You do not wish to go inside?" he asked.

"I do not wish to follow at your heels like a lamb,"

she replied, frost dripping from her tongue. "Proper etiquette requires that a gentleman offer his arm to a lady, especially in a place like this."

Ian studied her, studied his arm; then, shrugging, he stuck the arm not burdened with his staff straight out so she could hang on to it.

She tilted her head so even he could read her incredulity. Humming a tune that resembled the rebellious ditty of earlier, she caught his elbow, tugged it sharply downward, and lifted her skirt with her free hand. "You must have been raised in a cave," she concluded.

Thinking of his mother's safe haven at the foot of the volcano, Ian nodded. "I was, until I was old enough to go out alone."

This time, he ignored the look of disbelief she cast upon him.

Five

Located immediately next to the Palais de Justice, La Conciergerie prison was part of the medieval palace of Philip IV, and the hall's immense vaulted ceiling and rows of Gothic columns reflected its origin. Had the marble floors been empty, the palatial space would be awe inspiring.

Instead, the dregs of humanity mixed with soldiers, lawyers, and a host of visitors—elegant and otherwise—and the stench and the noise in the echoing chamber were overpowering.

Clinging to Monsieur d'Olympe's arm, Chantal hurried to keep up with his brisk stride. His robe swung around his boots like the cloak of a general, and he behaved as if not another soul existed but himself. For the most part, the mob aided his impression. People drifted aside ahead of them, creating a wide path to the iron grille at the rear of the chamber that marked the prison's boundary.

Perhaps it was his monk's robes that caused people to step aside, but Chantal doubted it. She assumed that if he had *her* following like a sheep despite her resistance, he might impose his wishes on others as well.

Praying that Pauline and her children were close by prevented Chantal from thinking beyond that. There wouldn't be time before dark to traipse about Paris to look elsewhere. The city was filled with prisons.

Monsieur d'Olympe apparently intended to march right past the desk and guards and part the grille with his bare hands. Evidently her task was to remind him that he was not God. A cave, indeed! Perhaps his parents were wolves.

A little shaken upon realizing that the man with whom she'd just had sex—it certainly hadn't been lovemaking, she had no illusion about that!—reminded her very much of a beautiful wolf stalking his prey, she tugged his arm and refused to walk farther.

At his impatient glance, she nodded toward the uniformed man behind the desk. "You cannot enter without his permission. Pauline will be here under her married name of Racine."

She wanted to search for Pauline among the prisoners strolling about on the far side of the grille, but watching over her determined companion took all her attention. Fierce features scowling, he twirled his gnarled staff against the floor while he followed her gaze and took note of their surroundings.

"I should have brought Kiernan," he said in disgust. "I cannot sense anything in this confusion."

That made about as much sense as anything else he'd said so far. Taking a calming breath, Chantal tugged him into the line in front of the desk. She might think rebellious thoughts, but she disliked actual conflict.

"I am not accustomed to waiting," he practically growled at her.

"We can't go through without a pass," she explained tightly.

"We could be here all night." He started to twirl his staff, realized what he was doing, and pounded it impatiently on the floor. "The chalice is more important than their petty concerns."

"Maybe so, but—" Chantal gaped as the slovenly couple in front of her looked around nervously and abruptly walked off.

She glanced at her companion to see if he might have threatened them in some way, but he was glaring at the next person in line—a black-coated, bewigged lawyer. The man suddenly checked his watch and apparently realized he needed to be somewhere else.

"That's better," the monk muttered, studying the weeping young woman now blocking their progress. He twirled his staff, studied the vaulted ceiling for a minute, then shook his head. "I detest this place."

Abandoning Chantal, he left the line and stalked toward the desk. The burly soldier ignored his approach until her audacious companion slipped a coin from a pouch in his robe, set it on the desk, and leaned over to whisper something in the man's ear.

Coins of any denomination were extremely scarce. He'd have a mob attacking him for his purse if he were not careful.

Chantal held her breath as other soldiers inched closer. She shivered, uneasy at being left alone in this crowd. She had foolishly felt safe at Monsieur d'Olympe's side. She ought to know better than to equate size with intellect. The idiot man could get himself thrown behind bars and never be seen again.

She surveyed the throng, praying she might glimpse sturdy old Girard, but a shift in the line ahead caused her to swing back to see what was happening.

A guard was opening the gate, gesturing for her escort to enter. Swearing under her breath, Chantal caught up her skirts and hurried to join him. To her surprise, all the others in line surged forward as well.

Monsieur d'Olympe—*Ian,* since he scarcely seemed a gentleman—patiently waited for her before entering. But there was nothing patient about his grip on her arm as he pushed her past the shouting, hugging couples and acquaintances who were meeting in the broad corridor.

"The guards have no compassion," he growled. "They think only of their bellies, like starving dogs in a manger."

"They have spent many years starving like dogs," she said tersely. "We had no grain, no bread, no coal with which to warm ourselves, while the nobility danced to Austrian musicians and competed to see who could wear the most extravagant imported laces and silks. If people are reduced to surviving like animals, they will behave like animals."

He wore his cowl over his head, so she could not see his reaction to her lecture. She had acquired her zeal for equality at her father's knee. She had no more respect for the monk's church than she did for the court. The church had hoarded its wealth while the aristocracy had squandered theirs. Fools all. Neither extreme aided the masses, but she politely refrained from completing the lecture. She still did not grasp Ian's connection to the church.

"How did you persuade them to let us all in at once?" she asked.

While the guard led them to Pauline's chamber, Ian responded, "The guards were bored. It was the end of their shift. The gates would close shortly. I offered them the opportunity to have a good time this evening."

He was a foreigner. How had he known the gates would close when she did not?

"In here." The soldier indicated one of the first-floor chambers, and Chantal sighed in relief. At least the children weren't being housed in the dungeons.

Choosing not to question this miraculous gift, she merely glanced at the monk's enigmatic features beneath the cowl, then brushed past him to enter Pauline's cell.

The chamber was narrow and filthy, and Chantal suppressed her rage that her beautiful godchildren and her frail sister-in-law were confined in such squalor. She had to get them out of here, at once. Somehow. She would worry about Pierre later.

Pauline cried out in surprise at her entrance, and the children raced to cling to her petticoats. Weeping at the sight of Pauline's gamin features stained with dirt and tears, Chantal hugged her. Wordlessly, she took comfort in her best friend's strong return of affection and sob of relief, then crouched down to wrap the children in her embrace. She kissed them and hummed beneath her breath to ease their fears and her own.

"We should leave now," the monk intoned quietly.

Chantal stared up at him in disbelief. "Leave? We have only just arrived."

"My supply of funds is not endless. I must still buy back the chalice and may not be able to pay our way in here again. Gather the children and hurry to the cart while you can."

Chantal almost bit through her tongue to keep from questioning this astounding order. Did he think they could invisibly walk past the guards at the gate? Had he bribed the guards not to see them? What manner of insanity inspired him?

Leaning down to lift her youngest, Pauline whispered, "Who the devil is he?"

"King Arthur?" Chantal suggested, taking the hand of five-year-old Anton. "But I am learning not to ask questions. Amazing things happen in his company." Given the embarrassing details, she could scarcely explain how amazing.

Without arguing, she hurried Anton past Ian's

motionless form into the crowded corridor filled with prisoners and their visitors. All were allowed to roam freely—until they reached the grille in the vaulted hall.

"We cannot go past the gates without a pass," she warned. "How can we reach the cart?"

"Ask nicely," he replied without inflection. "Or hum," he added after a moment's thought. "I enjoy the sound."

He confused her too much for her to know if he was being facetious. She had seen Ian move a line of people out of his way and fling open gates that were barred to most. That there had been no trial, no judge, and presumably no bail did not seem to deter him now.

Singing lightly to amuse the toddlers, she swung Anton's hand and hurried after Pauline, who was already halfway down the corridor, racing as if the hounds of hell were on her heels.

Chantal's heart was lodged too firmly in her throat to pound. That their party hurried toward the great room was not unusual enough for any to take notice. Passing the locked gate at the end, on the other hand—

Didn't stop Monsieur d'Olympe. Using his staff as a walking stick, he strode firmly toward the gate, nodded at the guard, and waited for the gate to swing open as if he were king and the soldier a mere footman meant to obey his orders. Given that during this turbulent time the king was a prisoner in his own palace, though, that was not a good comparison.

The gate opened. The guard waved them on without asking for visiting passes.

Not caring how this came about, Chantal shooed her small flock ahead of her, making certain they were safely past the grille before rushing out to join them.

The gate slammed, leaving Ian behind.

Gasping, Chantal sent him an anxious look, but he was already turning away, intent upon his own business. Humming a trifle frantically now, she held tight to her nephew's small hand and, shoulder to shoulder with Pauline, hastened through the medieval great hall until they reached the humid air of the darkening street.

A motley band of neighborhood militia stamped past—aging muskets and rusty sabers held over their shoulders, a drum and pipe playing marching music—leading a parade of idlers through the evening dusk. The military sights and sounds were increasingly familiar, and Chantal shivered as if she'd seen a portent of things to come.

"What just happened in there?" Pauline murmured, hugging her youngest and observing the normal street scene in confusion.

"We may have met a whirlwind," Chantal replied. "Did Girard find you?"

"He did. He said he was working on our release, but he could not say how long it would take." Pauline set Marie on her feet. "I did not expect it to come so precipitously. I owe you everything for this."

"You owe me nothing." Chantal dismissed the sentiment while watching the street in hopes of seeing a tall figure in robes striding after them. "Did Girard have my bell with him?"

"Bell? No, he carried nothing." Pauline threw her a worried glance. "Your friend did not trade himself for us, did he?"

Chantal shook her head. "As noble as I grant his actions are, I think they were in his own interest as much as ours. I just worry that he does not fully grasp our customs here. He claims to be Swiss and raised in a cave."

Pauline laughed shortly. "All Parisians behave as if

they were raised in caves these days. I fear what the wolves will do to Pierre."

"Your brother brought this on himself. We have not gone to the Palais yet to ask where he's been taken. My father can find him tomorrow and see what must be done. I wish Girard would come out. I need to take you home, but I hate to leave Monsieur d'Olympe."

Perhaps she could send Girard back to find him—

Which meant she was hoping the mysterious Monsieur d'Olympe would follow her home.

Gulping at that stunning realization, she hurried the children along and led Pauline to their waiting cart.

Six

Frustrated, Ian traversed the prison's corridors, attempting to locate the source of the faint tingle that told him he was on the right track.

The tingle abruptly ended.

Ian cursed. Either the chalice had left the premises, or his ability to sense it had departed in the tumult of violent emotions in the huge edifice. *He'd lost the chalice.* He clenched his staff and resisted the urge to swing it in the midst of the mob.

He needed the stars and an open field where he could meditate without the constant bombardment of human passions. He was better at Seeing than at Finding. The gods must be toying with him to send him here, or teaching him the meaning of living without their aid.

It did not take long to determine that asking questions was a waste of time. The chalice had undoubtedly been taken as a bribe, and no one would admit to accepting one. He left suggestions that he was in the market to buy such an object, and gave Chantal's direction should anyone wish to take up his offer.

Then nudging the mind of the gate guard as he had earlier to free Pauline, he walked out of the prison and into the street.

He was coming to appreciate Kiernan's difficulty in locating the elusive chalice. It was as if once the chalice had led him here to free the woman and her children, it had gone on to new pursuits. Ian prayed that whatever the chalice did next would not include Murdoch. The thought of having a dangerous rogue loose in the same city as the sacred object chilled him to the bone.

Perhaps his task was to find Murdoch first and hope the chalice would follow.

Unaccustomed to failure, Ian walked off his annoyance, returning to Chantal's home on foot. Perhaps the gods heard him only on Aelynn, and that was why he had not succeeded. He must learn to practice his gifts without divine intervention.

He had little difficulty using his ability to direct others out of his way. Opening a path through a crowd was a game he'd practiced since youth. Even men as gifted as Trystan and Kiernan seldom noticed when he influenced their direction, so these Other Worlders were no challenge.

But he could not extend the game to include persuading others to do what they did not wish. Had the guards not been bored and ready to go home, he could not have maneuvered them into allowing all the visitors entry. Admittedly, it was much easier manipulating people whose emotions he could read clearly. Genuine boredom was easy to detect even without his special abilities. Finding a soldier willing to take a valuable bribe like the chalice would be more tricky.

Ian wearily approached Chantal's elegant residence. He couldn't remember when he'd last eaten or slept. Perhaps with a little rest and meditation, his course would become clear.

Could he hope to share that rest with Chantal under her father's roof? The hope of once again attempting to create the child the island needed hurried his footsteps. He had no doubt that the gods had chosen Chantal as his amacara for a reason he had yet to grasp, but for now, it suited him just to know she was the most enchanting creature he'd ever met. Her music enthralled, and her sexual responsiveness was beyond anything he'd expected. He would welcome such enjoyment after a day's work.

Perhaps he would discover the mark of the gods on her and prove that she was a gifted Crossbreed of Aelynn blood. Except those born with the dark skin designs designating the favor of a particular god were rare and of greater ability than Chantal had revealed thus far.

The guard at her gate let him pass without question. Away from the river, the air was less chilly, and Ian opened his robe to allow a breeze to freshen his shirt as he strode toward the door. He still found the breeches confining, but considering his body's response to Chantal's presence, perhaps the discretion of confinement was necessary. Restraint had never been a problem until he'd met his amacara.

Food, rest, and bed play should restore him by morning.

As he had earlier, the servant at the door allowed Ian in after only a minor mental nudge. He offered to take Ian's robe, but Ian had some understanding that appearing without an outer garment was improper, so he kept it on. With his drab robe flapping at his boot heels, he took the wide marble stairs two at a time.

At this moment, Chantal's presence was much more vivid in his mind than the need to locate the chalice. Ian thought he could find her anywhere, if only by the music she radiated. By the time he reached the top of the stairs, he followed voices instead of instinct.

He came upon the women in a pretty room lined with flowered paper and filled with delicate-looking chairs he wasn't certain he dared sit upon. Pauline sat nervously on the edge of her seat, and Chantal was at a writing desk, pen in hand, looking worried.

Her expression of relief upon his arrival was so delightful that Ian crossed the floral carpet to kiss her. The gasp of the other woman reduced his enthusiastic salute to a less-than-satisfactory peck on the lips. He had to remember this was not his home, and Chantal not yet his.

"I was about to send Girard in search of you," she exclaimed with concern when he stepped back. "Have you eaten? I will send my maid for a tray."

She didn't wait for his reply to signal a young girl and order a repast. Ian's belly rumbled in anticipation. He turned to the woman clutching a china cup and staring at him in apprehension. The contrast between Pauline's dark hair and pale face was stark.

"I mean you no harm," he said reassuringly, answering the fear he heard in her mind.

"How did you release us?" Her cup rattled against the saucer, and she set them aside. "Will they come looking for us here?"

"Not until the court orders you presented for trial. The prison is too crowded and their records are"—he gestured to indicate his inability to explain—"not reliable."

"And Pierre?"

"I have inquired about your brother. He is to go before a judge tomorrow. I will seek him out there."

"You will?" Chantal's friend breathed the words with hope. "Please, what can we do for you in return?"

"I assume the gods have a plan. I will consult them later." Glancing around, he found a sturdy wing chair that might suit him and took a seat as if he belonged there. Sinking into concentration, he focused on Chantal to study his impressions of her . . . and her mysterious music.

Chantal stared at the man making himself at home in her feminine sitting room. At the moment, despite his declaration that he spoke to *gods*, Ian d'Olympe was very much a man, not a monk. His robe fell open to reveal the broad width of his shirt and the snugness of his fawn breeches as he crossed one booted foot over the other. She heard Pauline smother a gasp and could only imagine what her friend thought, especially after his kiss.

This was all happening too fast. Whether he intended it or not, Ian had assumed the role of lover with familiar access to her chambers. She had never before taken a lover, but apparently she had one now.

A thrill coursed through her as she realized his gaze conveyed a hunger for her as great as for the food the maid hastened to set before him. The silence after his rash statement stretched long, and she rushed to fill it.

"The gods normally consult with you?" she asked in what she hoped was sophisticated amusement.

"Do you not consult with your god?" He tasted the wine set before him and nodded in approval. "Pure ambrosia. Your wine is a part of your . . . country . . . that I fully appreciate."

He bit into a round of cheese before realizing they were waiting for an answer.

Chantal noted he ate with a gentleman's manners, using his napkin appropriately and not guzzling his drink, but he also ate with the enthusiasm of a healthy, famished male. She was unaccustomed to seeing food disappear so quickly.

With the damask napkin, he removed a bread crumb from the corner of his mouth and studied her with a piercing gaze. "My mother's wisdom in the matter of gods is greater than mine. She claims the ones we worship are the same as your god and saints. We simply speak of them differently. If your brother is a priest"—he nodded at Pauline—"I would like to discuss such matters with him. There are many aspects of your . . . country . . . that I wish to learn more about."

Chantal noted that Pauline relaxed at this reply, but she had heard Ian's hesitation over the word *country* several times now. Why did she feel as if he substituted *country* for *world*?

"I'm certain he would be delighted to have that conversation," Pauline said shyly. "But I fear my brother must leave France immediately should he ever be released from prison."

Chantal knew her sister-in-law well. Pauline was one of the queen's ladies-in-waiting, as her mother had been in her youth. Jean and his sister came from noble parentage, with estates near Versailles and Le Havre. Pauline's older brothers ran those estates now. Her late husband had left her a small townhouse in Paris where she left the children with governesses while she was at court. Since the royal couple had been effectively incarcerated in the Tuileries Palace, Pauline now spent most of her nights at home.

Pauline had no desire to leave Paris, but she doted on Pierre, her youngest brother. It would break her heart to see him exiled.

"Perhaps Pierre can live in Brussels with the émigré court until things settle down," Chantal suggested to soothe her friend's anxiety. Marie Antoinette, the queen, came from the Hapsburg Empire that extended from France's borders all the way to the English Channel. "He will have friends there."

Pauline twisted her hands in her lap and feigned a

smile. "I hope you are right and that someday the Assembly will recognize that they need the king as much as he needs them. And then perhaps King Louis will be able to bring back the real church. But I fear that before that happens, his brothers will raise an army to free him, and the result will be war."

In the brief time they'd conversed, Ian had consumed half a plump hen, a small loaf of bread, a carafe of wine, and Cook's famed creamed vegetables. Chantal waited with interest to see whether he would belch and slide under the table, or surprise her as he had been doing all day.

Using his finger bowl and napkin, Ian angled forward in the chair, indicating his interest. "You are expecting war? With whom?"

"Pauline is afraid of change," Chantal answered for her, "and admittedly, the political climate is uncertain these days, but I'm sure it will right itself once the country has wealth again. The theaters are still open. We entertain as always. The duchess gives her usual ball tomorrow night. Only the royal ducs are sulking because they can no longer rob the poor as freely as before. You will see. We'll be fine."

"The queen is virtually a prisoner," Pauline argued quietly. "She could not even leave the palace to attend Easter services, and she is questioned and followed within her own walls. She cannot attend parties! It is not the same at all."

After that unexpectedly heated diatribe, Pauline hastily stood and shook out her skirts. "I apologize, Chantal. I am not myself today." She turned to Ian. "I owe you my deepest gratitude, monsieur. Please, if you ever have need of anything, do not hesitate to call on me. As soon as my family is made aware of the great favor you have done us, they will feel the

same. I beg your leave this evening, however. My children are sleeping upstairs, and I wish to join them."
She curtsied and departed.

Chantal was relieved to note that the monk knew
to rise when a lady did. Her relief was short-lived
when he turned a heated gaze in her direction. She
could feel that look straight through flesh and blood
to her womb. No man had ever reminded her so forcefully of her sex.

"I have not found my chalice," he said formally. "I
must speak with your servant about it. There is much
I have yet to learn about your country. Is your father
home yet?"

"No, I've not heard from him"—which worried her
more than she would admit. Until today, the constant
piping and drumming of marching soldiers had not
bothered her greatly, but now, the military notes drifting by outside created cold shivers of alarm. "He may
have been delayed and decided to wait until morning.
Shall I have a maid show you to a room?" She rose
from her chair to offer him a candle to light his way.

"I will find you later," he said gravely. "First I will
speak to your servant. Then I must meditate on what
I have learned. I will not be long."

His voice rumbled deep inside her with an erotic
promise she shouldn't acknowledge. Instead of cor-
recting him, she wanted to walk into his arms and
refuse to let him leave. Only, giving any man everything he desired would be a serious mistake and a
certain path to heartbreak. Giving this man all he
wanted would only encourage his presumption.

"You'll find Girard in the kitchen. I can call for him
if you prefer."

"No, I will find him. I thank you for the delicious
meal." He approached her, and Chantal's heartbeat
escalated.

Now that they were alone, she ought to straighten out matters before he assumed too much. Unfortunately, her tongue had difficulty speaking what the rest of her disagreed with.

"Do not assume we will repeat what happened this afternoon," she managed to admonish despite her arguing body parts. "I live a respectable life and do not wish to mar my father's good name by behaving in a less than circumspect manner."

Ian's lips parted in an intimate smile that reached his eyes and said he'd like to consume her. The effect was so devastating, her knees nearly buckled. He could have carried her off in that moment, and she would not have protested. What the devil was wrong with her?

"I am glad to hear that," he said solemnly. "I do not like to share a woman with others. When your father arrives, I will make whatever arrangements you desire to satisfy your need for respect. And if that is your wish, I promise I will not repeat our earlier encounter."

Somehow she thought they were not quite speaking the same language, but she nodded anyway. "You assume too much on the basis of that encounter. It is as if it never happened. We will find your chalice and you can be on your way."

His smile widened against his exotic dark features until she feared she would fall forward and into his arms unless she escaped his magnetic attraction.

Before she was forced to run, Ian bowed slightly, sending his long queue tumbling over his shoulder. Then he straightened and retrieved his walking stick.

"Later," he promised, and strode briskly from the room, leaving Chantal to simmer in desire alone.

Seven

Wearing only a light muslin nightshift, Chantal sat up against the pillows of her bed and listened to the noise of the city from her open window.

Paris never slept. When militia weren't marching, or mobs gathering on street corners to protest the latest vitriolic political pamphlet, she could hear the sounds of a normal city. Carriages careened down stone streets carrying jovial theatergoers and inebriated young men. Farm carts rattled through the city gates bearing the products and produce the city's inhabitants would consume on the morrow. Passersby sang and chatted and argued on their way home. The clip-clop of metal-shod horses bounced against buildings and carried down alleyways.

And in the carriage yard below her window, a steady thud and grunt drifted upward. She hugged herself tighter, fighting the urge to look again.

Earlier, she'd given in to fear and crept to the window. The sight below had sent her scurrying back to bed, blood coursing heatedly to her cheeks.

So now she sat here, fretting about her father's absence while trying to avoid thinking about the incredible man practicing some form of weaponry in the carriage yard.

She did not want to admit that the brave new Paris of the Revolution was less than perfect, but she feared for her father's safety. His oratory was brilliant, but it irritated the more radical members of the Assembly, who thought all aristocrats ought to be executed for their crimes against the people.

Her father wasn't a violent man and believed reason would prevail. For the first time, Chantal wondered what would happen if he was wrong.

The muted sounds in the yard reminded her of the danger beyond these walls. She had expected to see thieves and murderers when she'd peeked out earlier. She hadn't expected her eccentric lover.

She couldn't resist the temptation any longer. She might be a well-bred lady, but she was also a woman. Throwing aside the coverlet, she crept on bare feet to the mullioned doors opening onto a small balcony above the yard.

Below, Ian had scandalously stripped to his breeches and boots. Lantern light shadowed and accented the awe-inspiring muscles of his brown arms and chest. His long dark queue hung down his back, and perspiration streaked his bulging shoulders as he twirled his heavy staff over his head, apparently lost in thought and unaware of his surroundings. Lean, trim, and in fighting shape, Ian was definitely no scholarly monk.

Chantal grew warm just watching him. He was a Greek statue come to life. What would he look like fully naked?

The blur of motion he created terrified and thrilled her. No mortal man could move with such speed. His staff was a whirlwind—its force dangerously invisible.

And he was her lover.

She was still trying to adjust to that fact. As much as she would like to pretend she hadn't behaved so wantonly, her body told her otherwise. She craved a chance to experience such sensations again, to prove she was still female and desirable to a man who looked like a god.

She must have made some sound, for he glanced in her direction. The blur of his staff slowed to a more natural speed, although his muscles still bulged with his efforts.

Chantal didn't look away this time. Ian held her gaze as he brought the staff to waist height and began spinning it hand over hand around his torso, eventually slowing it to lazy figure eights. Enthralled, she admired the fluid movement. But mostly, she wanted to see what he would do now that he knew she was there.

When he finally brought the oak to a halt and hid it in the shrubbery beneath her window, she should have fled and locked the door. But kneeling on the balcony's tiled floor, she clung to the wrought-iron rail and let excitement pound through her as Ian studied the ancient vines covering the stone exterior.

No civilized man in his right mind would attempt those thick, leafy ropes. Certainly no gentleman would. But no gentleman would be standing half-naked in her carriage yard either.

Perhaps he was some throwback to medieval knights. If so, she was the maiden in the tower he meant to carry off. He was already halfway up the wall, fitting his boots into crevices between the stones and hauling his weight up with his arms, looking as if he regularly scaled walls while the rest of the city slept.

Thrilled to the very marrow of her bones, she lingered to watch. She could argue that she wished only to make certain the foolish man did not fall and kill himself, but she could have done that from behind locked doors.

Instead, she felt bold and eminently desirable while waiting for her prince to come. . . .

Scaling a wall . . .

For her.

She stood and eased backward as Ian's powerful hands clasped the top of the railing. He wasn't even breathing heavily as he vaulted into the narrow overhang. Bronzed, half-naked, gleaming in the moonlight, he stood not six inches from her nose, his male musk strong and enticing. And she had yet to scream for help.

"I need a bath," he growled in husky tones that brooked no argument.

She heard, *I need you.* This time, her knees did buckle at hearing what wasn't said. His voice held that kind of power. She grabbed the wall to steady herself, but it wasn't necessary. Ian caught her waist and carried her inside. To the bed.

"We won't repeat this afternoon," he assured her, laying her crossways over the bed so her lower legs dangled over the edge, scarcely covered by her filmy gown.

Before she could scramble up from that vulgar position, he slid the muslin above her hips with a strong caress of her buttocks, then kneeled between her legs. As his tongue stroked the aroused bud of her sex, Chantal finally cried out.

But calling for help was the furthest thing from her mind.

Ian gentled his nervous mate by stroking her hips and cupping her buttocks while he applied his mouth to give her what she wanted without offending her with his perspiration-soaked body. She dug her fingers into the covers and bucked and writhed against him.

She aroused him to painful proportions, but he was a man who knew restraint.

He deepened his kiss, and she moaned, then froze with the tension building within them both. He didn't need any empathic ability to know what to do next. Suckling the sensitive bud of her sex, he filled her with his fingers, and she came apart in his hands.

He would have liked to linger and take his time bringing her to the crest again, then hunt for a mark that might prove she carried gifted Aelynn blood. He would have liked to take a bath and come to her clean. But trouble was on the wind. This time, his vision had shown Murdoch riding at the head of French troops somewhere in the countryside.

He did not need the stars to hear the more immediate danger riding this way now. He might have only this one opportunity to give her the child her body craved and his family needed.

Standing, he peeled down his breeches. For now, he would be crude and give her pleasure without subjecting her to his offensive stench. He lifted Chantal's legs to his shoulders, and kissed and nipped his way along her delicious flesh. She tensed as his ministrations woke her from her lethargy, but it was too late to stop him now.

Before she could pull away, he thrust deep within her tight passage. Arching his spine in a paroxysm of gratification at this joining, Ian closed his eyes and absorbed the wonder of her inner muscles convulsing around him.

He needed so much more time. . . .

But already, the galloping of horses in the distance rushed to end this moment.

He leaned forward and greedily suckled at her breast through the gauze of her bodice. She moaned and moved against him. That was all the encourage-

ment he needed. Lifting her hips to adjust the angle
of their joining, he thrust even deeper until he touched
the entrance of her womb.

He'd spilled his seed inside dozens of women without creating a child, but the gods had promised him
this mate. Sending up a prayer, he freed the animal
inside him, plunging without restraint until the wave
of lust reached its pinnacle. As Chantal arched eagerly
to accept him, the beast broke free and, with a growl
of possessive delight, filled her womb with the seed
of life.

Beneath him, Chantal shuddered and writhed in release, while Ian relentlessly held her in place, preserv-
ing their joining as long as he could. He wanted to
start all over, lick her skin, kiss her senseless, and find
new ways to excite her, but the rattle of carriage
wheels had already rounded the corner and entered
the street outside.

Still, he waited to feel that spark of life he'd been
told he'd feel when his seed found hers and a child
began. Trystan had sworn he'd known the instant his
twins were conceived. If Trystan could, surely Ian
would.

Maybe not. Ian felt an immense physical relief at
the power of his release, and deep gratitude for the
woman who even now reached for him again, but
nothing that spoke of life. Still, he didn't want to part
from her. Sheathed in her tight passage, he felt a new
rush of blood quickening in him.

But there wasn't time. As ever, duty called. Even
Chantal heard the shouts and musket fire now. Reluctantly, he released her, shuddering as he slid free into
the chilly night air.

She scrambled to her knees, letting the gown cover
her again as she stared in fear at the window. Ian
regretted that he had yet to see her fully undressed

so he might learn if the mark of the gods was on her. His path would be simpler if so. All Aelynners either had changeable eyes or a mark to show the gods' approval. Crossbreeds had them only if they were gifted.

He pulled up his breeches and began buttoning them, while admiring the way her thin gown clung to her plump breasts, slender waist, and curved hips. Next time, he would see all of her, he vowed.

"What is happening?" she asked in panic.

"I believe your father is returning. Dress quickly. You will be needed downstairs."

The peaceful street erupted in shouts and curses.

Without so much as a by-your-leave, Ian rushed out the glass doors and swung over the rail before the gates to the drive could burst open.

Chantal grabbed her robe and ran to the balcony.

Her father often kept late nights, but he never arrived at this speed and with this commotion. How could Ian know who it was? The crack of a whip, pounding hooves, and racing carriage wheels resounded across the cobblestones beyond the townhouse walls.

She saw Ian hit the ground running, snatching up his staff and racing for the entrance, but she couldn't see what happened farther down the drive.

She could still sense the blunt force of Ian's masculinity inside of her. Jean had been scarcely more than a boy when they married. Ian was a full-grown man, twice Jean's size. She would be sore for days, pleasurably sore, since each movement reminded her of what they had done and aroused her all over again.

Her father would be disappointed with her if he knew. If she came with child, she'd have to leave Paris and abandon their work here. Still, she could not regret what she had done.

She jumped back, startled, as the rusty carriage gate slammed open faster than she'd ever seen it swing. Galloping horses foaming at the mouth rushed in, dragging a coach that appeared to fly on two wheels before it crashed to a halt at the entrance.

Musket fire and shouts ensued, and she tugged her robe closed, terrified. Part of the mob slipped through the open gate, before it swung closed with a force that caught a man's hand as he tried to shove inside. He screamed in agony, but no one attended him.

She didn't know whether to race downstairs to offer help if that was her father in the coach, or run to Pauline's room and rush her and the children out a back door for fear of arrest. She kept searching for some sign of Ian, for some signal as to what was happening.

A mob formed behind the gate, waving weapons and cursing as the guard secured the lock. Even though she could barely see Ian's shadow, she knew he, not their aging gatekeeper, had been the one to open and shut the gate.

The yard was black except for the flickering of torches beyond the wall. She could see only shadows and hear grunts and scuffles. One of the intruders groaned after a particularly hard thud, and in her mind's eye, she could see Ian using his staff to double his assailant in half. She didn't know how, but the image was there, reassuring her that he had matters under control.

The coach driver and a footman climbed down to help out the carriage's occupant. Wearing a familiar cockaded bicorne and powdered wig, a tall man stumbled out of his own volition, grabbing the footman's shoulders before he fell.

Without further question, Chantal flew from the room and down the stairs.

Her father was injured.

And like a knight of old, Ian was single-handedly fighting off their enemies.

Eight

"I'm fine," Alain Orateur said, waving his hand dismissively as Chantal raced into his study. "I've just hit my bad knee. Have Girard arm the servants and send them into the yard. That should suffice to turn the rabble away."

Her father's face was white beneath the sweat-streaked dust of the road, and Chantal's heart lurched with fear. But understanding the wisdom of his order, she hurried back to the corridor. She nearly bumped into Girard hastily tugging on his coat, his shirt half outside his breeches. She repeated her father's command, sending him back to the kitchen to find help. She was much more accustomed to telling servants what to do than acting on her own, but she couldn't leave Ian out there alone. Retrieving the loaded pistol her father always kept in the foyer armoire, she bit her lip and approached the front door.

It was unlatched. She'd heard no one but her father enter. It was hard to believe that anyone in her beloved Paris would attack her generous father. It would be akin to attacking the beloved revolutionary soldier Lafayette. But the mood of the city swung with the tides these days.

She tugged the handle, and the door swung in effortlessly. Still barefoot and in her robe, she couldn't venture far without knowing her purpose. Attempting to stand behind the door and peer around, she scanned the darkened drive.

A mob still jeered and struck weapons against the iron bars of the closed carriage gate. She winced at the thuds coming from the graveled drive and smelled the stench of spilled blood.

Now that her eyes had adapted to the dark, she could see Ian more clearly, and she had to bite her lip to keep from screaming.

Ian's staff held his opponents at bay, but despite their bruises, the swordsmen were quick on their feet. If one feinted to draw Ian's blow, the other rushed in on his undefended side. Ian was deftly transferring the staff from hand to hand, holding them back, swinging surely and soundly, landing quick blows, but he did not have eyes in the back of his head. A man wearing the Phrygian cap of a radical, with hair straggling to his uncollared shirt, crept up from behind him.

With no time to think, Chantal shouted, "Behind you!" and hurried down the drive with pistol raised. She nearly slipped on a wet patch on the bricks, and fought back an urge to gag when she realized it was blood.

Without turning his head, Ian spun his staff behind his back, slamming his unseen assailant in the ribs, before swinging the stout oak low to the ground, forcing the other two to leap out of its way.

From the other side of the gate, the mob shouted as if they were watching gladiators.

Chantal was struck with the sudden impression that now that Ian had locked the mob out, he was toying with the invaders for his own amusement.

She had seen him spin his staff in a blur so quick that the human eye couldn't follow. He could have brought all three men to their knees in a heartbeat. For some reason, he chose not to.

Men! She could easily smack them all. The mob had deteriorated into a bunch of drunken louts looking for entertainment. A cockfight would do just as well, as long as blood was spilled.

Let Ian play his game with the swordsmen. She needed to return to her father, and she couldn't do that until the mob dispersed. She donned a smile for her own sake since it was unlikely that anyone could see it. Waving the pistol above her head, she began to sing "Ça ira!"

Thud. A sword clattered across the stones, and one thug went down. The mob jeered.

She sang louder, using the tenor of her voice in a manner she'd learned to encourage others to join in. Someone in the back of the crowd took up the refrain. This was why she loved Paris. Even in abject misery, the people remained proud and defiant. She poured her love for her home into her song, and the crowd responded.

The ruffian with the cracked ribs staggered in retreat toward the narrow arch of the pedestrian gate. Hands reached over the wrought iron to haul him across to the other side.

More voices sang in triumph, as if they were winning this battle.

Oomph. Ian's third opponent doubled up from a blow to the midsection.

Chantal switched to a laughing child's song and marched forward, gaily swinging her pistol. Ian grabbed his crippled adversary by the back of his shirt and flung him across the low pedestrian gate with his companion.

The mob cheered, apparently transferring its allegiance to the winner.

The man who'd lost his sword had finally retrieved it. Instead of rushing at Ian, he raised the weapon in salute and sauntered toward the exit, happily singing Chantal's tune.

Ian let him through, then slammed the gate shut and shot the bolt in place.

Chantal gleefully called out, "Farewell, my friends. We will see you when our flag flies in freedom and equality!"

The mob began to disperse, singing drinking songs and shouting rebellious verses.

Staff in hand, Ian approached her. She felt his disconcerting gaze piercing her as if he could see into her head. "You have a remarkable voice," he said dryly, dropping an arm over her shoulder and steering her back toward the house.

"People like to sing. I learned long ago that it's hard for people to be angry if they're singing." Taking in Ian's male musk and sweat as if they were fine wine, she was nearly dizzy from his proximity. She caught up her robe and hurried beside him.

"And this is the usual result when you sing?" he inquired off-handedly, as if they hadn't just confronted a mob and won.

"I don't usually sing in public, and turning away rabble is scarcely a habit, but, yes, whenever I have the opportunity to join others in song, I do feel better."

"I would hate to see you truly angry, then." He nodded at the servants gathering up their brooms and axes while humming under their breaths. "They act as if they're preparing for a party."

"You saved us from being terrorized by thugs. They have every reason to be happy. Ask them for anything you like, and they will most likely hug your neck." In a more seductive undertone, she added, "I would like to hug your neck. Thank you."

He squeezed her shoulders but didn't offer flattery

in return, as a normal gentleman might. He still seemed remarkably calm about the evening's events. He exhibited more interest in her singing than in a radical mob crazed with bloodlust.

"We have much to learn about each other," was all her suggestive gratitude elicited before they stepped into the hustle and bustle inside.

Girard handed Ian his discarded monk's robe, and he shrugged it on, enveloping his admirable shoulders, to Chantal's disappointment. But it was time to return to reality. She hurried in the direction of her father's study with Ian at her heels. She had no idea how she would explain his presence.

She sighed in relief at the sound of Pauline's voice coming from inside. Maybe she wouldn't have to explain after all.

Still captivated by the thrilling image of his mate in filmy white, her golden hair tumbling down her back while marching across stones with pistol raised, singing triumphant war songs like a Valkyrie of old, Ian stepped into her father's mahogany-paneled chamber and hastily returned to the present.

With curiosity, he regarded the larger, distinguished man reclining in a large leather chair with his injured leg propped up on a matching stool. The man was leaning his gray wig wearily against the seat's high back, but he abruptly sat up at Ian's entrance.

Interestingly, Ian couldn't read him at all. This must be where Chantal had learned to mask her thoughts. Since they did not have Aelynn eyes—and he had yet to find an Aelynn mark on Chantal—he had to err on the side of caution and assume Alain and his daughter were Other Worlders, not Crossbreeds. So their stillness was a phenomenon that he appreciated. The chaotic thoughts and emotions of most people in this world—even untrained Crossbreeds—were usually torturous to an extreme.

Chantal dropped to her knees at her father's side and examined his bandaged leg, but her father continued gazing at Ian with—fear? suspicion?

"I have been told, monsieur, that I have you to thank for Pauline's release," the older man said. "I would stand and offer my hand, but I fear my daughter would cut me down should I try." Humor and affection laced his words.

"I'm sorry, Papa; I've been rude. This is Monsieur Ian d'Olympe. He is trying to locate a stolen chalice. Ian, my father, Alain Orateur," Chantal said from her position on the floor.

Ian's gaze lingered admiringly on her slender form draped in the silk robe. When he lifted his head to greet his host, he encountered resignation in the other man's eyes.

He knew. Somehow, Alain Orateur knew who Ian was. That was inconceivable. The Other World knew nothing of the Mystic Isle. Only an Aelynner . . .

Immediately, he glanced at Orateur's left hand, but her father had already discreetly dropped it to the side Ian couldn't see.

Ian suspected what he hid—Aelynn's ring of silence!

That would explain the ability to shut off his mind as Other Worlders did not, and the name *Orateur* as well. Once upon a time, Aelynn had had a family of orators. Alain could be a descendant, and if he wore a ring—

He had to have come from the island.

It wasn't entirely unusual for an Aelynner to leave and not return. Many died in foreign parts. Some refused to leave their Other World mates and children. The reasons for leaving paradise and not returning were as varied as the individuals.

Ian thought it might be unusual for an expatriate

not to acknowledge a fellow countryman, especially one of Ian's rank, but he was new to this world. Perhaps the ring of silence prevented acknowledgment of his origins.

Ian was certain that Orateur recognized him—perhaps more by name and purpose than by presence, since they'd never met. Orateur must have left the island in his youth.

But if he did not have Aelynn eyes, which Aelynn god would mark an orator? The god of peace? War? *Chaos*? Ian shuddered at the possibility of the latter two. They'd been bred from Aelynners long ago.

That Alain Orateur was an Aelynner explained a great deal about Chantal. For a few minutes, Ian had begun to wonder if Other Worlders had an amazing form of power of which he'd known nothing. Singing a rioting mob into peace was not a skill he recognized. It was no wonder that Chantal thought her chaotic world was a pleasant place. She created her own small bubble of peace with her voice.

Music was a disappointingly useless gift on Aelynn since the island was already peaceful, which ought to make him anxious about his future with her, but he had more immediate concerns.

"It is an honor to meet you, monsieur," Ian stated, as was proper. There was no reason to reveal his knowledge of the man's origin, and it was impossible to speak of it with others present. "Please do not stand on my account. If you do not need my aid, I would like to retire so I might bathe." He was accustomed to bathing regularly in the hot springs of his home. The difficulty of doing so in his travels had been distressing.

"We have a heated bath in the cellar," Chantal offered. "Papa had it built, and it's the most marvelous place. The Romans could have none better."

Ian let his appreciation show in his expression as he glanced at her father. Resigned, Alain Orateur caressed his daughter's fair hair and nodded. As an Aelynner, Alain would appreciate a heated bath far more than Other Worlders who knew little of such conveniences.

"My house is at your service," his host said. "If there is anything we can do to aid your search, we are at your disposal. These are uncertain times, and I would not have you harmed."

Ian accepted his offer as an oblique acknowledgment that Alain would not challenge him. This was good. He was always prepared for battle, but he preferred peace. "I would like to understand more of your country," he agreed. "The more I know, the easier it will be for me to complete my task."

"Tonight was not a fair example of our ways," the other man protested. "I have a habit of saying more than I should, which angers instead of heals. I addressed the Assembly on behalf of the king today, and the more radical elements objected. There are those who would extract justice from the innocent for past wrongs, but once people see the wisdom of allowing the Assembly to counsel the king, the monarchy will survive in some form."

Ian approved of this insight, but to his surprise, he sensed anger, fear, and disagreement from elsewhere in the room. Trying not to look too startled, he bowed and turned for the door. His eyes met Pauline's defiant ones.

A flare of intense loyalty to the king and queen briefly eclipsed rational thought, and he sensed that this loyalty was in opposition to that of Chantal and her father. Loyalty to leaders was a positive attribute as far as he understood, since he was a leader. That there could be different forms of loyalty was puzzling but, again, not his concern.

He nodded in farewell and departed.

In the morning, after he had bathed and everyone was rested, would be time enough to ask for Chantal in marriage.

Of course, if Alain Orateur knew who Ian was, he also knew that Other World vows were meaningless on Aelynn. Ian hoped that wouldn't create a complication.

Nine

Chantal tried not to hurry down to the breakfast parlor the next morning, but her step was light and eager on the stairs.

Ian had not come to her chamber last night. She assumed it was out of courtesy to her father. She had thought that was what she wanted—to protect her father from unseemly behavior. But this morning, she felt otherwise. She wanted Ian in her bed again for whatever brief time he could be here. She didn't wish to miss a minute of the pleasure they could have together. If a child came of it, so be it. She'd never conceived in the early years of her marriage, before Jean became ill, so considering the possibility was mostly an intellectual exercise.

She had not realized she'd been living as if half-dead for so long. She wanted to feel truly alive again, and Ian did that for her.

She walked into the parlor to find Ian and Pauline with their heads cozily together over cups of coffee, and her spirits dropped to her feet.

What had she been thinking?

He was a strikingly exotic stranger, a traveler who took his pleasure where he found it. She *knew* that, had acknowledged that by assuming they didn't have much time together. So why was she so disappointed that she wasn't the only woman he had his eye on?

She supposed she shouldn't be so old-fashioned as

to believe men and women should have only one partner at a time, but she'd just discovered a strong streak
of jealousy she had not known she possessed—for a
man who had not even acknowledged her entrance.

Apparently caught up in his conversation with Pauline, Ian didn't rise from the table as he should have.
After Chantal poured coffee from the silver pot on
the sideboard and sing-songed her good mornings with
false gaiety, he slowly rose to tower over the table,
wearing a quizzical expression, as if he'd been kicked
into doing the proper thing and didn't understand
why. Perhaps her song had been a little too false.

He wore his monk's robes open over crisp linen
and lace that someone must have laundered for him
overnight, but he exuded a raw maleness that was far
from saintly.

She had to wonder whether Ian had gone to Pauline's bed last night instead of hers, if he preferred
her friend's more experienced lovemaking. She
couldn't bear to look at Pauline to see if she wore a
satisfied expression.

She could barely unclench her teeth as she took a
seat while Ian returned to his chair. "I see you have
learned more of our etiquette, monsieur," she said
politely.

Did she sense amusement beneath his serious exterior? Was her jealousy that evident? Maybe she ought
to kick him into rising again.

"I do not fully grasp this word *etiquette*," he acknowledged, "or the reasons for bobbing up and down
like a puppet on a string."

"Etiquette is how one shows *respect*, another word
you do not seem to fully grasp," she replied sweetly.

His amusement seemed to heighten, and he regarded her as if she were a particularly ripe plum on
his plate. "Your voice is an enchanting song in my

ear, even though your intention is to drive nails into my flesh. I am to show respect for this fascinating talent?"

Chantal tore off a bite of croissant with more force than the flaky pastry deserved. She did not recall anyone ever laughing at her. Perhaps she did not want this stranger here so much after all. She'd forgotten that the pleasures of sex came accompanied by the nuisance of submitting to the annoying notions of men.

"Monsieur d'Olympe believes the chalice has been taken to the king," Pauline interrupted Chantal's snit with excitement. "I am to go to the Tuileries this morning and see what I can learn. Isn't this fascinating? He rescues me, and then it turns out that I can be of help to him!"

Chantal feigned a bright smile as she examined the monk over the top of her cup. He'd let his cowl fall back, and his inky hair gleamed. Fine curls sprang from the tight queue. His high bronzed brow spoke of wisdom and intelligence, and his eyes . . .

She shook her head. They were so changeable that she could never tell if they were brown or black or just a very deep blue. They had the power to enthrall her, so she dipped her gaze back to the table rather than let him heat her blood.

"The king might appreciate coins rather than a bell that doesn't ring or a chalice too clumsy to drink from," Chantal responded, trying to think clearly when her soul was crying ridiculous protests. "But he is so tightly guarded, I cannot see how such a thing would be smuggled out, or even how we might get in to see His Majesty."

"I do not understand why the leader of your country is not free to do as he pleases. I understand it might be difficult to see a busy man, but that is not what you're saying, is it?"

Pauline's pointed chin lifted while she waited for Chantal to answer this very complicated question. They'd argued over it before, without coming to any good conclusion.

"Our kings held the power of gods for too long," Chantal responded carefully. "It is never wise to give any one person that much influence. People are human, not gods, and they have weaknesses. So it has become necessary to take some authority away from the king and queen and give it to the Assembly. There are some who disagree with this change." She cast a glance at her friend. "But that is mostly because it takes away the authority of the nobility as well as the king's. Since all of France is bankrupt, power is our strongest currency."

"Ah, I think I begin to see," he said. His eyes flashed with understanding. "Those who wish to return to the old ways guard your leaders in hopes of retaining what they once had."

"And those who wish to change the world overnight would lock our rightful leaders in cells and never let them out," Pauline finished for him.

"Without a leader, there will be chaos," Ian predicted.

"We are not trying to be rid of the king!" Chantal protested. "But he must put the needs of his own people above those of foreign popes and corrupt aristocrats. It is all much too complex to argue now. We should make some plan of retrieving the chalice once Pauline discovers if it is truly at the palace."

She would like to ask why Ian thought it was there, but instinct told her there were some things about this man that she'd rather not know. "Where is Papa? Perhaps he can help us."

"He has gone to find Pierre," Pauline said with a return of her worried frown.

He should be resting his injured knee. No judge would be about to set bail at this hour.

Chantal glanced at Ian. He had said he would speak with her father, although she had no certainty about what, since they barely knew each other. And she wanted nothing to do with a rogue who bedded every woman who smiled at him. Still, she'd like to know. . . .

He returned her gaze enigmatically.

She'd like to smack him.

That was not like her. She seldom let her impulses overcome her to the point of acting on them—but Ian seemed to have broken the barrier she'd built around her passions. Humming under her breath to pacify her turbulent emotions, she tapped her fingers on the table and wished for the bell back. If wishes were horses . . .

Understanding Pauline's concern for her brother, Chantal shoved aside her selfishness. "I cannot think it is safe for you to leave the house until Papa has settled this matter."

"I can always take sanctuary with the queen," Pauline said stiffly.

"The queen can't provide sanctuary for herself these days. I am terrified every day you return to her."

Ian intruded upon the argument. "Perhaps, while Madame Racine attends the queen, you might show me about your city?"

Did she imagine it, or did she detect a strong desire behind his words, one that could not be translated easily? Just because she heard harmonies in the breeze didn't mean she heard things that weren't being said. Ian d'Olympe was simply a very . . . forceful . . . man. She would say *intense* except she sensed no tension about him, as if he fully expected everyone to comply with his suggestions. And he wanted his chalice back.

"Usually, Papa leaves me a speech or pamphlet to edit and take to the printers. If he has not done so today, I'm at your disposal this morning. My students arrive in the afternoon."

Insanely, she was already squirming in her seat beneath Ian's penetrating gaze, wondering what he intended, if they could find a way to steal off somewhere private . . .

She had to *stop* this.

"If it would not be too much trouble, I would enjoy a tour. Perhaps you could show me this palace of your king. Are there other places I should see while I am here?"

"If Papa is looking for Pierre and arranging for his release," Chantal said with an assurance she didn't feel, "perhaps we could look for them while we're out and about."

"Would you?" Pauline asked. "I'd be forever grateful." She still looked anxious.

As she had every right to be. Pierre must leave Paris if he still refused to take the oath of loyalty. What would Pauline do then? Little by little, all the royalists were fleeing France. If Pauline took the children . . .

Chantal would be deprived of all her family except her father. Already her heart cried in loneliness.

Ian was now thoroughly convinced the gods meant to teach him the humility of living without the power of his position.

On Aelynn, his rank and abilities gave him almost complete control over his environment. If he wanted a woman, a woman came to him. If he wanted the Council's support, he could call on Aelynn to smoke and rumble. He could ignite fires if he was cold.

That he generally chose to do none of these things was irrelevant to his current frustration.

On Aelynn, he would have the status to order Chantal's father to a meeting of the Council where he could negotiate the terms of marriage or amacara. That was a power he would use now, if he could. But Alain's deliberate disappearance prevented it.

On Aelynn, he could easily locate the chalice and go back to mediating disputes, instead of wandering aimlessly, dealing with the irrational, like the bloody-minded mob last night.

On Aelynn, Chantal would be delighted to grace his bed without question. Instead, he was forced to woo her with subterfuge and promises, and even then, she remained frustratingly elusive. He had no idea why she had vibrated so strongly with what felt like jealousy this morning, then looked at him as if he were the dirt beneath her feet.

Despite her attempts to conceal it, the emotion in her voice had been so strong that he'd actually sensed her desire for him to stand up and had done so. He'd never acquiesced to the command of another in his life, not even for his powerful sister, and it irked him immensely that he had now. Still, although he had no certainty of how he could bind her to him, he was determined to have this maddening female.

Of course, the one thing he had not been able to control on Aelynn was Murdoch, and that remained unchanged here in the Other World.

Strolling through the garden of the Tuileries Palace, Ian glared at the medieval stone buildings housing the king and his guards and knew Murdoch was not inside. Ian was just realizing that France had many soldiers, but they did not all share the same loyalty. He didn't know which side Murdoch was on. Although Ian had Seen Murdoch leading troops, he had sensed that his nemesis did so outside of Paris. Last night's efforts to Find him had been as unsuccessful as earlier attempts.

He didn't know if that meant Trystan was wrong and Murdoch was now completely powerless, or if Murdoch was simply beyond the range of Ian's abilities in this world.

"Isn't the garden lovely?" Chantal asked, strolling along the riverbank and admiring the imposing view of gnarled old trees against ancient stone.

She wore another confection of a hat today, one that concealed her eyes but exposed the curve of her nape beneath her heavy chignon. Ian wished she would let her hair loose, but he could tell from the people around him that only the lowest of slatterns did so in public. Another pointless custom he must adjust to.

He disliked the palace immensely. The very stones reeked of terror. The crowd in the park seethed with resentment, hostility, and fear. Only the children chasing a rolling ball and a few heedless lovers enjoying a summer's day seemed content with the beauty of the greenery.

And Chantal. Living inside her own enchanted bubble, humming happily to herself, she whirled her frothy umbrella and glided along sunny walks, admiring fountains as if all was right in her world. He would think her an idiot except he'd seen her happiness expand to capture others. She was far more complex than even she was aware.

After meeting her father, Ian was convinced she had Crossbreed powers. He simply must observe her more carefully to understand them.

"Your king does not mind having the public cavort on his lawn?" he asked.

After talking with Pauline this morning, he had begun to form a plan that might accomplish all he needed, while rescuing the besieged royalty behind the moldy walls of their stone prison—walls that concealed the sacred chalice, as he'd seen in his meditations last night. Pauline had warned him not to tell Chantal, and instinct verified her conclusion that Chantal would not approve of their scheming.

"Since the king preferred to isolate himself from his people by living in a vast palace in Versailles until forced to return here, I daresay he's not thrilled," Chantal admitted. "Paris is rife with rumors of escape attempts. I would not want to be royalty. Too much is expected of them."

"Granted, one should not give power to leaders who are incapable of wielding it wisely, but one assumes there is some reason your royalty inherits their power."

That had been his experience, at least. He was the nominal leader of Aelynn since his father's death because he possessed the abilities to carry out the duties of that position, abilities inherited from both parents. In Chantal's world, he assumed those abilities included the power of influential connections as well as vital strengths such as diplomacy and foresight.

"Our royalty claims they were appointed by God and stand second only to the pope. That may have been true a few hundred years ago, but no longer." She shrugged, and the red, white, and blue ribbons of her hat fluttered in the breeze.

Ian's family had been appointed as caretakers of the island by their gods on the basis of his family's powerful attributes. Should his people attempt to imprison him and render him helpless, he'd be appalled and furious, and the gods would surely scorch the land with fire. Such treason went against the natural order of things.

He thought the poor beleaguered French king de-

served better than this cold fortress at the mercy of
bitter, angry mobs like the one last night. Rescue
seemed obligatory, even essential, if he were to retrieve the chalice.

He would never consider interfering in the Other
World, except rescuing the king meant rescuing the
chalice, and possibly capturing Murdoch by drawing
him out, thereby keeping his mate safe. All of which
were perfectly legitimate and approved by the gods
and laws of Aelynn.

"Your gentlemen dress colorfully here," he observed, studying the garish blue and gold stripes and
red accents of the uniform of a soldier near the palace's entrance. The bulky breeches were no doubt easier for warfare, but the ruffled collar looked most
uncomfortable.

Chantal followed his glance. "You are not familiar
with your own Swiss Guards?"

He shrugged. "I do not associate with military
men."

She still looked at him oddly but seemed to accept
his explanation. "The Swiss Guards protect the royal
family. You will see them only at the palace. The king
has hired mercenaries in the field who wear the uniforms of their regiment, but they're usually led by
French nobility. Officers of the nobility favor blue and
scarlet." She nodded in the direction of two soldiers
parading in front of the Swiss Guard. "Those blue
uniforms over there identify the Assembly's National
Guard."

"And the ones outside the prison yesterday?" he
asked dubiously, uncertain why a country needed so
many soldiers. "They wore stripes and trousers and
looked nothing like these."

"Those were local militia. Each sector of Paris and
every town and half the aristocrats in France have

their own soldiers. The ones here usually wear trousers instead of breeches, and favor patriotic red, white, and blue. Some are loyal to whoever pays them that day."

In Ian's last vision, Murdoch had worn the ornate blue and scarlet of a royalist officer. One more piece added to his knowledge.

"How do the National Guard and the king's officers differ?"

She looked uncomfortable. "The king hires mercenaries to guard the interests of the nobility. The Assembly instituted the National Guard two years ago to protect *all* the citizens of France. The king shouldn't doubt the loyalty of his people."

Ian raised his eyebrows at her naïveté, but she obviously lived in a happy world of her own making. He could see the problem of hiring a mercenary like Murdoch. Hired troops were loyal only to their ambition. And from the anger he was picking up, he suspected the National Guard had no love for their king. The whole situation fermented and simmered unhealthily.

Finally discovering that some small part of Pauline's plan was, indeed, in place, Ian indicated a tall, blond gentleman in an elegantly tailored frock coat who waited near a bench that his fellow conspirator had described earlier. "I would talk to that gentleman over there."

"That's Count von Fersen." Chantal tilted him a look from beneath her hat. "He's from Sweden, not Switzerland. How do you know of him?"

"Mutual acquaintances," Ian replied without breaking stride. Pauline's explanation had been that the count was the queen's lover and desperate to save the royal family from their imprisonment.

Chantal hurried to keep up with him. "Except for your coloring, there is some resemblance between you—you are both tall, strong, honest, and willing to do what is right at all costs. The count is truly quite formidable."

Ian slanted her a look. "I am formidable?"

"How could you not be? Given your skill with weapons . . ."

Inexplicably pleased that his intended mate found him formidable, Ian continued on to the next curiosity. "You know this man well?"

She waved away the question. "I've met him at salons. It is rumored he is a ladies' man," she continued, "and enjoys the queen's favors."

Which was why the handsome count was willing to aid the beautiful queen, Pauline had said, and from Ian's glimpse of the count's anxiety now, he concurred.

He cast Chantal another sideways look to see how she expected him to take her comparison of him to a ladies' man. "I shall have to challenge him if he should look on you as I do," he said solemnly.

He fully meant that. He would challenge any man who came between him and his amacara, but Chantal did not quite understand his intent. Ian hid his smile when she darted him a look but couldn't ask her question because they'd reached their destination.

"Madame Deveau," the count said as they arrived. "It is a pleasure to see you again. Madame Racine said you were entertaining a friend of mine."

Count von Fersen, the queen's lover, held out his hand, and Ian knew his plan to rescue the royal couple was already in place. He stiffened, assessing any challenge the other man might present, but the count exuded only concern for the queen and her children.

As he shook the other man's hand, Ian had the feeling that Chantal and her father would heartily disapprove of his intentions, which would certainly complicate his already complicated courtship.

Ten

Chantal had always recognized and admired the courage in the count's voice; only now, comparing him to Ian, she realized the shallowness of his character. Von Fersen might be golden, handsome, and smiling, but his gallantry was that of the court. Beneath the pleasantries he bestowed upon her, he was assessing her loyalty to the royal couple, testing her intelligence, and clearly dismissing her as useless for his purposes, whatever they might be. She felt no attraction to the man at all, although she was aware he had several mistresses and that every other lady in Paris swooned over his beauty.

Ian, on the other hand, was dark, mysterious, and unsmiling. She could almost swear he was a Spartan warrior poised for battle as he discussed the king's health and plans for the summer. Still, despite his enigmatic expression, Ian did not hide behind charm and subterfuge. He openly revealed himself as a friend to the court, even though he had to know that she disapproved.

Ian blatantly ignored her opinions when he did not agree with them, but he at least respected her knowledge enough to listen. That he chose to dismiss her view on the king's imprisonment was not relevant. All Paris argued over it. She preferred Ian's honest rejection to the count's artificial pretense that all was well.

Despite her acknowledgment of her lover's superiority, Chantal was not inclined to be diplomatic after von Fersen made his bows and departed.

"Do you have any idea how much Marie Antoinette spent on refurbishing the Tuileries when they moved in here?" she asked. "And now you and the count discuss returning her to Versailles for the summer where she can quadruple her staff and build more useless follies while people starve? While no doubt plotting to let her brothers' armies invade to march on Paris and overthrow the Assembly."

"I merely inquired into their health." Idly swinging his long staff as a gentleman would his walking stick, Ian eyed the long, low building housing the Swiss Guard. "It is up to your Assembly to take charge of finances and prevent royal overspending."

"It's not that simple," she argued, but rather than launch into a political tirade, she switched to a more pleasant subject. "I hadn't thought, but if you are Swiss, then do you know anyone in the king's guards?" The king's Swiss Guards possessed an unusual loyalty to Louis and his queen. That might explain a great deal of Ian's interest in the king—except that he hadn't recognized the guards' uniforms.

Ian shrugged. "I have an . . . acquaintance . . . in the royal army, yes, but I don't believe he's here. Did you say your father keeps a stable?"

She cast him a curious glance as he stumbled over the word *acquaintance.* "North of Paris, yes. We once raced horses, but the upkeep has become prohibitive. Why?"

"Once I've recovered the chalice, I wish to find my fellow countryman. I thought it might be easier if I acquire transportation." He strode purposefully along the gravel path near the barracks, examining the grimy windows and doors rather than the garden.

"Unless you ride, you will have to ask my father

about our carriage horses. The stable contains brood mares and a stallion, but they are Thoroughbreds from England and not broken to the traces."

"Nevertheless, I would like to see your stable. We do not have horses at home. The count mentioned that yours possess great speed, and I have discovered an affinity for these animals."

Occasionally, Ian was more than passing strange. Chantal frowned, trying to remember the count saying any such thing, but she'd quit listening once she realized von Fersen wasn't interested in her opinions. "Perhaps tomorrow we could visit them," she suggested as they turned toward the river. She could not imagine any country that lacked horses, so perhaps she'd misunderstood. "I suppose Switzerland is too mountainous for racing horses?"

"Something like that," he agreed, studying the river and its environs. "Could we reach your stable by riverboat?"

"No, and it's best if we wait for news of your chalice before leaving the city. Then, if my father agrees, we could provide a horse for Pierre once he is released, so that he may quit this country quickly."

As Jean and Pauline's youngest brother, Pierre had been Chantal's childhood friend, too, though not a close one. She hated to see him go into exile, if only for Pauline's sake, but his departure seemed inevitable.

Ian considered her suggestion. "You are fond of these people, yes?"

"Yes, of course. Pauline is like a sister to me. We have our differences, but I am godmother to her children, as she would have been to mine, had I been so blessed."

Swinging his stick, he frowned at a punt drifting on

the river. As if refraining from asking the question on his mind, he turned away from the water. "I shall see what I can do, then."

"What you can do about what?" she asked in puzzlement, hurrying to keep up with his now rapid stride in a different direction.

"I have a friend in this country, one who married here and lives on the coast. He tells me that your families are very important to you, and that we should not disregard your ties to them."

"You have to be *told* that? What do you do in your country—throw your relations down the mountain when you tire of them?"

Ian snorted. "If you knew my sister, you would understand." Before she could comment, he redirected the topic. "Tell me, what is the name of that animal on the leash over there?"

Chantal glanced in the direction he indicated and saw only a lovingly groomed spaniel being walked by a fashionably garbed woman at a distance farther down the path. "The dog? You do not have dogs either? Are you sure you do not live on the moon?"

"Not precisely," he admitted. "Do you know the lady? I must speak with her."

"She is not someone I may publicly accost." Chantal tugged his arm to keep him in place when he seemed determined to ignore her opinion once again. "You can't go up to strangers and ask about their dogs." She had to set aside her questions about a land with no dogs or horses in favor of preventing his faux pas.

"I fail to see why not. There is no barrier preventing it." He continued determinedly on his course, forcing her to hurry to keep up with him.

"I am very liberal in my beliefs, monsieur, but my father would have an apoplexy if he heard I was publicly acknowledging a courtesan. It is bad enough that you ruin my reputation in the privacy of my home, but I cannot allow you to shame me like this!"

He halted and stared at her with perplexity. "Explain *courtesan*, please."

Chantal rubbed the place between her eyes that had begun to ache. "Does your country consist only of yourself? No men who pay for the favors of women? Or perhaps you have no women in Switzerland?"

He snorted in apparent amusement. "We have men and women in plenty, and many ways of courting and enjoying each other's favors. There is only pleasure and no shame in it. It is your customs that are odd. Explain, please."

"You do not have women who exchange their favors for jewels and gowns and other forms of wealth?"

He was watching the beautiful courtesan stroll toward them, a vision in fluttering ribbons and flimsy muslin and exposed bosom. Chantal wanted to elbow him for his interest, but she had no right to act on her newly acknowledged jealousy.

"Our men might compete for the hand of a woman, and women often compete for the attention of men they favor, but that is not the same, is it? You are saying if I offer her coins or a pretty pearl, she will share her . . . *favors*."

"She is not a prostitute," Chantal replied crossly, wishing she could drag him away. "She is an expensive courtesan. I was surprised that she did not follow the court to Austria, but she has apparently found a new lover in the Assembly. The lady trades in state secrets as well as jewels."

He stared at her in astonishment. "Surely that is a crime."

Chantal deliberately dropped his arm and took a

side path so she needn't acknowledge the other woman's presence. She wasn't an innocent. This was Paris, after all, the city of equality. She was sophisticated enough to attend fashionable salons that such creatures also attended, but she was sufficiently well-bred to know how to avert the nuisance of meeting when they needn't.

She'd hoped Ian would follow, but instead, he lay in wait for the object of his interest, twirling his stick, a breeze rippling his robes over his boots, his dark visage a study in curiosity. Chantal considered walking straight home and leaving the annoying man alone, but she couldn't resist eavesdropping from behind the lilacs.

He intrigued her far more than was wise. Sometimes, he seemed so oblivious to reality that he may as well have sprung full blown from the earth just yesterday. He wasn't naive so much as unmindful of anything resembling the common niceties that allowed civilized people to live in close confines—as if he were above the rules.

"Excuse me, madame," she heard him say. "I could not help but notice that your . . . dog . . . has an infected ear that pains him greatly. You might wish to take him to a healer."

A healer? Ian's understanding of her language must be more limited than she had noticed. And how the devil did he know the spaniel was hurting? Or was this a novel excuse to introduce himself to a beautiful courtesan?

The lady expressed no curiosity as to how Ian knew about dog ears, but merely conveyed appropriate feminine horror over her "poor, dear poopsie-whoopsie." In exasperation, Chantal imagined the woman bending over the pretty spaniel, exposing her generous assets for Ian's benefit while she petted and hugged the dog in a manner that would allow a gentleman to envision himself as beneficiary to such cosseting. Would Ian recognize the wiles of a courtesan?

Chantal would have walked away if Ian were any other man, but for him, she lingered. She simply could not resist hearing his thoughts on spaniels and courtesans and whatever else came to mind. He seemed to view her ordinary world through an unusual lens.

Or maybe it was just basic sexual attraction that held her hostage.

He strolled around the shrubbery a few minutes later, this time actually offering his arm rather than forcing Chantal to appropriate it.

"She is a desperate woman who keeps a young child sheltered outside the city. I feel sorry for her, but she spies on the king. You must warn Madame Pauline."

"I'm sure Pauline already knows," Chantal said brightly, attempting to disguise her shock at his knowledge after just one meeting. "Did she whisper all those sweet nothings in your ear?"

He didn't immediately reply. "I am unsure of how much I can tell you," he finally said, as if that answered her question. "You and I have no formal arrangement between us. And even once that matter is resolved, it will take time for us to know each other. Perhaps it is best to concentrate on our tasks for now."

"That *matter* won't be resolved," she informed him. "I like my independence. And once you have what you want, you will leave. So there is no future for getting to know each other."

"There, you are wrong," he told her matter-of-factly. "I understand that the heavens cannot predict the future with great accuracy, particularly the distant future, since we all have free will, and our choices affect the outcome of events. But there is no doubt that you are meant to be my mate, and I will do whatever is necessary to make that so."

His *mate*? Shocked at this outrageous declaration, Chantal halted in the middle of the gravel path and gawked. "You believe in astrology?" she asked, unable to find words to question his more bizarre assertion.

He studied the question in the same thoughtful manner he studied everything around him. "Not precisely in the science of which you speak, although if I had time to examine the theory, I might connect the interworkings of your planets with my heavens. You will simply have to believe what I have Seen until you understand better."

Believe what he'd *seen*? That he assumed they were fated by destiny was too close to the edge of madness—or the heights of arrogance. To admit that he could predict the future was beyond belief.

Dropping his arm and picking up her skirts, Chantal strode from the garden, humming under her breath. A dove squawked and burst from the bushes as she passed. An old nag pulling a dusty coal cart whickered and fought his reins. Chantal wished for her piano. Or the lovely bell—*chalice*, she amended. Perhaps she could have a bell made. She needed to calm herself.

"I thought you wished to look for your father and Madame Pauline's brother." Ian appeared beside her, sauntering and swinging his stick as if she weren't walking as fast as she could to get away from him.

"Why don't you just ask your *heavens* where they are?" she asked cynically.

"Is it the heavens you doubt, or the idea of us as mates that you reject?"

"Both. This is just some new form of male manipulation. I expected better of you; that is all. I live in a nice house and have the trappings of wealth, and you thought it might be pleasant to acquire them. But that won't happen. Ever."

"I have little use for nice houses," he said with what sounded like regret. "I must return to my country shortly, and houses cannot be moved. What I desire to keep is you. Surely you do not deny what is between us? I'm finding it very difficult to ignore."

She was finding it damned difficult to ignore, too, which made her even angrier. "I am not a possession you can pack in your trunk and carry away. I have a life here, family, friends. It is insane to think I'd throw them all away for the pleasure any man and woman can share."

"But you have not shared it with any but one other man, have you?" he said with confidence. "For whatever reason, the gods have decreed that we be together. I'm sure that in the fullness of time, we will understand why."

"Your gods cannot tell me what to do. I'm not at all certain that I even believe in *my* God any longer, not if His church lets babies starve, so don't expect me to comply with the wishes of fickle deities."

"Where I come from, babies do not starve," he said implacably.

They turned down the residential street of imposing mansions that Chantal called home. A familiar carriage was just pulling through the gates, and, relieved, she hastened to follow.

"And you expect me to believe your god only looks after your country and your people? Forgive me for doubting, but that is extremely selfish, even for a deity. Now, I must see if Papa has found Pierre." She picked up her skirts and began to run.

Ian arrived at the gate before she did, cool and neat

despite the summer heat, looking as if he hadn't exerted a single muscle. "And then I will speak with your father. This city will not be safe much longer."

He took her elbow and marched her up the front stairs as if she did, indeed, belong to him.

Eleven

The cold cave of marble and stone that Chantal called home had erupted in chaos by the time they entered the front door. Chantal angrily fought Ian's grasp, but he held on to her as a ship clung to an anchor in a raging sea.

In his world, he was nearly all knowing and all powerful. In her world, he did not even know how to answer his mate's questions without violating every law of Aelynn. How could he make her understand who he was, and that he was right, when he could not even tell her that he'd Seen the future?

Laughing, crying children and a crowd of servants surrounding a drawn and silent young man did not ease his disorientation. Chantal had persuaded her sister-in-law to leave the children here, where they would be safe. Their uncle appeared pleased to see them, but too confused to give them the hugs they requested.

"Pierre, you are free," Chantal cried from the doorway. "Thank heavens!"

"Your father paid my bail," the young man acknowledged over the heads of the children. "Thank him."

Ian held Chantal back when she would race to her brother-in-law. "He was in a prison cell of such filth that he fears to harm those he loves," he murmured close to her ear. "He needs peace and a bath."

She shot him another wary look but, surprisingly, did not argue.

"Marie, Anton! Let your uncle Pierre wash and get the fleas out of his hair while we go to the kitchen and fix his favorite meal," she called with a cheeriness that brought smiles to all the faces around her.

She did not seem in the least aware that it was her voice that eased their anxiety, Ian noted. She was too accustomed to everyone responding to her moods.

Even the weary priest smiled gratefully at her understanding. "You are a sight for sore eyes, Chantal." His dark gaze drifted to Ian. "Monsieur, I understand you helped free Pauline, for which I owe you much gratitude."

"Go, bathe, we will find clothes for you," Alain Orateur said, patting Pierre's shoulder and pushing him toward a waiting footman. "Then we will have a feast and tell our stories."

Ian assessed Orateur's haggard, weary look. His normally latent healing ability had eased the dog's pain earlier, although he lacked the necessary herbs and compresses to cure the infection. His healing abilities might be of little value in Aelynn, but they were greater than most in this world. He could conceivably ease his host's weariness and the ache in his knee, but first the other man would have to allow it. And it was apparent from the unbending shields in Orateur's mind that he was unwilling to submit to the access Ian needed.

"See to the children, and I will see to your father," Ian ordered Chantal, expecting obedience as he would at home.

"He'll want brandy and a footstool. The servants can supply them," she countered. "What we need is clean clothing for Pierre. Have one of the footmen accompany you to his rooms. They're not far from here. It might be best to take a portmanteau and pack everything. We need to get him out of France." Chantal strode briskly after the children, as efficient at giving orders and expecting them to be obeyed as he was.

The gods surely tested his patience by giving him this contrary woman when he already had more than enough of them in his family. Ian supposed Chantal's bossiness might be effective at other times, but right now, they needed to settle who was in charge here. Since he knew more, she must learn to listen to him.

"Find a portmanteau," he told a waiting servant as the hall emptied. "I am sure you know more of what Monsieur Pierre will need for a journey than I do. Be quick, if you please."

Without waiting for the footman's response, Ian strode after Alain Orateur. Here was one task he could accomplish immediately. They must come to an understanding about Chantal.

Her father was settling into a comfortable chair in his study while a maid provided a footstool and another poured a strong drink from a decanter. Alain grimaced at Ian's appearance.

"Do we have to do this now?" the older man grumbled.

"I don't believe there is time to waste, no." Ian mentally nudged the maids from the room. They fluttered a moment, throwing a comforter over their employer, setting the decanter close to his hand, but within seconds they were gone.

"I always hated how your kind could do that," Orateur complained. "My daughter won't appreciate it either."

"Life is short, and time is of the essence." Ian preferred pacing the intricately woven carpet to taking a chair. Motion helped him concentrate, and he needed all his wits about him. "At home, I do not need to use my psychic ability so much, but here, it is difficult for me to explain myself. And I cannot use it easily on Chantal. She is as resistant as you are."

"Just explaining why an Olympus has come off the mountain could involve hours," Alain complained, sipping his drink. "My abilities are of such insignificance that I daresay your family breathed a sigh of relief at my departure, if they noticed at all. So why are you here?"

"Chantal is my amacara. She could not come to me, so I had to come for her."

"That's ridiculous," Alain spluttered. "Chantal has no gifts other than her musical ones. Aelynn has no use for music, or storytellers, or actors, or any of the creative arts. You cannot take her where she will not be appreciated. She's my only daughter, and I would see her happy."

"I understand what you say." Ian refused to admit his own doubts about the match. Logically, he should agree with her father. But his desire for Chantal would not allow that. He was not normally a man who acted on passion, but he had learned from Trystan's experience that amacara bonds were not based on logic.

"I do not understand the choice of the gods, but that makes no difference," he continued. "Two years ago, the Chalice of Plenty left Aelynn. Since our duty is to guard the chalice, the gods have expressed their displeasure, with droughts and hurricanes that even the Weathermaker has been unable to alleviate. I have foreseen that Chantal and the chalice are connected in some manner that I cannot comprehend. You know I can do no less than take the chalice back with me, and to do that, I must have Chantal. You are welcome to come with us, if you wish."

Ian thought Alain might have an apoplexy. He tried to send healing thoughts, but they didn't penetrate the older man's thick skull. Chantal's father pounded his fist on the chair's arm.

"Stop that! Stay out of my head. I don't need you or your kind, I tell you. I have everything I need, more than I ever had on the island. I have a say in how we are governed. I am respected for my ability to speak clearly and forcefully. I married a woman of great wit and beauty without permission from your damned Council. Why should I return?"

"Because Chantal loves you. But I would not force you to live where you do not wish, as you cannot take away Chantal's choice for your own selfishness. You know what an amacara match means. You know my family. You know she will be safe with me. And you must be aware that this country will soon go up in flames. Perhaps you have never experienced war, but surely any man of intelligence would understand what happens to women at such times."

"There will be no war. The king has agreed to consult the Assembly. We have a new constitution. I will be a man of great power in this new government. Chantal can have any man she wants. She doesn't need to breed more arrogant monsters like you."

Ian clenched the book he'd picked up but refrained from heaving it. He was a rational man. He could win this battle without physically pounding sense into thick heads.

"There *will* be a long and terrible war. When the stars show devastation of that magnitude, there is no denying the event will happen. And if you think I am a monster, then you have not met Murdoch. He killed my father, was stripped of his powers and banished by my mother, and still attempted to burn one of your ports with Greek fire. He's on the loose in France as we speak. I have come to suspect that he is a Lord of

Chaos who should have been thrown into the volcano when he was born."

Orateur looked alarmed and tightened his shields more. "Then go after him and leave my daughter alone. If he's all that you say, then he's after the chalice as well. Find it, and go."

"I will, but your daughter will go with me. You can name your price for her, and I will see it delivered. You know that I have every port in the world at my fingertips, and that an Olympus does not break his promises."

Unflinchingly, Ian met the other man's glare. Before he could negotiate further, Chantal burst into the study. She'd discarded her short jacket, leaving her breasts covered by a teasingly diaphanous scarf tucked into a bit of printed muslin. Ian couldn't drag his gaze from her breasts.

"I have come to see . . ." She halted in perplexity at seeing Ian. "I thought you had gone for Pierre's things."

"I told you I needed to speak with your father. A footman is far better suited to packing bags than I am."

"Of course, whatever was I thinking? Asking a monk to help a man in need—how foolish of me!" She turned her back on Ian and faced her father. "May I bring you some broth or one of Cook's tea cakes to hold you until dinner?"

Ian's patience stretched thin, but he held on to it in order to correct his mate's erroneous assumptions. "As you are fully aware, a man is not the clothes he wears. I am not a monk. It is important that your father and I come to some agreement as quickly as possible, or I will be forced to use other means—"

"Stay out of her—" Alain's shouted command

broke off with a wince, apparently from a tug of a reminder from his ring.

Chantal's big silver-blue gaze darted in concern from one man to the other. "My father does not have your chalice. We must wait for Pauline to discover its whereabouts."

"That man is not what you think," Alain tried to warn her, but his ring would not allow him to say more.

Ian was glad he wasn't the only one who was having difficulty talking around the very large elephant in the room.

"Oh, I daresay he is everything I think and more," Chantal replied. "But I am not the woman he thinks I am, so it matters little. I have sent word to Pauline that Pierre is free. She should be here in time for dinner."

Almost ethereal in her blond loveliness, she flounced out with the air of an angry goddess. They both fought the almost tangible bond of desire between them. Ian could sympathize. He did not like his hand being forced either, not even by the gods.

"I am a decade younger than your mother," Alain said wearily, pouring another glass of brandy, "but I remember her well. She had just married your father and taken her place as Oracle about the time I left. She was proud and unyielding in her belief that she was right and anyone who disagreed with her was wrong. If she has not changed, she and Chantal will kill each other. You are in over your head."

"My mother was the reason you left?" Ian asked, skirting around the argument presented in search of its deeper meaning.

"She would not allow me to marry her cousin because my family was too far beneath the mighty Olym-

pians. I saw no future in staying. I could talk the
Council into agreement, but it would only take her
veto to turn me down. She is far stronger than France's royalty."

"But more concerned about the welfare of her people," Ian pointed out. "It is difficult being responsible
for an entire population. My father was strong enough
to support and guide her. Chantal will do the same
for me, once she is free to grasp who I am."

"Are you sure of that?" Alain asked in disgruntle-
ment. "Haven't you once considered that your gods,
or your interpretation of them to suit your needs,
might be mistaken? Are you prepared to stand up in
the Council and take her for your wife and their
leader?"

No, he wasn't. Ian acknowledged the truth with a
nod. The Council would have great difficulty accepting
an Other World leader, and he did not know Chantal
well enough to believe she might be a good one. But
his faith in Aelynn was strong.

"I have a sister. There are alternatives," he argued.
"I only know that Chantal is my amacara, and she
will give us the heir we need for the future. How can
you deny your homeland, your own kind, the leader
they require?"

"I am not denying anything. Chantal makes her own
choices. I give you permission to court her, but I do
not give you permission to take apart her mind to
convince her to think as you do. If she says no, you
must accept her decision. That is the promise I will
have of you."

Ian hesitated, and his gut churned. He had skills,
experience, and knowledge beyond the comprehension
of most of humankind, but he could not tell Chantal
any of that—until she formally bound herself to him

at the altar. She shielded herself well from his mental skills, but he knew that given time and circumstances, he could seduce her into lowering her shields.

He did not have the luxury of time. If he gave his promise now, he would have to woo her as would any normal man.

Orateur watched him with wry amusement. "Wishing for that magical altar of yours, aren't you? Tie her up, seduce her, and have your way with her. That's what they did with your mother's cousin. Took her away from me with that foolish magic. I'll not have the same done to my child."

The gauntlet was thrown. Ian bowed his head in acceptance of the challenge. "I will not take her against her will, but you must remember, that 'foolish magic' is from the gods. I cannot control how they will use it."

"As long as I know you're not controlling her, I'm satisfied."

Ian knew he did not need the altar to seduce Chantal. He'd already done that. Or she had seduced him. The attraction seemed astonishingly mutual.

The act of procreation wasn't the problem. What he needed was a miracle to convince Chantal to bond with him for all eternity and leave all she knew and loved behind, when she had no idea of who or what he was or where he would take her.

If he failed to make that bond, he could doom his home to the same chaos that reigned here, which meant that failure was not acceptable.

Twelve

Tucking three-year-old Marie between the sheets, Chantal smoothed the child's fine blond hair and kissed her forehead. "Your mama will be up shortly to check on you, so show her how well you rest, *ma petite*."

"Will Uncle Pierre have to go away like Mama said?" Anton asked gravely from the other bed, sounding much older than his five years.

She hated seeing the children grow up so quickly. They should have no more concerns than she'd had at that age. They should be chasing butterflies through the fields.

She remembered Ian's talk of a country with no war and plenty for all, then reminded herself it had no dogs or horses either. No place was perfect.

"Perhaps for a while, little one, but Papa Alain will talk reason to people, and they will see this new law is wrong, and soon we will have Uncle Pierre back again." She did not fear making such a promise. Her father could talk the sun from the sky given enough time.

"Will you sing to us, please?" Marie asked.

"Yes," Anton agreed, snuggling beneath the linens. "I sleep good when you sing."

"Close your eyes, then. And I will sing of rocking horses to fill your dreams."

She'd created this song when Anton was born. It

reminded her of happier times and always eased her petty angers and anxieties. Preferring the nursery to the argument that was going on in the rooms below, she sat down in the rocking chair and began to sing softly.

Pauline, Pierre, and Ian had appropriated the study after dinner, presumably to discuss matters of which she would not approve. Her father had left to attend one of the many political salons to which he belonged.

At the beginning of the Revolution, the salons had been filled with excitement and the promise of a glorious future. Lately, the discussions had deteriorated to angry partisan quarrels, and she no longer enjoyed them. She wanted to play her music and laugh, watch the children run and jump, and dream of a man with whom she might share such simple pleasures. Her father fondly called her frivolous. If anger and hatred were serious, then she preferred frivolity.

Which meant she much preferred wondering whether Ian would come to her bed tonight than fretting over what he was plotting without her.

By the time her song ended, the children were asleep. She brushed kisses across their brows and returned downstairs to her music chamber, deliberately keeping her distance from the study. She was no good at plotting. All she did was worry about consequences.

"Von Fersen has been driving Baroness von Korff's fancy carriage around Paris at all hours, so no one will be suspicious when he parks near the house of his mistress," Pauline explained. "He has been planning this for months. It is smuggling the entire family out of the palace that is problematic."

And no doubt the reason the chalice had found its way into the hands of the king, Ian assumed, although he could not say it aloud. He wished he knew the chalice's goal, if it had one, but it had freed Pauline, so he must believe it meant to aid the royal family's escape.

"And you want me to ride with the royals?" Pierre asked in confusion. "How can I help?"

"In exchange for my chalice, I will provide cash for their journey and arrange for loyal men to guard the king once he leaves the city," Ian explained.

"The king can trust no one," Pauline said bitterly. "Even our most loyal generals say their troops mutiny in favor of the radicals these days. Peasants, all of them!"

"Since the queen cannot even trust her brother, the Holy Roman Emperor, we can't say they are all peasants," Pierre said dryly. "All of Europe waits for France to die. What court would dare take in our king?"

"The queen's family must," Pauline argued. "Luxembourg is under Hapsburg rule, and the fortress at Montmédy is on their border. The marquis de Bouillé's troops can safely gather there. The duc de Choiseul will guard us on the road once we reach his lands. We still have some honorable men."

"I repeat, how may I help?" Pierre demanded.

Ian knew nothing of the people Pauline mentioned but hoped, for her sake, that she was right. He could explain only his part. "Von Fersen will escort the royal party to the city gates, but once outside the city, they will need my loyal guards and good horses to speed their flight. You will direct them to the place where they must wait. You need only ride in the king's company until he is safely on the road to Montmédy. Then you may accept the chalice as payment for our services, and I will arrange a faster route for you and meet you along the way."

"It will be safe; you'll see," Pauline insisted. "The

queen will be dressed as the governess of the baroness's children, and King Louis has the passport of her
steward. The baroness traveled east a few months ago,
so the guards at the gate shouldn't be suspicious if her
family returns that way. You need only dress as one
of her footmen. It will be simple.''

"Nothing is ever simple," Pierre argued, but at last
he entered the discussion with more attention than he
had earlier.

Ian had to concur with the unworldly priest, but he
would not complicate their schemes with his own.
How to retrieve the chalice, persuade Chantal to go
with him, and prevent Murdoch from intervening were
problems of his own that he would not share.

Playing a sprightly tune to buoy her flagging spirits,
Chantal faced the piano and not the music room's
entrance, but when her notes changed to a sensual
melody of spring breezes, birdsong, and love, she
knew Ian had entered. He radiated maleness in ways
that stimulated her senses, confusing and exciting her.

He bent to kiss her brow much as she had done to
the children earlier, but his broad hand cupping her
breast was not so innocent.

"The bath is being filled," he murmured suggestively against her ear.

She'd never bathed with a man, or even considered
it. To state it so boldly in a public room . . .

"Come, let us enjoy the warm water while we may."
Without waiting for her consent, Ian took her elbow
and urged her from the bench. He was already
barefoot!

Before she could so much as think of a protest, he
pulled her into his arms and kissed her, and the room
became a garden of lush roses, summer heat, and the
pounding of surf in her ears.

Or perhaps it was just her heart beating. She clung to Ian's neck, stroking the fine hairs at his nape to verify his physical reality while his lips and tongue performed a magic that reached her soul, erasing all objection when he swept her off her feet and carried her from the room.

If they simply enjoyed the physical sensations binding them, then she had no argument with him. Perhaps if they never talked . . .

He carried her down to the bathing room and barred the door. Here, they were far enough from the main floor that no one could hear them. The small marble-tiled room was filled with steam from the heated tub. The tub itself was built in the Roman style, sunken into the ground, tiled, and large enough for two or more. She knew her father had gone to great expense to install pipes from a well and a stove to heat them, but she had little understanding of how they worked. She merely laced the waters with bubbles and appreciated the result.

She inhaled the intoxicating scent of jasmine as Ian lowered her feet to the warm tile. Her bodice slid off her shoulders without her awareness that the sash had been unfastened, and she hastily caught the muslin before it slid past her bosom. She didn't wish for him to see her naked.

"I want to admire all of you tonight," he said, tracing his knuckles over the top of her breasts and gently removing her grip on the bodice. "This time, we will go slowly."

He paralyzed her with his gentleness. She didn't want to fight him. He ran his hands into her hair, scattering the pins. In the steam, her carefully fashioned curls fell limp, and her hair tumbled in thick tendrils over her shift.

Chantal panicked slightly when Ian leaned over to

kiss her jaw, lowered his hands to her waist, and untied her skirt. Her head spun from his caress, and she grasped his shoulders to steady herself. He ravished her mouth with increasing arousal and shrugged out of his robe. The heat through his shirt melted her hands as if they were wax, shaping them to his chest.

In the next instant, her skirt and petticoat slipped down her hips. Gasping, Chantal grabbed to keep them from falling. Undeterred, Ian began unhooking her corset.

This was happening much faster than she'd anticipated. She had never bared herself completely even to Jean. Even in her bath, she'd always worn a shift. She could pretend her body was unflawed if she kept some modesty.

But Ian had no concept of modesty. He'd lit all the lamps and set candles along the rim of the sunken tub. She could see the hairs on his chest through the fine weave of his shirt where the steam plastered it to his skin.

His hands teased at her nipples as he unfastened the last hook and cast aside her stays, and she shivered at the erotic thrill. His dark look scorched the flimsy fabric of her shift. When he untied the ribbons, she had to let her skirt go to catch the shift from falling, but her grasp served only to raise her bosom like a plump offering. His hungry gaze aroused wicked sensations, letting her forget, just for this moment, her imperfections.

In his shirt and breeches, he was all magnificent raw male animal. He was right—clothes did not make the man. Ian was no delicate gentleman or scholarly monk, but a muscled knight without armor.

If she had but this one night of pure pleasure, she would enjoy it while she could. If she kept his masculine gaze appreciating her bosom, she could do this.

Taking a deep breath to quell her fears, she released the chemise to untie Ian's cravat. She almost panicked when the shift fell past her breasts and caught on the fabric pooling around her hips. Instead, she diluted her anxiety by sliding her hands beneath his shirt so she might admire the hard strength of his broad shoulders.

Muscle rippled beneath taut golden skin as he tugged the shirt over his head and flung it aside. Her breasts ached to be crushed against his nakedness.

As if understanding that words were unwelcome, Ian bent to capture her mouth again. He slid his palm along her cheek and into her hair, holding her so that his tongue could invade, incite, and persuade hers into retaliation.

At last, her breasts brushed his flesh, and she could feel the swelling of his arousal against her belly. She did not notice when her clothing finished the journey to the tile. She wanted to unfasten the buttons of Ian's breeches, but her hands could not abandon the breadth of his shoulders and strength of his back as his embrace lifted her from her feet.

"Sweetness," he murmured as his hand slid down her buttocks and a long finger swept along the crack between.

She shuddered and almost came undone right then. She had never bared that part of her person to anyone since she had learned of her defect. His wickedness elicited a thrill of arousal.

"I would hear you sing for me," Ian whispered, releasing his buttons.

She wrapped her legs around him so that he could not see what he had just touched.

Chantal clung to his neck, humming a song so sweet that Ian feared he would have to dive into her before he had his breeches off. Cursing Other World clothing, he shoved the cloth off his hips while her song teased and aroused. He nearly exploded from the pressure in his loins.

Steam enfolded them as he carried her down the steps into the tub. If he had less faith in his gods, he would insist on searching her beautiful body for the mark that would assure him that she would be the helpmeet he needed—before he committed an act that would seal them for eternity. But he could not release her when he was only a heartbeat away from paradise.

Among other things, he was a priest in his land. Not only did he have faith that Chantal was meant to be his, but he knew the vows he must make to bind her to him. That she did not understand did not deter him so much as knowing he endangered the future should she refuse him. Once he said the words, he would be bound forever. If she did not repeat the vows, she would be free to walk away, leaving him without an heir—and without relief. Then he might as well become a monk since he would find no other woman to satisfy him as Chantal did.

It was an enormous risk, but the prize was worth the peril. He trusted in the stars, his gods, and his senses. All three claimed that this sensuous, rebellious, and contradictory woman was the life mate he needed. Whether she was gifted did not matter.

After he took her to Aelynn, they could have a formal ceremony at the altar where he would give her his ring. For now, all he could offer were the promises and his body.

The tub was deep enough to immerse him to the waist. He rested Chantal's shoulders against a pillow on the tub's sloped edge. Her hair floated in long tendrils as she slid down to keep her legs around his back. Suggestively, she rubbed her heels over his buttocks. Ian's arousal strengthened, and Chantal smiled seductively through the steam as she urged him closer.

This time, he would take her slowly, as he had not before. Letting her float, he cupped her beautiful breasts and suckled gently. She moaned and writhed and grabbed his arms for support, then urged him with her heels to hurry. He did not succumb to her generous offer.

While his arousal slid temptingly along her cleft, Ian played an erotic tune upon her nipples with his thumbs and forefingers, and stared down into her eyes. "I worship thee with my body," he said with feeling. "I take thee for amacara, keeper of my future. With these vows, I do promise to cherish you in sickness and health, from now until Aelynn calls." The promise filled and became a part of him, providing the hook that would hold them as one.

Her silver-blue eyes widened as if she felt the connection, too. His arousal pushed at her nether lips, eager for the physical manifestation of his vow. As the pull between them increased, her lids lowered in sleepy desire, and her hips rose to urge him to complete their union. She did not understand. Not yet.

"Repeat the words after me," he requested, teasing her nipples into tight buds and nibbling her ear. "I take thee . . ."

She lifted her mouth to nip at his jaw. "I take thee any way I can," she repeated with a husky giggle.

If time wasn't so short, he wouldn't resort to such devious means of binding her. Her father had forced his hand. If he was not allowed to urge her to do this with his mind, he must use his body. He limited the vows to words she understood, hoping the gods would accept this truncated version from an uninitiated Crossbreed.

"In sickness and health," he rumbled enticingly, caressing her buttocks and finding the place that had excited her earlier.

"I've done that before," she murmured, arching eagerly into him, pushing him farther inside her. "Health is more fun."

"Play along with me," he purred, "or I shall turn you over my knee like a naughty child."

"I like the sound of that. Maybe later." She tried to slide down and take all of him, but he clamped his fingers into her sweetly rounded derriere and slid backward.

"In sickness and in health," he insisted.

"In sickness and in health," she agreed, "so long as you are around to pleasure me."

"For all eternity," he corrected, using terms more familiar to her.

She wriggled upward, caught his neck, wrapped her legs tighter, and sank down on him.

It was a wonder his eyes did not roll back in his head at the white-hot heat suddenly enfolding him. Ian shuddered in ecstasy. He had to be as large as a ship's mast by now. She still had not taken him fully, although she rocked against him with enchanting little gasps as she realized what she was doing to him.

"For all eternity," he insisted, holding still.

"For all eternity," she agreed, without an ounce of understanding beyond the fierce need pumping between them.

Ian's blood heated to boiling, his ring flared, and the candle flames shot high into the darkness, as if a breeze had entered from beyond. The gods had accepted their vow. The bond was irrevocably knotted in ways more deeply physical and spiritual than their sexual congress.

Thank all the heavens; he could have her now. And into eternity.

In triumph and gratitude, Ian gripped his amacara and gave her all she wanted and more—he plunged his sex to the hilt, until she screamed and opened herself entirely to him, body and soul. Feeding on the desires stretching their bond taut, he tilted her to the angle that most suited her, rubbing the center of her pleasure with their movement. He closed his eyes as her ecstasy became his.

The knot between them was too new and too close to resist her mounting need. Abiding by the pace she set, he thrust repeatedly and deeply. Even as she convulsed in glorious release, he did not let go.

Grateful for Chantal's trust and unquestioning acquiescence, Ian applied all his considerable skill and desire to making the moment of conception perfect. He suckled her breasts until she wept with need, angled her so he could reach her womb, caressed the sensitive cleft of her buttocks, and when she was quivering and moaning and bruising his arms with her grip, he reached outside of himself to let her ride the sky.

The energy of the universe flowed through him and into her as he plunged still deeper, taking her higher, opening the heavens to reveal the secrets there. She cried out her joy, and he succumbed to her cries. They quaked with their mutual release, and he flooded her with his power and his life.

Chantal exclaimed in startlement as her body seemed to come apart in a thousand tiny pieces. A joyous vision of children playing on a grassy lawn came to her, and then dissipated, and she became one with the water in which they lay. The stars exploded inside her head, and the man whose hot seed seared her womb seeped into her blood until she felt him under her skin as well as under her heart. He was so huge, he nearly cleaved her in two, but the caress of his hands and the water molded them together again until he was a part of her in a way that did truly seem eternal.

If she did not conceive after this mind-opening cataclysm, then she never would. She did not care either way, as long as she knew they could repeat this ecstasy. She felt possessed with a desire that was not quenched but increased with satiation.

Ian leaned over to ply her mouth with tantalizingly tender kisses. She was too spent to do more than nip at the corners of his mouth and settle more comfortably around him. He was already growing hard within her again. Excitement tugged at her womb, and to her amazement, her body easily adjusted to accept him.

"You are humming with pleasure," he said, smiling down at her.

"You should smile more often," she told him drowsily, admiring the way his stark features softened with tenderness. "It makes you almost human."

A hint of sadness crept behind the midnight blue of his eyes. "Almost," he agreed. "Too human, sometimes."

Leisurely, he stroked her from within, and a growing knot of anticipation vibrated.

"I did not know such pleasure was possible," she whispered as he played her as masterfully as she did the piano keys. "Will you visit me often so you can teach me more?"

"I doubt I will return," he said without regret. "I will show you my home, instead."

Chantal knew her tasks and her life were here, in France, and disappointment washed over her, but she wouldn't let tomorrow ruin the moment. "Perhaps someday," she agreed, so he would not stop his caresses.

He pushed deeper inside her. "Soon," he warned, "you will have no choice. But it will not be bad if we have this."

The stars sparkled inside her again, and she was well beyond arguing. Convulsing in his hands, she took his seed and let pleasure seal the bond between them.

Perhaps, when he was gone, now that she knew what pleasure was, she would find another lover.

"You can't. You are mine for eternity," Ian's voice murmured seductively as he pulled her into his arms with her last shudder of climax.

As if he could read her mind! Chuckling softly, she snuggled against his shoulder while the water lapped between them, soothing the pain of hearing him admit that he would soon be gone, never to return.

Thirteen

Striding across a field to reach her father's stable, Chantal felt decidedly odd after experiencing an awe-inspiring night of lovemaking in a bath and still waking alone. She decided to approach this day's tasks with more caution. That she still longed for Ian's company when her physical needs ought to be satisfied told her she was becoming much too attached, too quickly, to a man who had said he would not stay.

The promised expedition to the country should have provided the distance she needed, but her tight satin jacket chafed at her aroused nipples, reminding her of the previous night. She firmly diverted her attention by seeking the right horse to safely spirit her brother-in-law from France. She refused to be distracted by the barbarian striding swiftly ahead of her—instead of offering his arms to assist her and Pauline across the manure-strewn pasture.

"Your father is generous in offering Pierre one of his horses," Pauline said, regret tinting her gratitude. She stepped delicately through the grass with her skirts lifted and her eyes on the ground. "I only wish he need not leave at all. I am losing everything that is familiar to me."

Chantal swept Marie off her feet before the little girl could explore a particularly ripe horse patty. "We must learn to adapt to survive," she declared bravely, mouthing phrases she knew were true but with which she did not feel comfortable. "We have dallied too long in a past that no longer suits the present."

"Change comes too fast," Pauline protested.

Watching Ian striding confidently toward some goal she could not detect, Chantal had to agree with Pauline's sentiment. The revolutionary transition from abstinent widow to sexual playmate had certainly left *her* off balance.

Ian had left his monk's robe on the farm cart they'd taken for this visit outside the city. A breeze indecently plastered his shirt linen to his powerful torso. Despite the strength in his square shoulders, he was more lean hipped and sinewy than broad. He moved with the agility and grace of the thoroughbred that had caught his fascination.

"Does your friend know horses well?" Pauline asked, also watching Ian's eager step. "Pierre is not a good horseman. He needs a gentle pony, not one of those great beasts."

"As far as I'm aware, Ian does not know horses at all." Chantal watched in puzzlement as her lover leaned on the paddock fence to survey the mares, then turned his head as if listening to a distant call. Bypassing the docile animals, he headed for a fenced area past the stable.

Still holding Marie, Chantal bit back a squeal of fright as she recognized Ian's destination—at the same moment that Papa's stallion caught wind of an intruder.

Muttering an oath, she handed Marie to Pauline, then lifted her skirt to race across the grass toward the fence Ian was vaulting with the ease of an athlete. "No, Ian! Not that one! He's mean." Worse than mean. Just last year, the stud had trampled a jockey.

Ian didn't appear to hear her.

"Ian, wait!" she cried.

He didn't even turn around to see what she wanted, drat the man. She had spent her life among musicians, courtiers, and gentlemen. She had no experience with uninhibited beasts who did not believe the rules of society applied to them.

"Ian!" she screamed as the distant stallion angrily tossed its head and flared its nostrils.

Seemingly blind to the danger, Ian still didn't turn around.

She had no one to call on to help. Pauline was wisely hustling the children into the stable. They'd left Pierre in Paris. The stable boys seldom appeared except at feeding time.

At Ian's continued advance, the stallion reared, whinnying his displeasure. A descendant of England's champion Matchem, the thoroughbred was no mere Arabian, but a powerful animal bred for strength and stamina.

"Ian, no! Stop!" The gate was too far away. She clambered on a fence rail, tugging her skirt and petticoat to an indecent height so she could sit on the top rail and swing her legs over.

The stallion offered another loud challenge, then broke into a trot—straight toward Ian.

Perhaps, if she could run along the fence, she could distract the animal—

The stallion charged into a gallop. Ian halted in the center of the pasture—too far for Chantal to prevent disaster. She covered her mouth to keep from screaming her horror and prayed frantically as her feet touched the ground inside the fence. Maybe if she distracted the stallion quickly enough, he wouldn't have time to trample Ian into a bloody pulp.

The idiot man didn't even see the danger when the horse was almost on top of him. He stood still, as if *wanting* to be run over. Terrified, Chantal couldn't bear to stay sensibly near the fence. She ran toward him, screaming bloody murder, hoping to terrorize the animal into changing course.

She stumbled and almost fell on her face when the stallion pranced to a sudden halt and nudged Ian's shoulder with his muzzle, for all the world like a friendly puppy looking for treats.

Heart pounding so hard it left her light-headed, Chantal watched the amazing, terrifying, beyond-annoying man scratch the stallion's nose and rub behind its ear as if he didn't recognize a miracle when he saw one. Uncaring of her fragile muslin, she sat down in the grass and bent her forehead to her knees while she learned to breathe again.

Ian was so much a part of her that she felt as if she would have died if he had.

She vowed to make him pay for that. She'd been perfectly content living without the responsibility for anyone but herself. . . .

At the sound of pounding hooves, she jerked her head up.

With only a bridle to control the temperamental animal, Ian had gained the horse's back and was racing across the field straight toward the fence on the far side. And he'd said he didn't know horses!

She couldn't endure any more terror. Her stomach clenched, and she squeezed her eyes shut as the stallion's muscles bunched. *He will break his neck taking that jump.*

She waited for screams of agony. Instead, she heard only the sound of hooves racing away, and she looked up again. Horse and rider rode merrily across the next pasture without any evidence of disaster. A man who had never ridden a horse could not instantaneously

ride like an experienced cavalry officer. If the
wretched man had lied about his knowledge of horses,
what else had he lied to her about?

She hummed in growing fury, stood, and shook out
her skirts. So much for trusting her instincts. She could
have been making love to an assassin, for all she knew.

Meshing his mind with the magnificent animal's, Ian
stretched out and let his muscles move in tandem with
his mount's. The wind tore through his hair, and he
was riding the universe in a manner that exceeded
even that of his exercises with his staff under the
night sky.

Why had no one ever told him of this astounding
animal? Had Sky Riders in ancient times been denied
this powerful instrument of knowledge? To what
purpose?

The forward rush of motion focused all the frag-
ments of his thoughts, impressions, and instincts into
a steady stream of visions clearer than any he'd ever
known. The images hit him one after another with the
power of terror and fury.

Despite his joy in his newfound skill, Ian suffered
gut-wrenching horror as his mind's eye collected pic-
tures of human heads rolling into a basket, beautiful
women reduced to rags and shame and dragged in
carts through jeering mobs, cities burning, armies
marching—

And Murdoch there, in the center of it all.

Gagging on his nausea, Ian shut down his senses
before the psychic violence destroyed him. Closing his
eyes and taking deep breaths, he rubbed the stallion's
proud neck, whispered in his ear, and slowed him to
a cooling trot. Still linked muscle to muscle with the
horse's motion, he let his head clear slowly, gradually

coming back from the heavens and taking in his surroundings.

Somewhere in their mad race, they'd jumped the fence and left the stable far behind.

Chantal! She'd been terrified. Enrapt in fascination with the stallion's mind, Ian had ignored her foolish fears, just as she would ignore him if he tried to tell her of his vision—and his terror that she would one day be one of the women in a cart, rolling to her doom. The sky was red with blood that would soon rain down on all of France.

Stomach roiling, he asked his mount to turn home, promising rich feed and much gratitude in return. The animal shook its mighty head, enjoying the wind in its mane, but it obediently broke into a canter in the direction from which they'd come.

Ian mentally reexamined his fleeting visions. The horse's steady pace eased the task, but not the pain, of revisiting the violence.

By the time the stable came into view, Ian knew that Murdoch, the king, and the chalice were all intertwined. He was on the right course. He just hadn't planned far enough ahead. He needed to save the king and the chalice from treachery, then capture Murdoch and return to Aelynn before true revolution erupted.

He needed Chantal to go with him, sooner and not later.

He was prepared to die in his effort to stop Murdoch, if Murdoch's ambition was to control France with the aid of the chalice. He could not allow an Aelynner to wreak any part of the violence he'd just Seen. But he refused to leave Chantal alone and helpless in the terror to come. Which meant he needed to change his plans and transport her and the chalice safely from Paris *before* he went after Murdoch.

She wouldn't want to go. That knowledge gnawed at his innards.

The party of women and children sat in the cart, eating the picnic lunch they'd brought with them. Ian would think it a cheerful domestic scene if he did not recognize his amacara's rigid posture. Even from this distance, he could tell she was frightened and furious.

He'd known that taking a mate at a dangerous time like this was a risk, but not taking her would have been equally risky and decidedly less pleasant. At least, knowing she was angry with him, he wasn't riding around in a state of unrequited arousal. When she thought about their lovemaking, he knew it, and his body responded accordingly.

The amacara ties were already binding them, despite their unorthodox vows. He did not dare explain to Chantal that if she thought lustful thoughts, he would respond in kind. And vice versa. She had too much control over him as it was, and he needed to act on his own for now.

He supposed he ought to be grateful that she had yet to conceive his child, but the failure nagged at him. If only he'd been able to find that blasted mark, he could be convinced she had a talent of great worth to Aelynn, and he might understand the motive of the gods. But the candles had guttered out before they'd left the bath, and he'd been too besotted to examine her when she'd tugged her sheets tightly to her chin and fallen fast asleep. He'd have to be a brute to wake her by lighting lamps. Besides, his decision was already made. The mark wouldn't change it. Perhaps the gods meant for them to conceive on Aelynn, where Olympian spirits waited. Taking Chantal to Aelynn complicated his life beyond measure, but he needed to do it.

He slid off the stallion and walked it around the

paddock, delaying the moment when he must face Chantal's ire. When a stable boy finally arrived, Ian handed over a coin, and, translating the images in the animal's mind, he asked for the best oats and some carrots.

Then, unable to dally longer, he approached the cart.

"Did you have a pleasant gallop, monsieur?" Chantal called sweetly. "I had no idea you were such an accomplished rider. Do you practice on racing dragons in your country since you don't have horses?"

Ian uttered impolite oaths under his breath as he rested his boot on the cart step and reached for the hunk of bread the little boy offered. He had no way of telling her about Aelynn or his mental skills until she wore his ring. "I have never before encountered such an intelligent animal," he said truthfully, avoiding a direct answer.

"Or a better-behaved one. Tell me, do all creatures do as you ask?"

He didn't have to read her mind to know that dart had two prongs. Even the old mule stirred restively at her pointed barb.

"Some creatures are more contrary than others. Usually the more intelligent ones," he admitted, tearing off a hunk of bread with his teeth.

At home, he was a peacemaker. Here, he was a roil of turbulent emotions he had little experience handling. Apparently, it took time to temper the raging lusts induced by amacara bonds. Even in their anger, desire hung in a sheet of shimmering translucence between them.

"Intelligent creatures with minds of their own," she agreed, maintaining her sweet accents so as not to disturb the children, although Pauline looked at her oddly and the mule shook his head. "It must be diffi-

cult dealing with contrary minds that disagree with
your omniscience."

Ian wondered what would happen if she learned
how her voice affected others and deliberately directed her ire in his direction. He expected it would
be painful.

"If I knew all," he replied, "I wouldn't be here
trying to find the best solution to our mutual problems. I'm always open to suggestion." Well, perhaps
not always. He'd ignored her fears of the horse. And
he had no intention of leaving her in Paris. So perhaps
she had some right to complain. Eventually, she'd understand that he knew best.

"Then I suggest, in your omniscience, that you
choose a steady mare for Pierre so he can leave. Papa
is obtaining his passport as we speak."

After the visions he'd seen today, he'd changed his
mind about the plans they had made last night. They
needed to be modified.

"I don't think the documents will be sufficient to
see him safely from the country," Ian declared, reaching for the cheese and a cup of wine that Pauline
handed him. He was always starving after he'd had a
vision. "I have been listening, and security between
here and the north has tightened. The soldiers fear
invasion and are wary of spies."

"You mean, they are afraid the king will escape,"
Pauline said with bitterness.

"That, too." It took more time to plot his actions
than to process his visions. He had to think quickly
on how best to accomplish everything at once. "A
lone man on a rich horse that he rides badly would
arouse suspicion. A cart or carriage carrying women
and children going to a wedding would pass more
freely."

Chantal glared as if she saw inside his head.

Fortunately for all concerned, she could not.

"You want us to go with Pierre?" Pauline asked in dismay.

"For your king and country, I think that wisest," he agreed without inflection, hoping Pauline understood.

She did, and her expression grew thoughtful. Von Fersen had set the escape for tomorrow night, with the light of the full moon to guide them. It would be a matter of coordinating the escape of Pauline and the children instead of just Pierre—and without their being aware of the king's escape, persuading Chantal and her father to accompany them. Even without his premonitions, Ian could see that Alain Orateur would be murdered within months if he stayed, and that Chantal would never leave without him.

That, he could not allow.

Fourteen

"*Non, non!* This is inexcusable," Pierre protested, pacing the music room, where they had gathered that evening. "I cannot endanger my sister and the little ones with this reckless plan."

Chantal thoroughly approved of her brother-in-law's wisdom in this matter, even if she questioned his wisdom in his choice of loyalty to the church instead of king and country. He, at least, saw the fallacy of involving the innocent in his escape.

"I will not be talked out of it," Pauline insisted. "We will go with you wherever you choose to go. Paris is no longer the home we once knew."

Chantal tapped her friend's tones out on the piano keys and knew she was speaking falsehoods. But what was Pauline hiding with her brave words? Fear? That was very likely. But there was more than fear in her voice. What had happened to the flitting butterfly of society that Pauline once was? She'd had reason to change, Chantal supposed. With most of the French nobility, and even the king's brother, gone across the borders to the safety of the Hapsburg courts, society was not what it had been. And Pauline was not cut out for revolutionary thoughts.

Perhaps her friend would be happier with the exiled court. Chantal wanted to weep at the thought of letting her and the children go, but she had no right to prevent Pauline's happiness to aid her own. She could only hope the separation would be short.

"I have reason to believe the countryman I seek is traveling north," Ian said from across the room.

He'd physically removed himself from the family discussion by setting up a chess game on the far side of the salon and playing against himself, but he'd obviously been listening.

Chantal sat at the piano to avoid looking at him, but she was intensely aware of his presence just the same. Even though he was quiet and appeared scholarly, Ian was not the kind of man one could easily dismiss from one's mind. Sometimes, she thought she felt the vibration of his enormous energy from across the room.

Her father had lent him one of his old frock coats. Perhaps that was the difference tonight. In freshly starched lace, stockinet breeches, and newly cleaned boots, his long dark queue spiraling down the royal blue of his coat, Ian appeared the epitome of every gentleman she'd ever known. He sat with one long muscled leg sprawled out to the side of the chess table, the other boot tucked under his seat, as if he might leap from the chair at any moment.

All heads turned at his comment.

Not looking up from the chessboard, he continued, "I think it might ease all our minds if we traveled together."

Despite his casualness, Chantal felt the force of his determination. Odd, that she felt it without using the piano to test his tones. She clenched her fingers into her palm so tightly that her nails bit through skin. She didn't even know where to begin protesting his mad suggestion.

"You *see* the safety in that?" her father asked with a nonchalance to match Ian's.

Again, Chantal sensed an undercurrent she couldn't decipher, as if there were more meanings to *see* than she understood.

Ian moved his queen into position and glanced up, directly at her. His eyes glowed with an incandescence that held her captive and burned through to the places that he'd touched the prior night, inside and out.

"I See the danger of remaining here," he remarked, answering her father with the same emphasis, but holding Chantal's gaze as if he spoke only to her. "There's safety in numbers. The journey is not so long that you couldn't return later if you so desired."

"Of course we so desire." Chantal looked away first. Her fingers unconsciously stroked the keys, trying to play what wasn't being said. Ian's remarks were often strange, but her father's participation unnerved her. "This is our home. We cannot just up and leave it."

"But you understand the sense in traveling with your friends and the children until they have safely crossed into Austria?" Ian asked, not raising his voice.

The Austrian Netherlands were the closest country to Paris, a day's ride away. Silence filled the room now that their thoughts had been said aloud.

"He speaks truth," her father finally admitted. "The roads north are littered with checkpoints, and the soldiers are not always obedient to their orders. Thieves are everywhere. Larger parties aren't as easily intimidated."

Chantal stared at her father in surprise. His face seemed more lined with worry than usual, and the strain of his tasks had aged him. He rubbed his injured knee as he spoke, and her heart bled for him. He had lost as much as she had these past years. She wasn't certain he'd even looked at another woman since her mother's death last year. Her grief welled.

She usually played her piano or hummed to block out unpleasantness, but with all eyes on her now, she had to face reality. "Liberty and equality" had different meanings to different people. Some thought it meant they need abide by no law. Although she felt safe in her small world, in reality, much of France bordered on anarchy.

She bowed her head in grief and acceptance. "I cannot bear to think of you and the children leaving us," she whispered, holding back a sob. "You are all I have left of Jean. I would stay with you for as long as possible."

Pauline openly wept, wiping her tears with her lace handkerchief. "Perhaps, by next year, we can gather in Le Havre and enjoy the simple pleasures we knew as children. I want that for Anton and Marie."

Ian turned back to his chessboard as if he'd lost interest in the discussion now that he'd had his way. Chantal watched as he tilted his queen to knock over the black king. White had won. Why did she think this had some significance for him? She was surely losing her wits beneath the strain of all these upheavals.

"I will begin making the arrangements," her father said with an unusual heaviness.

Chantal wanted to rush to him as he struggled to stand, but she knew her offer of aid would be brushed aside. Her father did not require her help, but the children would. And, perhaps, Pauline. More than anything right now, she needed to be needed.

"I will help you, sir," Pierre said with a sad solemnity that indicated he'd accepted his banishment. "I sincerely regret the trouble I am causing, but I think it is for the best that Pauline leave." He stood and followed his host from the room.

Chantal was torn when Pauline, too, rose to retire.

She wanted to hug her friend and go with her to admire the sleeping innocence of her godchildren, knowing it might be the last time she saw them beneath her roof. At the same time, she was aware of Ian crossing the room. She felt desire for him coiling in her womb, causing her breasts to swell against the thin muslin of her chemise so that the sash at her waist was suddenly too tight.

He ran his hand proprietarily over the nape of her neck, and she was amazed that her hair didn't curl from the electricity of his touch.

"I must go out this evening," he said with regret. "I need to make arrangements for the return of my chalice."

Of course, it was about the chalice. Always the chalice. The object was more important to him than she was. In this irrational world, that almost made sense.

"I will go upstairs with Pauline and look after the children, then," she murmured, rising from the bench and meaning to walk away, just to show she retained her independence.

She couldn't do it. His hand drifted to her shoulder, and she looked up to meet Ian's dark eyes. The impact of what they had done together last night hit her when he pressed her closer, and she gravitated into his arms as if she belonged there. She circled his neck and stroked his nape.

"I know you have no reason to believe me," he said gravely, "but leaving Paris is for the best. You will understand someday."

"Shredding my heart into little pieces is for the best?" she asked, unable to keep the cry from her voice. "They are all I have left besides my father. This house will echo empty when we return. I think losing them may kill me."

She refused to acknowledge the possibility that losing him might be the worst of all.

She disentangled herself and hurried away before she could melt into a puddle of tears beneath the concern and understanding in his eyes. He didn't even have the decency to appear cold and proud in the face of her grief so that she could hate him.

Ian could feel his mate's grief deep down inside him where he couldn't work it off with a few spins of his staff or a good long hike through city streets.

Even knowing she believed she'd return to Paris, Ian couldn't ease the pain, because much of it was his own. He would have to offer her the opportunity to stay with her family in whichever country they settled. That meant giving up all hope of taking her home with him.

Providing he lived through his encounter with Murdoch, he amended. Best to take one obstacle at a time. Rescue the royal family and the chalice, pry Chantal and her father out of Paris before it exploded in rage, find Murdoch, then pray Chantal would come home with him. The odds of any of these happening were so close that even the stars could not predict the outcome.

Life had been much simpler when he could deny his need for anyone. He should have been a hermit.

Ian walked the city streets to the Palais Royale without encountering more than a rowdy band of revelers who demanded to see the revolutionary cockade in his hat. Forewarned about this symbol, he removed his borrowed chapeau from beneath his arm and waved it like a flag that allowed him to sail freely past their narrow straits.

He met Count von Fersen at the Royale as agreed

upon. Ian's ability to sense the emotions of Others verified Chantal's judgment about the handsome Swede's integrity. The count was their best hope of rescuing the royal family—and regaining Aelynn's chalice.

The Palais Royale was another matter entirely. An arena designed for amusement and built by the duc de Chartres, it mixed drunken soldiers with lewd courtesans and men of political power in a crowd pulsating with discontent and greed. With so many people crushed together in one place, the cesspool of vile sins simmered and festered in the summer heat, until the noxious fumes had to explode. It would be best if the royals were far from here when they did.

Although Ian picked up the occasional earnest conversation based on what was best for all, the stench of evil rose like a miasma from the cobbled stones. The revolution had not improved the morals of this city, where lawlessness and anarchy had reigned for too long. He did not need the stars to tell him he was sitting on a powder keg.

Joining the count at a café table where they could keep an eye on the mob, Ian hoped his uncomfortable borrowed frock coat allowed him to blend in without notice. He'd even donned a sword rather than carry his staff.

"My party will be ready to set out by tomorrow evening," Ian told the count. He nodded at the waiter to indicate he'd have a glass of wine, and relaxed into a lounging position against the chair back as he saw others do at nearby tables. "They will chatter of the gala wedding they're attending. I will be certain to mention that we hope the rest of our party is close behind us."

Von Fersen nodded his agreement. "The guards

should recognize my carriage and let us pass without difficulty. But our company's choice of the berlin for the journey is not the wisest and could cause you problems," he warned. "They insist on traveling together in comfort. You will have to schedule many stops so you do not get too far ahead of them."

Ian had second thoughts about risking all for a royal couple so removed from reality that they thought only of their creature comforts while their country was perched on the brink of destruction, but he could see only more bloodshed should he leave them here. "If you have the Russian passports, there shouldn't be any difficulty. They will smuggle out the chalice?"

"All is arranged, if you have the cash to exchange for it. They need money more than silver and gems. I have already provided them with attire suitable for a baroness and her servants and children. They have sent wardrobes ahead, and the carriage is well supplied. It is only escaping the palace guards . . ."

The count glanced around to make certain no one could overhear. "They practiced tonight and failed. Tomorrow, they must try separately, the children first. I will be driving, so they will know me once they circumvent the guards. I cannot say how long that will take, but it may be in the early hours of morning before we can depart."

"The roads are well marked?" Ian asked in concern. He'd learned that traveling at night was difficult at best in a country where the roads were often no more than dirt paths.

"The baroness has just come from that direction. She says they are safe and easily passable. The moon will be full, and we'll carry lanterns. If the weather holds, the journey should take no more than fifteen hours to the first meeting place. I have notified all concerned of their schedule so no one lingers too long and arouses suspicion."

Ian knew that von Fersen referred to the hussars and royal officers assigned to meet the carriage and escort it to the safety of the border fortress. He preferred not to mention the real danger that awaited them on the north road—not suspicious villagers, but Murdoch. Very little escaped Murdoch's preternatural notice. He might currently be wearing the uniform of a royal officer, but that did not mean his loyalty lay with the king. Ian knew of a certainty that if Murdoch realized the Chalice of Plenty was within his grasp, he would seek it out. If naught else, he could hold the sacred object for ransom in exchange for concessions from Aelynn, forcing the Council to back his ambitions with wealth or power.

"I will do what I can to divert any obstacles," Ian agreed, understanding that for the safety of the royal family it would be best if the chalice went one way and they went another. "Beyond that, we can only hope for good fortune."

"After tomorrow, none of us will be able to return safely here," the count warned, rising to depart. "Is your party prepared for that?"

Ian could not lie. He merely shrugged and looked unconcerned. "This is the best for all." And that was the sincerest truth as he knew it. Chantal and her father might despise him when all was said and done—although he suspected Orateur already accepted the necessity.

"I will owe you a great favor when next we meet." The count bowed, and his tall, striking figure strode off—a dashing, romantic hero who would sacrifice all he owned to save his endangered lover.

Ian sipped his wine and pondered philosophical

thoughts of sacrifice and romance, but he did not feel particularly glorified about saving lives by driving a wedge of deception between him and the one he wanted most. Instead, he prayed that he could capture Murdoch so both his party and the count's could safely reach France's border.

Given Murdoch's ambition and abnormal abilities, any other outcome was likely to be fatal to all.

Fifteen

Chantal held back her tears as she completed each task on her list. It wasn't as if she were leaving home forever, she reminded herself. They'd be back within a few days, and everything would return to normal, except Pauline and her children would no longer be in her life. Her heart already ached with grief at their loss.

Perhaps she should adopt a child of her own. There were orphans aplenty running through the streets. She would think of it later, when she returned.

Ian hadn't said where he would go, but his gestures spoke what his words did not. He'd climbed into her bed in the early hours and simply held her tight until daybreak. She'd understood then that he would be leaving once he had his chalice.

She refused to cry over that as well. He was *nothing* to her. Could never be anything to her. Except the best lover she'd ever had or would ever have again.

They'd made love again at dawn, and he'd left her bed while she dozed afterward. On the pillow where his head had rested, he'd left her a perfectly pitched silver flute. She'd wept over its beauty and his thoughtfulness—and the fear that it might be a parting gift.

She'd barely seen him since, but then, she'd been as busy as he apparently was. She'd helped Pauline pack trunks for the children, advised the servants on the food to send with them, arranged for enough fresh linen for everyone, and carried out her father's errands as if it were an ordinary day. There were spies everywhere, and if anyone surmised they were contemplating illegal actions, the militia would be at their door.

All except Pierre had proper documentation, and even he had the best facsimile her father could arrange. Her father had devised a story of their attending a wedding party in their hometown, so she'd packed a small trunk as well. For Pierre's sake, they must act relaxed. Pauline went to the palace to bid her adieu to the queen. Papa had gone to his usual political salon. The children chased each other around the house and kept the servants too busy to gossip.

Ian had returned from his tasks by dinnertime, and they'd all sat down to enjoy the meal together. But the hours had passed swiftly, and the summer sun had set, taking with it the heat. Now it was time to depart.

For some melancholy reason, Chantal felt as if she'd never see her beloved city home again. The rising moon illuminated the clean lines of pillar and post, and the decades-old vines twining up the limestone. Watching the flicker of lantern light in the glazed windows, she tried to put herself in Pauline's shoes and be grateful for escape. She could not. Pauline would not want to lose her home any more than Chantal wanted to lose her friends and godchildren. Or Ian.

So she hugged a sleepy Marie and passed her into the carriage; helped Anton in with his toy soldier; checked that the trunks were double-tied on top and that Cook's basket was under the seat. Garbed in a coachman's attire, holding a whip, Pierre huddled on the driver's seat.

Out of the corner of her eye, she watched her father and Ian talking quietly, holding the steeds they would ride beside the carriage. She still could not believe her father had agreed to this plan. There were important bills to be discussed, laws to be made. It was her father's participation, more than anything else, that rattled her secure little world.

"See that the beds are freshly made before we return," she ordered the head housekeeper. "And the brandy barrel is almost empty. Have the supply replenished. It will probably be late when we come home, so bread and cheese will suffice upon our arrival. That will give Cook time to go to market the next morning. Is there anything else you can think of?"

"The candles, madame," the servant reminded her. "Shall I restock?"

"Yes, excellent thought. Girard will be in charge of purchases, so check with him. Just look at the moon! It will be such a lovely, cool night for traveling, don't you agree?"

The housekeeper did not look reassured, but she nodded obediently.

Ian took Chantal's elbow. "The horses are restive. We need to be on our way."

"Of course." She scanned his face in the light from the carriage lamps, but she could see nothing beyond the grim set of his lips to indicate his state of mind. He hadn't shaved since morning, and his beard shadowed his jaw, adding a raw masculinity to his striking bone structure that tugged a primal chord inside her. "Thank you for the flute," she whispered. "It is beautiful."

His hand squeezed her elbow harder, as if he felt the same as she. It was unnerving how he did that. "I know you need your music with you. I am sorry we cannot bring more."

Touched that he'd thought of her in such a way, she accepted his assistance and climbed into the shadowy carriage to take the seat facing Pauline. The city gate would be the first test of their documents and Pierre's disguise.

As the carriage horses trotted into the open street and tension mounted, Chantal wondered if this was how the king and queen would someday attempt their escape. Rumors were rife all over Paris that the queen had purchased a berlin and sent an enormous wardrobe ahead to Brussels. Chantal did not understand why the king would want to leave his throne and people when France most needed a strong leader, but she assumed his brothers and the war cries on the border had much to do with it.

She hoped the royals would not be so foolish as to try to escape, but she couldn't stop thinking about it. Putting herself in the place of the queen, she shivered uneasily at the sight of soldiers lounging on street corners, peering into every vehicle that passed. The little bubble of her secure world weakened as she finally realized that this task they undertook was not a pretty game.

The beautiful, sophisticated Paris she knew had become a tinderbox. Intellectually, she'd known any little incident could incite a riot. But until this moment, she'd not feared these skirmishes. She'd always thought of herself as part of the protesting crowd. She feared now that she'd been living an illusion. If the soldiers saw so much as a suspicious face or form, they would stop the carriage, and violence-prone mobs would descend to search them.

Music and revelry rang out in the street ahead, and Pauline huddled her children closer under her cloak. Chantal could not see her face, but she sensed her tension. What was the world coming to that they should fear a party? Paris was known for its gaiety, was it not?

And sadly, she realized, the city had not been gay for a very long time. There had been many triumphs, yes, and there was hope for the future, but years of bankruptcy had taken their toll. People were angry.

She tried a few soft notes on her new flute to play away her unease, but she could not find the right tune. She should have asked Ian if he had his chalice yet, so she could hold it awhile longer. If she could just tap it one more time—

Music played outside, abruptly interrupted by sharp voices as the carriage attempted to traverse a street filled with revelers. She dug her nails into her palms as she listened to Ian's deep voice reply in a soothing manner that almost reassured her. He had a magical way of making people do what he wanted. Something in his voice must produce such excellent results. Except, she remembered, he'd said nothing at the Conciergerie, and people had still moved out of his way.

Her father called jovially to some of the merrymakers, asking the reason for the celebration. Lewd jokes about weddings followed, with her father and Ian explaining they were attending one also. The party in the street shouted their good wishes, and the carriage rolled on under the harbor of false pleasantries. Chantal breathed deeply when she realized she'd been holding her breath.

"I believe your lover has as persuasive a tongue as your father," Pauline whispered. "He could make pigs fly with his silver words."

"And stallions behave and women make fools of themselves," Chantal agreed grimly.

"All very worthy attributes," Pauline agreed with a chuckle, trying to ease the tension.

"A pity we will never see him again once he has what he wants. Did you help him trade his coins for the chalice?" Chantal tried to keep her tone neutral, but she knew what the king would do with the money. In some manner or another, she feared Pauline was helping him escape. She stroked the flute and tried not to believe that Ian was a spy or worse.

"There were messages exchanged," Pauline agreed quietly. "It would not be fair to keep him here by concealing what he came for, would it?"

"No, I suppose not." She stared out the window as they approached the first custom post. Ian rode one of her father's carriage horses and not the stallion. He still looked as if he were one with the animal, controlling its nervous sidesteps with his powerful thighs while speaking with authority to the guards to whom he handed their documents.

Ian was in all ways a stronghold of influence, a veritable prince among men. Even she could see it now that he'd discarded his robes and donned a fashionable costume. Before, his deep eyes and grave expression had fooled her into thinking him a spiritual man, but she knew better now that he'd taken her with a carnal lust that left her hungering for more.

As if he sensed her desire, he turned his head and saluted the carriage with a touch of his whip to his hat. Just the acknowledgment thrilled her as if she were a lovesick adolescent.

Once they were past customs, the full moon lit an easy road through the countryside. On any other occasion, she might have thrilled to the beauty of trees thrown into silver silhouettes. A song would have appeared in her throat, and she would have had everyone singing along with her.

Tonight, her songs were silent. Perhaps that was a good thing. They most likely would have been dirges.

Drums rolled and a small band of local militia drunkenly paraded through the single street of the village where her father kept his stable. Only a few days ago, the drums would have reassured Chantal that all was well. Now she waited tensely as her father greeted the militia leader and exchanged pleasantries. Alain tipped his hat as the guard let them pass. Just one wrong word, and all could end badly.

In silence, they stopped at the stable to exchange horses. Rather than ride one of the nervous Thoroughbreds, Pierre retained his seat beside the coachman. Chantal was not surprised when Ian emerged riding the stallion, but the string of brood mares her father led out shocked her. They'd not been bred this winter, so there were no foals, but these horses were not trained for traces.

She opened the carriage door and leapt down. She didn't dare approach the stallion, although the animal seemed calm in Ian's hands. Instead, she confronted her father.

"Where are you taking the mares?" she demanded.

"I'm selling them," her father said with a trace of sadness. "The military would only confiscate them otherwise. It is time to admit that our racing days are over."

Pierced by the sharp arrow of truth, Chantal crumpled, and her tears fell in a deluge. The horses were her father's pride and joy, representing decades of careful breeding. Sobbing, she rested her wet cheek against the neck of the old mare he rode. Her world was tumbling rapidly out of its orbit.

Wordlessly, she wiped her eyes and returned to her seat, not glancing toward Ian. Her father would not sell his horses to just anyone, so she knew he had a buyer already. And that buyer must be Ian. He was far richer—and more ruthless—than his monk's robes revealed.

Ian deliberately shut his mind to the sorrow emanating from the carriage. Chantal had the ability to close off her thoughts, but the new bond between them opened channels he'd just as soon not yet explore, not while he had harsh duties to accomplish. He didn't need her regret interfering with his awareness.

He'd not met the royal household and could not differentiate their thoughts or emotions from hundreds of others in the countryside through which they traveled. But he'd learned the thought patterns of the Swedish diplomat and kept his inner ear attuned to von Fersen's mind, as well as the chalice's presence in the king's trunk. It was finally within his reach.

He had caught a whiff of the count's concern when his coach ran into the wedding festivities at the Paris gate. But Ian hadn't sensed the horror of capture, so he assumed the royal party had passed safely. They were to exchange von Fersen's carriage for the royal berlin in a village not far from Orateur's stables, where Ian's chosen guards would meet them, dressed in the baroness's livery.

Hours later, as the moon sank toward the western horizon, Ian dropped the stallion behind Chantal's carriage, hoping to catch some sense of von Fersen's whereabouts. Dawn brought new dangers, and he would feel better if the chalice were closer, especially since the count would part company with the royal household once the switch was made.

Ian knew when Chantal finally fell victim to the carriage's rocking and slept. An entire layer of awareness fell away, opening his mind more clearly to the stars. He frowned at the realization that his attachment to Chantal caused an interference with his abilities. His parents had never told him of that handicap.

With the stallion walking smoothly beneath him, Ian connected with the sky and let his mind float over the moonlit landscape. He found the chalice first, carefully wrapped and concealed in the royal luggage. He offered a prayer of thanks to the gods, then sought von Fersen.

He read the count's impatience at the slowness of the royal couple, their children, and the servants as they switched from his speedy carriage to the cumbersome berlin. Haste was not a familiar attribute for a court bogged down by ceremony. This did not bode well for their ability to act with swiftness under pressure. They would have done far better to have taken horses and flown like the wind to the border—as Ian planned to do once he had the chalice in hand.

He was tempted to ride the ten miles or so back to the royal berlin and ask for the chalice now. All his instincts urged him to hurry west toward the sea with Chantal and her father before Murdoch could arrive.

But he had promised to deliver Chantal's in-laws to the Austrian border, in the wrong direction for the sea, and Murdoch must be returned to Aelynn, so Ian's hands were tied. The royal party traveled east as the Russian passports allowed. The duc de Choiseul's loyal hussars would meet the royal berlin on the road after noon. Once Ian was relieved of that burden, he could claim the chalice and lead Chantal's family on the faster road north. From there, if all went as planned, he would take Chantal west toward the sea and Aelynn.

Murdoch was the unpredictable element in this plan.

The stars told Ian that Murdoch was with the duc's troops on the road ahead, waiting for the arrival of the king—and the chalice. Murdoch could read the stars as easily as Ian. Or once, he could have. Once, Murdoch could have moved the earth, stopped the wind, and raised the sea, although never predictably. Even before his banishment, Murdoch's gifts had been dangerously erratic. Now, for all Ian knew, he could cause earthquakes and destroy villages if angered or distracted.

Ian gnashed his teeth at the slowness of the royal parade on the road behind him. But his own party appreciated the extra time for breakfasting at an inn while they exchanged the carriage horses again. And the train of mares appreciated a chance to rest before moving on.

A ragged brigade in the striped trousers of local militia stopped to study them with distrust and question the innkeeper. Suspicion and wariness marked all the roads of France. Ian mentally nudged this motley troop along its way after providing coins to buy their breakfast, but he could not do the same for the royal party.

As Orateur's carriage pulled away from the inn in the coolness of a sunny summer morning, Chantal's lovely voice broke into a children's song that had even the horses trotting to a happy beat. Other voices chimed in, and Ian allowed himself a brief moment to relax and enjoy their merry mood.

In that moment, on a cloudless June day, the blast of a northerly gale rocked the carriage, terrified the horses, and shattered Ian's tranquility.

Murdoch!

No one else could harness the wind in such a remarkable manner—and from such a distance, for Ian hadn't sensed him nearby.

The frail carriage tilted sideways, flinging its precious human cargo to one side. The driver screamed and clung to his perch, barely controlling the reins.

Shoving his fear deep down inside him, Ian drew on the center of his power and sent his reassurances to the bolting animals. In moments, the brush with death subsided, the carriage's wheels rested properly on the ground, and the animals pranced under control.

As the children wept, and the women's pale faces appeared in the windows, Ian leapt from his steed to examine the axles while Alain finished calming the horses and sent him a questioning look.

To Ian's chagrin, he finally recognized the danger of placing innocents in the path of Murdoch's superhuman powers and ambition. He'd trusted too much in the friend Murdoch had once been.

He must correct that error instantly. If Murdoch could raise a wind from miles ahead, he had evidently not lost as much of his unpredictable abilities as the Aelynners had hoped.

Sixteen

The wild rocking of the carriage cut off Chantal's song in midnote.

She grabbed the strap hanging from the ceiling to steady herself. The children screamed, then scrambled to look out the windows along with the adults. White-faced, Pauline clutched Marie as the carriage miraculously settled back to its normal roll.

At the sound of pounding hooves behind them, Chantal pushed open the sash and leaned out. The sky contained only a few puffy white clouds against the clear blue. Alarm shot through her at the sight of Ian's stallion raising dust, riding back the way they had just come.

She tried not to reveal her fear to the children as she waited for her father to ride up and explain what was happening. But when he arrived, he looked as puzzled as she was.

"Ian said he would meet us at the next stop," he said, leaning down to speak through the window. "He has some idea that there is trouble behind us."

Pauline drew in a quick breath, and Chantal glanced back to note her sister-in-law's eyes widening with fear. There was no reason for alarm as far as she knew.

Which meant Pauline knew something she didn't. "What?" Chantal demanded. "What is back there?"

Pauline could only shake her head and bite her lip.

Chantal clicked her fingernails against the flute in her pocket and tried not to let her nervousness get the best of her. "You know something," she insisted, even though Pauline shook her head. "Fine, don't tell us, but can you say if it's safe to go on?"

Pauline bobbed her head. "Yes, and hurry, please."

Chantal exchanged glances with her father, who suddenly looked as troubled as she felt. So he, too, was unaware of whatever Ian and Pauline had plotted.

Her instincts cried to turn around, but reason told her that was foolish. Ian was a grown man, and skilled in the use of weapons. He could take care of himself.

"If there's treason afoot," she murmured to her father, "then it's best we hasten away."

"Treason?" Her father looked astonished at this suggestion, but narrowing his eyes and glancing in at Pauline and up to Pierre, he nodded and ordered the carriage to roll on.

"It is not treason," Pauline said in a hushed voice beneath the children's chatter.

"The king has the chalice Ian wants, doesn't he?" Chantal asked calmly, while her mind added up possibilities and reached a horrible conclusion. "And instead of going directly north, we're heading for the duc de Choiseul's holdings, where the duc has loyal troops who can escort the royals out of France."

Pauline stiffened and stared straight ahead. That was all the admission Chantal needed.

"Ian is a stranger here," Chantal chided in a whisper. "He does not know our customs or the danger he faces. Surely there was a better way for him to obtain his sacred vessel."

Pauline didn't deny the accusation.

Ian was a man on a mission that he would never abandon. Guilt ate at Chantal's heart as she realized how thoroughly she had embroiled Ian in her family's troubles. Had she waited only a few hours to trade the chalice for Pauline's freedom . . .

But it was too late.

Had she been on her own, she might have attempted to ride after Ian in hopes of saving him from whatever treason Pauline had plotted. But even her father seemed to acknowledge that the children must come first. With a grave expression, he rode beside the carriage as it raced to the next inn. Helpless, Chantal played the flute to quiet her inner turmoil.

The tension, or the music, eventually silenced even the children. Pauline kept her petite nose determinedly in the air as she watched the passing landscape. Chantal tried to forgive her for endangering everyone for a weak king, but Pauline's actions had created a rift between them that she couldn't easily bridge.

If the king escaped to another country, it would mean civil war—or worse.

If the king were *caught* escaping . . . the streets would fill with irate mobs, and Paris would burn with their rage.

If Pauline and Ian were responsible for the escape, everyone traveling with them would be implicated, including Chantal and her father.

Her fury with Pauline and Ian knew no bounds. She couldn't even excuse Ian for his ignorance. He knew what he was doing, and he chose to do it anyway. She couldn't call him a traitor to the cause, because France's politics had nothing to do with him. He had just high-handedly decided to act without any consideration of the consequences.

Stretched thin, the bubble of illusion she'd lived in finally popped. The pretty iridescent colors disappeared, and dread took over.

Her flute began an angry tune, and she put it away,

only to rap out a harsh beat with her fingernails on the door.

Anton tugged Marie's golden curls, and she began to cry.

The strain inside the carriage escalated to reflect the pressures building in the larger world.

It had taken tense, hot hours, but Ian now galloped on the wings of joy down the road the Orateur carriage was taking.

Murdoch's cruel gale had frightened the royal party's horses and toppled the heavy berlin into the stone edge of a rural bridge. If the intent had been to stop the carriage entirely, it had failed. Murdoch had never perfected control of his gifts, so Ian still did not know how dangerous he was, but he knew now that Murdoch retained his ability to harness the wind—and that he could Find the chalice as easily as Ian could.

Emptying the terrified royals, their crying children, and the servants onto the roadside had taken all of Ian's empathic skills. Helping mend the broken wheel of the berlin without revealing his superhuman strength had required even more talent. He hadn't sensed Murdoch's presence, but the delay would cause trouble with von Fersen's rigid schedule, placing the royals in even graver danger of capture. Ian had done all he could to speed them on their way.

For his efforts, and his purse, of course, he'd been rewarded with praise and promises—and the chalice.

Wrapped in purple velvet, the sacred object rested in his saddlebag. Ian's relief at the ease of acquiring it was infinite. Aelynn's future was ensured! If he had Chantal's gift, he'd burst into song—an unusual reaction for a man who'd spent his life mastering serenity.

He was far from accomplishing all his goals, but he rejoiced in achieving one. The peaceful life he led seldom offered serious challenges, so until now, he'd been deprived of the experience of triumph. He relished its sweetness while he could.

He might despise the turbulence of his mate's world, and fear the dangerous effect on his abilities, but this thrill of triumph could be addictive.

With the acquisition of the chalice, he was free to take Chantal and her family directly to the northern border. Chantal's presence pleased him far more than praise and promises.

He patted the stallion's neck. "Ready for lunch, old friend? Shall I call you Rapscallion as your master does?" The horse threw its head up and down in response to his name. "Excellent. Rapscallion it is. We'll let you cool off while the royal party toddles on to meet their escort. Perhaps my lady would like to rest through the afternoon heat. Rooms for us and a nice stable full of oats for you."

The horse whinnied his approval of this plan. Eager for the reward of Chantal's bed, Ian spurred the horse on. After the hard physical labor of removing a wheel from a heavy carriage, he'd have liked a bath, but he was unlikely to find one in these rural surroundings. If he weren't in such haste to return to his party, he might take the time to find a stream or pond, but with one duty done, he was ready to complete them all. He wanted to take his prizes and go home.

Murdoch still endangered his goals, but Ian preferred to hope Murdoch would be too caught up in his schemes to easily follow the chalice. If they could stay a few days ahead of him . . . Chantal and the chalice would be on a ship to Aelynn and safety.

He rode into the town where von Fersen had said they might take luncheon.

Still savoring his victory at finally possessing both chalice and amacara, Ian hadn't paid close attention to the whispers on the wind until he rode into town and sought Chantal. He was immediately struck with a wave of rage and fear and grief.

He reached for the oak staff he'd tied to his saddle and eased it from the loop. Unable to read his ama-cara's mind, he reminded himself that she'd already been considerably upset, so he couldn't know whether she'd stubbed her little toe or was in serious danger. He had to resist panic.

Steeling his heart, he dismounted and cautiously walked the stallion toward the town square, examining the winds and trying to focus on separating thoughts from fears. He cursed his visionary skill for being so weak that he could not use it except when he was physically occupied and mentally open. His skills did not fit drawing rooms, of a certainty.

Reaching the top of the hill leading down to the posting inn, Ian inhaled sharply. In the town square below, ill-dressed militia clashed with furious farmers and shrieking housewives. Rakes and brooms swung dangerously at swords and muskets, and a shot was fired into the air.

Ian searched frantically for Chantal's fair hair. He picked up Pierre's confused thoughts as the riot swirled around him. The young priest had little experience in dealing with mobs, but he apparently knew Chantal was in the midst of this one.

Straining to hold back his superhuman ability to run, Ian hurried down the hill, wishing for a better link with Chantal, one that reached beyond her emotions. Even their strong sexual bond would not let him invade her thoughts. But racing down the hillside faster than a galloping horse would terrorize the villagers. Better that he study the situation than act in haste.

That rationality lasted until he recognized Chantal's straw bonnet rolling through the dust.

"Find the inn and your master," he told the stallion, looping the reins over the saddle, forming the image the stallion would understand better than words. With only that admonishment, Ian broke into a run down the hill, staff firmly in hand.

At the edge of the mob, he caught a housewife's flailing broom and parried it with his staff into an opening between two thick farmers. Judiciously using the oak and his mental nudges, he poked his elbows into stout ribs and shoved a path through shouting, angry villagers. He couldn't tell whether the militia held them off or urged them on or were simply shouting like all the rest.

His innards roared in rage when he finally heard Chantal. Her voice was not the ladylike melody he knew so well, but more that of a shrieking fishwife. Goosebumps covered his flesh, and irritation shredded his eardrums. He smacked a soldier's sword with his bare hand, sending it skittering beneath the feet of the crowd.

He never got angry. He had no experience with explosive fury. Yet he wanted to rip the crowd apart— and he had no idea why.

Realizing that, he still didn't stop and reconsider. Chantal was angry, so he must be, too.

With the strength of ten men, Ian lifted a soldier and flung him out of his way, grabbed a burly farmer and twisted him around so he'd take his curses elsewhere. He shoved aside men and women alike until he reached the whirling eye of the storm—Chantal.

Holding a . . . chicken?

His peaceful, enchanting, melodic-voiced Chantal was screaming hysterically at a skinny boy in tattered military garments.

The whole town screamed with her. Never again would he doubt the power of her voice.

Ian strode into the circle, wrapped one arm around Chantal's waist, slapped his other hand over her mouth, and hauled her off her feet.

She kicked furiously, hitting his shins with unfailing accuracy. The chicken squawked and flapped its wings. Men cheered. Women railed. The skinny boy just looked dazed.

Ian paid no heed to anyone except the woman in his arms. The stiffness was draining from her backbone, and she hugged the miserable chicken like a child, sniffing back tears.

Hands full, Ian could only glare at anyone in his way and send them scurrying from his path. Once free of the crowd, he was able to see the inn and the carriage.

"Do you wish to take the chicken to the kitchen or a henhouse?" he asked in his calmest tones, when, in fact, his head shrieked with a thousand damnable emotions—hers *and* his.

Carefully, he lifted his hand from her mouth, prepared to cover it again should she emit another scalp-raising screech.

"Kitchen," she whispered. "Put me down, please."

He didn't want to. He wanted to fling the chicken to the cook and carry Chantal straight upstairs to a chamber where he could close the door on the world and straighten out his spinning head in the best way he knew how—with his amacara in his bed. Barring that, he needed to take his staff to an empty yard and work through his serenity exercises until he had set his mind straight.

Instead, he had to figure out what had just happened here, and he suspected the answer would only make his head whirl more.

He returned Chantal to her feet. Not meeting his

eyes, she cradled the stunned chicken as if it were a long-lost friend.

"Are you sure you want to take it to the kitchen?" he asked.

"Papa loves chicken soup." Straightening her shoulders, she marched toward the inn, back ramrod straight. Golden ringlets had escaped their pins and fallen flat in the heat and humidity. Her skirt was covered in dust and adorned with chicken droppings.

Ian's mouth twitched and his insides softened at the sight of her vulnerable nape and swaying hips. Whatever she'd done, she'd scared herself, and he itched to reassure her. He would make a rotten leader if he couldn't handle one small woman.

"I don't think we have time for soup," he informed her, following her to the back of the inn.

"We will make time. Papa collapsed in the stable. He's barely conscious. I'll stay here with him," she said boldly.

That did not bode well for any of his carefully laid plans.

Apparently having circumnavigated the crowd, Pierre hurried to catch up with them. "Chantal, I think you're possessed," he muttered angrily. "Or bewitched. How can anyone start a riot over a chicken?"

Ian sensed the young priest's confusion but didn't trespass further into his mind.

"I think your entire country is possessed and bedeviled," he said to distract the priest from thinking of Chantal in such offensive terms. "Do people have nothing better to do than riot in the streets here?"

"Not any longer," Chantal said, shoving the chicken at a startled cook.

Apparently deciding this was an argument he couldn't win, Pierre dropped out of the fray to sample a sweet roll a maid offered him. Now that they were free of Paris, he'd returned to his clergyman's attire. A priest's collar had some benefits, like free sweet rolls.

Lifting her bedraggled skirt, Chantal walked past staring scullery maids and into the inn's hall. "The nobility has all run away," she said scornfully, continuing her tirade. "What is left for people to do if they have no employment? Priests are in hiding. Artisans have left for other countries where people actually pay for their talents. Shall I continue?"

"No. I can read a pamphlet if I want a political diatribe. I just want to know what set off this particular mob."

"I yelled." She said it simply and coldly, as if it explained all.

Ian feared it might.

Her father was an Aelynner with a gift for oration. Chantal was a Crossbreed, born outside the aegis of his gods. For all he knew, her gifted voice could cause emotional discord and incite violence. It certainly seemed to have done so here.

He followed her upstairs in hopes—and fear—of learning more.

Seventeen

A s hard as it was to do, Chantal ignored Ian and opened the door to her father's chamber in the inn. She was too shaken by her unusual behavior over the chicken to accept any more upsetting arguments. She needed her father's calm understanding.

"Chantal!" he called as they entered. "I heard the commotion. What happened?"

That he hadn't left his bed to find out spoke more than a volume of words. Without his wig, he was nearly bald and looked shrunken against the pillow. Escaping Ian's presence, she hurried to her father's bedside to stroke his brow. He felt too warm for her liking, but the room had little air, and the sun baked the roof. It could be just the heat, and perhaps his extreme anxiety, that caused his collapse, but his breathing wasn't normal, and his color looked unhealthy.

"I purchased a chicken for your soup, and some foolish soldier tried to take it from me. I boxed his ears," she said with a bright smile. Actually, she'd screeched. Helpless against her fear for her father and their situation, confronted by a boy with a gun, she'd screeched like an Irish banshee—and the entire town had started yelling with her, rushing out in the street to take sides for no discernible reason. Perhaps everyone's nerves were as on edge as hers.

Her state of anxiety ever since Ian had ridden off

had no doubt added to her hysteria. She really didn't want to know what he'd been doing. She was coming apart at the seams just fine without also knowing he was involved in sedition.

"You can usually sweet-talk an apple into falling into your hand," her father chided, not understanding the extent of the damage she'd done. "You did not sleep well last night. Go rest, and I'll be ready to ride by dinnertime."

She was grateful he had not seen the near riot, but her father was not a man who hid from reality. Alain turned his sharp eye to Ian. "I would speak with you, young man."

Chantal assumed that meant she was dismissed. She preferred not to hear Ian explain himself. *If* he could.

She needed to settle her nerves. She didn't need to know whether the king and queen were escaping. That would surely be the end of the world as she knew it— and not conducive to serenity.

The flute wasn't sufficient. She needed her piano. Or the bell—

Ian hadn't brought Rapscallion with him when he'd raced in to save her from herself. Had he retrieved his chalice? Was it still tied to the saddle? Nothing else could calm her so well.

On that hopeful thought, she ran down the stairs in search of the horse and her lovely bell.

"Tell me you didn't help the royal family to escape in exchange for the chalice," Alain Orateur demanded the moment the bedroom door closed behind Chantal.

"I'm not in the habit of lying," Ian said, taking a seat in a barrel-backed chair, folding his hands over his chest, and stretching his legs. He might as well relax while being interrogated. He seldom found it necessary to explain his actions, but this was Chantal's father. "I did what was necessary to save the chalice and my amacara. That I abetted a deed that was already under way, preventing possible harm to valuable lives, should meet with your approval."

Alain paled at the word *amacara.* "She would never agree to those vows," he whispered in horror, dismissing the political argument for the personal one. "What have you done?"

"What I told you I would do. I'm an Olympus. Did you expect any less? I must still put a halt to a wayward rogue named Murdoch. I don't have much time. Do you know the nature of your illness?"

Shocked, Orateur ran a hand over his balding pate, not looking at Ian. "She's all I have left. I cannot believe . . ." His voice trailed off on a note of grief.

"Have you even attempted to assess her talents?" Ian asked, diverting the topic away from any question of how he'd persuaded Chantal to take vows she did not understand. "The altercation outside just now wasn't quite as simple as she made it seem."

Alain shook his head. "She is extraordinarily gifted musically, a talent your people do not appreciate."

"They're your people, too," Ian reminded him. "Where else but Aelynn would you go when war breaks out here? Or do you plan to keep Chantal exposed to violence and danger?"

"She creates her own safety," Alain argued, glaring at Ian. "Have you not noticed? When she smiles, the whole world smiles with her. Or at least the portion who can see her."

"Hear her," Ian corrected. Until now, he'd almost convinced himself that Chantal had no Aelynn gift, but he'd been fooling himself. Since she did not have the changeable eyes of most Aelynners and gifted Crossbreeds, she must possess an unusual gift from the gods. He needed to find her mark and see what he had done by binding himself to her. He knew of no god of music.

"She charms with her voice," Ian continued. "And perhaps with her song, although that is less easy to ascertain. And since we all have a flaw in our gifts, she may also cause havoc when she is angry. I'd rather not test that last bit if the episode I just witnessed is any example." Ian hid his shudder at an image of an angry Chantal on Aelynn, an island filled with trained warriors and highly sensitive people. Could he possibly keep her happy enough to avoid causing mayhem? Had musicians been bred out of the island for their ability to arouse strong emotion?

"I have never seen her angry," Alain protested. "She is like a ray of sunshine, always humming and singing."

Apparently, Alain had kept her happy. Somewhat. "I do not have time for this." Ian rose in irritation. "Did she hum with happiness after her husband died? Will she do so if you die?" he asked pointedly. "I have some healing talent, if you are willing to submit to it."

Alain's lips tightened. "I'll be fine, for a man who can never go home again. Go about your treason."

Ian winced. As a leader, he'd done what he'd had to do to protect his home. But Alain was right—they could not return to Paris. He regretted that for Chantal's sake, but on Aelynn, he could provide a better life for her than she would have in this brutal world. He had to believe this was what the gods wanted.

But at his next realization, alarm streaked through him, and he nearly raced for the door. *The chalice had just disappeared!*

"I have no allegiance to France and therefore cannot be a traitor to it," Ian corrected, speaking hurriedly. "Your true home is on Aelynn, and you are always welcome there." He held up his hand to stay Alain's retort. "Saving a king is not treason. I would certainly hope I'd have people loyal enough to do the same for me, were I in such a position." Without arguing further, Ian stalked out.

Throughout these various altercations, his limited Finding ability had remained aware of the chalice's presence safely in his saddlebag. But within the last few minutes, the damned object had disappeared from his consciousness. The chalice might be sentient, but he doubted that it had feet. He hurried down the hall, toward the stable.

The only time he'd known the chalice to disappear from his awareness was when it was far away—*or with Chantal*. Since there hadn't been time for a thief to go far . . .

He reversed direction and hurried back down the hall, picking up traces of thoughts and physical sensations behind each door. He recognized Pierre and Pauline tucking the children in for a nap. Turning a corner, he felt the absence of thought or emotion behind the closed door on the end. The room could be empty—in which case, it wouldn't hurt to look.

He approached the door with a degree of caution. If this blank hole was Chantal, thankfully her grief and fear had subsided. But feeling no vibrations from her at all was unnatural. He'd been aware of her in some manner since the sky had revealed her to him more than a year ago. Since they'd exchanged vows, her presence had been like a second part of him. Her absence now was palpable.

This is what it would be like if he lost her. Ian stood still, trying to assimilate all his rioting reactions to the empty space where his mate should be. Bleakness. Despair. *Loneliness*.

He had never realized how alone he'd been. How

empty. He was a busy man, of course, and he had his mother and sister, friends. . . . But he'd always stood outside their lives, acting on his own, shouldering his responsibilities without help. He'd never needed anyone.

He shouldn't need Chantal. She was an emotional woman with no ability to lighten his weighty duties. But in some manner he couldn't grasp, she provided what he was missing.

Once, he'd expected to spend his future without a mate, but since finding Chantal . . . He rejected any idea of continuing alone. Chantal's many moods might be a serious irritation and obstacle to his goals and chores, but she was *necessary* in some way he could not explain.

Sending up a prayer, he opened the door without knocking. To his enormous relief, Chantal sat on the window seat with the chalice cradled to her breasts. She smiled sleepily at him as he entered.

He was fortunate she did not heave the chalice at him. Ian was envious of the damned thing. He doubted she would hold him so lovingly if she guessed that he'd assisted the king.

He understood now why she and the chalice disappeared together. They apparently nullified each other's vibrations. Odd, but not extraordinary. Very useful, actually. When he returned home, he ought to test whether his mother had the same effect on the chalice. If so, it might explain why the gods had left it to the inhabitants of Aelynn to conceal.

"Are you feeling better?" he asked.

"No, just more in control. Did I have a fit of some sort?" she asked.

"From all reports, it appears so." He'd have liked to linger and explore the fascinating aspects she presented, but he couldn't ignore Murdoch's menace. Ian had hoped they could outrace Murdoch, but Alain's illness ended that possibility.

Murdoch was apparently still able to sense the presence of the chalice. Ian would not underestimate the renegade's determination and imperil innocents a second time. He had to place himself between the chalice and danger.

Later, if all went well, he'd question Chantal more thoroughly. "Your father claims you're never angry."

She wrinkled her nose in thought. "I'm no angel. I get angry. I just usually find some way of diverting my temper into music. I like the tone of your bell. Chalice." Remembering who had held it last, she narrowed her gaze. "You helped arrange the king's freedom in exchange for this, didn't you? Do you have any inkling of what you've done?"

"Your queen lives in dire fear of poisoning, and your king is a prisoner, unable to even worship with his own priests. Their children are under constant threat of maniacs who despise the monarchy. I doubt that I have exposed them to more risk by offering them a choice."

"You have made it impossible for my father and me to return home." Cradling the chalice, she stared out the window to the street below. "Paris is not so large that our departure wasn't noticed. Two and two will add up eventually. We'll be arrested as soon as we return."

"You will go home with me," he assured her. "You will like it there."

She threw a pillow from the window seat at him. "I like *my* home!"

He caught the pillow. "You will not like it so well a year from now, when the streets run with blood. Think on what you would like most in this world, and I will provide it for you."

"I want my home and my life back!" she said angrily, before stopping to think of what he'd just said. Her eyes grew wide and apprehensive. "You did this deliberately so I could not go back. Who are you and where are you taking us? And more importantly, why?"

"I did not mean to permanently separate you from your home." Actually, he'd given it no thought at all. He'd simply done what needed to be done. But he assumed she was in no humor to hear that. Now that he had a mate, he needed to discover how best to keep her happy. "And I am taking you north, to the Netherlands, as you asked. We will discuss what you wish to do after that. I still must find my countryman before we can head in that direction. Will you kiss me before I leave?"

She shot him a glare. "In these last few years, I have lost my husband, my mother, and my grandparents. Now you separate me from what little family I have left, and you expect me to be grateful?"

"I brought your family with us," he reminded her. "And your father's horses." It would have been much simpler to have taken his amacara without moving her household, but he didn't think she'd be receptive to that reasoning. "I cannot move houses, but I can provide any house you desire."

She stared at him. "Do you really think I will follow you anywhere simply because of what we've done in bed?"

"Yes," he said simply. "That is how it is with amacara matches. The current circumstances are unfortunate, but we will adapt over time."

"Never! You cannot kidnap me and expect me to be grateful."

"I don't ask for your gratitude. Right now, all I ask

is a kiss." And he didn't know why he was adamant about that. Reason said she was angry and would not comply.

His newly discovered desires insisted that she feel the same as he. Foolish, even he must admit.

"Maybe I will kiss you if you come back alive," she said with a shrug. "I have lost all I've ever loved, so it's much simpler if I hate you."

Her words flayed Ian as sharply as any whip. This wasn't how he wanted it to be between them. But for the sake of his people, he must bear her scorn and anguish. And possibly, her hatred. Amacara matches were physical for the sake of heirs, so he held no illusion beyond that—although there was an odd longing in his chest for her understanding, at least.

"I am trusting you with my chalice," he said without inflection, hiding how her words hurt. "In your hands, it is invisible to me, so it will be invisible to others like me. Guard it well. I cannot begin to describe what might happen if it should fall into the hands of the wrong people."

"Others like you? *Are* there others like you? How extraordinary."

"You have no idea," he said, grateful that she listened to reason, however sarcastically. "Perhaps all happens for a purpose. You will be safer here than with me. Rest. I hope to return in a few hours."

"And if you don't? What do we do then?"

An excellent question, one he wasn't equipped to answer. He had been prepared to die fighting Murdoch, but he could no longer afford that luxury.

Shaking his head at that conundrum, Ian bowed out of the room.

The Chalice of Plenty was now invisible and safe in his mate's keeping. He had only to conquer a man who once had the unique ability to affect all four of the earth's powers, with strengths equal to Ian's own or better.

Perhaps he should test how much strength Murdoch still retained before he attempted to truss him like a pig and bring him back to Aelynn.

If excitement was what he craved, the journey home with an unwilling mate and a dangerous hostage ought to be the highlight of his life.

Eighteen

Even before Ian reached Rapscallion, he sensed troubled vibrations in the air.

He would have to hope the heavens showed him the way. Thanking Aelynn for the gift of the horse's motion to focus his energies, he climbed back in the saddle and struck out for the road the king's berlin had taken toward the northeastern border.

He had met the royal party long enough to recognize their thought threads among the hundreds of others around him. Letting the stallion have his head on the open road, Ian collected the threads carried on the winds. He recognized the queen's unease but not the reason for it.

More disturbing was the fury building in the minds of thousands in Paris—a cloud of rage so enormous that he could sense it even from a day's journey away.

It was late afternoon. The palace guards would have had time to discover the royal family's escape. The alarm would have been sounded. The Assembly would be forced to send out their National Guard, if only to stop the rioting, but more to the point—to prevent the king and his loyal troops from raising arms against them. There would be messengers racing down every road. The overloaded berlin barely covered a few miles an hour. Horses under saddle could travel three or four times that speed.

If the duc's loyal soldiers were in place . . . the

berlin might reach safety before the National Guard learned their direction and sent an army to stop them.

Where was Murdoch as the world teetered at a cosmic crossroads?

Ian knew he had no more excuses to interfere in the Other World by saving the royal party. He had the chalice. Chantal was safe. Fate would have to deal the cards of the royals.

His only purpose now could be to stop Murdoch from interfering, because Murdoch would not be so close to such momentous events if he did not have some scheme in mind to further his ambition. Whether the chalice was part of that scheme, Ian couldn't discern.

Knowing that Murdoch, with his Olympian strengths, had once hoped to be Aelynn's leader, Ian couldn't help fearing that his banished countryman had deliberately found a country on the brink of self-destruction so he could use the turmoil to his own advantage. To conquer an entire nation would require taming armies with terror, easily done should Murdoch unleash earthquakes or hurricanes or fire. Except—even if he meant well—Murdoch had never been able to reliably control these forces. People would die by the thousands.

It was Ian's duty as nominative leader of Aelynn to prevent one of his own kind from wreaking disaster on innocent Other Worlders.

As Ian drew closer to the village where the duc's forty hussars were to meet the royal party, he sensed as much confusion as anger ahead. The populace seemed to be puzzled and resentful about the duc's soldiers lingering where they didn't belong. Their greatest fear seemed to be that the soldiers meant to collect the rents that hadn't been, and couldn't be, paid. And there was relief that the hussars had abruptly departed.

Yet Ian still sensed the presence of soldiers somewhere in the distance. The days were at their longest now, and even past the dinner hour, there was sufficient daylight to see no sign of the berlin or the troops along the road as planned. The berlin had been scheduled to arrive hours ago, but the broken wheel had delayed them. Had the duc's troops not waited?

Opening his mind to accept all the energy generated in the area, Ian urged Rapscallion faster and let his surroundings flow through him, capturing the thought threads and analyzing them as best he could in his haste.

There, some miles from the road, a mass of men and horses wandered in confusion in the shadows of a forest—the duc's hussars. Retreating from the angry villagers after hours of waiting for a royal coach that hadn't arrived as promised, they'd become lost looking for a route through the trees to the next outpost. There was concern that the king had failed to escape as planned.

Some miles farther down the road toward the border, Ian sensed a few familiar threads from the royal party exhibiting fear and bewilderment at the failure of their escort to appear. They'd decided to drive on to the next outpost, where more soldiers should be waiting.

Not far ahead of Ian, weary from long travel, scared, and excited, was the messenger from Paris, riding to notify the countryside of the king's escape, carrying an order to the National Guard in each town to halt the berlin and arrest the occupants on sight.

And there, right before the village where the hussars were supposed to be waiting, before Ian could act on the disaster in the making—Murdoch. Ian grasped Rapscallion's reins and tugged him to a prancing, protesting halt.

If he could sense Murdoch, then Murdoch knew Ian was here.

It had been more than two years since he'd seen his old friend. More than two years since Murdoch had called down lightning, exploded a barrel of fireworks, and killed Ian's father, Aelynn's Chosen Leader.

Ian had nothing but mixed feelings about the man Murdoch had become. As youngsters, they'd been raised together—Ian, the heir to the most powerful family on Aelynn, and Murdoch, the baseborn child of a mere hearth witch, a woman who was little more than a housekeeper.

Normally, a child of Murdoch's background would be left to find his place among the island's laborers, but Murdoch had exhibited such astounding abilities that his talents couldn't be wasted. Ian's parents had taken Murdoch in and tutored him along with their own offspring.

Except Murdoch's erratic abilities had resisted training. If the lesson was in moving rock, he would shatter hillsides. If asked to fill a well, he would flood a town. He had a rage inside him that drove all his energies beyond the limits of others.

Most Aelynners had one strong ability that they cultivated and, if they were lucky, a minor one to complement it. As the son of an Oracle and Council Leader, Ian had many abilities. He'd been expected to develop his gift for Seeing, but even as a child, Murdoch had been so competitive in the same area that Ian had learned that the future was too unstable to predict. He and Murdoch had inevitably foreseen different outcomes for every event. At best, they'd each been half right in their interpretations.

They'd shared long philosophical discussions over the reasons for this and many other things, including Murdoch's inability to direct his gifts—which is why Ian doubted that Murdoch was guilty of more than accident by rage. Though, for all anyone knew, in the heat of anger Murdoch could very well have wished his leader dead, and the gods had answered.

Ian missed the friend Murdoch had been. He did not know the man who had killed the Council Leader or used Greek fire in an attempt to kill Trystan, the island's Guardian—or the man who waited somewhere in the shadows on the outskirts of the village just ahead, his thoughts hidden and his passions reined in as they never had been before.

Ian saw no sign of the king's berlin or the duc's troops as he approached the village. More people than was normal roamed the street, whispering and arguing. He scarcely needed his extra senses to know that the messenger with the news of the king's escape had just arrived.

One lone officer in royal blue and scarlet waited, hidden from the setting sun by a pergola outside a rose garden filled with vibrant blooms. The rich scent engulfed Ian as he swung down from his mount. If there was to be combat, he wanted the horse clear of it. The tension of challenge shimmered in the air as he approached on foot.

"You have grown wiser since I saw you last," the soldier said without inflection. "Up until an hour ago, I felt the chalice, and now I can't. Concealing it from me is a gift worthy of an Oracle. Did you bring the old crone with you?"

"Dylys is your mother as well as mine, in all ways

but one," Ian replied. If Murdoch meant to insult him into losing control, he'd forgotten the differences between them. "You owe her respect, if naught else."

"She nearly killed me," Murdoch replied conversationally. "She tried to steal my soul and turn me into a husk."

"She left you alive. That's more than you did for my father."

Ian was close enough to see now. Murdoch appeared taller and more finely honed than Ian remembered. The sharpness of his angular cheekbones could have cut through his browned skin. He wore a sword and scabbard as soldiers must, but he carried no musket. Given Murdoch's explosive tendencies, that might be for the safety of those around him.

"Killing Luther was an accident. You had to know it was an accident." Murdoch did not plead, simply repeated the same statement he'd uttered before.

Ian believed him, but it was still no excuse. "A fatal accident, one that could have been avoided had you refrained from showing off after arguing with Lissandra. You are too dangerous to be allowed full use of your powers."

"How is your charming sister these days?" Murdoch asked. "Married to tedious Trystan by now? Or has she killed him for taking an amacara?"

Murdoch had aspired to Aelynn's leadership by courting Ian's sister, Lissandra. The relationship between the pair was close enough that LeDroit would never be amiable on such a loaded subject. Ian steeled himself, concentrating all his energies in hopes of predicting where Murdoch would strike first. He did not fool himself into believing this was a genial talk between old friends. Murdoch wanted the chalice, and Ian was in his way. "Trystan married his amacara. He is one of the reasons I am here."

Murdoch absorbed this information. "Lissy must have been in a rage for my head to send you after me. I never expected you to leave your mother's apron strings."

Ian smiled coolly. "You know insults will not bait me. I offer you the opportunity to return in peace so you might make better explanations to the Council now that the fury of the moment is past."

A cynical expression marred Murdoch's already harsh features. "After Trystan has filed his complaint? In retrospect, the Greek fire was a mistake, although admittedly intentional at the time. No, I think I'll pass on your offer to return for my own execution."

"Then can you give your word that you will not use your gifts to cause harm in this world?"

"I cause no harm here," Murdoch insisted.

"It is your fault that the duc's troops wander lost in yon forest, is it not? You are pushing this country toward a bloody terror that will scar this world for years and forever change the course of history. How can I leave you here to wreak destruction?"

"We See things differently, as usual. The course of their history needs changing. As does Aelynn's. I can no longer change Aelynn," Murdoch continued, "but I can bring this country out of the dark ages of sloth and greed and corruption. Inherited power is danger-ous, especially when founded on arrogance and not leadership. France will fare far better with strong guidance."

"Your guidance," Ian said cynically.

Murdoch did not deny it.

They'd reached an impasse. They both knew it. Yet neither man reached for his weapon. Neither was will-ing to be first to draw arms against the other.

"I cannot let you interfere. I have no choice," Ian said, letting his sorrow show.

"Everyone has a choice," Murdoch said scornfully. "You've made yours." His sword materialized in his hand faster than Ian's eye could follow.

Prepared, Ian balanced his staff in front of him, gripping it with tense fingers. "We have ever been evenly matched in this. We know each other's moves before we can make them."

"Then you know you cannot take me," Murdoch replied. He swung his sword first.

Ian brought up his staff in self-defense, yet Murdoch hacked swiftly and brilliantly at the stout oak, no matter how quickly Ian moved. Splinters flew where the blade whittled precise notches despite the staff's tremendous speed.

With all his mighty strength, Ian swung his staff at Murdoch's ankles. His opponent danced in place to avoid being crippled, then slammed his boot against the swinging stick in an attempt to crack it at the weak point he'd carved. Failing that, he leapt backward out of range and flung fire circles at Ian's feet.

Ian would give him credit for restraint, but he knew Murdoch must hide his strange gifts here as much as Ian hid his, or risk death at the hands of superstitious Other Worlders standing not yards away.

It was more difficult to bring down rain on a cloudless evening than to throw fire in summer heat. Rather than waste his energy dousing the fire rings, Ian simply strode across the flames. Heat seared his boots, but his attention was focused elsewhere. Hoping to render his adversary unconscious, he spun his staff in a blur, with Murdoch's head for a target.

Ian was a man of Aelynn, of law and of science, not a warrior by nature. He possessed no bloodlust or even a desire for revenge.

Murdoch had spent these last years training for war. He easily parried Ian's staff. The blow of metal against wood shuddered the ground beneath their boots and strained muscles and nerves. The blade had come within inches of severing the front of Ian's despised coat. They were both hampered by the clothing required in this world.

"You can't win against me, Ian," Murdoch warned. "I do not want to kill you. Go home. Tell them I'm dead. Leave me alone before you cause me to do more harm than I wish."

Although they were on the edge of town, fighting in the twilight shadows of a forest, Ian sensed they had attracted the attention of the agitated inhabitants of the village. In moments, they would be surrounded. If Murdoch called down lightning, people would die. It was Ian's duty to prevent that.

"I would leave you here," Ian said, recovering his balance and positioning himself for what he must do, "if I could believe you would cause no harm, but I can't. You must come with me or die." Spinning in reverse on his heels so fast that even Murdoch would have difficulty following him, Ian came up on his challenger from his unguarded side. With staff extended fully, Ian connected with Murdoch's skull.

Murdoch flew face-first into the dusty road.

And immediately rolled upright, calling the wind in a blast so powerful, it threw Ian as well as half a dozen villagers backward. Even in wrath, he concealed his gifts—an admirable restraint he must have learned recently, Ian thought, rising and dusting himself off.

"The Chalice of Plenty is on my side," Murdoch declared. "Let it be, and all will be well. You have hoarded it for your own purposes for too long."

"We protect it," Ian protested, erecting a barrier of impermeable air between them. "Aelynn has no reason to exist if we cannot guard it. We will all die."

"Or emigrate," Murdoch said scornfully, "like the royal cowards. Leave, Ian. Go home."

Without warning, Murdoch disappeared, leaving only a rippling iridescence where he'd stood.

Ian blinked to clear his eyes but saw only a blurry mirage where Murdoch had been. He shook his head in disbelief.

Invisibility was not an ability Aelynn bestowed upon the island's inhabitants. What had Murdoch done?

Nineteen

"I hope you are well rested. We must leave for the border at once."

Bathing her father's brow with cool water, Chantal stared at the disheveled man who barged into the room. The normally unflappable, arrogantly assured man she'd come to know had metamorphosed into the equivalent of unstable gunpowder. Ian's boots were scorched and covered in dust. With his queue undone and his thick curls windblown, he looked as if he'd fought an army. Fear clawed her insides at the glitter of fury in his midnight eyes and the rigidity of his unshaven jaw.

"What happened?" she demanded.

That her father let her speak for him revealed the extent of his weakness.

"The king has lost his escort. It will take a miracle for him to escape now. Messengers bearing the news from Paris have already reached these outskirts. The bloody future I predicted is almost upon us." For a moment, regret etched lines about his mouth.

She might feel sympathy for him if the words *future I predicted* had not lodged in her brain, preventing any immediate reply.

Instead, Pierre rose from his prayers beside the bed to intrude upon the conversation. "I'll ride alone to the border. There is no sense in endangering everyone for my sake."

Taller and broader than the younger man, Ian did not move from the doorway. "Your sister and her children require your presence. We stay together," he ordered, as if he had a right to do so.

"I cannot go with you," Chantal pointed out. "Papa is too ill to travel. The border is not that distant. The rest of you should go and leave us here."

After the words she and Ian had exchanged earlier, she was more determined than ever to be rid of him. He assumed too much if he thought he had any claim on her, or that she would trail after him like a camp follower—no matter how much she inexplicably desired him. He and Pauline had endangered her entire world, and now it seemed they had brought it crashing down. She could not forgive him.

And insanely, she still wanted him, clear down to the marrow of her bones. She wanted to cleanse his sweat-caked face with her cloth, press kisses to his bristled jaw, and comfort him with caresses. And much more.

The heated look he bestowed on her said he felt the same, and she almost burst into flames. This adolescent lust was *impossible*.

"You do not understand," Ian said patiently. "The roads will soon be crawling with National Guards preventing anyone from crossing the border. We must go *now*." Tearing his gaze from Chantal, he turned to Pierre. "Fetch your sister and the children; have the carriage brought out. Chantal, help them gather their belongings. I will tend to your father."

He stepped aside to allow Pierre to pass. Chantal had expected Pierre to protest again, but he abruptly clamped his lips closed and hurried to obey Ian's wishes—just as everyone else did.

Despite the terror Ian's appearance struck in her heart, and the authority of his commands, she would not be so easily ordered about. "I have sent for a physician. We will not leave before he arrives. Take Pauline and her family, and we will follow later."

Not wasting his energy to argue, Ian strode to the bed and tested her father's pulse. "Orateur, tell your daughter she has no choice."

"I suppose besides being monk and warrior, you are a physician as well?" she asked cuttingly when her father failed to reply.

"I can work some healing," Ian agreed without dispute. He sent her a meaningful look that she felt in every place he'd ever touched her. "I can do it better without your charms to distract me."

Just when she was prepared to smack him for his temerity, he offered flattery to rearrange her thinking. That he even hinted at such vulnerability drained her of all her righteous anger.

"Go, Chantal," her father said hoarsely. "Do as he says. I'll be fine."

"You are not fine for traveling," she argued, but neither man listened. Tense and unsettled, she wanted a rousing quarrel, but upsetting her father wouldn't help anyone.

Channeling her irritation into a low hum, Chantal picked up the chalice she'd hidden under her skirts beneath her foot, prepared to walk out and not come back until Ian was gone.

"Take time to calm yourself," Ian called after her. "We do not want to stir the populace into another riot."

Calm herself, indeed! His presumption knew no bounds. She should heave the damned lump of silver at his inflated head. That would show him what happened when she wasn't calm.

She was not as good at persuasive argument as her father was, one of the many reasons she buried her soul in music. Thinking rebellious thoughts, hugging the chalice, she flounced out. Only after she slammed the door did she feel Ian's pain. Or was that her father? And why, by all that was holy, would she think she felt anything except her own wounds?

At least the children had had a nice nap and did not complain when they were loaded into the carriage again. Their driver had decided to return to Paris, most likely to report their escape, Chantal thought grimly. It was full dark as Pierre retied the baggage and she harnessed the horses. The moon was losing its plumpness, but it was still bright enough to see.

As much as she enjoyed cradling the soothing chalice like an infant, Chantal needed to tend to the real children. She stored the valuable object under her seat and played games with them while they waited for the rest of their party.

Pauline was too distraught to be useful. Tears flowed down her cheeks, and she wrung her hands in her skirt. Pierre had evidently told her that the escape plans were falling apart.

Chantal preferred not to think about it. A king so weak that he would abandon his people was no king at all, in her opinion. She would contemplate no further than that. Except, in her heart, she knew nothing would ever be the same again.

No longer protected by her cozy bubble of security, she recognized the danger of Paris erupting in flames, and a tear crept from her eye. Her home was lost to her.

Ian arrived, acting as her father's support until he settled the older man on the seat beside her. She would curse Ian for dragging an ill man into the night, except she sensed the urgency of the situation. She wanted to be furious with him, but no matter how hard she tried, reason ruled her head. Or maybe it was lust clouding her reasoning.

She tried to test her father's forehead, but he shrugged her off.

"I'm well enough. I have all eternity to rest. Let us be on our way."

Ian leaned through the doorway. "Hold the chalice, Chantal. Do not let it go again. Sing songs, and all will be well." He shut the door without waiting for a reply.

How could he see through the darkness to know the chalice wasn't in her arms?

In the street outside the inn's yard, a pipe picked up the notes of the "Carmagnole," and a drummer pounded the beat as the local militia began their nightly parade. She shivered in fear at what would happen should they suspect that the inn's guests were not heading to a wedding party.

She would have to disturb everyone to kneel on the floor and lift her father's seat to gain the chalice. It was much safer where it was. But because she thought it best to keep the children happy, she began singing while the men tethered the string of horses.

Once that task was completed, she expected Pierre to roll the carriage out of the yard. Instead, Ian returned, yanked open the door, and bodily lifted her father to the ground, propping him against the side of the carriage. When he reached for her, she smacked his hand.

"I am not a piece of luggage," she hissed. "What is wrong with you?"

"You must *hold* the chalice," he insisted. "I ask no more of you than that."

He asked a great deal more, and they both knew it. "You are mad! It's a lump of silver and not a child that needs coddling."

Ian growled and reached for her again. Hastily, Chantal kneeled on the floor and opened the seat. Pauline leaned over to help her hold the velvet cushions while Chantal dug around to find the chalice among the carriage blankets and children's toys.

"Thank you," Ian said stiffly once they'd located the object and returned the cushion to its place. "Think of it as an infant you must care for." He assisted her father back in and strode off.

"Honestly, who does he think he is?" Chantal muttered, but she'd already unwrapped the cloth and stroked the chalice to calm herself, so her anger had no edge to it.

"You brought this on yourself," her father replied tiredly. "Do you have any idea what you did by promising yourself to him?"

"I did no such thing," she murmured while Pauline sang to the children and the carriage lurched into motion.

"He thinks you have, and he's not the kind of man who would make a mistake in that."

"You would take his word over mine? I barely know the man." The chalice grew warm, and she snuggled it beneath her breasts. The warmth seeped through her skin and radiated through her blood. She suffered an embarrassing desire to share her body with Ian again.

What was wrong with her? She never felt such strong urges, and now she couldn't think of anything else. But she was no longer angry with Ian. Instead, she sensed the genuine concern beneath his curt orders, and a loneliness in him so strong that she longed to comfort him.

"Then he tricked you into doing his will," her father said wearily. "I don't have the knowledge to unbind that kind of vow. You will have to go with him to find out more."

Chantal tested her father's forehead to see if fever

had addled his brains, but out of the inn's heat, he felt cooler. "I don't know what you mean. I go with *you*. Do you think there is any chance that the servants will not mention our absence? We could go home, if so."

"No, damn his blasted foresight, Ian is right, and I have been a fool. All hell will break loose now, and the streets of Paris will run with blood. Maybe someday we can return, if you still wish to do so, but not now."

With that, he fell silent, leaving Chantal cold and afraid. How would they survive without their work? Their homes? Her father lived for his duties in the Assembly. The piano she had left behind was her life. Stunned, she sat back against the seat as her heart slowly turned to stone.

It might be some consolation that she was free to stay with Pauline and the children, but she could not picture such a future. She'd never been one to plan ahead, because it was too impossible to predict the disasters that inevitably occurred.

Ian seemed to think he could predict the future, but he was wrong. He had to be. Seeing the deaths of loved ones would be too devastating to endure. She would far rather embrace the moment.

Which was how she'd ended up in this position in the first place.

"We are not following the Châlons road," Pauline whispered over the head of the sleeping child in her arms.

"If that is the route the royal party took, it would be too dangerous," Chantal whispered back. "Pierre must have decided to go straight north."

Pauline wiped her tears on the shoulder of her gown rather than disturb Marie. "I hate this," she whispered vehemently.

Chantal nodded her agreement, but there was nothing she could say that would ease her friend. Beside her, her father snored lightly.

The moon was visible out their western window, and Chantal had nodded off when she heard Ian's stallion take off at a great gallop. She was riding on the rear-facing seat next to the eastern window. Ian had been trotting nearby just a moment ago, but when she looked out, he and his horse were merely a speck disappearing over a hill to the south.

The carriage faltered and lurched in a rut, then continued, more slowly than before. Pierre was not an experienced driver. What was happening?

She stroked the chalice to ease her anxiety, but it did not seem to calm her as well as usual. Oddly, she could sense Ian's fury and his fear for her and their party. Most likely, she was dreaming. Groggy from lack of sleep, she shivered and wished for her cozy bed.

She nodded off, dreaming of what she and Ian had done in that bed. Aroused, she squirmed in her seat while desire rose like a heated arrow into her midsection.

She could almost hear Ian's soft murmurs of assurance, feel his fingers where she needed his touch. And if she concentrated hard enough—

She quivered as her inner muscles spasmed with release. Briefly, she almost sensed Ian's sorrow at parting, but the lethargy carried her back to sleep.

In the distance, lightning flared and thunder boomed, even though not a cloud blocked the stars' light.

Twenty

Crushing the stallion's reins, Ian closed his eyes and cast a mental shield against the psychic blow vibrating the universe—*the royal party had been captured*. Despite the shield, his mind suffered terror and despair as grim soldiers in the unadorned blue uniforms of National Guardsmen surrounded the king's berlin.

Emotions he'd contained for decades abruptly tore through the newly opened crack in his heart. How could he hope to lead Aelynn into a safe future if he could not manage even a small part of this chaotic Other World? The anguish of loss and failure reduced him to a spill of ash.

Into this momentary weakness, a bolt of lightning exploded, splintering an oak tree not a hundred yards in front of him. Rapscallion reared, nearly unseating Ian, startling him from despair.

Murdoch. No thundercloud darkened the stars. No other bolts lit the sky. Only Murdoch could produce lightning from the blue.

Murdoch was the reason Ian had put a distance between himself and the carriage. The renegade had left the company of the duc's guards and abandoned the royal party to their fate. If it was Murdoch's desire to end France's monarchy, as he'd insinuated, he'd all but sealed the death warrant.

Ian set aside his anguish and lowered his shield to

search his surroundings. He found his nemesis approaching, no doubt intent on gaining the chalice. Now that the royal party was captured, Murdoch was free to take the next step to further his ambitions. That he meant to aid the revolutionaries was evident. That his resentment of the Olympus leadership of Aelynn had led him to his choice was equally evident, and right now, Ian blocked Murdoch's access to the chalice.

Rapscallion pawed the ground, refusing to proceed farther. Reluctantly, Ian acquiesced. He had no bloodlust for the duel Murdoch demanded, and the horse should not be made to suffer for the decisions of mankind—or of Aelynners.

Apparently Murdoch had been so attuned to the chalice that he'd sensed the brief moment when Chantal had let it out of her arms. Now that he knew where it was and how easily it could be obtained, there would be no stopping him.

With Chantal as his incentive, Ian could no longer afford to fail in this final task.

With a heavy heart, he dismounted. He removed his staff, tied the reins to the saddle, then smacked the creature into following the mares. Rapscallion willingly departed without his rider.

Shrugging out of his coat, Ian studied the battlefield Murdoch had selected. Tall trees surrounded the narrow deer path leading away from any form of civilization. No eyes but those of the forest would see them. They could use their gifts more freely here. For now, Murdoch was some distance away. Ian had time to choose the best position.

Unfastening the scabbard he'd borrowed from Chantal's father, he worked his way to the top of the nearest hill, regretting his amacara vows. Chantal's desire coursed through him, and his own body mindlessly responded. Desire was a powerful inspiration to avoid warfare. He wanted to be breeding heirs, not fighting with a man who'd been like a brother to him.

Finding a clearing beneath the stars, Ian clenched his staff in both fists and slowly began to twirl it. Chantal's desire flooded through him, destroying any hope of concentration. With his mind, he sought hers, touching it briefly, thinking of her lovely breasts, the downy patch between her slender legs, probing with his mind until he felt her clench on the brink of orgasm, then gently pushing her over.

Her release flowed through him, easing some of the ache in his own loins. He hoped she slept now. He did not want her to feel his pain. He'd known the amacara connection was strong, but he had not realized how strong. Chantal was already learning to recognize the sensations of his body that he could not block from his mind—and he, hers. In an ideal world, that would guarantee open communication between a couple, but this world was far from ideal. It would be convenient if Chantal had the same mental powers that he had to relieve his aching lust.

He spun his staff in front of him, hoping to return his focus to the stars and Murdoch. If anything happened to him tonight, Chantal and the chalice should be safe—as long as she held it so Murdoch did not know where they were.

Those were not thoughts conducive to concentration. Ian worked harder, spinning the staff around his waist, lifting it higher, straining his muscles to carry the stout oak above him so he might find the future in the stars.

Blood stained the constellations. Death shuddered along the heavens. A barrage of heavy artillery exploded in the night sky. Through it all rode Murdoch, his uniform untouched, at one with his horse.

Ian reached higher, shoving aside regret and focusing on Murdoch, trying to see what drove him, but the barrier of pain Murdoch had erected prevented any deeper probing. Murdoch was a man in agony, tortured by his past and his dreams, with a mind so complex, even the Oracle had not been able to penetrate its depths.

Without knowing what motivated his opponent, Ian was at a loss as to how to fight him. He could nudge people in the directions they wanted to go, but he could not nudge them to do what went against their natures. Murdoch had seldom been susceptible to Ian's mental shoves, but sometimes, if his desire was strong enough . . .

As with Chantal this evening, Ian could manipulate minds through desires, whether for sex, wealth, pride, or ambition; there was always a means to use those insights. He seldom needed to, though, except when healing the ill. With Murdoch, he needed every weapon in his arsenal.

Blindly spinning his staff, visions whirling as he reached deep down inside himself where knowledge lurked, Ian could see the death of his father more clearly now. Luther had opposed Murdoch's marriage to Lissandra for good reason. Lissandra's spouse could someday become Council Leader, and Murdoch was far too unstable to lead the island. Murdoch's desires were such that he would have rebelled against Luther's opposition, if Lissandra had agreed to take vows at the altar. Rightfully, she had refused. No wonder they had argued.

Were they amacaras? Appalled, Ian had no way of knowing. Surely Aelynn would not be so cruel as to match Lissandra to Murdoch for eternity.

Stunned by his insight, Ian was unprepared for the bolt of lightning that struck a tree on the slope below

him. The tree cracked and began to fall. Its branches
swept toward Ian's position at the top of the hill. He
leapt aside with the speed and agility of his kind, but
even so, some of the outer branches struck him, tearing his clothes and slicing his cheek. He remained
on alert.

"Just give me the chalice," Murdoch's voice intoned
on the wind. "I do not want to kill you."

Spinning his staff in figure eights, Ian located his
opponent climbing the hill behind a thicket of brambles. He still wore the garish blue frock coat and
scarlet breeches of a royal officer. "I don't intend to
make it easy for you; you know that," Ian called
back.

"It's foolish not to. You have a lovely amacara waiting. You can breed many new Olympians to hunt for
the sacred object. She promises nights of pleasure and
days of wonder. What does the chalice promise?"

"Survival of the home I love," Ian replied without
hesitation. "You cannot manipulate me so easily. If
we must do this, it will have to be a battle of strength
more than will."

"You never fought fairly," Murdoch said with disgust, emerging from behind the brambles. "It would
have been far simpler if you'd just removed my
head earlier."

"Messier, you must admit," Ian replied dryly, gaug-
ing the extent of his opponent's temper as well as the
weapons he carried.

"There's no escaping bloodshed this time, old
friend," Murdoch replied with regret. "The fate of the
world is greater than you are."

Ian didn't waste words after that. He swung his staff
in a broad arc meant to break Murdoch's upper arm.

Murdoch responded by producing a long-barreled
pistol and firing.

*   *   *

Chantal woke up screaming.

Marie and Anton began to cry. The carriage jolted into a rut and shuddered to an abrupt halt.

Chantal kept screaming. Frantically, she leapt from the seat, letting the chalice fall to the carriage floor so she could climb over her father's knees and throw open the door. Without waiting for aid, she gathered her skirts and jumped down, her breath searing her lungs as she gasped for air and screamed louder.

"Chantal, for heaven's sake, what is wrong?" Her father eased from the carriage after her.

She didn't know what was wrong. She just knew it was wrong—horribly, awfully wrong. "Where's Ian? Where did he go?"

Fields and woods stretched around them, but ahead, she could see a village. Smoke curled from the chimneys of a few early risers in the hours before dawn. Her stomach rumbled at the scent of strong coffee and bacon, so she knew the others were hungry, too. But she didn't care. She'd never eat again if she didn't find Ian.

"He took off several hours ago, something about pursuit. His eyes must be sharper than mine," Pierre said, climbing down from the driver's perch. "We're not far from the border, but I'd rather have a man of Ian's authority with us to help us pass customs."

Frantically, Chantal turned and scanned the road they'd traversed. In the distance, a riderless horse cantered toward them.

Rapscallion.

No-o-o! her soul screamed.

She would not see Ian die, his strong body cut down in the prime of life to become dust in the ground. She could not, would not, let it happen, not while there was an ounce of breath left in her. All her life had been spent waiting for events she could not control. She refused to ever sit idly by and wait again—even if it meant riding a killer horse.

She yanked the hem of her skirt between her legs, tied it up in front, and, ignoring her father's gasp of shock and Pierre's outrage, caught the reins of the terrifying stallion as he slowed down to approach them.

"Behave," she told the fearsome beast as she led it to a fallen tree trunk. "Take me to Ian *now*." The stallion snorted and pawed and shook its mighty head. She ought to run for safety. Instead, she climbed up on the trunk, and put her foot into the stirrup, while clinging to the reins.

Her father was too weak to follow, but Pierre ran up and caught the folds of her skirt, preventing her from gaining the saddle. "Wake up, Chantal! You must be dreaming. You cannot ride that horse. Come down from there."

Once upon a time, she would have listened, but not now.

Surely, she must be dreaming, but she could not wake. Pain engulfed her, and she nearly doubled over with anguish. She only knew that she must find Ian, prevent still more deaths. That this certainty was not rational did not matter.

Rapscallion danced restlessly, but she was beyond heeding fear and caution. She caught her hand in his mane, shook off Pierre's grasp, and hauled herself into the saddle by sheer strength of will. Her skirt tumbled down around her legs, loosened by Pierre's grip, but she had enough of it under her to ride. She kicked the stallion and turned him back the way he'd come.

"Lots of oats," she promised the prancing animal, "after we find Ian."

Pauline and the children had clambered out of the

carriage, but Chantal ignored their weeping. "Find Ian," she commanded again, as if expecting the stallion to obey her.

The powerful horse broke into a canter. Clinging to Rapscallion's neck, she gave him the reins and let him run with the wind.

Not until then did she remember that Ian had told her to treat the chalice as an infant and never let it go, but she'd dropped the damned thing before she'd left the carriage. Let Pauline mother it. People were more important than objects.

This time, she would stop the Grim Reaper in his tracks. She would fight and not give in unless he took her along with Ian.

Chantal no longer held the chalice. Ian grimaced the instant she dropped it.

Murdoch sensed it, too. He'd cast aside his empty pistol and been prepared to track the sacred object, until Ian had pulled his sword and, despite his wounded shoulder, cut into his opponent's arm. Murdoch had been forced to draw his saber and fight back.

What had happened that she'd dropped it so hastily? Needing to ensure Chantal's safety was the one reason Ian still stood upright, battling with the last breath in him. He sensed the chalice traveling beyond his Finding ability, but Chantal was coming closer. If he could just hold on . . .

With the physical strain of combat keeping the bullet wound open, Ian's shoulder bled freely, draining him of his life's essence as metal slammed against metal. Unable to divert his concentration to halting the flow, Ian wearily swung his borrowed sword. With his left shoulder incapacitated, he'd lost his ability to wield his staff.

He still had the strength to swing a sword with one

hand. He could only be grateful that Other World guns were notoriously unreliable and Murdoch had missed his intended target—Ian's heart. Still, Murdoch's two-handed saber blows were taking their toll.

Dawn sent feelers of light through the trees and cast a reddish glow over the clouds. Sweat poured down Ian's face, and he knew he'd have to find Murdoch's weak spot soon or die in the effort.

"Your lover comes to your rescue," Murdoch taunted, "leaving the chalice to tempt another. How does she hide it, I wonder?"

Distracted by this confirmation of his fears, Ian momentarily hesitated.

The tip of Murdoch's sword sliced through Ian's shirt and drew blood before he raised his weapon to counter it.

"Remember how we used to fight to the skin in melees?" Murdoch taunted. "I will beat you this time. Surrender now. Let me fetch the chalice, and you'll live to fight another day."

Grasping his sword hilt with both hands, knowing this might be his last chance to save the chalice and Chantal, Ian gathered the remnants of his strength. Concentrating, he swung his blade in an arc so forceful that the wind cried. It caught Murdoch beneath his upper arm and sliced deep, driving him backward.

Chantal's shrieks pierced the dawn.

The birds took up her cry, squawking and screeching, bursting from the treetops in a massive flapping of wings.

Chantal cried out again, a war cry of such high-pitched potency that Ian wondered the trees did not bend from it.

With a groan, Murdoch fell to his knees, holding his hands over his ears to protect his eardrums.

Staggering but still upright, Ian heard Chantal's

cries with a delight that eased his hurts and brought a smile to his lips. He did not entirely understand her ability to incapacitate Murdoch while reassuring himself, but taking the slim advantage offered, he dropped his sword, grabbed Murdoch's hands from his ears, and twisted his wrists behind his back.

"Surrender, or I'll tell her to shriek you a lullaby," Ian said with genuine mirth. With Murdoch paralyzed by pain, Ian easily bound his wrists with tough vines, using his mind as iron reinforcement.

Ian's shoulder throbbed. Blood ran down his shirtsleeve, and his head spun. Red seeped through the front of his tattered linen from cuts on his chest, and dried blood caked the scratches on his cheek. He was exhausted beyond all mortal limits. But he exalted in this triumph as if he'd just been given the keys to a kingdom.

And maybe he had. The chalice had found someone else to carry it on its journey to the unknown, but watching Chantal riding down the path, her lovely hair streaming behind her, concern and grief etched on her heart-shaped face, Ian learned true happiness. He was no longer alone in the world. Someone thought him human enough to care about.

This was what being a mate was about—his pain had called her, and she'd come running.

Of course, she would probably murder him shortly, but the triumph of watching a woman of Chantal's gentle nature racing to his rescue was worth whatever price he must pay.

Finally able to let down his guard, Ian crumpled to the ground.

Twenty-one

*S*he was too late!

In horror, Chantal watched a blood-drenched Ian collapse on the forest floor. His agony mixed with her fear, and waves of despair threatened to crush her. She cried out in frustration as she fought to untangle her skirts and petticoats from the stirrups and saddle. Her gaze fastened on Ian . . . on the blood soaking his garments . . . so much blood . . .

His arm moved. His chest rose.

Not too late . . .

Fighting the crippling anguish of his pain, she grabbed a stout branch so she could swing one leg over the back of the horse and climb down. "Damn you to Hades, Ian! If you die, I shall follow you to the gates of perdition to kill you again," she shouted to steady her rampaging emotions. The stallion stood patiently as she struggled from her high perch.

With obvious effort, Ian pushed to his knees and strained to remain upright while holding his wounded shoulder. "Meet my sweet-natured amacara," he responded dryly.

Chantal gave a hasty prayer of thanks that he was well enough to keep his wits about him. His pain kept her moving forward instead of collapsing into a weeping ball of uselessness. "Uncouth beast, you're supposed to introduce the lady first," she informed him, finally noting the other man—the one who'd nearly brought Ian to his death.

Tears sliding down her cheeks, she ignored the royal officer with his hands tied behind his back. She fell to her knees in front of Ian and cupped his bristled jaw. He'd bound his unruly hair, but strands escaped to fall across his cheek. She brushed them back as he watched through blazing eyes that seared her soul. She could not bear so much passion directed toward her.

Glancing away from his penetrating vision, she caught the torn edges of his shirt and ripped it off. His chest was strong and hard, and she felt his heart beating soundly beneath her fingers. She would not think prurient thoughts while his wide chest ran with blood. She tore the clean portions of the linen to use as a bandage.

"Chantal Deveau, meet my oldest friend and greatest foe, Murdoch LeDroit," Ian said with a trace of amusement, using the good manners she requested.

"I cannot say I am happy to make your acquaintance, Madame Deveau," Murdoch muttered, twisting at his bonds. "The circumstances could be better."

"Oh, shut up," she said crossly, causing Murdoch to grimace and nearly topple. "Men are like little children who think the only way they can get what they want is to take it. I have no sympathy for either of you."

Ian flinched as she probed his shoulder wound. "Did I mention that my amacara has the voice of ten thousand angels?" he asked.

"I probably missed that after she deafened me," Murdoch responded in the same dry tone. "Is she your mother's secret weapon? A voice that can shatter walls would be valuable."

"Use the water skin on Rapscallion's saddle," Ian told her when she glanced around in search of a stream in which to soak the cloth.

"I'd swear you were reading my mind except you'd be stung with a thousand barbs if you could see my thoughts right now." Furious at Ian's imperturbable confidence, trembling with fear at the amount of blood that still spilled, she located the water skin and brought it back.

"Where is your family?" Ian asked upon her return.

Chantal assumed he really wondered about his damned precious chalice, although mentioning it in front of his enemy was probably not wise. "I left them near an inn. I daresay they're eating a lovely breakfast as we speak. You will notice I cannot climb on and off horses as easily as you, and I thought your life a little more important than carrying extra baggage."

"Pierre?" Ian inquired with an intensity she did not understand.

"Probably riding for the border. It is only a few miles away, and he's anxious to prevent his presence from harming us. He's been praying for your safety." As if prayers would help, but Chantal left her opinion in her tone, without saying it aloud.

She thought the men exchanged a glance over her shoulder, but she was obviously on the verge of hysteria and could not trust anything she thought.

"Her voice cuts like a knife," Murdoch complained, wincing and sitting back on his heels. "Have you taken to wearing hair shirts as well, or is she sufficient torment?"

Her breath flowing more evenly with every foolish insult, Chantal ignored their false valor. She wished she had her piano so she could play the complex notes of Murdoch's voice. She sensed in him a strong honor and idealism that had little to do with a man who would kill his oldest friend.

She tensed to say something scathing, but Ian's gaze dropped to her perspiration-dampened bodice, and a different passion slid through her. They may as well have been one, the way their thoughts traveled together. She held her tongue and pressed a folded cloth to his cleaned shoulder wound. His gaze torched the frail cloth over her breasts, and even though he could scarcely have an ounce of blood in him, she noted that what was left had traveled southward to stir his breeches.

"Chantal's voice reflects what's in her heart," Ian explained through teeth clenched in pain. "She wants to kill you and save me. I don't recommend earning her wrath."

"That's preposterous," Murdoch muttered.

"Sing sweetly for the oaf," Ian recommended caustically. "Elsewise, he will stupidly wear out what little strength he has left attempting to undo his bonds."

Chantal picked up the sword lying in the blood-saturated dirt and handed it to Ian. "There, finish the job you started. Hack his head off."

She actually *felt* the shock rippling through both men. She didn't want whatever this connection was between them. She simply wanted her safe, sane life back.

"If you do not kill him, he will kill you," she continued ungraciously, now that she'd said it. "I'm sick to death of people I love dying, so why not be done with it now? Just die and leave me be before I become too attached to your rotting hide."

Ian did not react to her words of love, and Chantal wished she could take them back. Love and sex were not the same thing, she reminded herself, biting her lip to stifle a sob.

Ian set the sword aside and curled a tendril of her hair around his finger. He rubbed his thumb over her tear-streaked cheek. "Murdoch's soul is likely to come back to haunt us if I waste it in such a manner," he said in that illogical manner of his that drove her mad. "I prefer to let others judge him. Sing, Chantal. I fear I will pass out otherwise, and then he will free himself."

Jarred by the quiet urgency of his command, she studied his taut jaw, realized how much effort he was expending to stay upright, and relented, although she saw no logic in his request.

She tried "Ça irà!" just so she might sound bold and brave, but it did not ring true. Ian looked paler and more fatigued than before. Behind her, Murdoch actually chuckled. "War tunes do not suit his priestly tastes. You might try a child's lullaby."

If she had her piano or another singer, she could create a harmony that would soothe the savage breast, but she did not. Fine, then. If they spoke in riddles, she would take them literally.

She switched to the children's lullaby she'd composed. Relaxing, Ian picked up the sword and used it as a brace to unfold his knees and sit down properly. He breathed easier, as if her singing truly did ease his pain. He leaned his head against a tree trunk while she struggled to wrap a pad of linen to his shoulder. The bullet had torn through the muscle and fortunately gone straight out the other side. He had to have been shot at close range.

Battening down her rage in favor of her concern, she continued singing while she examined the long scrape bleeding on Ian's bronzed chest, but he caught her wrist and halted her.

"It's a scrape. Tend Murdoch, please. I would take him back as prisoner, not corpse."

"You would do better to leave me here to die and spare me the fate of having my soul ripped from my body," Murdoch muttered.

Thinking him delusional from fever, Chantal

frowned. She crossed the clearing to rest a hand on his forehead. He felt as cold as death, and she jerked her palm away. He had not seemed so injured as Ian. She hated touching him, but she would have to remove his clothing to reach the area that was bleeding beneath his torn uniform.

"You would escape as soon as I was distant enough for you to overcome your bonds," Ian said wearily. "I cannot allow you to roam free after what you have done. You must see that."

The anger had gone out of both of them, Chantal noticed. She continued singing, hoping reason would return soon. Besides, the song soothed her frayed nerves. She was not usually so easily pushed to the brink of hysteria. She needed the balance of believing that she was helping, that she was needed, to continue.

"I am no danger to our kind," Murdoch protested as Chantal tugged his torn coat over his bulging shoulders.

With his hands tied behind his back, Murdoch could not aid her in pulling the coat any farther than his elbows. A gash bled copiously from his upper arm, saturating his fancy red waistcoat and shirt. She was amazed he still remained upright, although trying to sit down while on his knees with his hands tied would be difficult. He just resisted toppling.

"You are a danger to us simply by hoping to keep the chalice for yourself," Ian countered. "Without it, the weather has become erratic, wells dry, and crops fail. There is no reason for our existence without the sacred objects."

They continued to talk in riddles as far as Chantal was concerned. Humming softly, she probed Murdoch's wound. It was a good thing her mother had taught her how to care for injuries. She'd nursed Jean for years, so she knew how to tend fevers and bedridden patients, too. She feared these two would die before they could ever do anything so sensible as retire to a bed.

"There is no reason for the island's existence," Murdoch asserted. He sounded weaker than earlier. "You do nothing for the greater good despite all your gifts. You have the power to command kingdoms, bring peace and prosperity to multitudes. Instead, you selfishly cower behind the walls you erect to keep the rabble out and cling to your wealth like dragons hoarding gold. I have no sympathy for your plight."

"Power corrupts," Ian replied without hesitation. "Already, the rot has invaded your soul. Tell me you covet the chalice for the greater good and not your own ambitions."

"This is a charming argument," Chantal intervened, "and I'm sure if we returned to Paris, you could join the Jacobins and Girondins or the troublemakers on the street and argue all day. May I suggest you use your energy more wisely and figure out how I will get you out of here?"

Murdoch grimaced as Chantal attempted to draw the raw edges of his wound together. Instead of responding to her suggestion, he addressed Ian in a voice dripping acid. "Her tongue may be sweeter than honey, but your mother will cut it out when you bring her home."

Tired of being talked around, she ripped his linen off the crusting wound until it bled again. "This needs cauterization," she told him. She chose to believe them delirious and shut out their nonsensical talk. "I don't suppose in all your wisdom that you carry fire on you?"

When Murdoch glanced down at the knife in his

belt, Ian shook his head. "Not now." Resting his
naked back against a tree trunk, he drew up his knee
and propped his injured arm upon it.

Chantal thought she could easily expire of desire
just watching his muscles ripple. As if he sensed her
thoughts, he watched her with boldness. Amusement
twitched at his lips, and she had the urge to smack
him, even as she wondered when and how they could
share a bed again.

"Your father will send the carriage after us shortly,"
Ian claimed. "You need only sing us to sufficient
health to walk down to the road."

"It's a strange gift," Murdoch murmured groggily,
beginning to sway as she tried to staunch the flow of
blood. "She charms and enchants in one voice, and
shatters nerves in another. Can she really use her
voice to heal?"

"Will the two of you quit speaking as if I'm not
here? My head and ears work as well as yours, better
most likely, if you think singing heals."

"It's a wondrous gift," Ian agreed. "Trystan was
right when he said we did ourselves no favor by ignoring Crossbreeds. Their talents are different from ours,
admittedly, and not so obviously useful. They cannot
defend with sword, perhaps, but with knowledge and
creativity—"

The rattle of carriage wheels on the road below interrupted this wildly improbable philosophical discussion, none too soon, in Chantal's opinion. Without
bothering to explain herself, she finished tying a knot
in Murdoch's bandage, then took off running down
the path.

"She doesn't understand, Ian," Murdoch accused as
soon as she was out of earshot. "It is like taking a
baby sparrow from its mother and placing it in a
hawk's nest."

"Only death can sever the bond between us." Ian leaned heavily against the oak, acknowledging the guilt Murdoch bestowed upon him. "And the ring prevents me from explaining. By all rights, our kind should never leave the island."

Awkwardly, Murdoch braced his back against a tree trunk, using it for support so he could climb to his feet, although sweat poured from his brow with the pain of his effort. "There, we disagree. Take her and leave me. The chalice is gone. You serve no further purpose by remaining in my world. Go back and hide from reality until the end of time."

Ian closed his eyes against a great weariness and pushed aside Murdoch's temper to focus on the imperative. "I cannot hear Pierre's thoughts clearly, but I suspect the chalice offers promises to go where it wishes. He probably believes running with it will make his family safe."

Murdoch glared at him. "The chalice talks?"

Ian shook his head. "I doubt it. It's sentient in some manner, but I suspect its power lies in influencing the minds of those who behold it. It lured Trystan's wife to take it from the island. I thought it had been leading me to Chantal. Or to you. If so, now that I've found you, it's changed course. Pierre seems to be heading for the coast instead of Austria."

"Perhaps he is catching a ship to Ireland. Or the Americas. What does it matter? The chalice is gone again. What will you do now?"

Ian heard the thread of hope in Murdoch's question and shook his head. He had found Chantal and Murdoch. He was in no condition to attempt to hold them and capture the chalice as well. He fought the weakness of sorrow and anger at his failure. "My task is to return you, the chalice, and Chantal to Aelynn. I cannot let you go in hopes of achieving the chalice."

"You have to sleep sometime," Murdoch pointed out. "You cannot hold these bonds forever." He'd already made it to his feet.

Ian knew full well that Murdoch had the ability to set fire to rope stronger than those vines, once Ian's mental reinforcement collapsed. Iron might hold him, but such manacles would be hard to come by in the few hours remaining before Ian passed out from exhaustion and loss of blood. They had reached another impasse.

"Give me your word of honor that you will not harm me or mine, and I will let you free so we can go after the chalice together," he suggested.

"Why?" Murdoch scoffed. "I need only wait until you fall asleep to free myself."

Ian shook his head sadly. "So much talent, so little wisdom. You are reacting without thought again. You were taught better than that."

"I was taught I ought to rot in your grotto thinking how wonderful it is to be an Aelynner and submissive to your god–almighty parents," Murdoch said scornfully. "I have better things to do than regret what I can't have."

Ian understood that Murdoch meant Lissandra. If the pair truly shared an amacara bond . . . He shook his head at the impossibility of such a cruelly disparate match.

The overwhelming realization that he would undergo the fires of the damned if he had to give up Chantal didn't hit Ian as hard it should. It simply *was*. He'd already accepted the bond, even though it hampered his ability to go after the chalice. He could only imagine Murdoch's torment at being forever denied his mate. Ian didn't understand why the gods chose to torture them with such impossible companions, yet he would not go back to his former sterile life.

"I think I will make you suffer a little longer for your insults," Ian said genially, hearing Chantal returning.

Murdoch gave a derisive snort. "At least I'm on my feet."

Relaxing against the tree, Ian grinned. "I have good reason to save my strength."

Chantal entered the clearing as he uttered this and shot him a look that boiled his blood.

"I should hope so," she said. "There's apparently a troop of National Guards asking after us already." She stood aside to reveal two strangers in the sabots and tunics of farmers. "Pierre generously hired these gentlemen to act as drivers in his place, since he seems to have run off with your precious chalice."

Murdoch slid down the tree trunk, unable to hold his ears against the agony of her sharp words.

"Do you begin to understand, my friend?" Ian asked softly. "She only wishes to beat me over the head with my staff. You, she would flay to shreds."

Murdoch twitched from the pain. "How do you turn her off?"

"Not angering her helps," Ian answered in satisfaction, climbing to his feet and catching Chantal's arm before she could decide to swing at him.

And once she was in his arms, it was too much for a man to bear to resist kissing her.

"I came back," he reminded her with a murmur. "You owe me for not dying."

Twenty-two

On the carriage ride back to the inn where the rest of their party had taken refuge, Chantal closed her eyes and leaned against Ian's uninjured shoulder, sheltered by his wide chest and strong arm, his heated kiss still burning on her lips. She had stood on her own for so long that even though she knew better than to depend on anyone else, she craved the comfort of sharing a moment with a man who at least pretended to care about her. She loved her father, but she knew she came second after his zeal to make France a better place—rightly so, but once in a while . . .

Of course, she would never have dared accept this luxury had Ian been awake, but he'd dozed off some miles back—after his prisoner in the seat across from them.

Both men were striking in their harsh, angular features and lean, hard bodies, but Ian's mouth could be tender, and his gaze held peace and assurance, whereas Murdoch possessed nothing soft or safe about him. She wished Ian could have left him behind or turned him over to the authorities for whatever he'd done. She could see no good coming of traveling with a man who was willing to kill for what he wanted.

"Just shriek if he breaks loose," Ian murmured into her hair, proving he did not sleep at all.

She should have jumped in startlement, or at least eased away so she was not so comfortably ensconced in his embrace, but she remained where she was, absorbing the steady beat of his heart. "I do not shriek," she asserted. "I merely hit notes others cannot."

Ian chuckled, and she loved the rumble of it coming from deep in his chest.

"His ears are more sensitive than mine. Speak to him sharply and he stumbles. Shriek—" He winced as she elbowed him. "Speak more loudly, and he falls. You are my secret weapon."

"That is nonsense. Go back to sleep."

"I warned you not to let the chalice go," he murmured again. "Learn to heed me, and all will be well."

Fine for him to say. He intended to go home. She couldn't. She wanted to rage against the unfairness, but she still couldn't believe they were forever banned from her beloved France. She loved the sea and fresh scent of scythed grass at their country estate. She adored the hotbed of ideas and discussion in their circle of Parisian friends. She couldn't live without her piano. It simply did not seem reasonable that she should lose everything because the king had chosen to escape the same day they'd left town.

"Maybe I'll listen to you when you listen to me," she retorted, to fight back tears.

"I listen," he said. "I just do not always agree. Your tongue is persuasive, but not always reasonable. You have your areas of expertise, and I have mine. We will learn together."

He gave her more confidence than she deserved, and she enjoyed the idea of learning together too much. He did not even scold her for abandoning the precious object he'd come so far to recover. She tried to sit up, but Ian tugged her back. She didn't fight him.

She had to blame the madness that was Paris these days as much as she blamed Pauline and Ian for their predicament. Keeping a king hostage was an open invitation to war. Blaming everyone else for their problems would not provide solutions. Filling the streets with weapons carried by unregulated, desperate men was a recipe for anarchy.

So perhaps her home was not the home it once had been.

Her bubble of contentment had finally burst, leaving her vulnerable to a riot of thoughts and emotions she could not wrestle into place.

The carriage rocked to a halt in the shelter of a beech grove, and Ian instantly stiffened. The driver slid open the speaking door. "There's soldiers blocking the road ahead," he said in his crude accent. "If ye're after avoiding them, I'll let you out here and pretend I'm working on the wheel until ye've gone around out of sight."

Chantal glanced questioningly at Ian, who nodded agreement. Murdoch was already awake and watching them.

"They'll be my men," he said.

"You wear the colors of a royal officer," Chantal objected. "Men loyal to the king have no reason to pursue us."

Murdoch shrugged. "The king is now a prisoner, and those loyal to him are fleeing the country. Those men out there are mercenaries who follow me now, and I've set them to hunting you. Let me go, and I'll call them off."

Ian sent him a look of scorn, then clambered from the carriage and offered his good hand to help Chantal. She clung to it, needing the reassuring squeeze of his fingers to keep fear at bay.

Murdoch remained inside. "Come and get me," he said with a weak chuckle.

"I could, but I told you I'm saving my strength," Ian replied peaceably. "Chantal, he is endangering your father and godchildren by his recalcitrance. What do you have to say to him?"

"That I'll come in and drag him out by his bad arm?" she suggested, still thoroughly puzzled by Ian's and Murdoch's odd quarreling.

Silence from within the carriage.

Ian nodded approvingly. "Now say it as if you mean it and directly to him."

"Will the two of you quit playing games!" she said in her lowest shout. "You could both bleed to death if we don't find a physician soon."

Murdoch miraculously appeared in the doorway, leaning heavily against the frame, looking haggard and pale. "The Inquisition could have used her talent," he grumbled.

Ian used his good arm to help his prisoner down. "Who says they didn't?"

Chantal knew her voice wasn't that bad. Murdoch's pretense that her fury with him hurt must be some kind of game he and Ian played.

Briefly, she remembered other people wincing at her angry words—like the printer who'd escaped under his press when she'd received the note about Pauline's imprisonment. Perhaps she spoke more sharply than she realized.

"The two of you don't look well enough to walk two steps, much less half a mile." Deciding to ignore the nonsense about her voice, she gauged the distance between the carriage and the curl of smoke ahead. The path through the woods would not be difficult for her, but she would never be able to lift either of the men should they fall.

"Do not worry about us," Ian told her, keeping his hand wrapped around Murdoch's uninjured upper arm. "Start down the path ahead of us, and we will follow. Don't go too far ahead, though, in case

Murdoch thinks me unarmed and helpless, and tries something stupid."

Since Ian wore both swords and carried his staff, he was scarcely unarmed, but loss of blood had left them both close to helpless, as far as she could see. Still she saw no point in arguing with opinionated men who thought they were invulnerable.

Instead, she addressed the driver. "You will tell the soldiers you merely went in search of the stallion?" Rapscallion was tied to the back of the coach.

The driver raised his crop to his cap in a salute of agreement.

Gathering her ruined skirt and petticoats, humming under her breath, Chantal proceeded down the rocky shortcut through the woods. She heard the men trampling the underbrush behind her. They moved with remarkable speed despite their weakened conditions. She hurried a little faster. Their speed increased.

She was all but running by the time she reached the inn's kitchen garden. The men were right behind her, striding comfortably as if taking a stroll in the park. She didn't know why she'd worried about them.

She abruptly swung around and was nearly crushed by the two giants stumbling into her. She started to scold them for their haste, then noted how pale they were beneath their stoic demeanors. Blood seeped through their bandages. She'd found Ian's robe to cover him with some decency, and pulled Murdoch's clothes back up his arms again, but they still looked as if they'd survived a royal battle—which they had, apparently. She had no intention of asking over what. Cocks fought, in her experience, and these were two prime cocks.

"You'll scare the maids to death. Let me go in first. I'll send them on errands and distract the cook."

Murdoch started to object, but Ian quelled him with a look. "Do what you can. We'll handle the rest."

She didn't know what that meant, but eager to settle her patients somewhere safe, she hastened into the kitchen. Facing the entrance so the maids had to turn their backs to it, she set them to heating water to take up to her father's room, then engaged the cook in a discussion of healing broths for invalids.

Neither maids nor cook seemed to notice the blood-stained, bedraggled ruin of her clothes, which she thought odd, but she used her most charming voice to keep the cook's back to the door until Chantal saw Ian and his prisoner slip safely past. With a grateful nod, she thanked the cook for her understanding and wisdom, and scampered after them.

The inn had only three doors upstairs. Ian unerringly aimed for the center door and went in without knocking. She followed her father's voice inside. He was sitting in a wooden chair by the window, appearing somewhat less gray than when she had left him. He smiled at her appearance, until he took note of her clothes. Then he scowled at the two bloody men entering with her.

"This is a pretty predicament," he growled. "Perhaps we ought to send Chantal and Pauline across the border on their own. They'd be better off than burdened with the lot of us. What the devil do you intend to do with a king's officer?"

Ian studied Murdoch's tattered uniform. "In my country, he is a criminal."

"You have criminals now?" Alain snorted in derision. "My, how the mighty have fallen. You can't even hold on to that damned chalice anymore."

Arms still tied behind his back, Murdoch rested his good shoulder against the wall beside the bed and slouched as if distancing himself from the argument, yet Chantal had the distinct impression that he was absorbing a great deal more than it appeared.

"Chantal does not yet understand that the chalice is worth more than all of us together," Ian replied. "But now that we have Murdoch, we should be able to catch up with it. Did Pierre take one of your horses?"

"The oldest one," Alain agreed. "But even though he's a poor rider, he'll have time to catch a ship before we escape this mess."

Although Chantal sensed Ian's tension, outwardly, he didn't appear worried. "Why the sea when the border is so close?" he asked, reasonably enough.

"I don't know what got into the boy. He's always had an idealistic bent. Perhaps he hopes to sell the chalice to save the church." Alain looked tired. "Le Havre is our home. His parents have an estate there. And that was his direction."

Ian nodded as if filing this information in the appropriate corner of his formidable mind. "Our ships can find him on the sea. The main problem is how we will travel to the coast."

"The main problem is finding a physician who won't go running for the National Guard," Chantal said when none of them seemed to care that both men were swaying from their wounds. "The bed is empty. Sit down, both of you. You make me dizzy just watching you."

Both arrogant roosters remained standing in an apparent challenge to see who submitted to his weakness first.

"Fetch your sewing kit to mend Murdoch's arm. That is better than cauterization," Ian suggested. "We do not need physicians. Once we've eaten and rested, we will set out again. I think the local troops can be made to look the other way, if Murdoch's men can be diverted."

Murdoch snorted but remained otherwise silent.

"Fine, have it your way," Chantal replied with a shrug. "I have nothing left to lose. But if you don't start listening to me . . ." She raised her voice sharply on the last words.

Murdoch visibly shuddered and collapsed into a sitting position on the bed's edge. With a degree of weariness, he leaned against the headboard and dragged his legs up onto the mattress. Grinning, Ian did the same.

Her father stared from them to her in astonishment.

"Don't ask," she told him. "I'll fetch Pauline's sewing kit."

She opened the door and let in a maid carrying a bucket of water and another with a tray containing bowls of broth. Bread was still too expensive, so she had not asked for it. She did not know how they would draw on their bank funds if they were forced to leave France, so she must mind their small store of coins. Perhaps Pierre had seen the chalice as a king's treasure and an opportunity to provide for his sister and the children.

Her stomach rumbled in protest, but she hurried to Pauline's room first. She needed to see for herself that the children were safe and sound.

At her entrance, Pauline looked up with relief, then widened her eyes at the state of Chantal's clothes. "Are you all right? Shall I send for a bath? A physician?"

Chantal couldn't let exhaustion catch up with her. She crouched down to hug the children and kept her voice warm. "After a while, a bath. I must do some mending first. Do you have a needle and strong thread?"

"Pierre?" Pauline asked in fear. "I know he means only to help, not harm."

"He's safe, for all I know. I'll explain later." She kissed Marie and Anton on their foreheads. "I will read to you later, yes? You have been such good children, I will have to think of a lovely reward for you."

"Candy?" Marie suggested, her blue eyes lighting with hope.

Making promises she feared she could not keep, Chantal took the sewing kit offered and hurried back to her father's room.

As much as she loved the chalice, she saw no purpose in risking the children's safety to follow it. She could not imagine what had inspired Pierre to steal the cup, but knowing his idealism, she was certain it was for the good of all, as Pauline said. If he had chosen the road to his and Pauline's childhood home, she couldn't blame him. She longed to return to the carelessness of youth as well, but she feared he hadn't made a wise decision. The roads of France were no longer safe, and the route to the coast was long. She would not feel comfortable until they rode the few short miles to the border. Once safe in the Netherlands, they could decide where to go.

Ian must choose his own course. If he elected to chase after the chalice, it was no matter to her any longer. Her family came first.

She hummed to shut out the sickening wrench of her heart at that decision.

Twenty-three

He lacked the required concentration to keep Murdoch bound by mental restraints, Ian decided wearily as the whole family gathered in the sickroom to discuss their next step.

It was one thing to focus his gods-gifted mind while performing serenity-enhancing exercises on a barren hill. It was quite another to do so while confined in a small chamber with a woman whose presence kept him in a perpetual state of arousal. It was still another to do so while surrounded by an irascible diplomat with a sharp tongue; two laughing, quarreling children; and their weepy mother; not to mention Murdoch—a man with unknown gifts, some greater than his own.

For the first time in his life, Ian felt the helplessness of Others. How did they survive? He could scarcely think straight, much less filter out all the conflicting thoughts and emotions while keeping Murdoch mentally bound.

Obviously, there was a reason he'd been alone all his life.

Ian couldn't tell how much of his pain his amacara could sense. He knew that once the vows were said, mates shared their gifts, even if in a small way, but until now, Chantal had exhibited little awareness of anything extraordinary. *He'd* certainly not taken up singing as a means of dealing with this damned violent world. So he watched her every action for a sign that they were matched in all senses of the word.

That she'd come after him was both wonderful and appalling. It suggested she had felt his pain. And that she must suffer as he did now.

"You're not eating," she murmured worriedly, perched beside him on the edge of the bed. She stroked his brow and offered him a spoonful of broth from the tray in his lap, as she had offered Murdoch before he'd turned up his nose at being spoon-fed. "Would you like to rest?"

He could interpret that offer in many different ways. Perhaps she sensed his weariness as well as his pain. Or his desire to have her to himself. Or she could just be trying to get rid of him. Ian wanted to pound his head on something hard at this inability to understand even the simplest of questions. He was a complete and utter misfit in her world.

And he didn't want to be. He wanted to conquer her world as surely as he had his own—a true challenge fitting an Olympus.

"I don't wish to leave you alone to guard Murdoch," he grumbled with an irritation he seldom exhibited. "Holding him prisoner is difficult enough while I'm fully armed, but this way it is nigh impossible."

"I can ask the local militia if they have chains," she said dryly. "I doubt Murdoch's royal mercenaries will provide them, and I can't see how we'll leave as long as his men are out there. It's a wonder both sets of soldiers haven't taken to shooting each other in the street."

"I don't suppose you could sing them to sleep?" Ian asked facetiously, too weary to guard his words.

"Why don't I *shriek* and make them drop their

weapons?" Apparently annoyed, she stood up and straightened her skirt.

She'd changed into what appeared to be one of her oldest and simplest gowns. This one was a dismal dark green without a hint of the frilly delicacy of the other confections she'd worn. Ian had the urge to rip the rag off and provide her with the luxuries that would make her smile again, but the inhabitants of his home seldom wore silk. His mind was obviously wandering.

He caught her hand and prevented her escape. "I need your help," he said before he could think better of it.

She halted instantly, offering him an uncertain— almost hopeful—gaze. "How?" she whispered. "I feel so useless. . . ." She gestured at the room bursting with people.

On the feather-stuffed pallet beside Ian, Murdoch watched them both, one sardonic eyebrow lifted.

"The chalice is more important than I can explain to you," Ian said slowly, groping for the words to convey what his ring would not let him say directly. "But so are you. I cannot leave you here while I chase after it. And I understand that you go nowhere without your family."

Chantal's eyes widened, as if surprised that he'd understood the difficulty they faced. Ian supposed he'd surprised himself. Since taking Chantal as amacara, his horizons had broadened perceptibly.

Murdoch snorted. "Bit off more than you can chew, haven't you?" he said with a sneer. "Can't hold me and have her and chase the chalice all at the same time. How do you plan to win this one, wise man?"

"Do you know a funeral dirge?" Ian asked Chantal in exasperation. "Perhaps we could bore him to death."

Murdoch rolled his eyes heavenward. "Gods forbid," he muttered. "I don't doubt that six feet of dirt would fall on my head should she try."

Ian was aware that Orateur was watching them with eyes narrowed, but the older man had a lap full of children demanding a story, so Ian hoped he could not hear their conversation. Orateur appeared immune to the effects of his daughter's voice, perhaps because she lavished only love on him. Had her father turned a blind eye to abilities she'd inherited from a world he'd left behind? Or tried to make her life normal by not acknowledging them?

Ian clasped Chantal's hand tighter when she tried to tug away. "For all his wits, Murdoch has the common sense of a conch shell. Ignore him, but listen to me and consider my words carefully. Does your father not say that you speak sweetly and can sway the angriest man to reason?"

A tiny frown formed between her eyes. "Men are prone to fall for feminine charms, for a small while, at least," she said with a shrug of discomfort. "What has that to do with anything? I cannot charm a troop of militia or a dozen mercenaries."

"Lovely as you are, my lady, it is not just your looks that sway men; it is the beauty of your voice." Ian waited to see if she fully grasped what he said.

She wrinkled her nose in distaste. "Then men are fools to let a pretty song sway them. How will this help us escape?"

The urgency of the situation forced Ian to phrase his idea delicately, but firmly. He still had difficulty thinking straight and hoped he'd worked out all the angles—and that he knew Murdoch as well as he thought he did. "Murdoch is overly sensitive to your voice, especially if you direct it at him. First, do not talk *too* sweetly to him." He shot his prisoner a warning that brought the familiar mockery to Murdoch's harsh face. "He may get ideas he shouldn't."

Chantal smiled faintly. "I doubt there's any chance either of my being sweet to him or of him forgetting where he is."

"Sensible," Murdoch muttered, shifting to a less painful position.

"Just something to keep in mind," Ian warned. "He does not trust me, for good reason. But he is a man of his word for all that. You must try your most charming voice on him to persuade him that it's in all our best interests for him to work with us."

Chantal laughed. Murdoch grunted and strained against his bonds.

Ian raised his eyebrows expectantly. Chantal had no idea how her presence reduced him to a groveling imitation of himself. Instead of *ordering* her to do as he asked, he waited for his lovely, talented amacara to trust him. She gave him unreasonable hope.

Possibly some of his hope reached her, for she turned a sweet smile on his captive.

"Ah, Monsieur LeDroit, I did not understand!" she cooed in a mockery of a coquette. "So charming a man should not be treated in such a despicable fashion. *S'il vous plaît,* would you listen to Monsieur d'Olympe's reasoning? Unless, that is, he has knocked all the brains from your simple head."

Murdoch tried to sink deeper into the pallet, and Ian chuckled. His amacara might be a sweet confection on the outside, but on the inside, Chantal was a double-edged sword. She was still angry at him, but her fear and fury were directed at Murdoch. If Ian could feel her cut, Murdoch must truly be squirming.

"Very good," Ian complimented her. "A little less tart and a little more sweet, and he will be putty in your hands."

"This is ridiculous." She jerked her hand free and propped it on her lovely hip. "It is unfair to tease me in some jest I do not understand."

"I do not tease. Watch." He turned to glare at Murdoch. "We can work together to recover the chalice, or I can haul you home trussed like a pig. Which would you prefer?"

Murdoch replied with a string of curses that had all heads in the room turning.

Chantal picked up a pillow and swatted him with it until he stopped. "There are women and children present, monsieur!"

"Ow, ow, cease and desist, woman!" Murdoch cried in a pained voice.

"Milksop," she said in disgust, throwing the pillow to the bed. "It is but feathers."

"No, it is your voice," Ian insisted. "Your anger is like a bludgeon to him. Ask him the same thing I did. Use the exact same words, if you like, but mean what you say."

Torn between feeling as if she were a figure of fun and wondering if Ian had lost what little remained of his mind, Chantal tapped her toe. Since she could think of no good solution to their difficulty, she played the game just to appease him. She groped for the phrasing he'd used.

"We can work together," she said reasonably, "or Ian can haul you home trussed like a pig." She added her contempt to her tone. "Which would you prefer?" she demanded.

"Damn and blast you all to hell," Murdoch muttered, writhing. "Hack my head off. Give me my sword and let me fight fairly. This is cruel torture."

Chantal shrugged. "Do I sing him a lullaby and put him out of his misery now?" she asked with sarcasm.

"Did he tell you no and curse you as he did me?" Eyes laughing, Ian straightened, looking stronger than he had just moments ago. "His resistance is strong, but your charms are stronger. Try again, in your own words. It seems you have had much practice at this."

"Since I don't even know what 'this' is, I cannot say." But Chantal's heart flipped with delight at Ian's laughter. He was actually handsome when the burden of his responsibilities was lifted from his shoulders. If it would make him happy . . . It would make her very happy.

She considered a moment, channeling her true desire into her tone. "We are in a bit of a pickle, monsieur," she said with less sugar and more wile. "The chalice is on its way to the coast, you are both injured and in no condition to race after it, and there is a troop of militia on our doorstep who might decide we're traitors. A little cooperation might aid all our goals, do you not agree?" she said, willing him to accept.

Murdoch sighed deeply and closed his eyes. "Yes, I agree."

Ian grinned like a fool. Undeterred, Chantal pushed her odd advantage. "Then, if we unbind you, will you ask your men to help us locate the chalice instead of foolishly chasing innocent people across the countryside?"

"If you will give me real food instead of this swill," Murdoch ground out from between clenched molars.

"He always did insist on keeping the upper hand," Ian said almost jovially. "Have him swear that he will help and put his men at our disposal. He will attempt to wiggle out of his promise otherwise."

Chantal was aware her father had set the children aside and limped weakly over to stand behind her.

She didn't know what to make of what was happening, but if she were being made jest of, her father would soon put an end to the nonsense.

With more confidence, she said, "Murdoch, please swear that you and your men will help us find the chalice."

With an air of resignation, he swore, "My men and I will help you find the chalice, but no more than that."

Chantal waited expectantly.

Ian appeared to be considering the vow. "He means to keep the chalice when we find it, but you cannot force a man to go against his nature or his conscience, and I suspect forcing him to give up his goals would be asking too much. Perhaps have him promise to protect you and cause no harm. Let's see how far he's been corrupted."

"Damn you, Ian! I am not corrupt! I won't hurt your charming amacara and her family. There is no reason for me to. All I ask is that you leave me alone, go home where you belong, and let the chalice do as it pleases."

Chantal's father put his hand on her shoulder and squeezed it gently. "I see Monsieur d'Olympe exploits your talents already. Be very careful that you do only as you want to do, *ma petite*. He has a manner of twisting people to think as he does."

"How do you know this?" she asked, puzzled. She'd sensed before that her father and Ian knew each other in some manner, although neither man had said as much.

Her father hesitated for the first time in her memory. With a sigh, he admitted, "I know his family. They are cut from the same cloth."

Ian rubbed his shoulder and protested, "If she speaks with her heart, I twist nothing, and I would never harm Chantal."

"You already have," her father replied angrily.

Chantal rubbed her temples, attempting to straighten out the nuances in their voices. There was more her father would say, but he seemed restrained from adding it.

Murdoch unexpectedly burst his bonds and began rubbing his wrists. He winced at the disturbance to his upper arm but otherwise looked relieved. "Madame Deveau, I can send word that you were visiting sick relatives and had no part in the king's escape. Go home. Stay out of Ian's clutches."

Chantal watched Ian stiffen and grow wary. Murdoch's offer caught her by surprise. On top of her astonishment that he had actually capitulated to Ian's request—if the capitulation had not been something planned between them—she didn't know how to respond. How had Murdoch so conveniently broken free immediately after swearing he would not escape?

She felt as if she'd not only left her safe world behind, but entered one on the moon, where she did not know the customs.

Murdoch offered to give her back her home. He dangled temptation . . .

"He has a better chance of escaping if you are not with me," Ian said. "That is why he is being so agreeable about sending you home. But it is your choice. Paris is no longer possible, but I can arrange for you to proceed to Le Havre. If Pauline wishes to follow her brother, I can help."

Ian might as well be offering her the choice between the devil she knew or a step off the brink of the unknown into the valley of the unseen. She was torn in two, her sensible half demanding that she pack up and go home where all was safe and comfortable and predictable.

But she'd lost her blinders and knew Paris was no such thing any longer.

The buried half of her—the one that had trusted Ian from the first, taken him to her bed, and caused her to throw caution to the winds and do appalling things like sweet-talk a uniformed officer into a bargain against his will—clamored to continue on this wild adventure. That a strong man like Ian needed her . . .

Perhaps she did not want to be parted from him just yet.

She looked up at her father, who looked sad and vaguely disoriented. He'd not been telling her the whole truth any more than Ian had. These two knew each other in some way that she did not understand.

"Let us see what Pauline wishes to do," she said decisively. "I go where the children go."

Twenty-four

"I want to go with Pierre," Pauline whispered wearily. "I want to go to Le Havre and my parents. I want the madness to end."

Chantal directed a challenging look at the two large men now restlessly roaming the small room. "Can you take us safely there without fear of arrest?"

Even now the revolutionary militia in their crude striped trousers strutted defiantly down the street, playing fife and drum in the face of the king's boot-and-breeches-clad mercenaries lounging against buildings and grooming their horses. No doubt the Assembly's National Guard or spies blocked the roads. She could not imagine how they could escape, but obviously, her imagination was lacking. She certainly couldn't have imagined influencing a surly rogue like Murdoch to do anything against his will, yet he did not immediately slay everyone in sight and flee.

For all that mattered, she wasn't entirely certain how he'd been bound. It wasn't as if drying vines were a deterrent to a man of his evident strength, even when wounded. And why would the king's men follow Murdoch? So many odd things had happened since Ian had walked into her life that she wasn't certain what was normal anymore. She, who had woven her home into a secure nest of peace, now teetered on the brink of falling into thin air.

"To Le Havre?" Ian asked, directing the question at Murdoch. "West of here?"

"On the coast," Murdoch agreed with a snarl as he paced the floor like a caged beast. "Not near Trystan," he added, inexplicably.

Pauline caught Chantal's hand and whispered in her ear. "Are we all talking about the same thing, or is this some riddle I do not understand?"

"I believe we are talking different things with the same outcome," Chantal concluded. "Pierre has their chalice. Pierre goes to Le Havre. We wish to go to Le Havre. They want the chalice. *Alors*, to Le Havre we go."

"How do they know where Pierre is?" Pauline asked sensibly.

"Magic," Chantal decided. "Who cares as long as we get what we want?"

Her father had returned to his chair and poured a large goblet of wine. Swirling it in agitation, he scowled at the room at large. Chantal felt his gaze become thoughtful as it fell on her, but she was too rattled to understand what was happening.

Her voice could not possibly have persuaded a desperate man to reason—or brought him to his knees with her shouts. That was not credible.

And yet, she had nearly caused a riot by screaming over a chicken.

She needed her piano to sort all this out, but she did not even have the bell . . . the chalice . . . to calm her. By dropping the valuable chalice instead of holding it, as Ian had requested, she'd allowed Pierre to succumb to temptation. This was all her fault.

Why? Why must she be the only one who could guard the chalice? Ian was bigger. Her father was smarter. Pauline was prettier and more deceptive.

She was simply a musician.

Ian stopped his pacing to lift her chin and kiss her nose. "All will be clear soon, I promise. Will you trust me?"

"Do I have a choice?" But when he looked at her like that, his deep soulful eyes full of mystery and admiration, she would promise him anything. She had grown up with Jean and adored him like a brother, but he had never stirred deep sensual longings in her with just a look.

She yearned for the privacy of a chamber alone with Ian. He smiled hungrily as if he wished the same and pressed his mouth to her lips. She shivered in expectation, aroused by this simple caress.

"You always have choices," he murmured, "except in how we feel about each other. That is granted by the gods."

"I doubt my God has any interest in carnal appetites," she said dryly. "You must have more primitive ones."

"Let us say, more practical ones."

He released her and strode over to confront Murdoch. "We have agreed to try not to kill each other until we have found the chalice, correct?"

"Reluctantly," Murdoch growled. "It would have been simpler if one of us had hacked off the other's head as your amacara so pleasantly suggested. You do realize that I cannot order a dozen mercenaries to traipse across half the country for no reward? The king has been caught. Their goal now is survival, and that lies across the border."

Pauline gasped and dug her fingers into Chantal's arm. "I thought Louis merely lost the hussars. He may have met the other soldiers. How could you know that he did not escape?"

Murdoch performed a stiff bow. "I never lie. I served in his troops until I understood that the rabble are right—leadership without knowledge and understanding is no leadership at all. I am sorry, madame, but all the king's troops failed. The rebels have discovered him."

Pauline sagged against Chantal's arm, and grief hung heavily in the room. It did not take a Gypsy to predict the end of an old regime. Wrapping an arm around her sister-in-law's shoulders, Chantal gestured at the children. "Come along, *mes petites*; let us take your *maman* for a nap. While you sleep, I will find those prizes I promised you."

The children cheered and raced each other to the door, oblivious to adult concerns and sorrows. Chantal threw a glance to the men they left behind. "I assume we leave tonight?"

"The carriage is too slow," Murdoch said scornfully. "You have an entire herd of swift beasts out there who could catch up to the thief before he reaches the coast."

Chantal shot him an unsympathetic look and replied with the disdain Ian seemed convinced reduced argumentative men to tatters. "If you think we are slow, you should see Pierre ride. Pauline and I wish to go to the coast. We will take the carriage."

To her pleasure, Murdoch winced at her tone and seemed to acquiesce. Ian grinned. Normal men tended to scowl at her attitudes, but she liked thinking that after a lifetime of feeling small and helpless, she could actually affect two great beasts like these.

Hugging Pauline's shoulders, she did her best to flounce out of the room with her friend, though her old gown lacked sufficient petticoats to be effective.

"She has always twisted people around her little fingers," Alain Orateur complained as the women and children departed. "Encouraging her will produce a monster." He glowered at the other two men in the room. "Just like the two of you."

"Another rebel in the Olympian court," Murdoch murmured sarcastically. "But I doubt we will convince the crown prince that his mother is as ineffective as French royalty."

"I'm not a prince, and my mother is not royalty," Ian replied without hostility. "If we did not fulfill our duties, the Council would remove us."

"In favor of Lissandra." Murdoch laughed. "No wonder you seek so eagerly after a chalice that can only be caught if it wishes to be. Lissy as Oracle would drive half the island to emigrate. And I cannot imagine your amacara would be any more acceptable to Aelynners."

"Those are not our concerns now." Ian discarded his own unease on the subject in favor of the present. "If you cannot bribe your troops to escort us to the coast, what will you do with them?"

Murdoch attempted to shrug, winced at the pain from his shoulder, then walked to the window and stared down. "The king's troops have two choices, to follow and fight for their king, or to slip away while they can. A few down there are more loyal to me than to their pockets. I can order those few to do as I wish. The others, I must release to find their own way."

Ian recalled the bloody images he'd seen in the stars and tried not to picture Murdoch leading trained soldiers into riot-torn Paris, but the image persisted.

"Do you see yourself as king in this land?" he asked, masking his horror that an Aelynner would interfere in such a manner.

Orateur looked equally horrified. And very tired.

"Someone must lead this country out of the dark ages," Murdoch said without inflection. "If not me, then someone equally strong. Anarchy cannot exist forever. Usually, the most corrupt with the willingness to kill without qualm will win out. I, at least, have some scruples and a greater than average ability to lead. I don't expect you to see that."

Ian shook his head. He'd experienced Murdoch's arrogance and ambition firsthand. In some ways, he understood them, but that did not mean he approved. "It is not an argument either of us can win. My duty is to return you and the chalice to Aelynn. We will seek the chalice first. The gods will decide who wins in the end."

Still watching out the window, Murdoch crossed his arms and leaned his uninjured shoulder against the frame. "For old times' sake, then, we will see who is the better prognosticator. Perhaps you'll see sense by the time we reach the coast. I'll send two of my men ahead to find the trail of your runaway, and we'll keep two guards with us."

"You retain your capacity to guide men's thoughts?" Ian asked warily.

Murdoch shrugged. "As in everything, it's erratic. It was never my area of expertise."

"Monsters," Alain muttered. "Monsters who play with the minds of men."

"No more so than you with your persuasive oratory or Chantal with her enchanted voice," Ian corrected. "With our gifts come responsibilities."

"I'll take Chantal to America," Alain grumbled.

"If anything happens to me, you'll take her to Aelynn," Ian said, doing his best to think calmly. Chantal belonged to Aelynn, to the chalice, and to him. Any other outcome caused a buzz of rage in him that defied rational thought. "She deserves the explanation I promised her. She's made her vows, so Aelynn will accept her if she is accompanied by you or me.

Trystan, our current Guardian, lives in Brittany and will help you, if need be."

Alain looked even more gray at that pronouncement. "If anything happens to you, there is no one to force me to do anything against my will."

"Besides Murdoch, you mean?" Ian said, doing his best not to offend his amacara's father. "Besides the reality that your heart is failing and needs more healing than I can provide, we have other means of influence. Trystan is Guardian these days. His wife is a Crossbreed who has dominion over the sea's depths and speaks with the fish. How long do you think it will be before Kiernan the Finder comes looking for my amacara?"

Murdoch lifted his surly glare from the window to Ian. "The whole world's your oyster, isn't it? I don't suppose that you have questioned why the gods do not grant you an heir?"

Because the gods were waiting for Ian to bring Chantal to them, was Ian's belief. But his personal life was of no concern to others. Without explanation, he opened the bedroom door. "I leave you to sort out your men. I will see to the horses."

Chantal did not protest when Ian sought her out in Pauline's room and quietly led her into the hall. She was exhausted beyond measure, and the idea of the long ride ahead did not fill her with joy. But Ian's presence did.

He did not say a word, yet she understood his desperate desire and need for time to themselves. Lust that she had not thought possible in her weary state immediately made its presence known.

"You cannot be serious," she murmured as he drew her inexorably down the hall.

"Test me," he replied, opening the third door.

Inside, he discarded his robe, and she glanced down to his breeches placket. Testing was not necessary. Heat formed in her womb just from imagining her fingers releasing his buttons.

"Exactly," he said, as if she'd answered him.

Swiftly shutting the door behind them, he pulled her into his arms and pressed her back against the wooden panels. "I need to have you to myself all night and day, but this will have to suffice for now."

Ian's mouth clamped down hard against hers. Chantal grabbed his arms to thrust him away, but she fell under his spell too quickly. Parting her lips, she offered him entrance, and clung to his iron strength when his tongue invaded and possessed like a conquering warrior, emulating the invasion he would impose on her sex if she did not stop him.

She didn't wish to stop him. She pressed her breasts into his chest, then, remembering his injured shoulder, tried to pull back against the door. With no patience for coddling, Ian crushed her against the wooden panels and unfastened the hooks holding her bodice in place. She gasped against his mouth as his hands shoved aside fabric to find her flesh. With a persuasive tease of her nipples, he had her melting in his arms.

"I want to see all of you," he said roughly when they came up for breath.

Before she could argue, he dropped to his knees and lifted her skirt and lone petticoat.

"Ian!" Little light seeped through the room's shuttered windows, but still . . . She was self-conscious of her less-than-flawless skin. She grabbed his shoulders and tried to push him away, but she may as well have tried pushing mountains.

His bare hands grasped her buttocks, separating them as he leaned in to kiss between her legs. Unpre-

pared, Chantal lost the use of her knees. She slid down
the door and collapsed in a puddle of skirts on the
floor to frantically tear at his buttons.

Without hesitation, Ian helped her, then lifted her
so he could bring her down on his straining sex. He
muffled her cries with his mouth as they came together, and she tasted herself on his lips. She shuddered and clenched him tighter.

"It's not enough," he muttered against her mouth,
while his sex filled hers. "I need more time."

More time? She could scarcely think as primal need
exploded in her brain, and she rose and fell with the
plunge of his thick staff inside her. She choked back
a moan as her climax broke and rolled over her, and
she fell limp in his arms.

Still engorged and in place, Ian lifted her and carried her to the edge of the bed, where he tugged her
skirts completely to her waist and ran his hand over
her belly and thighs. "I know somewhere you bear
a mark. . . ."

She lifted her hips, forcing his attention back to
where it belonged. To her satisfaction, he threw back
his head and groaned, and there was no more discussion of marks or time or anything so humdrum. He
drove home, rekindling her desire with thrusts as mea-
sured as a good melody, and as one, their bodies sang
a beautiful chorus. Replete, they clutched each other.

A pounding on the door prevented any further in-
vestigation of singing bodies. Ian cursed and leaned
over to suckle gently at her neglected breasts. Chantal
could almost feel the milk form, so primitive was the
hunger between them.

"In my home," he said. "We will create a child there."

With that odd promise, he pulled up her bodice to
cover her breasts and, buttoning his breeches, reluctantly returned to his duties.

Twenty-five

Ian rode beside the ponderous carriage in the fading moonlight. This new road to the west was barely more than a goat path. He empathized with Murdoch's restless need to drive their mounts to the speed for which they were bred and bring this prolonged torment to an end.

But his desire to win the chalice had been surmounted by the challenge of capturing Chantal's trust . . . and her heart.

Not that he knew anything of the emotion Other Worlders called love, but the physical bond of ama-cara had taught him to crave . . . more intimate rapport. He hungered to know more of her tender compassion and reluctant courage. Even though she understood nothing of him or his home, she didn't shy from his demands but met him as if they were equals. She fascinated him.

Until Chantal, his responsibilities had always kept him distant from those he served. Perhaps the chalice was trying to show him the error of his ways.

So Ian let Murdoch wear himself out riding back and forth between their forward and rear guards while he waited for Chantal to wake.

He ought to be ashamed that he'd treated her so crudely in their lovemaking. He'd always treated women with respect, tried to learn their likes and dislikes so he could reward them with the appropriate gifts. He'd always taken time to bring them pleasure. Never had he taken one as roughly as he had Chantal—or with as much uncontrolled, elemental passion . . . and joy.

They'd come together in equal need—against walls and doors and on floors—and she hadn't seemed to mind. He certainly hadn't minded. Their passionate couplings had been far more mind opening and fulfilling than any of his more . . . cerebral seductions. Apparently, the internal *connection* between him and Chantal was more important than material surroundings. That alone taught him a great deal.

With the first light of dawn, he watched the youngest child stir inside the carriage while the others slept. Should he ever be fortunate enough to have children, he would need to learn more about them. Could he learn to love children as Chantal did?

Just as Marie began to prod her grief-stricken mother for attention, Chantal woke and lifted the child to her lap. Crooning, she settled Marie into a welcoming cuddle and, as if she felt Ian watching, glanced out her open window.

The humidity and heat had been building as they neared the coast, and the passengers had left the windows open to let in the cool night air. Ian drew closer so he could speak.

"How is your father?" He'd known when Alain chose to ride inside that the older man's heart problem had worsened. Ian could only relieve the congestion around it, not cure it.

"He sleeps, but not well," she said quietly. "I do not know if it is his health, or the pain of seeing his dreams broken."

She kept her voice carefully neutral, for which Ian was grateful. She had no way of understanding the power of her voice when she could be told nothing of the advanced abilities of Aelynn's inhabitants or her father's origins. But she was at least heeding his warning. She apparently had much experience in wielding her enchanted voice in normal situations but had never had reason to explore the more dangerous extremes of her gifts.

"We have healers at home who will help him mend," he said with confidence.

"We go where Pauline goes," she reminded him.

And Pauline could not go to Aelynn. She and the children had no Aelynn blood, and the gods would not let them through the island's barrier of invisibility. Ian could find no way around that.

"Ships sail both ways," he said without arguing. "We can take him home, let him heal, then return wherever he wishes." Ian prayed that by then Chantal would see the wisdom of staying with him. Perhaps, if they had a child of their own . . .

She nodded, as if she had decided to be as reasonable as he was—or as if she pacified a madman.

"You do understand that I can give you silks and featherbeds and pearls, and that it is only circumstances that have led me to be so crude?" He was anxious that she not consider him a barbarian. He had no experience in courting a lady of refinement, but he assumed wealth was one of those factors women considered in choosing mates.

"I do not understand anything at all these days," she responded, pressing the child's head to her breast. "Perhaps after we return to Le Havre, and things have settled down, I will understand better. You are not the only one who has behaved badly."

She blushed as pink as the dawn's light, and Ian regained his assurance that she did not despise him for their hasty couplings. "There is nothing bad or wrong in what we've done together. The gods have blessed our joining." He reassured her as gently as he could. "You realize it's not likely to be safe in Le Havre? And Murdoch and I cannot stay there. Our home is elsewhere."

She searched his face and looked sorrowful. "I understand you cannot stay."

He wanted to emphasize that she could not either, but Murdoch chose that moment to gallop back to them.

He brought his steed to an unnecessarily abrupt halt. "There is a village ahead. We can rest the animals and eat there. The chalice has nearly reached the coast. I think we should leave the women and children while we go after it."

Ian did not need an interpreter for Chantal's questioning look. How Murdoch knew the chalice's location was not something he could tell her. She must trust his promise to explain later.

"*All* the horses need resting," Chantal said from the window, in a tone that apparently pained Murdoch's sensitive ears.

"We could trade them—" Murdoch started to say.

"For nags too bony to be eaten?" Chantal finished with scorn.

Ian noted that Murdoch's frustration matched his own of earlier. Nothing in this Other World could be accomplished with the swiftness to which they were accustomed. Even with the injuries he and Murdoch had sustained, they possessed the speed and stamina of horses. They could follow the chalice's trail with their extraperception and catch up to Pierre in hours. But they could not change Chantal's world to suit themselves.

People and animals would have to be fed and rested.

"We could run—" Murdoch started to suggest.

Ian rejected that idea with a shake of his head. "The chalice teases us. We only open the way for trouble if we allow it to goad us into haste. Your ambition still blinds you, LeDroit."

In anger, Murdoch reeled his horse back toward town. "Don't patronize me, prince," he called as he rode off.

"There is nothing wrong with ambition," Chantal objected, watching Murdoch ride away.

"Not when it is tempered with an awareness of the public good instead of selfish greed. That is a hard lesson to learn for someone who possesses nothing."

"That is a hard lesson for people who have *everything*." She slammed shut the window and turned her attention to her waking family.

Let her believe what she would. He did not need her approval—much.

Even though they were in town only long enough to eat and rest the horses, Ian insisted that Alain take a room and rest while he and Murdoch showed their passports to the local militia. Since her father seemed to fare better now that Ian looked after him, Chantal did not question his orders. Ian apparently had a bottomless pit of wealth, and she was sure the innkeeper would make good use of the coins.

But now it was time to leave, and her father would not wake.

"Papa?" She felt his forehead. His temperature seemed normal, but his breath rasped heavily in his lungs. She tried shaking him just a little, but his eyelids did not even stir. "Papa!"

Nothing.

With fear chilling her bones, Chantal fled down the stairs in search of Ian. Pauline was letting the children chase pigeons around the village green. Chantal hadn't seen Murdoch since they'd arrived—didn't want to see him. He frightened her in ways she did not understand. She didn't know why Ian trusted him.

Far better than anyone else, Ian would know what to do. She found him in the stable yard, checking over the mares, stroking the nervous creatures and talking to them as if they understood, while he examined their hooves.

He looked up before she even called to him. "What is it? Your father?"

She'd given up attempting to dress her hair and had merely pinned it at her nape. Strands blew free and brushed her face as she nodded. Her heart beat quickly. She felt flushed, and she did not know if it was fear for her father or proximity to Ian that did it. She could not even stand near him without embarrassing herself.

"Papa will not wake. We have to find a physician."

"There is none here who will do more than bleed him." Ian was already halfway across the yard and hurrying toward the inn. "We need to take him to my home. We have . . . physicians . . . there who can work miracles."

Chantal hurried after him. "He's never been ill a day in his life. Even when the fever struck Le Havre, he did not take to his bed."

"He is a stubborn man, but his weaknesses are catching up with him. Distress will harm the constitution, break it down faster than any fever." He took the stairs two at a time.

"But once we are in Le Havre, he will be fine, won't he? He'll have me and the horses and the children and . . ."

Ian halted and whirled on the stairs. "You can't stay in France, Chantal. You have seen the riots in Paris. What do you think is happening now that the angry mob realizes your king ran away in order to wreak war on your new government? You have seen the obsessive suspicion of the militia: they track every citizen for fear of royal spies and arrest innocents like Pierre who disagree with them. This country is about to go up in flames. Pauline and Pierre are aristocrats. You and your father are wealthy and publicly supported the king. Even without Pauline's involvement in the royal escape, you would be targets. Go, find your friend and the children. We must be on the road."

"But Papa! He can't travel like this." She could not absorb or accept his predictions. He had no way of knowing these things any better than she did. Her father was a more immediate concern than *might be*s.

"He will fare better with my people than here. My sister's healing skills are better than mine, and there are still others better than she. Your father needs their help. Go! Now!"

He dashed up the steps, leaving her behind.

The children whined about being returned to the carriage. Pauline sank into sullen grief. Papa groaned and slumped against the cushions after Ian helped him in. The only one who seemed happy about their return to the road was Murdoch, who raced his steed ahead of them.

Chantal had the oddest notion that Ian somehow controlled Murdoch's actions, or at least, the distance he could run. Each time, the angry man returned even angrier, with dark fires flashing behind eyelids he kept lowered to conceal his inner self. At least Ian had been able to wake her father.

Despite the disgruntled temperaments of his fellow travelers, Ian clenched his jaw and remained stoic. In the summer heat, he'd discarded his robes and frock coat and rode scandalously in shirtsleeves, breeches, and spotless boots, his hair bound and curling in a long tail down his back. And still, he looked every inch the noble prince.

Knowing the king's brothers, Chantal thought Ian looked *better* than any royalty or nobility. He possessed dignity and wisdom and a kind of . . . leashed power . . . that the drunken, greedy, spoiled fops of the aristocracy could never acquire. Perhaps the Marquis de Lafayette and a few of his soldiers exhibited a similar moral fortitude, but she suspected Ian could manage soldiers more intelligently than Lafayette had done lately. And Ian could do it in monk's robes or shirtsleeves without need of impressive uniforms.

Which meant she was in serious danger of falling head over heels in love with a man who would ultimately ignore her wishes. Men of power were dangerously arrogant in their beliefs, and Ian exhibited every sign of believing he knew best for everyone.

If he thought she was a woman like Pauline who needed someone to take care of her, he knew nothing at all. She might have been relatively frivolous, but she had not tended her home and loved ones all these years without learning to be strong.

So, as much as she might admire and desire Ian, as much as she would like to think he was the one man in a million who could be her match, she could not fall in love with him. She'd tucked her poor, shattered heart away long ago, and she had better sense than to open the box now. Her music would be her life, as before.

So she lifted her flute and taught the children to sing in harmony. The instrument would never replace her piano, but the flute was beautifully melodic, and she was grateful for the gift. She handed out the tarts she'd bought as prizes and began to rebuild the bubble of happiness she'd lost when she'd left Paris. . . .

Until she heard the firing of muskets in the distance, and Ian spurred his horse into a gallop, shouting at their driver to hide the carriage in the woods.

Twenty-six

Binding her fear tightly inside her, Chantal pretended that musket fire, galloping horses, and lurching carriages were part of a pleasant summer's day as the coach came to rest in a copse of woods.

"Open the lovely picnic basket and see what Cook has made for you," Chantal told the terrified children as the driver climbed down to water the horses.

The carriage's abrupt change in direction had scared them badly, and she was certain they could pick up on her fear and Pauline's. Marie was already weeping, and Anton's lower lip trembled. If her voice had any power at all, Chantal prayed it would soothe them. She sent Pauline a telling glance that brought her friend back from her own terror to the moment.

"I should think there are trees here you can climb," Pauline exclaimed with false gaiety, following Chantal's example. "It is gallant of Monsieur d'Olympe to find us such a lovely dining room."

While the children sniffled and tried to decide if this was sufficient reassurance, Pauline mouthed a questioning "Pierre?"

Chantal shrugged slightly, not knowing the answer. She recognized the countryside. They were nearing the coast. Chances were good that Murdoch and Ian had either found Pierre or encountered a swarm of soldiers. The shots did not indicate a peaceful resolution.

Papa opened his eyes and scowled. "With luck, our traveling companions have gone for good, and we can go home in peace."

Chantal knew better. She felt it deep inside her, where Ian somehow resided. But she did not let his fury or her fear appear on her face . . . or in her voice. She had to mind her voice, just in case Ian was right, and she somehow revealed or affected too much with it.

She did not feel pain, but . . . the heat of battle? Why would she think that what she was feeling had anything to do with Ian? Except last time she'd felt his pain, he'd been badly wounded, and this time, she felt as if she were angry and fighting, when she wasn't—which meant she was officially insane.

Ian had thought her voice *useful.* If she could help . . .

She desperately wanted to help, to be in charge of her own fate. She'd lost everything she'd owned while being cautious. She had little enough left to risk and no reason for caution any longer.

Her father watched her with suspicion, as if he knew something she didn't and wasn't very happy about it. She managed a polite smile. "I'd like to stretch my legs a little. I think I'll take one of the mares for a ride. Shall I look for berry patches?"

Pauline and her father knew she was lying to protect the children, but she escaped the carriage before they could voice a protest. The mares weren't saddled, but they were bridled. She'd been on horses since she was a toddler. If she rode without benefit of stirrups or appropriate habit, her skirts might drag the ground and kill her, but the horse wouldn't. At least, in this heat, she was wearing a minimum of petticoats.

Trying not to show her fear, she shakily unfastened the leading strings on the last mare in the train. The driver hastened to her side. "There's water for them just over the hill. I can lead them down myself, madame. It's dangerous for you to go alone."

Chantal took a deep breath to prevent shouting her hysteria. If her voice had any influence at all, now was the time to use it prudently. She conjured her sweetest smile and most reassuring tone. "That is thoughtful of you. Pierre chose wisely when he hired you. But I am restless and would like to explore the countryside a little. Would you give me a boost up?"

She could see his internal struggle. Ian had said something about not being able to force people to go against their will, but the driver didn't know her well and should have no strong inclinations one way or another if she chose to risk her silly life. She watched with interest as he obeyed her command, kneeling down to provide a stirrup with his hands so she could mount.

If she hadn't used her persuasive voice on him, would he have been so obliging? Papa was the orator in the family. The possibility that she had used her voice to persuade the driver was too inexplicable to ponder while she was in a state of panic.

There was no sense worrying over it while Ian could be in danger. Steadying the nervous animal, stroking and talking to her, she gained the mare's confidence, then led her into a polite walk back to the road.

In their flashy red and blue uniforms, the mercenaries that Murdoch had ordered to guard the rear galloped toward her, and she waited to direct them to the carriage. They seemed reluctant to follow her orders until she spoke to them in a commanding tone. Instantly, the armed and trained officers reined in and walked their horses down to the trees. If this kept up, nothing would ever amaze her again.

Her success in escaping her safe boundaries gave

her courage. Oddly, Ian had become part of the select group of people who were her family, so she must protect him as she did the others.

And he was still fighting. Her mind and heart felt the blows. And his determination.

Out of sight of the carriage, Chantal kicked her mount into a gallop.

The gunfire was muted with distance but still terrorized her. She'd seen blood running in the streets after soldiers fired on crowds, but it had never been the blood of anyone she knew.

Pierre and Ian were ahead. And fearsome Murdoch. And her childhood home.

She'd recognized the edge of the chalky plateau they'd entered some while back. If they still followed Pierre, he was returning to his parents' estate, as expected. They were north of Le Havre, close to the coast and her maternal grandparents' country house. The alabaster cliffs of Étretat were a mile or two to the north. She'd roamed these fields with Jean and Pauline when they were children, knew every dovecote and manor along the way.

The cliffs they raced toward were treacherous, composed of loose shingle and shale, and no place for horses or fighting. Farther to the south lay the lowlands of the Seine Valley and the port of Le Havre. If Pierre meant to catch a ship from France, he would go there—after saying farewell to his parents near Étretat. He would not suspect that Ian and Murdoch were so close on his trail, intent on reclaiming the chalice. She trusted Ian not to harm Pierre but feared Murdoch would not hesitate to shoot him.

She couldn't bear Pauline's grief if that happened.

Drawing on her love for her home, Chantal hummed a triumphant battle song to bolster her flagging courage and steered her horse along the road to Étretat. The chalk plateau did not provide shrubbery for shelter, but once she reached the safety of—

Galloping hooves trembled the ground, and her mare nervously tossed her head. Glancing over her shoulder, Chantal saw the blue uniforms of the Assembly's National Guard on her heels. Lost in concern for Ian, she'd forgotten she could still be taken as a traitor.

She did not have time to explain herself. If they meant no harm, they would leave her be. If not . . .

She whipped the horse across the field in the westerly direction of the cliffs.

The cavalry wheeled and galloped after her.

Following the sound of gunshots, racing the stallion across the chalk plateau with little or no cover, Ian sought Murdoch's mind—just in case the feeble idiot would open it to him.

Murdoch didn't, of course. But Ian did find the arrogant threads of Murdoch's two mercenaries. They thought to chase away a ragtag band of foot soldiers with their mighty steeds, greater training, and deadly weapons.

The fatal flaw in that theory, Ian realized as he came upon the scene from a distance, was that the local militia knew the countryside, and Murdoch and his men did not. They'd been surrounded, a dozen against three. One should never underestimate a man fighting on his own turf, especially one defending home and family. The power of Other World emotion seemed almost as great as his gods-granted gifts.

Which placed Ian in a dilemma. He and Murdoch were intervening in Other World affairs. Yes, the priest had the chalice, but did they have the right to injure anyone in their pursuit of it? Wasn't it, to some extent, his and Murdoch's fault that the chalice had escaped?

He had no stomach for killing a man who was fighting to defend himself and his own kind. From the militia's fierce thoughts he gathered that these men were loyal to Pierre's family, and they fought to shield their hometown priest until he could escape. Placing his desire for the chalice above theirs to protect loved ones would reduce him to Murdoch's level of selfish ambition.

He needed to find a path to the shore, in the direction the chalice had gone, except he couldn't abandon Murdoch and his men.

He definitely couldn't abandon Murdoch, whose anger had brought down lightning and killed before. Even if he wished to cause no harm, Murdoch might kill before he could control himself. Ian didn't wish to be an instrument of Murdoch's descent into his own personal hell.

With no place to run or hide, Ian sighed and rode straight into the fray.

The dozen or more militiamen broke line when Ian's staff swung methodically from left to right. He restrained his might, not only because his shoulder still ached, but also so as not to cause broken ribs or heads.

A musket ball ripped dangerously near his ear. He reined Rapscallion around to find the gunman and, with a mightier blow, knocked the weapon from his adversary's hands. It flew across the terrain and slid on a flurry of shale over a cliff.

It was then that Ian fully appreciated the trap in which Murdoch was caught. They fought on the brink of a crumbling cliff, with no visible path downward. How the devil had Pierre carried the chalice this way?

Rather than risk his gallant stallion on the treacherous shale, Ian chose to fight on foot. He let Rapscallion loose, ordering the horse to find a path back to the mares. Murdoch and his two officers had apparently already recognized the danger and released their mounts as well.

The local foot soldiers in their striped sailors' trousers must have used firearms to force Murdoch and his companions to the edge of this precarious precipice. One of Murdoch's royal guards had taken a bullet in the leg, quite possibly in error, given the erratic aim of the muskets.

Somewhere on the narrow shelf of beach below, Pierre raced in a southerly direction, toward the harbor. Not as foolish as he seemed, he'd apparently set his aristocratic father's hired soldiers to stop any pursuit, if Ian was reading their thoughts correctly.

"That was a stupid move," Murdoch complained as Ian spun his staff and daringly stalked toward the soldier blocking the southern edge of the cliff. "You should have left us and gone after the chalice."

"Or waited to see if you've learned to fly?" Ian asked with a touch of exasperation, giving up his target to knock a loaded musket from another man's hands. "I know I haven't. The chalice is down there, on the beach, and I don't see a path."

"You can't read their minds?" Murdoch mocked, lunging at a foot soldier who came too close, sending him scrambling backward at the point of his blade.

"They know the path Pierre has taken, and they're keeping us from it. Beyond that, I cannot tell if it's to the north or south or straight over the edge."

"You take the north, I'll take the south, and my men will take the middle," Murdoch ordered in the French that his mercenaries could understand.

Despite their injuries, the two officers spread out with rapier and sword in hand, but there were three militiamen to each of them. All must die if Murdoch's plan was to work.

"A waterspout might carry us down," Ian suggested, ignoring Murdoch's command and lashing out with his staff at the men on his right. They dodged and feinted and reloaded their muskets.

A waterspout would terrify the natives, but with the chalice slipping from his grasp, Ian was prepared to scare the trousers off them if necessary. Unfortunately, he was only a Sky Rider. Murdoch was the one who could harness the powers of wind and water.

Ian swung his staff and advanced menacingly. He'd lost sense of Pierre's thoughts in the assault of false courage from these brawny men.

"Your control is better than mine," Murdoch asserted in frustration, gesturing for his men to follow him in a show of strength behind Ian. For Ian's ears alone, he spoke in their Aelynn language. "I'd drown us and everyone within a mile. I vote we set fire to the lot."

This was the second time Murdoch had admitted that his abilities were erratic, which meant they must be even more skewed than Ian had supposed. Now he had to worry about not only Murdoch's allegiance, but also the survival of everyone on the cliff.

"And trap us with a wall of flame?" Ian replied blandly so as not to set off his companion's rage. He struck his staff downward, forcing men to leap and jump away from him, but they did not fall so far back as to free him from the cliff's edge. "Charming notion. I'd rather find a way down than burn alive. The men mean no real harm. They're merely hampering our progress."

"Is that all? I thought they meant to push us over the edge," Murdoch said sarcastically, glancing at the sea pounding the rocky shore far below. "Have you looked down? The rock spires along this coast are awe-inspiringly sharp."

Ian snorted at this show of bravado. Even with their ability to run swiftly and leap far, they couldn't soar past jagged stone to the uncertain depths of the sea. "We're no more than curiosities to them." With satisfaction, Ian whacked another musket so accurately that it spun over the cliff. To his left, the less injured mercenary engaged in a swordfight with a crude pike, without evidence of success. "They have no reason to kill us, just keep us from reaching Pierre."

"That doesn't mean I can't kill *them*." Murdoch lunged with superhuman speed and power at his nearest captor, and the soldier collapsed, clasping his shoulder with a cry of pain. "Let them see we're not cowards."

"Angering them is hardly useful," Ian objected as one of the rural militia ran to save his comrade and Murdoch's royal officer discouraged him with a sword. "I can read the heavens or their minds, but I can't force either to go against their nature. You're the one with earth skills. Aside from creating an avalanche to take us down, is there nothing you can do?"

The militiamen milled angrily.

Talking while fighting was second nature to Aelynn men, as was fighting for the sake of fighting, but Aelynners had known peace for thousands of years, so fighting to actually cause harm went against their inclinations. Ian sensed some of Murdoch's tension in doing so. He had to find some way out of this tangle before any of them unwittingly killed a man.

Wielding saber and rapier, Murdoch advanced slowly, pushing southward along the cliff's edge. "Your puling heart would object to a hurricane."

"You would drown Pierre and the chalice," Ian said in growing irritation.

He could feel the cup slipping away, along with his patience. Murdoch would have them embroiled in a real battle if he did not find a better focus for his temper. "Seek their thoughts."

"That's your ability, not mine!" Murdoch slashed his sword in the direction of a soldier aiming his weapon. "To hell with this!"

Fire erupted at the soldier's feet. The earth trembled beneath their boots, sending showers of shale crashing to the rocky beach below.

"*Stop it*, Murdoch, or you'll destroy us!" Even as the words emerged, Ian knew he'd have to act on them—halt Murdoch's explosive reactions before he endangered more than a dozen men.

But the only way to stop an out-of-control Murdoch was to slay him.

As if in protest of his thoughts, a shriek like the wail of ten furies carried over the wind and struck his heart with the force of a blow.

Chantal—in danger, and both afraid and furious.

Her cry pierced Ian's soul. Fear gripped him in a fist so tight that instantly, all his strength, all his talent, poured into one goal—reaching Chantal.

He spun around to face the plateau, and the staff in his hands began to vibrate as raw energy filled him. The ground stopped trembling. Murdoch bent in two and fell to his knees in pain—whether Ian had done that to him or Chantal had was impossible to tell. Ian's entire world narrowed to removing anyone who stood between him and his endangered amacara.

Grabbing one end of his staff with both hands like a cricket bat, he swung the oak with all the power in him, creating a wind of such force that the militia stumbled backward in astonishment. Had he time to think about it, he would have stumbled in surprise as well. He had many minor abilities and could raise a breeze for amusement, but never a hurricane's gale.

His amacara's call was too strong to ponder anomalies. He lashed out again, clearing a passage with the force of his will and the thunderous storm of his staff. Chantal's fear and fury tapped energies deep inside him that he'd long ago locked away. They exploded from their strongbox now, but unlike Murdoch, whose tempestuous anger was erratic and uncontrolled, Ian ruled his ferocity with an iron will, directing it toward a single purpose.

Any militiamen still standing fell over their comrades in their efforts to avoid the lashing of his mighty oak. They stumbled faster once Ian exercised the full fury of his mental forces. He'd never unleashed his abilities to this extent for fear of the damage he'd cause, but Chantal's voice held him steady.

Her screams were closer, more like war cries than panicked shouts. Knowing Chantal better now did not ease Ian's alarm. Her untempered wrath could wreak as much havoc as Murdoch's, perhaps more since she had little knowledge of what she did.

"By the gods, Olympus, you'll rip *all* our heads off!" Murdoch shouted as Ian's staff spun in circles, disarming those who dared rise behind him as well as those in his path.

The warning didn't hold him back. Ian swung his staff with such speed that men who raced to halt him now dropped to the ground to evade his blows. Chantal had released the beast he kept caged inside.

She streaked across the horizon, bareback, her hair streaming like a flag behind her as she aimed—not toward him, but toward the cliff to the north, with half a dozen blue-clad National Guardsmen in pursuit.

In her haste, she was riding directly toward the precarious edge of the cliffs.

Finally free of the trap of armed soldiers, Ian broke into a sprint, running along the cliffside. Until now, he'd not felt the sweat on his brow, but his hope of intercepting Chantal's mad dash pushed him to his limits. He could match the mare's gait, but neither the force of his mind nor the brawn of his muscle could stop animal and rider from bolting over the edge, or falling in a crumbling avalanche of loose shale.

In the back of his mind, Ian was aware that Murdoch might grab this opportunity to chase after the chalice on his own. It no longer mattered. Swinging the staff to send sprawling a soldier who approached from behind, Ian focused, seeking the connection that bound him to his amacara, hoping to warn her of the danger. He was almost there. . . . Just another moment . . .

Her thoughts were clouded with unheeding fury, and the recklessness of her intent nearly brought him to his knees—she thought to save *him*. In desperation, Ian swung around, knocking down two more men. He had no time for indecision. And no time for disobedience.

"Murdoch!" he yelled at his nemesis, who was already halfway down the crumbling rocks to the beach below. When Murdoch only hesitated, Ian channeled his amacara's compelling tones. "Waterspout, Murdoch!" he thundered.

The resulting reverberation forced Murdoch to scramble upward again. "Blast you to Hades, Olympus, I can't control the sea," he cried, but miraculously, he acted upon the command, running along the edge of the precipice to join Ian.

Intent on her goal—a point jutting toward the sea to the north of them—Chantal was merely a furlong away from the precipice, her pursuers an equal distance behind her.

In an age-old ritual of obeisance, Murdoch held out

his sword to Ian's outstretched staff. "You've never done this," he protested. "You'll kill us both."

"Better that I die than live without her. You needn't follow." Ian staggered as Murdoch's erratic power surged into the already pulsating staff. "Now!"

They opened their minds, as they once had as children. Only then, it had been child's play, and Murdoch hadn't needed guidance. Now, Ian had to take the full brunt of the storm, remain standing, and harness the energy in tandem with a man whose mind he no longer knew.

Surging through Murdoch, the force of wind and water slashed into and through Ian, wild and unmanageable, until he channeled his strength through the staff and sword, achieving the center of power that Murdoch desperately sought through a haze of pain.

Together, from that core of strength, they commanded the wind and waves. The air whipped and the tide rose, crashing along the jagged point where Chantal was headed. If they worked swiftly enough, they could catch her, prevent her fall. . . .

At the cliff's edge, Chantal wheeled her horse. Her pursuers hauled on their reins to prevent crashing into her.

To Ian's horror, as the National Guardsmen fought to control their mounts, Chantal's horse reared. For one startled instant, their eyes met.

In that one moment she was there, full of life and roaring her defiance. In the next, she tumbled backward off the horse and disappeared over the cliff, onto the rocks below.

Power and fury swept through Ian to Murdoch. The howling waterspout rose to its full menacing height— too late to save Chantal. With no other alternative, Ian raced to leap into the rising storm to follow her down, not caring whether he lived or died.

Twenty-seven

With a scream, Chantal flung herself free of the horse and tumbled off the edge of the cliff, straight into an unanticipated gale-force wind.

Dying for her cause was not her intent.

She landed on a grassy ledge hidden directly beneath the cliff overhang and hastily grabbed a boulder to keep from being blown into the sea below.

Above her, the mounted soldiers trampled the plateau a distance away, wary of meeting the same fate—not knowing what she had known: that the jut of the cliff hid a grassy area and a clear path down to the water.

Despite the wind, her heart pounded with terror and exhilaration. She could not describe the primitive rush of excitement she felt at outwitting and outriding a troop of trained cavalry. Bruised and filthy, she slid down the muddy path through the rising wind, toward the crashing waves, to duck under an outcropping of rock.

The full impact of Ian's grief abruptly blasted her exhilaration like ignited gunpowder. Panicking, she glanced from beneath the overhang. Where was he?

An unusual blast of wind whipped her skirts and toppled her sideways. Alarmed, she pressed back into the lee of the overhang. Below, the extraordinary wind caught the wild waves and whirled them ever higher.

She blinked in astonishment as a wall of water rose and swirled from the cove.

A waterspout!

Horses pounded the ground above her head, running to escape the dangerous gale. Shouts of alarm echoed over the wind's howl. She prayed frantically as water sprayed across the cliffs, raising fears of Neptune rising from his watery grave. She could think of no other reason for the wind and water to blot out a clear summer day.

Earlier, when she'd been riding, she'd felt Ian's presence in her head, giving her courage. It was as if he were the air current beneath her newly fledged wings. She'd felt invincible when she should have been shaking with terror. Now his agony tore at her heart.

Finding a strong handhold, she peered from her hiding place. Her gaze was drawn to the cliff on her left, where two tall masculine figures raised their weapons in salute to the tempest. Then, to her horror, they deliberately dived off the edge, into the howling maelstrom.

Ian!

The cries escaping her throat matched the silent screams echoing in her heart.

Not Ian, please, Lord, not Ian!

The waterspout sank to the sea as abruptly as it had risen, dragging Ian and Murdoch down with it.

Below, the waves crashed against rocky outcroppings, splintering any debris caught in the sea's deadly grip. The wind died as abruptly as it had arisen.

Releasing her handhold, Chantal fell weeping to her knees. This had to be a nightmare from which she would surely wake. No storm could behave like that.

Ian couldn't be gone. He'd been too vital, too alive, too . . . honorable! She'd scarcely had the opportunity to appreciate all that he was.

Now that she was faced with this sudden black hole in her existence, she was crushed by the realization of how much a part of her he had become. Shaking, sobbing, she knew this was the one death from which she could not recover.

Ian spluttered and shoved his wet hair out of his face as he climbed up on a tumble of boulders battered by crashing waves. The cliffs of this coast were little different from those of his home. He'd never descended them quite so precipitously, but treading deep water and climbing slippery rocks to escape the sea were second nature to him.

Murdoch emerged from the swirling tide a moment later, snarling and whipping his hair back as he, too, climbed onto the rocky platform. Sitting, he yanked at his boots. "You've been practicing diving," he growled. "It's a wonder you didn't split open your fool head."

Ian ignored his companion's complaint. He desperately scanned the bluffs above, looking for tatters of cloth or the broken body of his amacara. She'd thrown herself off a cliff . . . to save *him*. Saving lives was *his* duty. That she'd undertaken it for him . . . He rubbed at his suddenly blurry vision and continued his search.

Moments ago, her voice and mind had filled him with animation, helping him command energies he'd never dared release, opening his eyes to a future far wider than he could possibly have imagined, and now . . .

He couldn't deal with his soul-devastating grief.

His near-fatal dive had forced him to recognize what he should have seen all along: Chantal's spirit, her sincerity, integrity, creativity—her *love*—were her accomplishments. That the chalice had allowed Chantal to obscure its presence meant it *trusted* her. If the chalice was sentient, it had been telling him that it would welcome the shelter of only a man, or woman, of purity and enlightenment.

And he'd been fretting over worldly assets like Chantal's physical gifts and how they would affect him!

And because of his selfish carelessness, he'd lost everything.

Shattered, refusing to believe such life and love could be extinguished so uselessly, he continued to search the rocks towering over them. His mind was blank of everything but what his senses told him.

Oddly, instead of feeling her absence, he felt her heartbroken anguish.

She was alive!

Her mind was fully open, but he could not reach her through the storm of her grief.

Hope soared, but decades of experience had taught Ian to restrain foolish emotion. With Chantal by his side, maybe . . . Someday, please Aelynn, he would dare open his heart again.

"I've not performed the waterspout dive since we were foolhardy youths," Ian replied with only half his mind. He knew better than to ignore Murdoch entirely, but his senses were occupied with searching for Chantal.

For Chantal, he'd learned to coordinate his physical senses with his mental ones, call on his passion as well as his experience. She'd showed him how to be whole again, and he needed her to balance his energies while he continued to learn.

Barefoot and carrying his ruined boots, Murdoch waded through the receding surf to stand beside him. "I'll pull back the waves," he said quietly, with what sounded almost like sympathy. "If she's caught beneath them, perhaps we can still find her."

The tide began an unnaturally swift ebb.

Unable to utter his gratitude for his friend's compassion, Ian shook his head. "No, she's alive. She's
inside my head. I can hear her." He said it with awe.
He heard Chantal. She'd opened herself completely,
and the sorrow pouring from her heart was making
his ache.

Murdoch shook his head. "That's not possible. I saw
her—"

Fearful that he would alert any remaining soldiers,
Ian couldn't shout aloud. Instead, he shouted inside
his head, calling her name, pleading with her to listen.

He'd never begged in his life, but he was begging
now. Without the peaks of Aelynn at his back, he felt
abandoned by his gods, but still, he beseeched them.

And they heard. Just when he was beginning to
think his mind had cracked with grief . . . there, in a
crevasse to his left, the fluttering of moss green fabric.
Without a second thought, Ian began scrambling
across the rocks at the bottom of the cliff, looking for
a path upward.

In that same moment, he heard Chantal's startled
cry of surprise and relief—in his head. He could hear
her; he could see her— His sun would rise again in
the morning!

He felt Chantal's joy the instant she spotted him.
Her tender heart had grieved—for him. It was not an
experience Ian had ever expected, nor was this elation.
Perhaps there was something to be said about giving
way to emotion—it opened whole new paths of
insight.

Chantal half slid, half scrambled down the trail to
the shore. Ian hastened toward the bottom of the path,
climbing over boulders, watching her with a glow on
his face that warmed her all over.

He was drenched head to foot from the surf, but he looked very much alive and unbattered. Admiring his straight back, broad shoulders, and wind-whipped, curling queue of hair, Chantal succumbed to an up-welling of love and desire. She had to admit that no man had ever excited her as he did, might never do so again, and now that the time had come for him to sail away, she didn't want him to leave.

Now that she'd learned what living was really about, she wanted to be with him. Where that might be no longer mattered. The notion terrified and excited her.

Abruptly, she shut out the foolish images in her head.

She wasn't in any position to act on her impossible desires. Her family waited somewhere on the plateau. Ian had not yet intercepted Pierre and reclaimed the chalice, but they had reached the end of the road. The harbor was not far. There, she would be expected to say farewell.

The losses of her mother and grandparents and Jean had left their marks on her. But to lose Ian . . . Ian had been a breath of life. She wanted to spread her wings and fly.

Which was nonsense. She'd only get herself killed. That she even thought in such fantastical terms told her how close she'd come to the edge of madness. She couldn't fly away and leave her home and her family. She loved them too much.

As she loved the man wading through the crashing waves to meet her.

Reaching the pebbly beach where she stood, Ian looked down on her as if she were his moon and stars, and a frisson of pleasure coursed through her. Word-lessly, he hauled her into his arms and kissed her so thoroughly that she was immediately as soaked as he.

Chantal clung to his neck, weeping, and kissed him

back with all the pent-up sorrow, excitement, and longing inside her. It was as if his blood raced through hers, joining them in some inexplicable manner that would be fatal should they be parted. She couldn't bear it.

But they could not stand there with the undertow threatening to carry them out to sea. Reluctantly, Ian set her down.

"Is there some way to the harbor from here?" he asked, jumping to the next topic of importance, proving he was all male and not swamped with the wild swirl of joy and misgivings that crippled her ability to think sensibly.

She no longer heard his shouts of grief in her head, but he held her tightly, as if he could not let her go. He helped her climb over the rocks at the bottom of the cliff, squeezing her waist as if to reassure himself she existed. She clung to him in the same manner. Around the bend, they discovered Murdoch, to their amazement, still waiting on a boulder, looking grumpy and waterlogged.

"I saw you dive into a waterspout," she exclaimed. "I thought you were both dead!"

"Your soldiers would have to burn Ian to kill him," Murdoch growled, rising from his rocky seat. "You're the one who ought to be dead. Can you fly?"

Chantal laughed as he echoed her earlier desire. "No, but this is my home. I've tumbled down these cliffs countless times. I knew there was a ledge and a path there. I'm sure it's the same one Pierre took." She sobered as she glimpsed their faces. "He'll be far ahead of us by now. Those were his father's men delaying you so he could catch a ship."

"We'll find him," Ian said without a shred of doubt, lifting her past a rock covered in sharp barnacles.

With the joy of finding him alive ebbing like the tide with her knowledge that soon she must part from him, Chantal shoved away and fought to return to her feet. She gulped back a sob and tried to remain as coolly rational as he.

"The tide is *out*," she said, swiping at her eyes. "If Pierre was very quick, he's already on a ship in the channel. If there was no ship available, he's still there. We must hurry."

Ian caught the back of her head and pressed a kiss to her brow. "Thank you."

She glared at him and refused to ask for what, not in front of Murdoch. If that was his manner of farewell, fine. She would guard her heart and keep it for her family.

Chantal stalked the familiar beach past the slope of the cliffs. A steep path led down a hill to the low terrain of the river valley. She shook out her muddy skirts, but the men didn't seem in the least concerned about their soaked attire.

"Where are your mercenaries?" she asked Murdoch.

He grimaced and glanced at Ian, who merely lifted his eyebrows in what appeared to be an arrogant challenge.

"I told them to escape any way they could," Murdoch admitted.

The notes in his voice said he did not speak the entire truth, but Chantal had sensed his confused honesty from the first, so she shrugged this off as one more deception. "I ordered the other two to guard the carriage," she told him. "My family will be waiting for me. I must find some way back while you look for Pierre."

"No," Ian stated simply, pulling her down the dusty

path toward the town in the distance. "We will ask after Pierre together, then go back for your family. I won't abandon them."

Murdoch looked at him as if he were crazed but said nothing.

Chantal met Ian's unwavering gaze through eyes blurred with tears of gratitude. He wouldn't sail away immediately? Because of her?

Still, she had to let them know she wasn't entirely without help. "Once Pierre is safely on his way, his father's men will protect Pauline and my father. They're friends of our family."

"I don't suppose you can persuade them to protect us from the National Guard on our heels?" Murdoch asked dryly.

"They aren't trained as well as the guard," she admitted. "I wouldn't wish to see them slaughtered. They might hide us, if we asked."

"After what they saw us do up there, I don't think that's wise," Ian said. "Perhaps they'll all think us dead. Come along, let us find Pierre. I am not leaving you here, and that's final." Ian caught her elbow to help her down the next steep slope of the path.

She wanted to know where he thought he could take her with a troop of soldiers camped in town, but she was too grateful for the reprieve to ask. She wasn't entirely a changed woman yet. She had an even greater fear of death and separation than before, and now it was tearing her apart. To choose between Ian and her family would cleave her in two.

The chalice had all but disappeared from his ability to sense it. Ian knew it had taken sail.

After the terror of almost losing Chantal, the loss did not seem so significant. The chalice would always be somewhere. He could follow it anytime. But he couldn't bear to be parted from Chantal. If she was the gift of plenty that the chalice had granted him, he would not disrespect the bequest by letting any harm come to her.

What she had done on the cliff, the screaming war cry that had paralyzed an army . . . The energy that had surged through him at her screams . . . The way she had called out his rage and directed it safely . . . Their actions surmounted all the knowledge he'd been taught. He knew Trystan claimed he shared some small portion of his amacara's gifts, but Trystan and Mariel were formally bound by Aelynn vows.

Ian thought his connection to Chantal was more visceral than that. He couldn't read her mind as he might others unless she let him, but he'd never uttered a war cry in his life. He hadn't exploded with such fierce passion since his childhood. It was as if she'd burrowed into his heart and unlocked all he'd hidden there, and together, they'd ignited like fireworks.

Keeping a possessive hand on Chantal's shoulder so he would not lose her in the bustling port town of Le Havre, Ian let her choose an inn. She assured them that the owner was a friend of the family and would keep quiet about their presence. Ian used his mental ability to verify this and planted a warning that added urgency to her request. Then he commandeered several rooms.

Murdoch disappeared as he was wont to do. Their bargain was over. Ian would soon have to decide what to do about him. For now, he simply hoped Murdoch was discreetly searching for Pierre in a manner his worldly experience prepared him to do better than Ian could.

Perhaps it was a mistake to let Murdoch go, but the man had saved his life, fought beside him, and shared his mind when he could have run. Underneath the bitterness, Murdoch was still the friend Ian had once known.

"You should follow him," Chantal murmured as if reading his mind, while the innkeeper sorted out their keys. "He cannot be trusted."

"He could have escaped anytime these last hours. Instead, he protected my back. I think he does not trust himself."

She tilted her head as if considering the idea. "I suppose that's possible. He's very confused in some ways. In others, he's extremely determined."

"And how do you know this?" Ian asked in amusement as they followed their host.

"The same way I know you can be trusted, and that our host is loyal to Pauline's family. I read it in your voices." They were murmuring so the innkeeper couldn't hear them, but her answer was defiant.

"Your gift is foreign to me," he acknowledged, "but nonetheless, I find it amazing. You read voices, not minds?"

She shot him a glance so full of hope and disbelief that he almost kissed her right there on the stairs in front of all. Fortunately or not, the space was too narrow for him to reach up to her.

"I have never thought of it like that," she admitted, proceeding upward. "I thought it was something musicians noticed. I cannot tell what people *think,*" she corrected.

"People think a dozen things at a time. That is seldom useful. If you were to read my mind now, you would know that I am watching your wet garments cling to your lovely ankles, while wondering if the bed will be soft, hoping Murdoch returns with information, craving a good dinner, and trying to figure out if I can talk to porpoises. Such a clamor from dozens or hundreds of people around you would quickly drive you mad."

She waited until the innkeeper had shown them their rooms and departed before responding. To his relief, she did not immediately leave for the larger chamber she'd been assigned but remained in the one he'd chosen for himself.

The minute the door closed, she studied his face. "Talk to porpoises?"

He'd said it deliberately. If she could not accept what he was, she would never be happy on Aelynn. And with her apparent gift for causing all who heard her to feel as she did— An unhappy Chantal would be a disaster for his home.

The differences between them weren't as vast as the differences between their two countries. He understood her reluctance to leave the security of the familiar, but he wanted her not only to accept the necessity of leaving, but also to act on it of her own free will.

"I am a foreigner in your land," he said carefully. "I cannot easily explain our differences without showing you where I come from. Where your father comes from."

Stunned, she stared. "My father is from Le Havre."

Ian shook his head patiently. "He is not allowed to speak of it, and since he will not admit his weakness, he won't tell you, but your father was born in my land, and for his health he must return there. I will take you both with me, and you will see for yourself that our gifts are natural."

"My father's home is here," she protested. "He married my mother in Le Havre."

"No, he settled here as a young man. I do not know why he chose to remain. Your mother, perhaps, and then you. It happens that way sometimes. But those were peaceful times, and these are not. I must take you and your family to safety."

"Pauline?" She turned eargerly to him. "If we could take her and the children—"

Ian caressed her cheek and tangled his fingers in the fine hairs that had escaped their pins. "Pauline cannot come with us, *mi ama*. We will see her settled safely wherever Pierre goes. She will want to be with him, someplace where their parents can go when the time comes."

Her thick lashes closed over her beautiful eyes as she recognized the truth in his words. And his voice. A single tear trickled down her cheek.

"You tear me in two."

"I know," he said sadly. "But we are out of time, and I have no choice."

Murdoch had told him that he always had choices, but Murdoch was wrong. Ian's path had been carved from birth. Aelynn was his destiny.

Twenty-eight

With Chantal assuring him that the citizens of her childhood home would not reveal her to the National Guard and could be trusted to quietly fetch the carriage and her family, Ian reluctantly left her at the inn while he went in pursuit of Murdoch. He no longer believed that Murdoch was the reason for the chalice's disappearance or the means of its return. And while he might trust Murdoch's word, he could not trust Murdoch's control over his own powers.

He found his old friend at a tavern, seeking passage to England. Murdoch was highly capable of stealing any of the vessels in the harbor. It was good to know he wasn't a thief—yet.

Ian sat down on the chair beside him and mentally nudged a swarthy sailor from the table. When the sailor was gone, Murdoch shot him a cryptic glare and lifted his mug without speaking.

"Does the chalice show you its purpose here?" Ian inquired, because he had to know if Murdoch's abilities were stronger than his own.

"Obviously, it's here to make amacara matches," Murdoch replied in a voice dripping with scorn. "First Trystan, and now I must congratulate you on yours. She is stronger than she looks."

Ian would have liked to have heard Chantal's translation of Murdoch's tone. Would she hear truth? Perhaps it had been a mistake to leave her behind, but she was exhausted and needed fresh clothing, and he'd wanted a moment alone with his old friend.

Which told him right there that he was no longer capable of killing Murdoch. Something inside him had changed. Ian had spent the better part of his life knowing more than everyone around him, knowing he was right when others were wrong. But his had been a narrow world. And now it was much broader. He did not possess adequate experience or knowledge of this new world to act as judge and executioner.

He was treading in unfamiliar territory, and it was invigorating. He felt fully alive again.

"I can't see past the blood and war that surround Chantal and her family to my own future," Ian admitted.

"That is because the future isn't yet determined. You are not wholly bonded without the altar." Murdoch shrugged this off as obvious. "I, on the other hand, see nothing but blood for years to come. Whether I'm the cause or not may be up to you."

Ian shook his head firmly. "No. Your future lies in your own hands. I can choose to subdue you and take you home. Or I can choose to let you go. What happens either way is decided by your own actions. The Oracle merely addled your powers more, didn't she?"

Murdoch drained his mug and slammed it down on the wooden table. "Perhaps she did me a favor. I could not have restrained the waterspout without your aid. I no longer know what I can or cannot do, and everything has less strength here. Have you noticed that?"

"We draw our strength from Aelynn. Distance would impair it, yes. That's to be expected. In my case, it takes only the confusion of a million voices swirling in my head to diminish my concentration."

"I was never as gifted that way," Murdoch mused.

"The weather here is more turbulent, so there is a different energy to draw on than Aelynn's, but the future is still cloudy."

"Return the chalice to Aelynn, and I believe you will find a different welcome," Ian suggested, the words coming from a place inside him that hadn't existed when he'd left home. Perhaps from the heart that he hadn't known until Chantal had opened it.

Murdoch looked startled. "I doubt that. Dylys would fry the hairs off my head, should she ever see me again."

"She has passed her leadership on to me and Lissandra. We share her duties as well as that of Council Leader between us. The land is failing. Your return with the sacred chalice could make you a hero."

Murdoch shook his head. "No, it is too late for that. I can no longer pretend our world is the only one that matters. You have no need of me there, but they do here."

"They need you to burn villages with Greek fire and help rebels to imprison kings?" Ian asked in disbelief. "I think you have wreaked enough havoc and should have learned your lesson by now."

"I would not have used the fire near Trystan's village had I realized I could no longer control it. And the king's death has already been written in the stars. He chose his own fate by selfishly ignoring reality rather than enacting the necessary changes to help his subjects. How he dies is not my choice. I didn't even intend to kill you. I directed the musket ball to injure in order to force you to heal yourself rather than follow me. I am trying to relearn what I can or can't do without causing harm to others, but it is not easy. I didn't think I could still call on wind and water. Thank you for that. It is difficult to practice without my old friends."

Murdoch's sorrow was buried beneath his usual bravado, but Ian felt it—again, in an unexercised muscle he must call his heart. He'd forgotten until now what it meant to have friends, knowing Murdoch spoke only the truth. They had been brothers, closer to each other than any men on the island, but Ian had never acknowledged Murdoch as anything but a challenge.

"I knew you meant only to wound, just as I could not kill you. But you would have done better not to alienate Trystan," Ian said without sentimentality. Neither of them was accustomed to expressing his feelings, but Ian could grant the gift of understanding.

"Your Crossbreed will teach you what Trystan's wife has taught him," Murdoch warned. "That their people are as important as ours. The Council will not accept her as leader."

"That's an obstacle I will face when I reach it. For now, I need to remove her family from these shores and bring Chantal and her father home with me. The chalice must wait a while longer. I give you a head start in pursuing it." Ian prayed he was making the right choice in choosing Chantal over the chalice. Only time would tell.

Murdoch's eyes lit with fires of hope and challenge. "You will let me go after it?"

"Didn't I just tell you so?" Ian asked dryly. "I thought that was what this conversation was about."

Murdoch pounded him on the back in delight. Ian choked on his drink.

"There must be a stray strain of compassion in your breeding," Murdoch crowed. "No Olympus would ever be so broad-minded."

"No Olympus has ever left the island," Ian reminded him. "Experience is good for us."

"Then set Lissy to packing at once." Murdoch leapt to his feet and started for the door.

"Where the hell do you think you're going?" Ian called after him, hurrying to follow. "I didn't just release you so you can return to playing war. I need your help."

"Of course you do. It's nice to hear you admit it for a change." Cheerfully, Murdoch set out in the direction of the dock.

That was the problem with LeDroit. Give him an inch, and he took the whole rope. Ian grabbed him by the back of the fancy frock coat he'd acquired somewhere in the past hour and hauled him into the air. Ian was still the stronger man—when Murdoch was caught off guard.

The ground beneath their feet trembled. His nemesis still had stronger earth powers, Ian acknowledged, setting Murdoch down before his anger caused an earthquake that might swallow the town. The land settled again, leaving bystanders glancing quizzically around them, possibly recalling myths of giants who made the earth tremble with their rage.

The two men squared off, glaring at each other.

"What is the price of my freedom, then?" Murdoch demanded.

"I am coming to understand that friendship requires sacrifices." Ian stalked toward the water. "Chantal would see me sail away before she would leave her friends or family."

"Then she is an ignorant fool to give up what you can offer her. I do not see the benefit of this sacrifice for friendship."

"Then consider it payment," Ian responded dismissively. "I care not how you label it. I intend to summon Trystan and his ships."

"Trystan would kill me on sight." Murdoch turned a corner, and they reached the end of the road, where a barren strip of shale and sand stretched to the water's edge.

"Which is why you will be gone from here before he arrives. The chalice heads for England. I will hire the next ship out to transport you and Pauline after it. The horses will provide your entry into that world, so take care with them. I expect you to see Pauline and her family safely settled so I may escort Chantal there later to visit. With luck, Pauline's brother will seek her out, and you can retrieve the chalice."

Murdoch raised a derisive eyebrow. "And why should you trust me to do anything more than take the chalice for my own purposes?"

Ian snorted. "I don't. Your ambition precedes you. But try thinking for a change. If you leave Pauline in distress and Chantal discovers it, she will have the power of the entire island—including Lissandra—to come after you with a vengeance. Women are not so lenient as I."

Murdoch's expressive lips pulled into a wicked grin. "I could debate many of those assertions, but I need only point out that Chantal has agreed to none of this, and in fact, isn't likely to. You may not See your future clearly, but I See it without the filter of your denial. She or Dylys will kill each other before they will live together."

"All mothers have difficulty giving up their sons," Ian said without alarm, rather than give Murdoch the pleasure of seeing that he might be right. "Chantal is a peaceful, reasonable creature."

"You say that after those war cries she screeched today? Don't be too certain. Have you discerned her mark yet? She does not have our changeable eyes, so if she possesses Aelynn gifts, she must be a creature created of the gods. Which one does she belong to? I wager it's not the God of Peace."

Ian set his lips grimly. "That is not your concern. Are we agreed, or must we fight this out?"

Murdoch held back a smirk and waved his hand at the ocean. "Be my guest. Show me how you will fetch Trystan. Has the bonehead learned to hear voices in the wind?"

Ian sat on a boulder and tugged off his boots. He had no intention of explaining to Murdoch or anyone else what he was about to do. Diving beneath the waves with the intention of asking a passing dolphin to relay a message to Trystan's wife, Mariel, who could talk with the fishes, to send him a ship hardly seemed the act of a rational man. Nor was it likely to help him maintain the dignity of his position. And yet if by concentrating his psychic gifts he could communicate with the stallion, why not also with the creatures of the sea? Murdoch would no doubt laugh at him, but let him. Bigotry came in all flavors.

Walking into the channel until it was chest deep, Ian plunged under the surf and began to swim.

Chantal woke to the darkness in a large bed. Still groggy, she lay still, seeking the sound that had woken her while reorienting herself to her unfamiliar surroundings.

The bedside candle flamed to life without the spark of a flint. Startled, she blinked, then inhaled sharply.

In drenched breeches and linen, Ian stood beside her. He'd released his thick, curly hair and made some attempt to dry it so it didn't drip on her, but a rivulet of water accented one sharp cheekbone. The rest of his face remained in shadow.

"I feared you had left already," she murmured, reaching for him. After what he'd told her about her

father's origins, she feared many things, but she still
trusted Ian's honesty. If he said his home could heal
her father, she believed him.

He leaned over and kissed her, threading his fingers
through her hair. His kiss was sweet and hot and
blazed with desire, but she sensed that he held back.
She tried wrapping her fingers in his wet linen, but he
merely seared her cheek with his lips and let her tug
his shirt over his head, leaving her holding a damp
rag. The candle gleamed on the wet drops on his chest
hair and wide shoulders.

"Your family's carriage will soon arrive," he announced. "They will need our attention. With luck,
we can sail on the morning tide."

"They're not here yet," she said seductively, sitting
up but not pulling the sheet over her nakedness. She'd
never in her life been so brazen, but she no longer felt
uncomfortable acting so with Ian. Her nipples pearled
boldly under his approving glance.

"I always come to you in stinking disarray." He lit
another candle with the first, and the light emphasized
the breadth of his bronzed shoulders and chest.

"Have you heard me complain?" she asked in
amusement, enjoying the intimacy of the quiet conversation almost as well as his kisses. "You are more
human in dishabille."

He wrapped a leather tie around his hair, his gaze
never straying from her nakedness. "You are a goddess risen from the sea for the sole purpose of providing me pleasure," he said with a straight face, although
his eyes danced with delight.

She chuckled and pulled her knees up to her
breasts, punishing him for not taking advantage of
what she offered. "How much time do we have? And
why am I asking you that as if you'll have an answer?"

He grinned, then turned to wash in the tepid water

in a bowl on the dresser. "I feel like a groom on his wedding night, on the brink of a wondrous new adventure. I think I need the formal vows to push me from my lonely perch into the communal world that you prefer."

Stunned, Chantal could not immediately reply. She sifted through all his words, seeking the sense of them, but heard only his excitement and happiness, and those could be because he would soon be going home. "Vows?" she finally repeated.

Drying himself with a linen towel, he straightened and faced her again. His joyful smile struck her with the force of an arrow through her heart. She thought she might grovel at his feet to see that smile again and again.

"Marriage vows. I'm taking you home to meet my family. When your father recovers his health, he will be there to formalize the legal ceremony. Do I dare ask you now for your consent, or should I wait to show you how much I can offer?"

Chantal tried not to gape, but she thought her chin might have fallen to her chest. "Marry? Men do not marry their lovers. You're supposed to sail away, never to be seen again."

He laughed, tossed aside the towel, and reached for his breeches buttons. He brimmed with the pride of male possession as he approached the bed. "Men marry their *mates*—women who match them in strength and wit. You are mine."

It wasn't just the thrill of his words but the intense satisfaction with which he said them that won Chantal's heart. Without further question, she lifted her arms to accept him into her bed.

And into her life, forever, if such a thing were possible.

No longer shy, she let him explore her as he would,

and they kissed and tasted of each other's flesh until Ian tossed her over to begin on her back.

Chantal quivered as his hands cupped her breasts, and he threw his powerful legs across hers, covering her from behind. She was moist and ready to accept him as he raised her to her knees and stroked her into opening for him.

He was pushing his thick sex into her when she felt his hesitation. She froze at the image rising between them of the strange brown discoloration marring the skin at the base of her spine, a spiral with a broken arrow through it, curving into the crease of her buttocks.

"Chaos," he muttered with disbelief, and what she thought might be horror. "I should have known."

She tried to pull away, but he pushed deep inside until she cried out with the enormity of his filling. Then he bit her shoulder until she shuddered and began to move with him. Their mutual release sang a song to the heavens, but the harmony had already been tarnished.

Twenty-nine

The group of voyagers huddled between crates and barrels on the pier was unusually silent as the morning tide rolled in, carrying with it two sleek sailing ships. The sun gleamed on the flapping white canvas as sailors scampered through the rigging, rolling up the larger sheets and adjusting the smaller to catch the wind.

"Sorry, but they were sailing together," Ian murmured to a scowling Murdoch, who was lounging, arms crossed, against a barrel. "Waylan is less likely to rip your head off than Trystan. I'll load Pauline and the children on his ship while you perform that fascinating invisible act and slip aboard behind them. He can do nothing to you once you're at sea."

"The Weathermaker must have blown the storms off the channel for them to have arrived so swiftly," Murdoch growled.

Murdoch had been irascible all morning, Chantal noted, but his was a tormented soul, and she spared him no concern. Unreasonably, she blamed him for her family's plight. Had Ian not come here in search of him and the damned chalice—

She would never have known true lovemaking. Or learned the thrill of releasing the strength inside herself. Or found someone who understood her so well. So maybe she'd forgive Murdoch, eventually. Especially if

Ian trusted him enough to send him after the chalice so they could take her father home to get well.

She wished Ian had explained his comment about chaos last night. He'd been remarkably uncommunicative ever since.

Despite Ian's surliness, she still felt light enough to fly, so great was the freedom she'd discovered in his company. All her life she'd obediently poured her volatile emotions into her music and let others act for her. Never had she considered acting independently—until Ian.

The same Ian who had been pacing about with a black cloud over his head, constructing their hiding places, ordering people about until they were stumbling over one another to comply. No one questioned his commands, while she stood here with a million questions on the tip of her tongue. Even Pauline had acquiesced to his high-handed demand that she travel with Murdoch to England, and Pauline did not even *know* the man! But Ian was telling Pauline what she wanted to hear—that Murdoch would take her to Pierre and safety—so she'd agreed.

Chantal wanted to scream her protests, but she submerged them in humming as always. Just because she felt free to act didn't mean she was in a position to do so. The blue uniforms of the National Guard were all over town, hunting the "traitors" who had aided the king. Much of Ian's pacing and Murdoch's growling had to do with the tension of hiding everyone in plain sight, among boxes and barrels of cargo. How Ian had known the ships were coming was another of those questions she couldn't ask. All she could do was keep her questions to herself and calm the children.

"This is no way to prove our innocence," Chantal muttered as the tall ships sailed closer.

"The mob is not looking for justice," her father

replied wearily from where he sat propped out of the sun. "They are looking to lay blame. This day would have come sooner or later. D'Olympes do not hold power by being wrong."

Her father's pallor frightened her—another reason she waited here without questioning. Her father needed help, but the best physicians had departed Paris along with half the court. Last night, her father had finally admitted it was time he went home, although neither man would say where that was. If she truly meant to fly free, she'd tell them both to jump off a dock.

But she loved them, so she must restrain herself. Love bound her more thoroughly than her music, confusing her. She'd loved Jean, but in the pragmatic way of a good friend, always seeing reason and able to act on it.

There was nothing reasonable about the sensation of being so much a part of another person that she could not tell where she left off and he began. To part from Ian would be like cutting off her own head.

Last night, after they'd made love and he'd left her to meet the carriage, she'd known he'd stayed away because of her birthmark. And still, she followed him this morning. Love was irrational, and at the moment, she resented it.

As if he heard the confusion inside her head, Ian finally took the time to catch her elbow and drag her deeper into the shadows of the crates where they could not be overheard. "I did not want to have to say this."

His tone struck her with black fear. Eyes widening, she clutched her hands together and waited.

"You have gifts, abilities, that I do not totally comprehend." He held up his hand to stop her from objecting. "Your ability to hear character in voices is a gift of great import. But I cannot judge the significance of your emotional ability to use music and voice as both shield and weapon. The gods granted this gift for reasons I don't comprehend. I hadn't realized the consequences of your emotional gifts until last night."

He hesitated, as if searching for difficult words. Chantal held her breath, feeling her heart bleeding from the puncture wound of his tone. Ian was nothing if not honest, and anguish colored his voice.

As tonelessly as he could, he continued. "Because of your gifts, your unhappiness has the potential to destroy my home. For this reason, I promise that if you are not happy there, I will take you anywhere you wish to go. I simply ask you to bear with me for as long as you are able. Can you do that for me?"

He is not saying farewell. He accepts me as I am, flaws and all.

She covered her mouth with her hand rather than speak her questions. Tears welled, but she nodded her agreement. Ian looked miserable as he brushed his hand over her hair. She understood—if she was not happy in his land, he would send her away, but he would not follow. She was throwing away her home to protect her family, but he could not do the same for her.

A shout from one of the sailors gave warning of trouble, and Ian was gone like a shadow, slipping past her hiding place and into the sun, leaving her shivering with unshed sobs.

She clenched her precious flute in her pocket, understanding nothing at all except that the man who was joined to her heart and soul might cast her off.

The children began to quarrel, and Chantal hastened to rejoin them. She bit her tongue to avoid humming an angry tune. She had to watch herself. She didn't grasp how she could affect others with her voice, but horribly, so far, Ian had been right. She crouched down to speak soothing words that returned smiles to the children's faces.

Murdoch's blade-thin shadow cut across their pocket of safety. He spoke in a neutral monotone to prevent frightening Marie and Anton. "The soldiers are two streets away. We'll load the little ones first."

Chantal closed her eyes and prayed for strength at this parting. With a false smile, she hugged her niece and nephew and kissed their fair brows. "Your mama is waiting for you. Let Monsieur LeDroit show you how a ship sails."

The children eagerly looked to their new friend, apparently sensing none of his reluctance and discomfort. Murdoch muttered for Chantal's ears alone, "Ian is an ass because he was raised that way. Have patience, or leave him rather than kill him. There are others who will help you."

Lifting Marie and holding Anton's hand, he disappeared in a narrow alley between crates, leaving only a shimmering glimmer of air in his wake. Even knowing where he'd gone, Chantal couldn't see him. How did he do that?

Too stunned by his warning and Ian's declaration, she almost let Pauline escape without saying farewell. But she caught a glimpse of her sister-in-law's blue skirt hurrying past Ian's bulk, and she jolted back to the moment.

"I must say good-bye," she said fiercely, practically walking on Ian's boots when he would not let her pass.

"I don't possess Murdoch's talent for disappearing," he said without inflection. "I'll stay with your father. Follow Murdoch. He'll take you to Pauline."

The glance she cast at his stony expression was that

of fear and worry, but she nodded and hastened down the alley of crates in the direction of the tall ships tying up to the pier.

"I take it you are having doubts," Orateur said dryly, muffling his harsh breathing.

"I've arranged for your horses to be shipped on a more suitable vessel," Ian said, as if Orateur had asked. "I'm pleased that your friends have recovered the stallion. They have promised to look after the horses for now. Some of them may be willing to travel with the animals. The Weathermaker has family in England who will stable them until you decide what you want to do."

"They're yours now, and you know it," Orateur said with as much scorn as he could muster. "They go to Chantal when I die. I have land here, and wealth, but it will be worthless if she cannot return to claim it."

"You won't die. You'll live long enough to divide Chantal's loyalties for a long time to come." Ian's troubled anger simmered just below the surface. He'd sacrificed both Murdoch and the chalice for an amacara with the mark of chaos, one who might cause more harm than good for everyone but him. He was being selfish, yet he could not seem to help himself. "I do no one any favors by taking you home."

Orateur's shoulders slumped. "You've seen the mark, then."

"You know what it means?" Ian asked. "Only my family is familiar with the symbols."

Orateur gave a weak snort and glared at him through eyes glazed with pain. "It is a family mark. I bear it as well. Why do you think your mother prevented my marriage? Your family has done its very best to wipe out those who bear the symbol of change."

"That's not so. The gods mark few, that is all." The Lord of Chaos had marked none at all, Ian had believed, until he'd seen Chantal. Even Murdoch had not worn the symbol, although all declared he was a straight descendant of the bastard god of misrule. He wished Orateur would offer solutions to his dilemma, but so far, he'd only confirmed what Ian already feared.

"Then do us both a favor," Orateur said. "Don't let your mother anoint Chantal if you take vows. And unless you trust your sister, I'd recommend that she not see the mark either. I have protected my daughter from the disapproval of your kind all these years. Now it's your turn."

Ian frowned. The symbol of rebellion was troublesome, indeed, but to condemn the person wearing it—

"Nonsense," he said scathingly. "All marks are direct blessings from the gods. You've lived too long with your resentment, and it has twisted your thinking."

As his parents' beliefs were in danger of twisting his, Ian realized. He must keep a clear head, think this through on his own, and not allow his prior prejudice to influence his future.

"I don't resent you or your family," Orateur said. "I am grateful that I was given the opportunity to live in a wider world and raise my daughter in freedom and comfort. I am simply telling you that if you are intent on binding Chantal to you, then her protection becomes your duty."

That much, he already knew. "You may trust me with her life," Ian affirmed coldly. "Do not go filling her head with foolish tales."

"She knows more than I can tell." Orateur relaxed against the crate. "Perhaps Aelynn matches her with an Olympus for good reason. Your family resists change elsewise."

Achieving her father's approval was a mixed blessing, indeed, Ian decided.

Chantal reappeared, her tear-stained face speaking her heartbreak at this parting. In that moment, Ian suffered her grief and wished he could return the lovely bubble of happiness she'd lost, apparently because of him. Despite his concern for their future, he was thoroughly grateful that she had not taken the opportunity to run away with Pauline.

Distracting both of them, a towering golden god shivered the planks of the dock beyond their narrow hiding place. He halted, and his shadow blocked the morning light creeping between the cracks. "Do I just haul the crates into the hold without question, or will our fearless leader step out of hiding and introduce his new playmates?"

Ian was almost grateful for this reprieve from his turbulent thoughts. He rolled his eyes and glanced apologetically to Chantal and her father. "Trystan is a doltish clod, and an acquired taste. Pardon me while I remind him of his manners."

He had need to vent his pent-up frustration. Without staff or sword, or even fist, Ian smashed the force of his mind and the wind against the broad target of Trystan's chest, staggering him backward. Then he mentally tugged his feet out from under him.

The golden giant toppled like a fallen oak, crashing to the weathered planks and shaking the crates around them.

Ian stepped from the shadows to straddle Trystan's long legs and drop the end of his staff dangerously near his crotch. As anticipated, the oaf grinned back at him, sat up, and grabbed the end of the staff in a movement so swift that none other than Ian could see him. A tussle with an Aelynner of greater strength, someone against whom he didn't have to restrain himself, was exactly what Ian needed just then.

Trystan's attempt to leverage the staff into tumbling Ian to the dock failed as Ian spun the oak out of his reach. Calmer now, he resisted pounding the Guardian's head. "More respect, please," he commanded politely. "My amacara and her father await, and I would not have them think you are a buffoon."

Rising, Trystan lowered his hand dangerously near the hilt of his sword, but the competitive spirit of Aelynn men that caused them to fall into battle at the drop of an insult did not usually extend to Ian. The Guardian hesitated just long enough for Ian to mentally nudge his hand from the weapon.

"You still fight dirty," Trystan acknowledged with a nod. "But Mariel will be displeased should I shame you in front of guests. She is eager to know how you sent your message."

"I hoped she would be sailing with you." Aware that Chantal could hear all they said, Ian kept his words neutral so as not to arouse her fear. "We'll talk later. There are soldiers hurrying this way as we speak. I do not wish to disturb them any more than is necessary. If you have men strong enough to carry the crates, we'll transport our passengers on board in them."

Trystan glanced toward the town. "I'd advise you to find a hiding place as well. They have an arsenal." He glanced back at Ian's monk's garb. "And you are a tempting target."

"I go nowhere until the others are safe." Ian spoke without turning around. "Chantal, if you and your father will enter the containers, I will see you on board."

"*Bonjour*, Monsieur Trystan, it is a pleasure to meet you," she whispered tauntingly from behind him. "Good manners are seldom out of place."

Ian bit back a smile. It was good to know Chantal kept her sense of humor in even the most trying circumstances. "She is a lady," Ian explained. "Someday, you must teach me the meaning of *etiquette*."

Trystan grunted. "Someday, I must teach you the meaning of common sense. You are not lord over all you survey here." He nodded toward the half dozen blue-coated soldiers hastening toward the dock, sabers drawn, bayonets at the ready. "Even you are not invulnerable to cold steel."

"I know. I find the challenge fascinating." Twirling his dangerous staff into a blur that hid the people behind him, Ian faced the soldiers who had dared earlier to chase Chantal off a cliff.

They did not look pleased to see him. And he was feeling just mean enough this morning to welcome a bloody brawl.

Thirty

S till weeping at the loss of Pauline and the children, the home she knew and loved, for a man who did not know what to do with her, Chantal almost preferred to cower in the narrow crate. She knew nothing of ships or the men on them or even the unknown country to which Ian was taking them. When the crate was opened, and she stumbled out into the lantern-lit hold of a ship to meet the welcoming smile of another woman, she nearly toppled in short-lived relief.

The tall, dark-haired beauty greeted her with open arms and evident delight. "Are you the one who talks to dolphins?"

Chantal should have known Ian's friends would be as eccentric as he was. "I do not swim, so I hope I have no cause to speak with fish," she replied as politely as she could, shaking out her skirts and surreptitiously studying her surroundings.

Ian was nowhere in sight. Neither was the blond giant. Or anyone she knew. Pain clenched at her heart at the reminder that Pauline and the children wouldn't be stepping out of similar crates. They were in another ship, sailing to distant shores.

She stifled the anguish and bounced a curtsy to her hostess as a sailor pried loose her father's box. "If you will excuse me, my father"—she gestured as the crate opened—"he is ill."

Dismissing her earlier question, the stranger hurriedly replied, "Oh my, yes, of course!" Dark gown rustling, she hurried to lift the wooden lid. "You must call me Mariel, please. As you may have noticed, we do not rest on formality. It seems a trifle foolish given the circumstances."

Standing in a smelly, dark ship's hold, Chantal had to agree. She held out her arms as her father rose from his hiding place, but he was so weak, she staggered under his weight. The sailor stepped up to offer assistance.

"I'm Chantal, and this is my father, Alain Orateur. Is there somewhere . . . ?"

Mariel was already hurrying toward the stairs. "This way. This is a small ship, with only one cabin. We do not have far to go." She held up the lantern at the bottom of the ladderlike stairs. "It is a pleasure to meet you both. I am eager to make the acquaintance of another Crossbreed. You cannot know how exciting this is for me!"

With that remarkable statement, she ushered them ahead of her.

The stairs led to the living quarters below the main deck. The floor bobbed beneath Chantal's feet, and she could hear a clash of steel that sounded like fighting coming from above her head.

Fear wrenched her stomach, but her companions didn't seem concerned. Aside from Mariel and the sailor, no one was around to watch them navigate the trestle table and hammocks of the crew.

"What is happening?" Chantal whispered worriedly as they reached the door of the captain's cabin in the stern.

As the sailor helped the invalid into a bed inside the cabin, Mariel glanced upward at the shouts and clanking of chains. "Not as much as you fear. I don't know how well Ian does in this world, but Trystan is a diplomat. They will be fine."

As far as Chantal understood, there was only one world, and they were in it, but again, she held her tongue, afraid of the damage she might do should she unleash her voice in her current state of near hysteria.

She slipped into the cabin to hold her father's hand. To her surprise, two toddlers, both younger than Marie, played quietly under the doting eye of a slender young man.

"This is Hans. He's a healer." Mariel indicated the young man before swooping up the golden-haired girl who ran to catch her skirts. "Monsieur Orateur, if you will allow Hans . . . ?"

Despite the pain in his chest, Chantal's father observed the cabin's occupants with interest. He nodded at Hans. "Helen is your mother? You look just like her. She healed my broken arm when she was about your age."

The lad looked pleased. "She is, indeed. She works mostly with women these days, so she was happy I could take on some of her duties."

Chantal nearly bit her tongue in two at this confirmation that her father came from Ian's "world." As a child, she'd asked why her father didn't have parents like her adored maternal grandparents, but he'd merely said they were "gone." Later, she'd assumed that was a euphemism for dead. She'd worn blinders and assumed a great deal for many years, apparently.

Her father turned to Mariel. "I would not put your family out. I would be fine in the main cabin."

"Nonsense," Mariel said. "If I am understanding correctly, you are a man of rank and should be treated as such. My hooligans are more familiar with this ship than their own beds. Come along, Davide. Papa will join us shortly. Let us be ready for him."

Too confused and worried to absorb all this, Chantal followed Mariel and the children so Hans could visit privately with her father. With hair the gleaming ebony of his mother's, the little boy strutted over to a trunk, withdrew a wooden sword, and, holding it in battle stance, waited at the foot of the gangway.

Not to be outdone, the golden-haired cherub in Mariel's arms scampered down and did the same. Grasping tiny sword hilts, they both adopted fierce expressions and waited patiently for their father's arrival.

"I objected to the swords," Mariel said with a mother's sigh, taking a seat on a bench. "But Trystan said it was in the blood, and we could not resist it. Although I think even he was a little startled when Danaë insisted on having her own weapon." Mariel's smile was as proud as it was rueful. "My sister's daughter is nearly a year older, and she is terrified of them."

Chantal's heart melted at the sight of the two adorable toddlers. Would she ever have a child of her own? She had never worried about it while she had her niece and nephew to spoil, but now . . . if she married Ian . . . A rush of need and desire swept through her, and she had to clench her hands in her lap to hide it. He'd asked her to marry him, but then said he'd send her away. She did not know where she stood with him.

"They are beautiful, and so precocious," she said with genuine admiration. "Are they the same age?"

"Twins, a year old this past March," Mariel acknowledged, "although it's hard to tell they're brother and sister, they look so different. I had hoped one of them would take after me, but they are both determined to be Guardians. I can't blame them when they see their father conjure up an island and glow like the sun. My accomplishments as a mere mermaid must seem a puny thing after that."

Chantal's throat closed, and she didn't know what to say to this casual narrative of incredible deeds. Mariel's French was spoken in an unpolished Breton accent, a far different tongue from Chantal's aristocratic, Parisian French. Perhaps she misunderstood.

The shouts above became heated, and heavy heels pounded the planks. Canvas snapped as if caught in a strong wind, and Chantal half expected to hear a deluge of rain, although the skies had been clear. She glanced toward the stairs, instinctively starting to rise.

Mariel caught her hand to the table. "Don't. You won't see anything, and the children will want to follow you."

"I really wish someone would explain," Chantal complained, feeling her breath constrict in her lungs as the ship rocked with more force. At least she heard no musket fire.

"They are allowed to cause no harm except in defense of themselves and their families. They have the ability to slaughter armies, but spilling blood tends to make one unwelcome, so it's avoided. You never told me if you were the one who sent the message that we were needed. I've been told I'm impulsive, so I've been trying to be patient."

"I can't send messages to ships," Chantal murmured, still listening to the sounds above and marveling at the stillness of the two fierce toddlers. She didn't understand the question well enough to do more than answer plainly. "Perhaps if I had a carrier pigeon . . ."

"How odd. If you can't talk to dolphins, then who can? Your father? He did not look well enough to swim in the channel."

The image of Ian dripping wet, standing over her bed, appeared in her mind's eye. He'd been swimming in the middle of the night—in the sea.

"Dolphins can't talk," she asserted, although she no longer had confidence in anything she once thought she knew.

"Not the way we do, admittedly. They emit a series of squeals and high-pitched noises that would be difficult to learn if their vocabularies weren't so limited."

Chantal swung her dazed gaze to the seemingly normal woman sitting across from her. Mariel appeared to be close to Chantal's age, and wore an ordinary gown that might be outdated by Paris standards, but it wasn't worn backward or fastened crazily like a madwoman's.

Only—Chantal hesitated as she met her hostess's eyes. Hadn't they been a lovely clear turquoise a moment ago? Now they darkened to changeable shades of midnight . . . just like Ian's.

"You received a message from a dolphin?" she asked faintly.

Mariel studied her with uncertainty and didn't reply as openly as before. "I thought you were Ian's amacara. If I am wrong . . . Perhaps I ought to wait to explain until they return."

"Perhaps," Chantal agreed quietly.

"You did not even allow me to draw my sword," Trystan grumbled as they stood beneath canvas cracking in the stiff wind and watched the blue uniforms of the National Guard marching away. "It would have been in defense and perfectly legal."

Ian had been the one to wield his staff, and his mental abilities, to drive the soldiers back. There had been a few protests, a few swords drawn and fists thrown, but all in all, they'd escaped with little more than bruises and bad feelings.

Yet Ian was still itching for a fight. And the reason waited below.

"This land will see enough bloodshed in the years to come without our adding to it," he replied. "Should we need to return here, it's better that we leave the inhabitants confused rather than dead. I wish we all had Murdoch's trick for invisibility."

"Invisibility!" Trystan's golden brown eyebrows shot up. "You've seen Murdoch? Or should I say, *not* seen him, if he's learned invisibility?"

Ian glanced to Waylan's ship in the distance, lifting sail, fighting the channel's tide. The Weathermaker would be working the wind to allow both ships to leave the harbor before the French soldiers changed their minds and came after them. "With any luck, Murdoch is aboard the *Destiny,* where Waylan can keep an eye on him."

Trystan stilled and watched Ian guardedly. "You let him go?"

Turning away from the dock, Ian twirled his oak and watched the canvas unfurl. "Perhaps it is best if we do not mention this at home. Not yet, not until the future becomes more clear."

"He was once my friend, too," Trystan reminded him. "That he's still alive speaks well of your patience."

Ian laughed and took delight in doing so. How incredible that even in these trying circumstances, thanks to Chantal's effect on him, he could laugh. "I think it speaks well of my amacara. When she is happy, she surrounds me with peace and joy. Come, you must meet her." He started down the deck to the gangway.

"What happens if she's not happy?" Trystan asked with interest.

"Given that she was weeping when I left her, you are about to find out." And still, Ian didn't hesitate in his eagerness to see how Chantal had fared. Even her tempers were endlessly fascinating to him. He supposed he ought to hope his enthrallment wore off soon or he would never accomplish anything, but the experience was far too new to surrender it easily.

"Best let me go down first," Trystan said apologetically, brushing Ian aside.

As they climbed down the gangway, two fierce toddlers swarmed up the stairs to attack Trystan's ankles. Barely able to balance on their feet, they shrieked as if their cries could topple him, and waved their swords in a manner destined to send them tumbling backward.

Ian watched in amusement as Trystan laughingly conquered the toddlers, scooping up both children and carrying them into the cabin where the women waited.

"They are certain to trip and break the necks of any pirate," Trystan crowed, leaning over to kiss Mariel's brow. "Do you think we might make the next one a docile sailmaker?"

Ian noticed that neither woman was smiling with her eyes, although they both gazed fondly at the children. *Children.* That should be his purpose—creating a better world for the children. It would be easier to remember that if he had one of his own.

Ian didn't feel comfortable displaying his weakness by kissing Chantal in front of Trystan and Mariel. He and the Guardian had grown up together, but they'd always been aware of their unequal ranks and position. Since Trystan had once aspired to the hand of Ian's sister, their relationship had often been more combative than comfortable.

"Monsieur Orateur is with Hans," Mariel said, taking Danaë from her husband but glaring at Ian. "Perhaps you would care to clarify what's happening before I say anything else that I shouldn't? Keep in mind that I'm new at keeping your secrets."

"Your ring will prevent your saying more than you should. I hope," Ian added, since too many of his preconceived notions had been shattered lately. "What secrets were you revealing?"

"Perhaps you would care to start by telling me where we are going?" Chantal asked in modulated tones, saving Mariel from having to reply.

"I would rather show our friends your ability to spread cheer," he said dryly. "Why not choose a subject less apt to create chaos?"

"Chaos?" Trystan asked. For a blockheaded Guardian, he was amazingly perceptive. "I thought Murdoch was our Lord of Misrule."

"There is no such thing as a Lord of Misrule, only harbingers of change." Ian had spent the night trying to convince himself of this notion to justify bringing the Orateurs to Aelynn. "Chantal's father is an Orator. Her abilities are different. We have yet to explore them fully."

"Who sent the porpoise message?" Mariel demanded, cutting through his obfuscations.

"I did," Ian admitted. "It seemed reasonable to believe that if I have some small part of everyone's abilities, I should share yours as well. I have never been drawn to the sea, but it was an enlightening experience."

"You talk to dolphins?" Chantal asked, shielding her heart and using her pleasant voice.

Hearing the turbulence she hid from the others, Ian took her hand and lifted her from the bench. "We have sworn the vows of amacara to each other, but we have not yet done so before the gods. Until you wear my ring, it is difficult for us to speak of our home. You have said that you trust me. Will you take my word that all is well and will be explained shortly?"

To his relief, she seemed to consider his promise without protest. Rising on her toes, she pressed a charming kiss to his cheek before releasing his hand and stepping away.

"Of course, my love," she said sweetly. "If you will understand that I sleep alone until all is explained to my satisfaction."

Sweeping back her bedraggled skirt as if it were the silk and lace of a princess, she sashayed to the cabin where her father rested and quietly but firmly shut the door between them.

A moment later, she played a note on her flute, and the glass of the hanging lantern above Ian's head shattered.

Thirty-one

"If you would come with me, I'd like to show you the passage to my home." Ian stood diffidently outside the open door to the cabin where Chantal sat by her father's bedside.

She glanced up to see him in the garb he'd worn since they'd set sail. He'd discarded his robe, boots, and cravat, and now wore only breeches and an open-necked linen shirt. At least he had not cut the sleeves off his shirt like many of the sailors had. He looked so delectable just as he was that she wanted to lick the brown V of skin revealed by the open neckline. She did not dare look at his bare toes without thinking she could start there. . . .

Apparently the savages of his country thought nothing of going bare legged and barefoot. When she had joined the others for meals, Chantal had done her best not to stare at all the muscular masculinity barely concealed by thin linen, but she was feeling decidedly like a fish out of water. No wonder her elegant father had preferred the civilization of France and had not mentioned his barbarous background.

Only the music of her flute had kept her calm. She blessed Ian for the thoughtful gift every time she played. And cursed him whenever she did not.

In deference to the heat and humidity and the difficulty of navigating the narrow stairs of the companion-way, she wore a frock without petticoats as Mariel did.

But her stockings clung to her legs, and she wished she dared go barefoot, too.

She swallowed the lump of fear that had been with her since the ship cast off, and followed Ian into the main cabin. "We are there?" she asked with some trepidation. At least they had not sailed an ocean away from France.

"Almost. But you need to be at a distance to appreciate the full effect. Trystan is already pacing the bow. He feels it first."

She'd promised not to ask questions until he was free to explain. She didn't understand, but despite her fears and worries, she vibrated with eagerness to see the world he called his own.

"Try not to burst with impatience," he said with laughter as she ran up the companionway. "I would try to answer all your questions now, but your fears may sink the ship before I'm done."

"I can't sink ships." On deck, she glanced around with disappointment. She could barely see the dawn through the fog drifting over the water. No land was in sight. "You exaggerate."

"Possibly," he admitted. "Since you have no training, you do not truly understand what you're capable of, but I think you have a natural capacity to keep your passion tightly reined. 'Tis a pity you were not around to teach Murdoch such control. But I know you have driven even me to actions I cannot explain, so your effect on others would be multiplied."

"As usual, you raise more questions than you answer," she complained, leaning on the rail and watching the dolphins that followed the ship. Just standing alone beside Ian with her hair blowing free in the wind was exciting. If she did not have so many questions and concerns, she could learn to enjoy this adventure. "That we cannot stay in the same room without thinking of lovemaking may be obsessive, but I can swear I do not have that effect on anyone else."

"Thank the gods for that," he said fervently. "Admittedly, it is difficult for me to know whether I made love to you the first time because your voice called me to you or because you're my destined mate or if they are the same thing. But our physical attraction has nothing to do with my need to slay everyone in sight when you're afraid, or my berserk behavior when I thought you were about to ride your horse over a cliff. I am a man of peace, but your war cries struck chords in me that could have led entire armies to battle."

"That's still obsession," she scoffed. "I loved your chalice as much or more than my piano. But I gave it up for Pauline because I loved her more. Sometimes, we act against our best interests for those we love. Since you don't know me well enough to love me, you must be obsessed."

The fog thickened, but Chantal thought she saw black cliffs or tall boulders looming straight ahead. She prayed the ship's captain knew what he was doing or they would wreck very messily on those craggy rocks. Any normal captain would be frantically ordering the sails reversed to escape this death trap.

"I am not certain I grasp the concept of love," Ian admitted. "I cannot separate it from my physical need to be with my amacara. But I think neither would affect an inanimate object like my staff. And yet it vibrated when I thought you were in trouble."

"People can accomplish extraordinary things when they are frightened for their loved ones," she replied with careful nonchalance. He'd said he didn't know if he loved her, which was somewhat better than saying he was *certain* he didn't. He'd shattered her fledgling hopes days ago, but now Chantal heard notes in his voice that offered hope. "I knew a man once who lifted an overturned carriage to release his family inside. Once they were free, he could not ever lift it again, no matter how hard he tried."

"Your war cries stopped Murdoch in his tracks," he reminded her with a hint of humor. "That alone saved lives, since he'd become so angry that he made the earth quake."

She slanted him a look of disbelief. "Men don't make the earth quake. Your explanations are no better than the hallucinations of those who suffer from opium dreams."

His smile was so devastating that he made *her* earth quake, and she had to grab the rail to prevent herself from falling. She wanted to kiss him, but she was aware of Trystan in the bow not yards away. And sailors scurried through the rigging, no doubt watching their every move.

"I do not need to artificially alter my mind," Ian assured her. "My world already possesses more wonders than opium dreams, more than a man of science or blind faith can explain. The time has come for me to introduce you to my home. I hope that, in some way, you will help me understand those things that puzzle me."

"Like etiquette?" she asked tartly, unable to express her confusion elsewise.

He leaned over to kiss her cheek. "That, too. Now, watch Trystan." Standing behind her so that she could feel the length of him shielding her from the wind, he turned her chin so she faced Trystan in the bow and the ominous black rocks looming through the thick fog.

"He is our island's Guardian," he explained. "The volcano we call Aelynn—after our most powerful god—heats the waters and raises the fog that renders

our land invisible. Trystan creates the barrier that prevents all but the fish in the sea and the birds high in
the sky from entering these straits. Only Aelynners
may pass these waters. The vows we spoke bind you
to me so that you can cross the barrier, but Pauline
could not. She is not one of us. Your father is, and
thus, so are you, almost."

None of this made sense to Chantal, so she remained quiet, watching for this oddity that would
allow her in but keep Pauline out. She did not understand what vows she may have exchanged with Ian
other than those they'd made with their bodies, but
she was willing to believe those were strong enough
to create miracles.

The fog silenced even the cries of the gulls. They
sailed so close to the walls of the narrow strait that
Chantal thought she could reach out and scrape her
knuckles. But Trystan remained in the bow, his fists
clamped around the railing, his golden hair blowing in
the wind like that of some fierce god.

Then he straightened and raised his bare arms, and
a gleam of light struck the strange bands he wore on
his upper arms. It was a primitive gesture that shook
Chantal to her shoes. Ian wrapped his arms around
her waist and pulled her back against him.

The glow brightened, streaming down Trystan's
arms and chest, until in an instant, he gleamed like a
golden statue. The fog parted with an oddly colorful
shimmer, and the ship sailed out of the gloomy channel into a sunny bay that had been invisible just moments before.

Chantal gasped as an emerald island spread across
the horizon. A volcanic peak smoked lazily into a distant cloud. Gentle waves lapped against crystalline black
sand beaches. Strange trees dipped their fronds in a soft
breeze. The rich floral scents of exotic gardenias and

jasmine perfumed the air. Not since she'd been invited to walk through the king's orangerie had she inhaled such a marvelous fragrance.

She leaned back in Ian's embrace, and he hugged her tighter. If this was the world he'd brought her to, she heartily approved.

"Quite a sight, isn't it?" her father asked from behind them.

Chantal whirled around. Ian stood broad and tall behind her, with one hand remaining at her waist, keeping her close. She was grateful for his steadying influence.

Her father looked better already. Color had returned to his beard-stubbled cheeks. He had always kept what remained of his hair cropped short for comfort under his wigs, but the dark blond strands had turned an iron gray over the years. The brilliant sun revealed wrinkles and deep creases in his face that she'd not noticed until now. But his eyes gleamed in appreciation of the view.

"We should have traveled more often," she said softly. "The islands of the Caribbean are also said to be magical."

"In their own way," her father agreed. "I saw them as a lonely youth, learned their music and customs, but they could not match Aelynn. I had not realized how very much I missed her."

"You will overcome that impression momentarily," Ian said in a dry tone that caused Chantal to glance up at him.

He'd shaved closely that morning, and pulled his unruly hair into a tight knot bound by leather. But barelegged, with his loose shirt blowing in the breeze, he still appeared a pirate, especially when he scowled toward the shore.

Cautiously, she studied the people waiting there as

the ship prepared to dock. If this was to be her new home—even temporarily—she must learn the ways of its inhabitants. At least she did not feel underdressed for meeting Ian's family. The men on shore wore little more than Ian did, and the women were wrapped in what appeared to be linen sheets.

"Am I allowed questions yet?" She could not keep the mockery from her voice. Ian had shown her the marvel of freedom, then imposed limits on the one strength she possessed.

"You may do as you wish," Ian whispered against her ear, "but it might be safer and better for our future if we wait until we reach the grotto where no one may disturb us. And with luck, we cannot disturb others. There is a hot spring there we can enjoy."

His tone spoke of steaming waters and lovemaking and shivered down Chantal's spine. For a sensual promise like that, she might manage to hold her tongue—just barely.

"I assume that's your mother in white," her father said, in a note bordering on dread. "I thought she would be too busy to greet us."

Her father had once single-handedly brought an unruly Assembly into order. Angry aristocrats, clergy, lawyers, and merchants alike had bowed to his wise oratory. Why would he fear Ian's mother?

"She does not normally meet ships, but she fears for our future," Ian responded. "I do not always abide by her wishes, which causes her greater fear."

He spoke of his mother with fondness and respect. Chantal studied the older woman dressed in flowing white robes. She had high cheekbones, and silver hair caught in a long braid from which wisps as unruly as Ian's escaped. She stood straight and proud, slightly apart from the fair-haired woman on her left, who also bore a striking resemblance to Ian—his sister, no

doubt. Chantal doubted that his family expected Ian
to return with a fiancée. She shivered nervously.

Mariel joined them. "Council members," she murmured, explaining the men on the shore. "They're
waiting for the chalice and Murdoch. What happens
now?"

Ian's jaw muscles tightened, and Chantal sent him
a look of concern. She had not comprehended the
importance of his task—or its failure.

"Nothing happens," he claimed. "They wait until I
am ready to pursue them again."

The studious Ian she knew was disappearing behind
a haughty shield of arrogance. Gone, too, was the
sober monk and the seductive lover. In his place was
an implacable authority who ruled his world.

She recognized the truth of her shocking revelation
without need of proof. She heard it in the gravity of
his voice, finally recognized it in the deference of the
crew, who kept their distance, even acknowledged her
father's behavior in his presence. The man she loved
had the power of royalty in his home.

She recalled Murdoch's insulting tones when he'd
called Ian a prince. That Ian used no titles did not
mean he lacked nobility or power.

She despised men of rank who wielded their influence as if they were gods and no man was their equal.

Surely, not Ian—

Yet he'd just said the Council would have to wait
until *he* was ready to finish his tasks. That was like
the king telling the Assembly that he wouldn't accept
their terms—thinking he was a law unto himself, without any consideration of his effect on others.

Chantal stared at the shore in horror. What in the
name of heaven had she done?

Thirty-two

Ian barely noticed Chantal stiffening beneath his hands. That he arrived home with his amacara instead of the Chalice of Plenty or Murdoch was a slap in the face to everyone who relied on him. He regretted that, but he refused to regret his decision. If he was being selfish in following the stars and choosing Chantal over the chalice, then so be it.

"Mariel, take the children off first, please," he requested as Trystan leapt to the pier to tie the ship in place. "Then you can take them home without their witnessing adult quarrels."

Mariel snorted lightly. "And I was so looking forward to the fireworks." She reached over and squeezed Chantal's hand. "The Oracle is terrifying in her ability, but keep in mind she is still a mother, and Ian is her pet. Not that he looks like one," she granted, glancing at Ian's square jaw, "unless one thinks of panthers as pets."

Chantal managed a weak smile. "Haven't you heard? Ian claims I tame wild beasts."

Mariel's laughter trilled the air. "Then you ought to do just fine."

"Tame them and *rile* them," Ian corrected, keeping his hand firmly on her waist. He nodded at her father, who leaned against the rail, scanning the shore. "Orateur, would you like to go down with us, or do you prefer to disembark quietly with the crew?"

"Unless Dylys knows I'm here, it might be preferable for me to keep a discreet distance. I'll only exacerbate the situation."

Ian agreed. Bringing a potential Lord of Chaos onshore in accompaniment with his equally marked daughter could cause a riot. One obstacle at a time. At least no one knew Chantal's origins. Yet.

"Besides, I left a fine set of drums here after one of my voyages," Orateur continued. "If they haven't fallen apart, I would like to find them before the shouting begins."

Ian wasn't about to ask what he wanted with them, not now. There hadn't been music on Aelynn in his lifetime, but he supposed the talent could have departed with the Orateurs. He took Chantal's hand and led her toward the gangplank. She was such a whirl of emotions that they spilled past her usual serenity and into his heart. He did not have her efficient means of calming them. "You're not humming," he noted, wishing she would.

"You would risk toppling mountains with my voice?" she asked with sarcasm.

"I was thinking your humming might calm stormy waters, but maybe not." He squeezed her hand reassuringly. "Are you familiar with Shakespeare's plays?"

She shook her head, startled from her anxiety by his question, as he intended.

"I studied some in my youth. He often wrote about strong-willed women who accept no one's authority. Think of my mother in those terms, and you see the task we face."

"Like Marie Antoinette, who thinks herself above the king?" she asked derisively.

"Not even close." He squeezed her hand again, and amazingly, her apprehension seemed to settle another notch. "Your queen is weak, with little influence over anyone, including herself. Dylys Olympus has complete and total dominion over everything in sight, in ways you cannot fathom. She is the one who shattered a man as formidable as Murdoch and banished him from home. Only her wisdom prevents her from becoming dictator and keeps her power in check."

"Like the queen in a game of chess," she said coldly. "I never was good at games."

Nevertheless, Chantal followed him from the ship with her head held high. She might not understand the power struggle they faced, but instinctively, she prepared for it. Ian appreciated his mate's courage.

He knew his mother would not surrender her rank gracefully, especially to a Crossbreed, and particularly to an Orateur. He did not need the etiquette of explaining to her that Chantal was his amacara. He had declared his intentions by bringing Chantal home instead of leaving her in the Other World. The only question remaining was the legal one of marriage, and that had to be decided by the Council, since his wife traditionally became their Leader.

His family behaved politely while Ian introduced Chantal, using her married name to avoid the conflict over her father for now. His mother and sister weren't the warmest people on the island. From his own experience, he knew decades of bearing responsibility for an entire demanding race had taken a toll on their sympathies. He hoped Chantal understood that in the same mysterious way she had trusted him from the first.

"Your amacara does not have Aelynn eyes," his mother declared as her opening volley the moment the introductions were complete. "She is at least a Crossbreed, is she not?"

"I am a French woman and an Orateur," Chantal replied, revealing her dangerous identity before Ian could deflect the question. "Not a cross anything. Bigotry carries an unpleasant note that grates on my ears, so you cannot hide it."

Now that his queen had knocked all the chess pieces flat, Ian studied Aelynn's peak for signs of an impending explosion.

Dylys froze, and someone behind them gasped in shock. Ian squeezed Chantal's hand in warning, but her mental barriers were as strong as his family's, preventing him from nudging any of them to peace.

"Can you hear honesty as I do?" Chantal continued conversationally, as if she hadn't just offended an Oracle of the gods. "Ian sometimes hears things others can't, but I think he would have told me if he heard your deception."

"A Crossbreed is merely someone who has only one Aelynn parent," Ian explained in the resulting silence. "It is not an insult."

Chantal's long lashes swept upward and her silver-blue eyes turned to frozen tundra. "To your mother, it is. Her voice screams with dismay and fear and desperation. Despite what you've told me, I think your queen may suffer the same dislike and fear of those who are different from her as mine does. It is a universal hazard for those who isolate themselves."

Quite capable of eavesdropping, whether mentally or from a distance, the assembled members of the Council began murmuring among themselves. Ian had intellectually accepted the challenge of what he'd done by allowing his passion to rule instead of his head, but he was now experiencing the consequences of his choice. Chantal's very first words caused dissension.

Still, his faith held strong. "I will need to speak before the Council of the things I have learned," he said, diverting the tension of his family's shocked silence and overriding any retort his mother might make once her fury abated sufficiently to allow her to speak. "But Chantal and I need time to prepare for our vows so I may answer her many questions. And then we must find teachers who can help with her gifts."

He nodded at the elder who had stood in his place while he was gone. "If you would arrange to assemble the Council on the morrow, I would appreciate it."

Lissandra closed the distance between them and spoke in low tones. "You would make her Council Leader?" she asked with a horror she did not attempt to conceal.

"I will not allow it," their mother declared. "It is impossible."

"Nothing is impossible," Ian retorted, "although some things may be impractical. That is a discussion for the Council. It may be time to part with more of our traditions."

"Those traditions have kept us safe and in peace for thousands of years!" Dylys hissed. "We have lost our leader and the chalice, and the island suffers for it. It was your responsibility to correct the situation!"

"And I will, as soon as you allow me to complete what I have begun. You abdicated your responsibilities when you stepped down after your failure to completely strip Murdoch of his powers. If I am to act in your place, you must allow me to do as I think best."

"I will take back my position before I'll allow you to make this mistake!"

Chantal sighed, crossed her arms, and began to hum. Ian winced, but he couldn't resist a scientific interest in the result.

"If you marry her, *you* will have to abdicate," Lissandra insisted, escalating the argument. "You have to know she's unsuitable as leader."

Chantal's low hum took on a decidedly warlike edge. The council members began arguing more loudly, and Trystan's ship banged against the pier, bobbing on whitecaps. Ian considered the possibility that her voice might contain vibrations that resonated with matter. He would have to experiment, if Chantal didn't kill him first. How interesting, to find his equal in power in a woman scarcely half his size.

Caught in the midst of the three strong women in his life, Ian debated between creating a gale to drive them all home or simply picking Chantal up and carrying her off. Aware the Council leadership judged his every action, Ian resisted a malicious desire to appoint Alain Orateur as leader in his place. Instead, he nodded to his peers, caught Chantal's elbow, and practically dragged her toward the path away from the beach.

"We will discuss this in a more appropriate time and place," he declared firmly as the wind whipped the palm trees and Lissandra grabbed her sarong to keep it from blowing off.

"Stop that," he whispered to Chantal as they walked past their protesting audience.

"Stop what?" she demanded in a low, angry voice. "I thought I was behaving exceedingly well by not scratching their eyes out. How *dare* they speak to us that way? They do not even know me, and surely they know you do what is best for all."

With a surge of elation that his amacara thoroughly believed in and supported him, Ian halted at the edge of the jungle, lifted her from her feet, and kissed her soundly in front of one and all.

The wind died and the waves calmed. So maybe *he* was causing some of the turmoil.

Setting her back down again, Ian smiled in response to the gasps drifting up from their audience. Even Chantal glanced warily at the fronds now waving in a gentle breeze.

"Perhaps chaos is simply not knowing what to expect," he said cheerfully as he guided her into the shaded, flower-lined shrubbery. "We need new thoughts and ideas and people like you and your father to challenge us with them. I can see you now, raining plaster on the Council's heads when they defy us. Or perhaps you could just crack their eardrums occasionally. Or better yet, make them dance jigs upon their chairs!"

"*You* are the one hallucinating, not me," she muttered.

"Fine, then, don't believe me. But next time my family begins sniping like that—and they will look for an excuse to do just that—I want you to think of Anton and Marie, or maybe Trystan's twins. Hum prettily, or play a happy tune on your flute. Humor me and try, please?"

"May I think of them dancing jigs in their chairs?" she asked spitefully, although a smile tugged at her lips.

"That might be asking too much for a first try, but if it makes my lovely bride happy . . ." Unreasonably cheerful, Ian caught her shoulders and pointed out the temple of the gods in an oleander-lined clearing. "Tonight, at that altar, we will formalize the vows we've made, I will give you my family ring, and we will conceive our first child. All else is irrelevant for now."

Chantal stared at him. "I'm not in the habit of marrying mad princes."

His smile never dimmed as he stroked her dainty nose. "You already have, my lady. Until eternity, if you'll recall."

Those had been marriage vows? But there had been no priest—

Later, the steam and incense of the grotto brought

it all back—Ian's seduction, the bath, the giddy promises they had both uttered as he taught her body to climb to heights she'd never previously explored.

Marriage vows. She'd uttered them without a qualm. . . .

And would do so again. The realization brought a kind of peace, as if all the mislaid bits of her world had fallen into place. They were promised to each other, if only in their hearts.

Standing on the edge of the dark pool, Ian slid Chantal's bodice off her shoulders just as he had that first night. "You may argue until you turn blue, my love." He kissed her bare shoulder, and she shivered with the passion already building between them. "But this *obsession* we share is the result of those vows."

He shoved bodice and skirt to her feet and pressed both his thumbs to her midsection. "You feel me here, just as I feel you here." He lifted her hands and flattened them against the shirt covering the hard muscle of his waist. "It is a physical connection as well as a spiritual one, and can be severed only with death. And that is only an assumption, since we cannot know how the dead feel. Amacara bonds are quite rare, and I know none who share them again after a spouse is lost, so it may last into eternity as the vow promises. We are blessed with such a bond."

They were blessed with a passion for lovemaking that transcended all reasonable bounds, but Chantal did not think he meant that. Her hands trembled as she pushed up his shirt to stroke his flesh. "*Blessed* is not the word I would use," she said with an edge of hysteria. "We made no choices, no decisions based on logic and what is right. You have reason to regret that vow."

He shrugged and unhooked her corset. "I am learning that sometimes our hearts understand more clearly than our heads. I have faith that the gods would not choose unwisely."

Untying her chemise, he lifted her from her feet to suckle at the nipple he'd bared, and Chantal moaned in hunger, catching his wide shoulders for balance.

"Iason!" His mother's voice echoed from the cave's entrance, but she was barred from entering by the barrier Ian had said he drew from the earth. "You cannot exchange vows unless I initiate her."

Chantal stiffened and tried to push away. As if prepared for this intrusion, Ian refused to release her. "Chantal is a widow and no virgin," he called back. "She has no need of your rites any more than I do. I can anoint her as required."

Without waiting for his mother's reply, he lowered Chantal into the grotto's steaming water, where the only sounds she heard were the bubbling of the spring and the happy humming of her heart. As Ian began to strip off his clothes, the protests inside and out silenced without a whimper.

She might despise arrogant princes, be terrified of dangerous queens and the mother-in-law from hell, regret losing her home and her family, and have no rational reason to marry this man, but he was right about one thing. The bond between them required no thought.

And she trusted him, as she had from the very first.

She opened her arms as he stepped into the water beside her, pressed her wet breasts to his chest, and let nature take its course.

Tomorrow, chaos might reign, but today, she could pretend they were the only two people on the planet and all was well.

Thirty-three

"My head spins," Chantal whispered later that evening as Ian lifted her from the bliss of the grotto's mineral-infused water into the cloud of herb-laden incense.

"Do you see the stars?" Ian asked, needing to know how deep the connection was between them. They'd made love with their hands and their mouths, but he'd resisted planting his seed in her womb until the stars were in their proper place and the gods were ready.

"I do," she said in wonder. Closing her eyes, she rested her head on his shoulder, and he relished this moment of her vulnerability. She was strong, as she had to be, but he loved that she trusted him enough to lower her defenses with him. "They seem to be talking to me," she murmured.

Ian hugged her tighter. "As they do to me. Our bond tightens. I must warn you that what we do tonight can be dangerous since neither of us can predict your gifts or know which ones we will share between us. But if you are already seeing the stars as I do, there is no turning back."

"You see stars? Do you understand them?"

"I do. They led me to you. I cannot always understand clearly, but sometimes there is no denying their meaning."

They'd fasted since breakfast, but together they'd

consumed the traditional potion he'd mixed. It contained mildly hallucinatory herbs and aphrodisiacs and made Ian's head spin. The mixture was useful for virgins and reluctant mates, and expected as part of the amacara ceremony. In this instance, he thought it could be useful for tempering the merging of their gifts so as not to frighten his intended. He'd foregone all other traditions so as to keep Chantal and her revealing mark to himself, but he saw no reason to neglect the incense and potion if they might lead to greater insight and safety.

"Do you understand what the stars are ˎsaying now?" she asked dreamily as he carried her down the shell-strewn path to the altar.

She was naked in his arms. Although the rising wind of a storm cooled their overheated flesh, he'd seen no necessity in dressing for a ceremony that only the two of them would attend. The same barriers he used to block the grotto could be used to block any who came this way and to provide barriers of privacy at the temple. Perhaps in ancient times, public beddings were common, but no longer.

Despite all they'd done together, he burned with the desire to touch and taste her all over. "I am not listening to anything except the rush of blood as it flees my head," he admitted.

"I feel as if a river of fire flows through me," she agreed. "And the river's mouth is between my legs. Hurry."

He did. If the task of the aphrodisiac was to draw his blood and all other sensation downward, it was succeeding. His erection strained to bursting and preceded him like a tree trunk. At last he knew the torment he'd put countless other couples through at the gods' behest when he'd performed the rituals preparing them for their vows. He struggled to remember that this was an act of faith and procreation, but reason was rapidly diminishing to a feeble thread.

"Hurry," she whispered again, or perhaps it was the wind rustling in the trees.

A night bird called, and another answered. Heavy clouds swirled around Aelynn's peak, and the air was sharp with the welcome scent of rain. The woman in his arms was all ripe breasts, rounded hips, and graceful legs, and smelled of vanilla and honey. His sex throbbed and rose still higher when she wiggled in his arms to press her nipples into his chest.

He thought he might burst before they reached the altar. He didn't remember the temple being so far away. He might have to stop right here on the path and—

As he finally stumbled into the clearing, he saw that torches had been discreetly lit in the shrubbery. Lissandra would have seen to that, if only out of her duty as temple priestess. The altar gleamed soft and welcoming in the dancing light. Created of some sponge-like matter by the gods, the bed on which Aelynn's spirits waited looked firm yet gave easily. He laid Chantal upon it, and she immediately tightened her grip around his neck and tugged him down.

"Now, please," she said urgently, spreading her legs so the flower of her sex beckoned. He climbed upon the bed and kneeled between her thighs, his organ of reproduction straining to penetrate the blossom in a ceremony as old as time.

"The vows first," he retained sufficient willpower to say.

Although he had no approval from the Council, he did not hesitate over which vows to finalize, those of wife or amacara. He'd had a lifetime of isolation to recognize that he could never share a cold, rational marriage with a Council-chosen woman after the passion Chantal had showed him. And he'd had enough nights without her in his bed to understand that sending her away would destroy him.

He did not need the heavens to tell him that he would sacrifice his life to keep her.

"By Aelynn's will," he intoned before his gods and hers, "I take thee for amacara, keeper of my children, and as wife, keeper of my soul. Hear me, Aelynn, for I am yours to do with as you will."

The cloud-hidden stars seemed to chime their approval as he leaned forward to caress Chantal's breasts. It would make sense that the heavens would play music for his amacara. He waited with his heart in his throat for her to repeat the words he'd taught her.

"I take thee for husband, keeper of my body and soul," she said carefully, staring up at him with eyes glazed in rapture and expectation. "And amacara, father of my children, from now until the gods decree."

Overhead, thunder rolled, echoing the approval of the stars.

In relief and joy, Ian slipped his family's ring over her heart finger, and kissed her thoroughly, claiming her as an Aelynner and his own. The delicate music of the stars filled his ears, underscored by the deep bass of heavy drums. Her father's approval, apparently. All on the island would know that the Orateurs had returned.

This was it, the moment Ian had been waiting for his entire life, the binding of heart and soul and body into one and the resulting creation of new life. He didn't need the aphrodisiac racing through his blood to complete this joining. The song on Chantal's lips sang in his heart. Cupping her buttocks, he angled her hips to meet his, and thrust high and deep until she cried out with her surprise and pleasure.

With none but the gods and the spirits watching them, they mated beneath the whirling clouds, to the beat of drums and the roll of distant thunder. Their cries mixed with those of the night birds as the potion worked through their blood and poured from their skin, forced out by the binding strength of their promises and the desire to be as one.

As the moment of completion rose within them, Ian lowered Chantal's hips and covered her completely with his weight. With the power of the gods overtaking him, he held her arms pinned to the giving bed until she writhed and arched and clawed. He drove his teeth into her shoulder like the panther he'd been called, then licked the wound he'd made bleed.

She moaned and shuddered and arched higher, still possessing him so deeply he thought they could never come asunder. He held himself taut, letting her thrust and circle and plead until he could bear no more.

Giving himself to the elements, Ian threw back his head and let lightning enter his body.

Chantal screamed a long and haunting cry as Ian's sex plunged a path to her heart, thunder boomed, and a bolt of lightning illuminated the clearing like daylight. Electricity raised the hair on her arms and traveled through Ian into her, burning through blocked passages into her womb, making her whole.

Ian howled his release, pounding into her repeatedly until she jerked and shuddered and saw stars where there were none. As every muscle in her body convulsed, his seed spilled deep inside her.

But the hot flood of moisture was as nothing compared to the melding of her mind and body with Ian's.

She felt him inside her in ways that she could never express, saw his stars, felt his heart beat inside her chest, recognized the strangeness of his male member jutting between her legs. She felt his wonder, and oddly, his disappointment.

Perhaps sex made one insane. She couldn't explain what was happening in any other way. The distant drumming entwined with the thunder, surging through her veins like a heated elixir. And still, she held him.

Chiming notes of harmony and accord rang through the clearing, mating with the loud bongs of deeper instruments in an inexplicable chorus as she absorbed Ian's life force joining with hers in a manner that made her whole again.

"Have I hurt you?" he asked worriedly as the first drops of rain pattered the stones.

"I think you have brought me to life," she said with puzzlement. "I prickle all over, inside and out, as if whatever I'm made of has finally awakened and stirs."

He propped his weight on one elbow and stroked a hair from her brow. His deep-set eyes were the changing colors of midnight. He'd not shaved before coming here, and his beard shadowed his jaw. Unbound, his hair curled freely down his shoulders and tickled her breasts. He looked more primitive male than she'd ever seen him, and arousal began to heat her sorely used loins.

He smiled wickedly with understanding, and lifted his hips slightly until his sex almost, but not quite, slid out. "It is about to pour. Would you prefer to return to the grotto?"

"No," she said without hesitation, lifting her shoulders to reach between them and squeeze the masculine sac between his legs. "Nothing will cool me off. I plan to die here."

"If you did not die after what just happened, then

nothing will kill you." He shuddered at her caresses, then nuzzled and nipped her ear. "I had not fully appreciated the power of the gods in this place. But I agree, I do not think we can join the world until we play this out."

With a speed she could not grasp, he rolled over, carrying her on top of him. Startled, she sat up and looked around. The wind tossed her hair. A drizzle of rain sizzled against her skin. Dancing in the wind and threatening to go out, torchlight trailed shadows across her breasts.

She felt huge. She glanced down to be certain that her petite stature had not changed. Her breasts seemed larger, fuller, but Ian's lust-filled gaze as he drank in the sight could be responsible for that. His sex hardened within her. Perhaps she felt as he did, large and potent and prepared to battle the world.

Was this how men felt all the time? She gazed at him in wonder, as he grasped her hips and held them to push higher inside her as his strength returned. She was half his weight, barely reached past his shoulder, but she felt as if she had the strength, if not to overpower him, then to be his equal. She raised up on her knees, resisting his hold.

He slid his fingers over her mark to the sensitive skin between her buttocks, and she instantly came down on him again. He played a finger along the base of her spine and continued stroking her into deeper arousal.

"You carry the power of revolution," he told her, urging her to slide slowly back and forth until they both burned with renewed desire. "You will need my aid to learn to use it wisely."

"I don't have the slightest idea what you mean." But she did, if only with a sliver of comprehension.

The rush of the wind and the storm in the heavens matched the changes overturning all she knew and had been. The world was changing, and so was she.

"You do. You will. Perhaps we are not meant to have a child, but you are meant to be the instrument of change. It's happening already. Even Waylan has not been able to open the clouds sufficiently over Aelynn these past years. It's not the chalice they awaited, but you." He smiled in male satisfaction. "My choice was the right one."

She stared down at him. "What choice?" She wasn't at all certain that she wanted to know, but she would love to create that expression on his face more often.

"I chose you, *mi ama*," he said tenderly, brushing her cheek with his long fingers.

"You chose me—" She laid her forehead against his and choked on the rest of her sentence. "You chose *me* over the chalice. And Murdoch. No wonder your family is furious."

"It was the right choice," he stated firmly. "The stars have blessed us, and the heavens have sent us a storm after years of poor rainfall."

"What if it had been the wrong choice?" she asked hoarsely.

"It was not. The gods did not bless us with this bond without a reason." He rotated his hips and thickened even more inside her.

His arrogance knew no bounds, her mind insisted, but her heart agreed with Ian. She was drunk on love and lust and could not reason clearly. That he had risked so much for her was enough for her to know, to comprehend, and to love him even more deeply, if that was possible.

She raised her arms to beckon the lightning, let her breasts bounce freely in the increasing rain, then dragged her fingers through her hair to set it free from the confinement that once civilized it. She had no words to offer, just gestures.

And Ian understood. Holding her still with one arm around her waist, he rose to a sitting position, embedding himself deeper as he nibbled at the peaks of her breasts.

Even holding completely still, she felt arousal rise to the heights in an improbable instant. Chantal wrapped her legs around his back, moaning her readiness, and Ian caressed the bud of her sex. Thunder crashed, and lightning struck again, shattering a lintel of the temple.

The storm spiraled through them faster than the aphrodisiac. Riding Ian as she did a horse, Chantal gasped and grabbed his shoulders when Ian crushed her to him. They climaxed as one, with his hot seed shooting upward. Ian's arms tightened around her waist, and they shuddered in release. On fire from the inside out, Chantal collapsed against Ian's broad strength.

And then a miracle happened. Or a hallucinatory vision.

She saw a minuscule particle tear loose from the tunnel to her womb and tumble free into the golden light where Ian's seed swam. The particle instantly disappeared in a swarm of eager maleness. The explosion of contact, when it came, was so fierce, all the air left Chantal's lungs, blood drained from her head, and she passed out in Ian's arms.

Thirty-four

Chantal woke in the dawn light to find Ian resting on his elbow, leaning over her, in a room she didn't recognize, with rain beating on the roof overhead. Upon discovering her wakefulness, he caressed her hair and kissed her.

Pleasure and stormy memories rose in her breast, summoned by the magic of his kisses. But finally, they had reached some satiation, and she could resist his call enough to slide her fingers over his stubbled jaw and appreciate the length of raw male beside her.

"I feel very strange," she murmured, not certain where the strangeness began or ended. Perhaps just feeling replete was odd. The ring on her left hand weighed heavy.

"I feel what you feel," Ian marveled. "All those years I was told I'm heartless, I was missing the part of me that is you. I can feel you making my heart beat. Don't be scared. You have only to remember our loving to know this is right."

Briefly, she'd been a bit frightened by the newness of her surroundings and the realization that she'd bound herself forever to a man she didn't fully understand. But his acceptance banished all doubt, all argument. A man of his authority and ability had bound himself to her willingly, without remorse. Never had she been held so dearly by another, regarded above duty and family, first in his thoughts and in his heart. She was overwhelmed.

She grabbed his long hair and tugged. "You are real, aren't you? Will you explain now how a man who has never been on a horse can ride Rapscallion?" Of her many questions, she asked this first, because she did not know how to ask the deeper ones. And in truth, she didn't need to ask. Ian acted as he did because he was Ian, and his heart was larger than any she had ever known.

He wrapped his arm around her and fell back against the pillows, carrying her with him so she sprawled across his hard chest. "I read minds," he announced, as if he'd just said he'd eaten dinner. "Apparently, I can also see into the minds of certain beasts and make them understand what I want. There are not enough animals on Aelynn for me to have recognized this ability until I came to your country. It is something I must explore further, when we have time."

"You read minds?" she said in disbelief. "Then tell me what I'm thinking."

He chuckled. "You're thinking I am crazy, but I don't need to read your mind to know that. I can't read your thoughts unless you open them to me. Like most Aelynners, you have the ability to block me out. But the thoughts of people in your world spin crazily through my head like winter leaves in a storm. It's very distracting."

"So you can't live elsewhere," she murmured in disappointment.

"I can't live elsewhere because my people need me here. I am their Sky Rider, the only one who can read the heavens and help them see the future outside Aelynn. My sister can prophesy for individuals, but she cannot see what will happen beyond our shores. I saw you and the chalice in the stars and knew I was meant to go after you. By bringing you here, I've returned rain to our thirsty land."

"It could be a coincidence," she argued, not yet ready to believe he could have such mystical powers.

"I suppose it could be a coincidence that the sun rises every day, but usually, a pattern of behavior predicts cause and effect. I have a pattern of behavior that you will soon understand." He raised his head to kiss her jaw. "And predict," he said with a grin in his voice.

She grew warm all over at the idea of waking in Ian's bed every morning, listening to his plans in the evenings, walking beside him through his days— bearing his children. She reached between them to stroke her lower belly and wonder if her vision had the meaning she thought.

He covered her hand with his. "I saw it, too. The gods have promised children to all who mate in their temple. There is no promise that the child will live or that it will bear our traits, but that is the usual outcome."

"We will have a child who sings and reads minds?" she asked dubiously, attempting to absorb these oddities.

He toyed with her breast, and arousal tugged instantly at her.

"I'd rather not search the stars for an answer to that," he said with a seriousness that did not suit what he was doing to her body. "The island has always had an Olympus as a leader. Lissandra and I are the last of our line. I can hope our child will carry the traits he or she needs to take our place one day."

"But you doubt my traits are good for leadership."

She fell back against her pillows, remembering why she'd been reluctant to come here, remembering his mother's threats.

"Even you do not know that," he argued. "You have spent your life suppressing your gifts with music and believing you don't have the power to change lives, but you do. Very few of us are born with the symbol of one of our gods. Those who are have been chosen for a purpose. That purpose may be unknown or discarded or lost, but that does not negate the intent."

He traced the broken spiral on her spine. "Here, you bear the mark of the Lord of Chaos—or Change. He does not give such lightly."

"I can change lives?" The possibility seemed far-fetched. She'd done no more than nurse Jean, teach music to students, and manage her father's household. Ian and Pauline had been the ones who'd set her feet on the path outside of home.

"Perhaps not entirely on your own," Ian conceded, "but with practice, possibly. Your father's oratory helped bring about a revolution. If he'd possessed your ability to understand character and more of your ability to manipulate with his voice, he might be ruler of all France."

That was too terrifying a thought to consider. She did not have the wisdom to effect such changes. Or the need for such power. "You are seeking an heir to keep your family's position," she replied accusingly, "instead of seeking the very best leader the island has to offer. Our child could be like me—with no desire at all to be king."

"We don't have kings," he said, although she heard doubt in his reply. "The Olympus family is the only one with the ability to predict the future. That's necessary in a leader."

She made an inelegant noise. "Intelligence, wisdom,

experience, understanding, and a broad mind would serve as well. Lack of greed would be useful. Seeing the future serves no one unless they're prepared to act upon it."

"I hear the notes of certainty in your voice," he said with the delight of discovery. "Is this how you hear character when people speak? It's a vastly useful trait."

She punched his arm. The sun was rising through the open windows, and she would like nothing more than a lazy breakfast and a leisurely exploration of his home, but even she knew that wouldn't happen. His people were waiting for him.

"I never knew that what I heard was real. I thought it was my imagination. Don't start using my gifts against me already!"

She was gifted. It was a startling notion, but not so startling with Ian as her guide. He made her oddities seem real and potentially useful, if she had the courage to test and make use of them.

He chuckled and rolled on top of her, trapping her with his big body. "Read my mind."

And amazingly, she could. She was beautiful in his eyes, a complex creature of immense fascination to him, a gentle, courageous partner who would share his life, not exploit his position or abilities. His joy filled her, and she nearly burst with it.

He *trusted* her . . . and . . .

"You love me?" she whispered. "How can that be?" But she knew. He'd told her without the words, through his actions, his sacrifice.

"Is that what this feeling is?" he asked, pleased. "If so, you have brought it to me."

In wonder, she opened her own mind, let the feelings flow freely from her heart and soul as she had not done since she was a child, and acknowledged that the connection between them was far more than physical.

"I see me in your eyes," he whispered, kissing her tenderly. "Thank you for that."

"I lose those I love," she warned, gripping his arms. "I don't *want* to love you."

"But you do," he said with certainty. "I will do my best to cherish your love. And I am not so easily lost, as you must know by now."

A small laugh covered her sob. "You are right; you are very difficult to lose. And I think I love you for that most of all."

"Good. Keep that in mind when I'm at my most aggravating."

He pressed his case then, giving her no time to respond with words, only actions.

When Chantal woke next, the bed beside her was empty. She scarcely knew where she was, but she knew Ian was not here, and panic raised its ugly head.

"Good. You're awake," a cool female voice announced from behind her head.

Female. Not Ian. She grabbed the sheet to her breasts and forced her eyes open. Sunlight poured into a room of whitewashed walls and shelves of books. She would recognize Ian's room anywhere. Where was he?

"Ian has his hands full," the voice explained as if Chantal had asked the question aloud. "The Council has discovered your father's arrival, and our mother is attempting a mutiny."

Not good. *Danger.* She sensed things she had no right knowing. She turned over and met the multihued eyes of Ian's sister. Lissandra's silver-blond hair hung loosely to her shoulders this morning, crowned with flowers and braids. Her Roman-style gown fell to her feet in a ripple of white, like a vestal virgin's from an Italian painting.

"Can you tell if the child is a boy?" Lissandra asked, wearing a composed expression. She held a mug of steaming liquid but did not offer it.

"What child?" Chantal drew the sheet around her nakedness.

The movement reminded her of the ring she now wore. She glanced down, and a pearl glowed from a ring set in rubies and gold, a smaller version of the one she'd seen Ian wear. They were officially bound. Or married. Or whatever that meant here.

"Amacara ceremonies always produce children." Lissandra finally offered the mug. "Perhaps you are not sufficiently gifted to have seen the vision," she added sympathetically.

Chantal wasn't discussing visions of any sort with this woman who spoke in careful tones designed to conceal her every thought. "Where are my clothes? If Ian and my father are in trouble, I must go to them."

"Don't be foolish. They can take care of themselves. You need a restorative before you can go anywhere. You have Ian's heir to think of now, should he manage to keep his position."

"Excuse my bluntness, but I know what happens to queens who drink from the cups of enemies." Holding the sheet around her, Chantal swung her legs over the bed's edge. Dizziness swamped her, and she steadied herself with her hand while she studied her surroundings.

At least it wasn't a prison. It wasn't even a palace. The vaulted ceiling distinctly resembled thatch, with branching tree limbs providing support. The tree grew upward from beneath a floor of golden wood that gleamed in the sunlight streaming through enormous open windows. The chamber was beyond enchanting.

"Rivals maybe," Lissandra replied with a little more feeling. "But not enemies. Ian and I share the duties our parents once shared. If our mother's mutiny succeeds, we will both lose our authority."

"And this is not a good thing?" Chantal translated the notes in her "rival's" voice.

"It will set Aelynner against Aelynner as people take sides. Our mother has been under a great strain for years. Our father's death nearly broke her. She agreed to be relieved of her duties two years ago, when we learned she had sent Murdoch into the world without fully stripping him of his unpredictable powers. But she is still a strong, gifted woman."

In Lissandra's voice, Chantal heard grief, resentment, and determination. She didn't need her piano to play the notes and verify her instinct. If she believed Ian, this mystery was a gift, not madness.

"I believe Murdoch is learning some degree of control," Chantal said dryly, finally daring to touch her bare toes to the warm floor.

"You met Murdoch?" Lissandra gasped. "Where is he?"

Picturing the sardonic Murdoch walking away with two laughing children in his arms, Chantal dared a smile. "Well occupied for a while. Ian can tell you more. I need to go to my husband now. I am the cause of his distress, and I must be the solution."

"Don't be foolish. You know nothing of what we can do here. You know nothing of our ways." Alarm overrode Lissandra's initial startled reaction to Chantal's declaration. "Ian could very easily be the most powerful man on earth. He certainly doesn't need your help."

"There we differ." Chantal crossed the room to a trunk where a gleaming white linen gown awaited. Ruby embroidery to match her ring adorned the neckline and hem. She looked, but her corset and chemise were not to be seen.

Defiantly, she dropped the sheet, revealing the mark upon her spine.

Lissandra gasped again and went blessedly silent.

Chantal drew the gown over her head. Lined with delicate muslin, the folds of soft linen draped over her breasts, both emphasizing and concealing her form. The gown left her arms bare, but in this warm climate, that seemed sensible.

"You do not believe Ian is the most powerful man on earth?" Lissandra asked warily, avoiding any comment on Chantal's revealing mark.

"I haven't met every man on earth." She looked for a mirror and, not finding one, grabbed the hair at her nape and picked up one of Ian's leather strings to tie it back. "But I don't doubt that Ian is quite extraordinary. That doesn't mean he can't use a little help from time to time. You just admitted that your mother had your father's help, and you need Ian's. It seems reasonable to believe he needs mine. No man should have to stand alone."

Oddly, she felt his tension, almost as if she read his mind, but not quite. She thought he might be clenching his jaw to prevent his temper from exploding. And she thought maybe his temper needed to explode.

Besides, thinking of Ian kept her from thinking too hard about all the fantastical memories of the past night. She wanted to sit down to prevent flying apart, but she couldn't afford the luxury. *Change* hovered like a growing thunderhead. She might not see it, but she knew it was there, and she wanted to be with Ian when the cloud burst.

"If your presence affects him, it's to weaken him," Lissandra countered. "An Olympus has never mated with a Crossbreed in all our generations dating back to when time began. He cannot rule properly with your weaknesses flowing through him."

"Had your mother allowed my father to marry your cousin, their child would not have been a Crossbreed and might have been more powerful than I." She had no idea where that notion came from, but the paleness of Lissandra's face said she'd struck the right chord.

"You're saying the gods disapproved of my mother's decision," she whispered.

"I'm saying that, in my world, royalty claims they're chosen by the gods, and it's utter nonsense. Generations of inbreeding produce inferior stock. Any horse breeder knows that."

She needed shoes. She opened the trunk and rummaged among the garments she found there, locating an old pair of small sandals that might have been Ian's as a boy. She drew them out and sat on the trunk's lid to tie them around her ankles.

Lissandra looked both cross and thoughtful. Chantal ignored her. Ian had given her wings, and she must learn to use them. Perhaps it was just freedom that streamed through her senses, making everything seem sharper, clearer. Or perhaps it was the strange notion that her actions could actually make a difference.

"The mark of chaos was bred out long ago for good reason."

Lissandra had evidently found an argument that satisfied her, Chantal noted. It was not as if anyone had an answer to it.

"Bigotry," she replied, recalling the Oracle's distaste. "Every culture needs someone to despise, and it's foolishly easy to scorn those who suggest that things are not perfect and could be improved. We don't have time for this. If you wish to help Ian, then show me where he is."

"Aelynn is as close to perfect as it is possible for a

place to be." Despite her argument, Lissandra led the way into the next chamber, one twice as large as the bedchamber and supported by two trees.

Chantal wished she had time to absorb more than the bright primary colors of the furniture splashed against the golden floor and white walls, but she hurried to keep up with Lissandra's longer strides. "Ian said you've had a drought for years—that ended last night, if I understand correctly."

Lissandra grumpily refused to acknowledge this fact.

"And Murdoch is evidently not the product of a happy environment," Chantal merrily continued, relishing her newfound confidence by saying anything she wanted. "Your mother failed to train or restrain him, from what I can tell. He's a desperately unhappy man."

Lissandra cast her a glare that didn't quell the words spilling from Chantal's tongue like the notes she'd channeled into music all these years.

"The Chalice of Plenty has apparently escaped for some reason none of you understands, which seems a serious flaw to me." Hit by a bolt of comprehension, she added, "And if neither you nor Ian can find an . . . amacara . . . or a mate on this island, then your breeding program is failing spectacularly, isn't it?"

"It's not a breeding program," Lissandra grumbled. "Don't be crude. You come from a country that starves the poor to feed the rich, a place that is about to explode in fire and bloodshed that will kill men for decades to come. Don't tell me your *improvements* will help us."

Still learning to walk in the odd footwear, Chantal lifted the skirt flowing around her ankles and hastened to follow the shell path Lissandra strode with long-legged grace. She would like to enjoy the rich fragrance of the flowers lining the path, but the foliage dripped with moisture from last night's rain, and she didn't want to ruin her new gown before she found Ian.

She glanced over her shoulder at the shelter they'd just left. Built into the giant tree limbs, it was already nearly invisible.

"I do not have the arrogance to believe that my opinions alone matter." Hurrying onward, Chantal talked to keep from expressing her qualms in an inappropriate manner. She suspected if she hummed, she might cause the earth to vibrate as Ian claimed Murdoch could do. "But if no one on this island has any solution to your problems, then it seems reasonable. that you need to introduce new ideas. It is reassuring to know that it can be done without soldiers and weapons."

Lissandra halted abruptly, and Chantal nearly walked into her. Catching herself just in time, she eased to the right and glanced down into a clearing of houses where people hurried along sandy paths toward a long, low building. A chimney at one end of the building poured smoke.

"The smoke means the Council has called for a vote," Lissandra said. "Our men wield swords more deadly than any you've ever seen. They have been known to vote with the point of those swords. War here could be the end of our world." Lissandra broke into a run down the hill.

Thirty-five

"Enough discussion," Dylys shouted over the clamor resulting from her abrupt lighting of the fire of decision. Her voice was unusually weak and did not end the disruption.

All morning, the chamber chairs nearest the podium had filled with representatives from the island's elite families, those who held land and were blessed with the greatest gifts. To the rear, those with lesser abilities milled about rows of benches.

Trystan and Mariel stood in the rear, diplomatically waiting for Ian to call on them if needed. Once, Trystan had thought to stand at the podium as leader. He'd relinquished his high position in favor of taking Mariel, a Crossbreed, for wife, and dividing his duties between Aelynn and her home.

Kiernan the Finder also waited in the back of the room, along with Nevan the Navigator, both bachelors close to Ian's age. With Waylan and Murdoch sailing to England, these two were as close as Ian had to friends present. They were travelers who held little interest in owning land, so their Other Worldly views tended to be overlooked by the more powerful representatives. The success of this debate rested solely on Ian.

A voice of dissent arose from an unexpected corner. "She closes the floor to discussion rather than listen to reason," Alain Orateur stated loudly enough for those in the first ranks to hear. In the brief time since he'd returned to the island, he'd used his silver tongue to persuade the elderly lords to accept that he was entitled to his family's ancient position among them.

Muted arguments fell silent as Orateur's comment carried from front to back. Ian wondered if Chantal would have such power, once she'd been given the opportunity to speak. But she had no interest in his position as leader, so it would not benefit him to have her here.

"You forfeited your right to speak to the Council when you left Aelynn," Ian's mother said crossly to Orateur. Holding her left arm as if it hurt, she had taken a seat near the fire she'd lit instead of commanding the podium as she once had.

Dylys had lost her power of command, Ian noted with eyes opened by new insight. Once she could have forced the entire room to quiet and listen. Now she sounded like a querulous old woman—one who knew she was losing her authority. That startling thought jarred Ian from his reverie. He'd *heard* the desperation in his mother's words.

His power to read minds was almost useless against Aelynners, but Chantal gave him the power to read voices.

"I did not forfeit my right to speak but had it stripped from me by you and others who fear change," Alain countered. Already he was recovering his health, and his voice was strong and certain. "I am not the instrument of change, nor is my daughter. We are the tools at your disposal to guide you through what lies ahead. We do not create chaos but interpret and help ease disruption to bring harmony. Throw us away, and you throw away your future."

Lissandra ought to be here, Ian thought. Her future was at stake as well. He had seldom fully understood his sister, and if she possessed their mother's need for power, it did not bode well. But Orateur was likely to lead an uprising if Ian waited for her any longer.

He did not bother stepping to the podium. Gathering a powerful psychic surge, Ian nudged the room's occupants to respectful silence. They stared at him in confusion, since he'd never bothered to use his gifts so forcefully before. But with Chantal to balance him, he no longer feared the result of expressing his full power.

"The sun rises in a different position every morning for a reason," he said into the sudden silence. "The tides ebb and flow for a reason. Without their constant movement, the water would stagnate and marine life would die. For this same reason, we cannot expect to do things as we always have. Instead, we must correct our actions to make our land productive again."

His mental abilities did not extend to keeping everyone immobile forever. Dylys slumped against the arm of her chair and shook her head in what Ian assumed was despair. His gut knotted in anxiety at her weakness, but he had to concentrate on listening to his audience. Murmurs rose in the back of the room and flowed forward like the tide.

"She's coming," he heard whispered repeatedly.

His heart ought to sink in dread at the anarchy those words could represent. Instead, a deep thrill of pleasure caused him to hold his speech. There could be only one "she" who would so capture the Council's interest.

He'd wanted to protect Chantal from the political side of island life until she'd learned to love his home as he did. But he was still remembering the delicate lady musician he'd first encountered, and not the courageous woman who'd ridden a battle charge off a cliff.

He waited proudly, watching the entrance, so that his entire audience turned to look as well. His mother hissed her anger but remained seated. Even she knew better than to interrupt the drama.

Interpreting his nod correctly, Kiernan and Nevan leapt to open the chamber doors.

Chantal entered, displaying his family colors as she'd once worn the cockade of solidarity for the rebels in France. The gown had once belonged to Ian's grandmother, and he'd left it out in hopes that she would wear it for him. Even Alain grunted his approval as his daughter walked up the aisle, her golden hair streaming down her back, her head held high, her eyes steady on Ian.

She was terrified, he knew. It took immense courage for her to walk through a storm to be by his side. She had to have heard the anger and fear threatening to tumble the walls and known they were directed at her as well as at him. He thought he'd burst with love and pride and joy that his proper Parisian lady dared this public display for him. He opened his mind to let her in, and she gifted him with a radiant smile that reflected her equal love and determination.

He held out his hand to help her up to the raised platform where he stood. When he bent to kiss her cheek, the whole room murmured its approval.

"You color my world with joy," he whispered. "I'm glad you're here."

"Don't be," she rejoined, planting a kiss on his jaw. "I have a feeling that like Murdoch, I'm about to make the earth tremble."

"Then so be it. May the gods speak through you." He placed his hands on her shoulders and faced the people whom he was meant to rule.

"May I present my wife, with the Council's ap-

proval, my amacara, and mother of my child, Chantal
Orateur Deveau, daughter of Alain Orateur."

Gasps erupted in the front rows when he mentioned
his child. The Council must formally approve his marriage for those vows to be legal, but only the gods
controlled amacara bonds. Dylys could refuse the marriage, but an Olympus heir would be impossible to
deny.

"You are manipulating them," Chantal murmured.

"And your father does not? And you? Would you
speak now?" He tried not to laugh at her grimace.
Point and counterpoint.

"The marriage can be postponed until we are certain of an heir," Dylys pronounced from her chair,
looking more gray than she had earlier. "That is not
a matter for today."

"I am sorry for your grief and the loss of your loved
one." Turning to face her mother-in-law, Chantal
spoke in polite French, which not all the Council
could understand.

Her sympathy caught Ian by surprise, but he'd already said his piece. He did not interfere.

"It is impossible to replace a great man like your
late husband," she continued, addressing Dylys. "But
he lives on in your son and daughter. Would you deny
him his place in this house?"

Dylys clutched the chair arm to hold herself upright,
and Ian saw her overwhelming grief and frustrated
anger. He sensed an outpouring of compassion and
understanding from those in the audience who understood Chantal's sentiments and translated for those
who did not. Chantal opened whole new avenues of
connection between him and the rest of the world,
and in fascination, Ian studied the results, letting his
wife continue without his aid. *This* was what it was

like to be Chantal, to act on understanding and passion instead of coldly observing. Terrifying.

When Dylys uttered no response, Chantal turned back to their audience, even though she must recognize the opposition against her. As she spoke, her father stepped up to translate.

"I am here today because Ian taught me I must act when I see injustice. He has told me my observations can make a difference. I do not claim to be a leader or a ruler or a princess or any of the titles people give to those who lead instead of being led. I would far rather be sitting down there with the rest of you. And from what I'm hearing in your voices . . ."

She looked over the room full of rising murmurs and tilted her head as if listening to a symphony. "Many of you believe you could lead this discussion more fruitfully than we are. Perhaps that is where you must make your first change."

The chamber exploded with outrage and speculation and bursts of pure delight. Aware that Lissandra had crept in the back door and stood beside the platform, Ian signaled for her to join them. She resisted. Understanding her bitterness and disappointment better now that he knew she and Murdoch might be amacaras, he glared at her and gave her a mental swat.

She glared back and climbed the stair to stand beside him.

Unable to raise her voice, Dylys goaded Ian with a fierce frown. He obediently nudged the crowd to silence. With a strength of will that had marked her reign, his mother pushed from her chair to speak. "We are here to vote on whether or not Ian is the steady influence we need to lead us, not on whether we want chaos to rule."

Relieved that his mother was recovering from her momentary weakness, having made up his mind and

no longer worried about who ran the Council, Ian
wrapped his arms around Chantal and Lissandra's
shoulders. In astonishment, every eye turned to him.
He never hugged. He'd always stood aloof and gone
his own way. His action now was a signal of change
in itself.

"I am not at all certain I want to lead," he announced. "Not if leading means standing here arguing
and tearing the island apart when I need to be searching for the chalice. Recently, I have discovered a pref-
erence for doing instead of talking."

For the first time in living memory, one of the
Council's oldest widows rose from her chair and dared
interrupt an Olympus. "We need someone to act as
judge in questions of law. Is your chosen bride capable
of that?"

"Without a doubt, better than I am," he admitted,
aware that Alain quietly translated his Aelynn speech
for Chantal's benefit, "but whether my bride is willing
to act in judgment is another matter entirely. She has
a gift for knowing when we speak truly, but there are
others here who may have equal insight and certainly
more experience with our laws. We refuse to assume
leadership based solely on family name and wealth."

Gasps of horror and disbelief passed around the
room, not the least of which came from his mother,
who grabbed her arm again and used the chair as a
prop to remain standing. Without flinching, Ian
continued.

"Perhaps, after the war in the Other World passes,
Chantal and I may be wise enough to take our places
as leaders, should the Council agree. But for now, you
would be better served to *elect* a judge to settle matters of law, another as speaker to guide your meet-
ings." He glanced toward Alain, who scowled at him
from beneath bushy eyebrows. "And a spiritual

leader." He turned to Lissandra, who was too stunned by his suggestion to find her normally sharp tongue.

"There are three of us. We can do all that as we have been," Dylys rasped weakly, gripping the chair with one hand. "An Olympus has always fulfilled those duties."

"They should only do so if qualified," Chantal said pleasantly. Her words, and her father's translation, rang over the clamor and confusion rising in the audience. "Inherited power is not the strongest or the best means of leadership. Nor is power based on riches, or power for its own sake. You should choose your leaders on the basis of their ability to carry out their duties."

A cheer rang out from the back of the room, where those of minor position stood. The elders in the front rows looked less certain.

"How can you allow me to lead if you do not believe me when I say the Outside World is part of our future?" Ian asked over the growing din in the chamber. "How can I be a leader if I have no experience or understanding of that world?"

"Please . . . ," Dylys whispered with a note of panic.

Before Ian could whirl around to see what was wrong, Lissandra shouted "Mother!" and pushed past him to the chair where their mother had been standing.

Slowly, as if pressed beneath a heavy weight, Dylys was crumpling to the floor. Lissandra had felt the disturbance first. Now, without consulting the stars, Ian felt the impact as his mother lost her grip on consciousness. Grief welled inside him. Squeezing Chantal's shoulder, he abandoned her to help Lissandra lower their mother. Shocked silence filled the chamber—

Then Chantal's clear, high voice broke into a hymn

of prayer that rose high to the rafters and spread like wildfire.

She did not even speak their language. The island hadn't heard music for as long as Ian could remember. But her voice conveyed the power of prayer, and tears stung Ian's eyes as others slowly picked up her refrain and began to repeat it in voices rusty with disuse until the chamber echoed with pleas to heaven.

Even Alain joined in, translating rapidly for those who did not have an aptitude for language. That the man who'd been scorned and driven from his home by their Oracle could join in a prayer for her well-being spoke of a character strong enough to stand in Ian's place for as long as was needed.

Glancing at Lissandra, Ian saw tears streaming down her face as he lifted their mother and carried her from the room.

As predicted by the gods, Chantal had brought change and possibly rebellion to their quiet life. Whether it was for good or ill remained to be seen.

For once, he did not need to see the future. He believed Aelynn's wisdom in choosing her for him.

That was enough.

Epilogue

"I feel like an assassin," Chantal murmured, leaning against her husband while they watched the schooner prepare for departure. "No wonder your family banned ours from this paradise."

"My mother has been unwell for some time. And she is alive yet. You have not killed her. That you have changed me is for the better." He hugged her tightly and pressed kisses in her hair.

"Do the stars tell you that?" she whispered hopefully. "I am tearing you from your home when they most need you. How can that be better?"

She'd had months to adjust to Ian's home while he and Lissandra had helped develop a new political structure, and the island's most skilled physicians tried to save their stricken Oracle. Chantal understood why Ian loved this place of peace and prosperity. Her father had grown stronger and been elected to Council leadership. With no opposition from Dylys, Ian's marriage had been approved with little debate. She was a wife in all ways now, with so much to lose. . . .

Ian patted the slight swell of her belly. "Because I want this as much as you do. We'd be foolish to believe life is meant to be a cheerful rainbow. Paradise must be earned. Our purpose is to share our plenty, to work at making the world a little better for everyone. And you are doing that by carrying my child and helping me to understand how your world works so I know better how to help mine."

"In England," she said with only a hint of regret.

"Because the chalice is there and France is not safe," he reminded her. "It is still my duty to find the chalice or understand why it has left. You can help me understand Other Worlders anywhere we live."

"I love you," she murmured into his shirt. "I don't deserve you, but I'm never letting you go."

He chuckled and swept her into his arms. "Oh, you'll come around and want to argue with me just as everyone else does. I'm counting on you to remind me that I'm not the only person in the world."

She clung to his neck as he carried her on board. "I doubt I can cure you of arrogance. If you mean to breed my father's racehorses while learning about my world and chasing Murdoch and the chalice around England, you'll learn quickly enough that you cannot control the fates. I can, however, teach you etiquette so you behave in a more civilized manner. I believe even the English require some degree of politeness these days."

He snorted. "I am not the only arrogant one in this family. You're a snob." He set her down on the deck and turned her to face the beach.

Lissandra stood alone, watching from the edge of the jungle.

"She is so strong," Chantal said in admiration. "I'd be in a fit of hysterics if you left me to lead the island all alone."

"She's not alone, but she's lonely," Ian acknowledged. "Your father will keep the Council in line so she need not roar at them. But she needs a partner as much as I do."

Chantal wrapped her arm around her husband.

"You need a keeper to prevent you from diving head-first into trouble. Lissandra needs someone to take up the burden of power and allow her to be the spirit of peace she's meant to be."

She was aware of Ian's sharp look, but she resisted returning it. Instead, she waved her hand in farewell to the woman on shore.

"Spirit of peace? Lissandra?" Ian asked in disbelief.

Uncertainly, as if not accustomed to a friendly exchange, Lissandra waved back.

Satisfied, Chantal smiled up at her omnipotent husband. "She is strong because she must be, not because she wants to be. Come along, now, let's see if Trystan has gathered enough food to feed your babe. Surely he knows by now that a pregnant woman must be fed regularly. I wish he'd brought Mariel on this journey."

Ian laughed. "He knew he would have to surrender his cabin to us. You don't really think I'd wait until we reached England to celebrate our glorious adventure?"

She cast him a coquettish glance over her shoulder. "Oh, is that what you think? Perhaps it's time for your lessons to begin."

With that, she lifted her skirt and ran for the companionway.

Whistling leisurely, Ian arrived at the stairs before she did. Looking sufficiently rakish in loose shirt and breeches, his dark hair streaming down his back, he hauled her into his arms and carried her down to the captain's cabin.

"Consider yourself kidnapped and ravished by a pirate captain," he warned. "You will be a ruined woman by the time we land in England."

Chantal laughed. "Ruin me as you will, my pirate, and I will rule your ship before we land!"

Above, Trystan and Kiernan exchanged glances and snickered.

"Oh, how the mighty have fallen," Trystan sang as he signaled his sailors to cast off.

On his way once more to track the elusive chalice, Kiernan leaned over the rail and waved to the lonely figure who slipped back into the woods. But Lissandra failed to see him.

There was always tomorrow.

Author's Note

Much of the period of time recorded in this book contained terrible coincidences or events incited by master manipulators who have no place in a story that is, after all, about one couple and not an entire revolution. In addition, European politics and geography prior to the Napoleonic Wars were drastically different from those of modern times, so for the purposes of my story, I have simplified some aspects of history.

For readers interested in knowing more, I recommend beginning with Christopher Hibbert's *The Days of the French Revolution*. For further references or questions, I would be delighted to hear from you at www.patriciarice.com, or you can stop by my blog at www.patriciarice.blogspot.com.